PRAISE FOR JAMES
No Good Deed

"Once again, Jim Swain has presented a fast-paced, intricately plotted, informative, and ultimately pleasing investigative tale."

—*Deadly Pleasures Mystery Magazine*

"*No Good Deed*, the second title in the Jon Lancaster & Beth Daniels Series, following *The King Tides*, is a blessing for crime thriller fans. It continues to build the shaky relationship between the highly engaging and original lead characters while exploring a heinous series of crimes in human trafficking. What's happening is terrible, but the crafting of the tale is first rate. And the main characters, in values and style, are the 'Odd Couple' of crime fiction."

—Phil Jason, *Florida Weekly* reviewer

"Swain's characters are so real and so believable they jump off the pages and into the reader's heart in an adventure you won't want to miss."

—Cheryl Kravetz, Murder on the Beach Bookstore,
Delray Beach, Florida

The King Tides

"James Swain's *The King Tides* is a hundred percent adrenaline rush disguised as a detective novel. Its hero, an ex-detective named Jon Lancaster, is as adept at using the latest digital sleuthing software as he is shooting a gun. The pacing is terrific, the dialogue memorable, and the characters, including a tough-as-nails female FBI agent and some truly frightening serial killers, jump off the page. You will read this book in one sitting. It's that good."

—Michael Connelly, #1 *New York Times* bestselling author

BAD NEWS TRAVELS

ALSO BY JAMES SWAIN

BAD NEWS TRAVELS

A THRILLER

JAMES SWAIN

THOMAS & MERCER

Text copyright © 2020 by James Swain

Published by Thomas & Mercer, Seattle

www.apub.com

Amazon, the Amazon logo, and Thomas & Mercer are trademarks of Amazon.com, Inc., or its affiliates.

ISBN-13: 9781542016445
ISBN-10: 1542016444

Cover design by Shasti O'Leary Soudant

Printed in the United States of America

BAD NEWS TRAVELS

PART ONE

WARTS AND ALL

PART ONE

CHAPTER 1

Not many people could say that a chicken had saved their life.

But Jon Lancaster could. It had happened in the Republic of Mali, in West Africa. The region had been infiltrated by an Al Qaeda franchise called AQIM, which funded its terrorist activities by kidnapping foreign ambassadors and oil executives, and holding them for huge ransoms. It was nice work if you could get it, and AQIM had become one of the richest terrorist cells in the world.

Lancaster's SEAL unit had been sent to Mali to rescue an oil executive named Duncan Farmer. Farmer and his wife had been hosting a dinner party in their home when an AQIM team burst in, executed several guests, and spirited Farmer away. The next day, a ransom note was delivered to the local American embassy.

The SEAL unit's marching orders had been simple. Rescue Farmer and bring him home, and give AQIM a taste of their own medicine.

Lancaster was the front man, his relatively short stature and pot-belly allowing him to mingle easily with the natives. He'd been born with gastroschisis, a condition that gave him a big stomach. People thought he was fat, but it was an illusion. Dressed in flowing robes and his face darkened by charcoal, he shuffled down the dirt road leading into town without drawing suspicion.

He'd left before dawn. It was quiet, and he saw only a handful of people, mostly women going to fetch water. As he neared town, a chicken ran out onto the road, and started squawking up a storm. Not just any chicken, but a variety called a naked neck, a prodigious layer of eggs. He'd encountered naked neck chickens during missions in Africa before, and was ready. Reaching into the pocket of his robe, he removed a handful of corn, and sprinkled it liberally on the ground. The chicken quieted down and pecked away.

"Where are your buddies?" he asked.

It was an honest question. No one in Africa owned just one chicken; they owned a brood, and kept them for eggs and their meat. Having just one chicken would be like owning an aquarium and keeping a single fish. It didn't feel right. He needed to find out why there was only one chicken, or risk putting himself and his unit in danger.

The chicken cleaned the ground and squawked for more. Kneeling, he held the rest of the corn in front of the chicken's face, tempting it. Clearly irritated, the chicken flapped its wings, and the squawking grew louder.

A faint *bock bock bock* reached his ears, the sound originating from a mud house sitting a hundred feet off-road. The house had no electricity, the only sign of life a billow of smoke coming from its chimney. The *bock*ing sound grew into a chorus as the brood, which he assumed was locked in pens behind the house, joined in.

He let the corn sift out of his hand, and the chicken started eating.

He wondered why the brood was locked up. There had to be a good reason, only it wasn't coming to him. Had their owner been ordered by AQIM to lock up the chickens so they wouldn't be a distraction? If so, then he was walking into a trap.

He decided to leave. Using a Garmin GPS, he got his coordinates, then walked back to his unit, who were hiding in the bush a half mile down the road. He relayed his suspicions to the officer in charge, and gave him the reading off his phone.

The OIC called the base, and requested a reconnaissance satellite spy on the area. A half hour later, the base gave them the bad news. Twenty armed men were hiding up the road from where he'd met the chicken. He wouldn't have stood a chance.

The OIC asked for a drone to drop a bomb on the men. Then, the unit hunted down the villager who'd given them the bad information, and persuaded him to reveal where Farmer was being held prisoner. The next day, bruised and beaten but still very much alive, Farmer was flown back to the States with his family.

Lancaster thought about that chicken often. If it hadn't run into the road and made a fuss, he would have walked into a trap, and probably perished. He owed that dumb bird his life, and for the longest time, he hadn't ordered poultry when he was in a restaurant.

It seemed like the least he could do.

- - -

Memorial Presbyterian Church in Saint Augustine was a towering structure of poured concrete and crushed coquina stone, with architectural details painstakingly created with terra-cotta. Looking at the building took your breath away, and Lancaster couldn't think of a more fitting place for Martin Daniels's funeral to be held.

He had never met the man, but had heard so many stories from his daughter Beth that he felt like he knew him. Although it sounded trite, Daniels had been a pillar in his community. Surgeon, college professor, philanthropist, church elder. Everyone he had touched had come away better for the experience. He'd made the world a better place, and several hundred people had turned out to pay their respects.

"Dad would be embarrassed," Beth said under her breath.

"Your father didn't like spectacles, did he?" he asked.

"He hated them. Not that there's anything we can do about it."

He'd had to park several blocks away. As they neared the church, he asked if the knot in his tie looked okay. They stopped for Beth to check, and he gazed into her eyes. She'd been crying for days, and she looked like hell. It didn't matter how old you were; when your last parent died, you became an orphan.

"You going to be okay?" he asked.

"I'm managing," she said.

Grief had a way of robbing a person of their strength, and he knew of only one thing that would make Beth feel better. He hugged her.

"Thank you," she said, and kissed his cheek.

The church was on a brick-lined street called Sevilla. As they crossed, a black Charger with tinted windows and black exhaust billowing from its tailpipe caught his eye. There were a dozen parked cars on the street, but the Charger was the only one occupied.

He stopped to stare while Beth kept walking.

"It's nothing," she said over her shoulder.

They'd been dating for a few months. Long enough for Beth to be able to read him, and know what he was thinking.

"How do you know it's nothing? It looks suspicious," he said.

"It's broad daylight, and it's a church. Come on, we're going to be late."

"It doesn't look right."

"Get over it. Please."

He quickly caught up. Melanie met them at the entrance. The sisters embraced, and Melanie gave Lancaster a hug. She was a wreck, and barely holding on.

"Nolan and Nicki are in the front row. They saved you seats," she said.

"How many people are inside?" Beth asked.

"At least three hundred. It's standing room only."

"Dad would be mortified."

"I was thinking the same thing. I guess it's better than the church being empty. There are some FBI agents from the Jacksonville office who said they knew you."

"How nice. I'll have to make sure to say hello."

Lancaster's guard refused to go down. He shot a glance over his shoulder, and saw that the Charger hadn't budged. It just felt wrong.

"When did the people start arriving?" he asked.

The question caught the sisters by surprise.

"About an hour ago. Why?" Melanie asked.

"Just curious."

Holding hands, the sisters started to go in. They hadn't always been close, but that had changed when Melanie's daughter had become the target of predators, and Beth had joined forces with Lancaster to stop them. Since then, they'd grown tight, and were now doing a good job of emotionally supporting each other.

"I left my phone in the car. I'll join you in a few," he said.

"You better hurry. The service will be starting soon," Melanie said.

He hurried down the front steps, and walked around the front of the church to Valencia Street, then began circling back to Sevilla. If people had started arriving an hour ago, then so had the Charger, otherwise it wouldn't have gotten a parking space. So why had its occupants chosen to remain in their vehicle, with the engine running? That was the kind of thing undercover cops did, or criminals looking to settle a score. As far as he knew, Martin Daniels had led a clean life, but you could never be certain. As the naked neck chicken in Mali had taught him, it was better to be safe than sorry.

He hung a right on Riberia Street, and soon was on Sevilla. Not wanting to scare the occupants of the Charger away, he took off his sports jacket and folded it over his arm before approaching the vehicle from behind.

He rapped on the passenger window. It lowered, and a brutish man with a buzz cut and a boxer's crooked nose stuck his head out. His teeth were stained a hideous brown, and his neck and hands were covered in tattoos in praise of the gangster life.

"What do you want?" the man asked.

His accent was Russian. Every country had criminal gangs, and in Russia they were called khuligans. Down in Fort Lauderdale where Lancaster lived, the khuligans ran strip clubs and escort services, and didn't like to pay their taxes. They were harder to find in the rest of the state, and he wondered what brought this one here.

"Sorry to bother you, but I'm lost," he said. "Can you help me out?"

The khuligan gave him a hostile look. Lancaster pretended not to notice and removed his wallet. Kneeling, he extracted a slip of paper with the church's address and held it in front of the man's face. While the khuligan studied the address, he took a hard look at the driver, who was a slightly smaller version of his partner, his neck and hands also covered in jailhouse art.

"You are looking for the church?" the khuligan asked.

"That's right. Do you know where it is?"

He jabbed a crooked finger at the ornate building. "Right there!"

"Oh my God, is that it? If it was a snake, it would have bitten me on the nose. Sorry to bother you gentlemen." He slipped the piece of paper into his wallet. Clipped to the interior was the detective's badge that the department had presented him when he'd pulled the pin. He tilted his wallet so the badge was clearly visible, then waited a beat before speaking again. "So what brings you boys here?"

The khuligan struggled for an answer. Lancaster had dealt with Russian gangsters, and had found that their understanding of the American justice system was poor. Most of them didn't know about probable cause, or being read their Miranda rights.

"We came to pay our respects," the khuligan mumbled.

"You knew the deceased?"

He nodded. Lancaster glanced into the car, and the driver nodded as well.

"Tell me his name."

The khuligan's eyes locked onto Lancaster's.

"Dr. Martin Daniels," he replied.

"How did you know him?"

"We did work around his home. The doctor didn't like to climb ladders, so we cleaned his gutters and pruned his trees. He was a nice man."

"You're landscapers."

"I think the expression is handymen. We take whatever work we can get."

He was passing with flying colors, but there was still the question of why he and his friend were sitting in the car, and not inside the church.

"Why haven't you gone inside?" Lancaster asked.

"We wanted to wait and stand in back. People look at us funny. You know how it is."

The man was either a very good liar, or he was actually a friend of Martin's. Lancaster was starting to feel that the latter was true, and he stepped away from the car.

"Sorry to bother you," he said.

"You are a friend of Dr. Daniels?" the khuligan asked.

"Of the family. See you inside."

Lancaster headed toward the church. Beth would be furious if the service started without him, and he began to jog. Going up the steps, he found himself thinking about the Charger's interior. There were shift paddles mounted on the steering wheel, and they gave him pause. The only version of the Charger that came with shift paddles was the SRT Hellcat, which was the quickest, fastest, and most powerful sedan in the world, with 707 horsepower and 650 pound-feet of torque. He'd come into some money a few months ago and gone car shopping, and had seriously considered buying the Hellcat. Its base price was $65,000, but that didn't include the $1,300 destination charge and the $1,700 gas guzzler tax, or the sales tax. Throw those charges in, and it ran $73,500.

The average handyman made fifteen bucks an hour. Hardly enough to insure a Hellcat, much less drive it off the lot. The khuligan lied to him. Intuition was the messenger of doubt, and his gut had known that these two jokers were up to no good. Now, finally, his brain was catching up.

He spun around, sensing the worst.

The Charger was gone.

CHAPTER 2

In the natural order of things, we buried our parents.

It was how life was supposed to work. The parents pass away, the children bury them, and the cycle of life continues. It was how everyone wanted it, yet it didn't soften the blow when a parent died. The grief was overwhelming, the pain a dagger to the heart.

Staring at her father's coffin, Daniels found herself playing back their last conversation, wondering how she'd missed her father's obvious dismay. She knew that he wrestled with depression—he talked about it often, addressing his mental condition in the third person, as if he were his own patient—but suicide had never entered the conversation.

Dad had hidden his suicidal thoughts to protect her. That made sense. But what bothered her was that she'd never seen it coming. She was an FBI agent, and trained to see clues that other people missed. But that hadn't been the case with her father's suicide. She'd been in the dark, which had made the pain of losing him worse.

The tall, silver-haired minister took the podium. His name was Stan Dransfield, and he'd been a close friend of her father's since he'd relocated to Saint Augustine a dozen years back. Dransfield spent a long moment unfolding his notes. He was having a hard time composing himself, and the silence in the church was uncomfortable.

Melanie leaned into her. "Where's Jon?" she whispered.

"I don't know," she said.

"Is he checking out that suspicious car?"

She glanced sideways at her sister. "You saw it too?"

"Nicki did. She said it didn't look right."

"Jon felt the same way."

Daniels glanced down the pew at her niece. Nicki was taking CSI classes at her high school, and had developed a sixth sense for sniffing out suspicious behavior. Jon had been onto something when he'd called out the Charger, and she wished that she hadn't doubted him.

"Excuse me."

Jon had returned. Beth drew her legs in, and he sat down beside her.

"Where have you been hiding?" she whispered.

"Checking something out," he whispered back.

"Anything to report?"

"Nope. False alarm."

Dransfield cleared his throat and began to speak. He was a gifted orator, and his words brought a soothing calmness to the packed church. Beth looked straight ahead, listening hard. Not to the man on the podium, but to the man sitting beside her.

Within moments, she knew that Jon was lying.

- - -

While a student at the FBI academy, Daniels had been trained in the science of reading body language. Behavior analysis, as the bureau called it, was the ability to decode and interpret a suspect's silent tip-offs, commonly called "tells." How a suspect sat in a chair and held their hands was often as important as the words coming out of their mouth.

Reading tells was helpful during an interrogation, but it wasn't foolproof. If a suspect was on drugs, there was no telling what their body language meant. The same was true of sociopaths, who lied so convincingly that they even fooled themselves.

Environment also played a role. If the environment was controlled—such as a police interrogation room—then the job was easier. If the environment wasn't controlled, the job often became impossible.

Despite these limitations, reading tells was an important tool in crime fighting, and Daniels excelled at it. She would begin by asking a suspect innocent questions that she already knew the answers to. Then, she'd start tossing bombs, and watch the suspect's body language and facial expressions to see if they changed.

She'd discovered another tip-off to a suspect's truthfulness: breathing. Lying quickened a person's pulse, which caused their breathing to accelerate. Like a pant, you could *hear* the lie coming out of his mouth.

Jon had a similar tell. When he became agitated, he shut his mouth and breathed heavily through his nose, which produced a faint whistle. She guessed that his nose had once been broken, and left him with a deviated septum.

She could hear that whistle now. Like wind passing through a stand of bamboo, it made a faint *whee*. Something was definitely bothering him. She guessed he'd talked to the driver of the Charger, and not liked the conversation's outcome. Yet when she'd asked him, he said it was nothing. Which meant he lied to her.

Daniels considered lying an unpardonable sin. When she caught men in her life doing it, she blew them off. Without trust, there was nothing.

Jon had never lied to her before. He didn't always answer her questions, but he never lied. So why now? Was it because she was upset, and telling her more bad news would make her mood worse? That was a good answer, and she decided to go with it for now. Later, when they were alone, she would get the truth out of him. If he did it again, he was history.

- - -

The church service was mercifully short, as was the graveside service, as her father would have wanted. Had Dad expressed his wishes to Dransfield during one of their fishing trips? It was just like him to control the narrative, even in death.

They drove to her father's house in her rental. Jon was at the wheel, using Google Maps to guide him. She could still hear his whistling nose and knew that he was upset. She wanted to ask him what had happened with the Charger, but that would mean revealing the tell, and she wasn't ready to go there just yet. She enjoyed the occasional upper hand.

Jon pulled up the driveway and parked. Her father's house in Saint Augustine had been purchased not long after her mother's death, and was not what Beth or her sister had expected. They'd thought he'd sell the family place and buy a condo, but instead, he'd bought a house big enough for his family to pile into during the holidays. Nestled in nature and steps from the beach, it had a multitude of decks and covered porches, plus three extra bedrooms. It had become the family home, and a place she loved visiting.

Melanie had yet to arrive, and the place was quiet. Jon killed the engine and turned in his seat to look at her.

"How are you feeling?" he asked.

"A little better."

"Strong enough to talk?"

"Sure. What's up?"

"I wasn't up-front with you earlier. I'm sorry."

There. He'd come out and admitted it. Such a simple thing, yet so important.

"What weren't you up-front with me about?" she asked.

"I had a chat with the guys in the Charger," he said. "They were a couple of Russian khuligans, and they were on a first-name basis with your dad. Which begs the question, Why would Martin be mixed up with guys like this? Any idea?"

"Khuligans?"

"Gangsters."

The question hit her hard. Her father had committed suicide without leaving a note, and there were lingering questions never far from her thoughts. Now Jon had added yet another twist.

"Back up a second," she said. "Did these two guys tell you they were gangsters?"

"They told me they were landscapers who did work for Martin and came to pay their respects. But the model of vehicle they were driving was way above their pay grade."

"Maybe the vehicle was borrowed."

"That occurred to me. At the cemetery I got the name of your dad's landscaper from Melanie. I found his company page on Facebook on my phone. He has two employees. Neither were the guys in the Charger."

"So you established the guys that you spoke to weren't landscapers. How did you make the leap to Russian gangsters?"

"Their tattoos."

"So you've dealt with them before."

"Russian gangsters started popping up in Fort Lauderdale when I was a cop. They had suitcases filled with cash, and bought strip clubs to launder money. One of the ringleaders got arrested and did a short stint in jail. I heard his arrest was deliberate."

"The ringleader deliberately got himself busted?"

"He did it to network. Jail is a great place to meet other thugs."

"Sounds hard-core. How did he make his money?"

"Drugs and extortion. The drugs were sold in the clubs. They rarely strayed out of Fort Lauderdale, which was why running into them here was so strange."

"Did you get the Charger's plate?"

"Of course I got the plate."

"Send it to me."

As Lancaster texted her the Charger's plate number, Daniels gazed at the front of the house. The nagging suspicion that there was more to her dad's death had been there for a while. Her father hadn't talked about his desire to die, hadn't left a note, and to end his life had used a World War II vintage handgun that no one had ever seen before. And now, there was a pair of Russian gangsters in the mix.

She decided to start with the Russians. They needed to be run down, and possibly interviewed. The question was, Did she have the emotional fortitude to handle an investigation? She hadn't been sleeping well, and didn't feel strong enough to do it. As if reading her thoughts, Jon placed his hand on her wrist, and gave it a gentle squeeze.

"Want some help with this one?" he asked.

"I need all the help I can get right now," she said.

"I'm your man."

She closed her eyes and took a deep breath. She likened grief to standing in the surf on a clear blue day, and being knocked over by a powerful wave. Sometimes it took a minute to right yourself; other times, it took much longer.

When she opened her eyes, she discovered that Melanie had arrived. She kissed Jon on the cheek, then got out of the rental to greet her sister's family.

CHAPTER 3

"I hope they don't sell the house," Nicki said.

Lancaster and the teenager were taking a walk on the beach outside Martin's home. An annoying flock of screeching gulls circled overhead, hoping for a handout. Otherwise, the beach was deserted.

"You like coming here, don't you?" he said.

"I sure do. I remember the first Christmas we spent here. We were living in Virginia, and we drove down on a Friday. My mom wasn't too thrilled about coming. I guess she was still sad over losing her mom, and her dad selling the place up north."

"How old were you then?" he asked.

"Four."

"You have a good memory. What was that first time like?"

"It was the best. The outside of the house was strung up with decorations and colored lights, and there was a big Christmas tree in the living room and five stockings hanging over the fireplace. My grandpa pulled out all the stops. Did you ever meet him?"

"Afraid not."

"He was a cool guy."

They stopped, and he opened his hand to reveal the collection of flat stones he had picked up during their walk. Nicki selected one and skimmed it over the water. She would turn sixteen soon, and had started taking the long walk into adulthood. He was concerned about her. She and Martin had been close, and he didn't want her too badly scarred by her grandfather's passing.

"How many skips was that?" he asked.

"Six. My record is eight." She took another stone and gave it a heave. This one had *Guinness Book of World Records* all over it, and she clapped excitedly.

"Nine!" she said. "Should I quit while I'm ahead?"

"Never. You're just getting warmed up."

She threw another stone. This one plopped into the water after one skip. She groaned and dropped her chin. She began to cry, and he stood silently beside her, not wanting to disturb the moment. Drying her eyes, she lifted her head and gave him the thinnest of smiles. He had a supply of tissues in his pocket and handed her one.

"Let's head back," he suggested.

"Can we stay here? I need to tell you something," she said.

He said okay. She took the rest of the stones from his hand, and started throwing them. "A day before my grandpa died, we talked over the phone. He made me promise not to tell my folks, so I didn't."

"That wasn't smart, Nicki. Your parents are going to be upset."

"Are you upset?"

"Yes, I am. This isn't something you should have kept secret."

"I'm sorry. There's something wrong about the way he died, isn't there?"

She was looking at him, trying to gauge his reaction. He didn't want her jumping to any conclusions, and decided to put a lid on her suspicions.

"There's nothing wrong about your grandfather's death," he said. "There are just questions that need to be answered, that's all."

"Like why he didn't leave a note."

"That's right. What did the two of you talk about?"

"I was having problems with my science homework, so I messaged him. He called and answered my question, and then we talked. He sounded really depressed, and said he hadn't been sleeping. He told me how sorry he was for the things he'd done."

An icy finger ran down his spine. Nine months ago, pornographic videos had circulated on the internet with a young girl who looked remarkably like Nicki. The videos had set on fire the libidos of sexual predators far and wide, and put Nicki's life in danger. That danger had since passed, and Lancaster wondered if Martin Daniels had seen those videos, and been aroused by them. Was that what he'd been hiding?

"Did your grandfather elaborate?" he asked.

"He said that he'd been tempted, and acted foolishly, and hurt himself and his family," she said. "He asked me not to judge him. Before he hung up, he said that there was a passage in the Bible that would explain it. It was in Corinthians. I looked it up. I'm not sure what it all means."

"Please show me."

She took out her cell phone, got on the internet, and pulled up the passage. She handed him the phone, and he shielded the screen with his hand so he could read. It was from 1 Corinthians 10:13. *No temptation has overtaken you except what is common to mankind. And God is faithful; he will not let you be tempted beyond what you can bear. But when you are tempted, he will also provide a way out so that you can endure it.* "He did something bad, didn't he?" the teenager said.

He handed her the cell phone. Martin had gotten caught up in something, and it had spiraled out of control. This was his goodbye note.

"Let's go back to the house," he said. "We need to tell your folks."

- - -

They found Nicki's father in the living room, answering emails on his iPad. Nolan Pearl was a neurosurgeon at a large hospital in Fort

Lauderdale. He had a surgeon's temperament, and rarely raised his voice or lost his temper.

"How was your walk?" he asked.

"It was fine," Lancaster said. "Are Melanie and Beth around?"

"They're in the dining room, going over Martin's will and bank records."

He glanced at Nicki. There was no time like the present when it came to telling the truth. She sat on the couch beside her father, and told him about her last conversation with Martin. Nolan gazed out the window when she was done.

"This isn't good," he said under his breath.

"We need to tell Melanie and Beth," Lancaster said.

"My wife said they didn't want to be disturbed. Let's wait until they're done."

Turning to his daughter, Nolan said, "Nicki, I don't want you to blame yourself for what happened. There was no way you could have known that your grandfather was planning to take his own life. You're not responsible here."

The teenager slid across the couch and buried her head into her father's chest. She was crying again, and her father consoled her.

"I'm going to fix coffee. Want some?" Lancaster asked.

Nolan said no thanks. Lancaster went to the kitchen and poured beans into the fancy machine and fixed three individual mugs, assuming that Beth and her sister would probably enjoy a pick-me-up. He opened the refrigerator in search of cream, and was surprised at the amount of food lining the shelves. Eggs, an assortment of cheeses, a six-pack of Guinness, bread, a bag of bagels, plus a half dozen yogurts. In the meat drawer he found sliced turkey and ham with expiration dates several days away; in the vegetable drawer, several plump tomatoes and a head of lettuce that looked fresh. He'd dealt with suicides as a cop, and in his experience, the departed waited until the last item in the fridge was eaten before taking their life. That wasn't the case here, and he found himself struggling to understand Martin's mindset before he died.

The cream was nearly finished. He split it between Beth's and Melanie's mugs, and tossed the empty carton into the trash. A receipt caught his eye, and he pulled it out for a closer look. It was from the local Publix supermarket, and contained many of the items in the fridge. The date was from three days ago, which was when the police believed that Martin had driven his car to Anastasia State Park before dusk and walked down a hiking trail to a secluded spot where he'd taken a gun and ended things.

The receipt had a time. Martin had purchased the groceries at 4:10 p.m. That didn't make any sense. Why would Martin buy groceries, come home, put them in the fridge, then drive to the park and kill himself?

He didn't know, but was determined to find out. Folding the receipt, he slipped it into his wallet, then took two of the mugs to Beth and Melanie. He tapped on the dining room door with his foot, and Beth appeared.

"For you, my lady," he said.

"You're so thoughtful." Her face was puffy from a recent cry, and when he glanced into the room, he saw the same bereaved look on Melanie.

"Is something wrong?" he asked.

"I'll tell you later," Beth said, and shut the door.

CHAPTER 4

Martin's study was on the second floor and faced due east, with a panoramic view of the Atlantic Ocean. A comfortable-looking leather chair was situated in front of the windows, with a neat stack of newspapers on the floor beside it.

The room had cathedral ceilings to accommodate the bookshelves that took up three of the walls. Martin was a fan of the mystery genre, and there were autographed collections by Connelly, Child, Grafton, and James W. Hall, whose Thorn novels set in Key Largo he'd read and enjoyed. Thorn was an off-the-grid loner who helped people in need, and the kind of guy he could see closing down a bar with.

There were volumes on American history, with several shelves dedicated to the Civil War and Abraham Lincoln. Finally, there were books on medicine, several of which Martin had authored while practicing up north.

Lancaster sat down at Martin's desk. It was a double pedestal design with a walnut finish and brass pulls and dovetail construction. Martin's personal items covered it, a visual history of his life, and he examined each item carefully.

There were framed photos of Beth and Melanie as children, and several of Martin's late wife. Of more recent vintage was a photo of

Martin on a fishing trip with a group of his buddies, each of them clutching a can of beer. They were all smiling and looked toasted. There were multiple paperweights, a wireless Bose speaker, a cup filled with pens and pencils, and several pairs of reading glasses.

The desk drawers were next. They contained old files and tax returns and nothing that bore closer examination. It was starting to feel like a dead end.

He pulled out the center drawer last. A blank legal pad and a badly chewed pencil plus a book of stamps. Game over.

He shoved the drawer back in, and noticed how tight the fit was. It made him wonder if there was something stuck in the back, so he pulled it out, and had a look. There was nothing there. Yet something didn't feel right.

After a moment, he realized what the problem was. The opening was deeper than the depth of the drawer. A good inch wider.

He removed the drawer's contents and put them on the desk. Then he flipped the drawer over, and found the culprit. On its underside the drawer had a secret compartment held in place by Scotch tape. He peeled away the tape and lifted the flap. For his effort, a folded piece of paper was revealed.

He put the drawer back together, replaced the contents, and inserted it into the desk. Then he unfolded the hidden paper. Printed in block letters was a word with lowercase letters, uppercase letters, and symbols, which he assumed was a password. There were also three numbers printed on the paper—15, 25, 45. He wondered if there was a hidden safe, and he walked around the study, rapping on walls.

The wall containing the mystery novels was hollow, which he found appropriate. By removing the collection of Harry Bosch books, he discovered a wall with a secret latch. He turned the latch and gently pulled. The shelf swung outward.

He found himself staring at a circular wall safe. It was ensconced in concrete and looked recently poured. Martin had gone to a lot of trouble to install the safe, and keep it a secret, and he wondered why he'd done that.

He entered the three numbers written on the paper, and the safe popped open. The interior was lined with carpet, and contained a laptop computer and a checkbook.

He hesitated. There was no doubt in his mind that the password would give him access to the laptop's hard drive, and shed light on why Martin had taken his life. But these things were not his to discover. They were for Beth and Melanie to look at, and digest. This was a family matter, and he needed to tread delicately.

"Jon!" a distressed voice said.

The voice was coming from outside the house, and it sounded like Nolan Pearl. He opened the French doors, stepped onto the balcony, and went to the railing. Looking down, he saw Nolan and Nicki standing in the backyard.

"What's up?"

"We found something that you need to see," Nolan said.

Nicki was crying, her eyes beseeching him to hurry.

"Give me a minute," he said.

He went back into the study, shut the safe, and gave the dial a good spin. He shut the bookshelf and put the books back the way he'd found them. He folded the paper with the password and combination, and stuck it into his wallet.

Then, he headed for the door.

– – –

Reaching the bottom of the stairs, he stopped at the entrance to the dining room. Beth and Melanie were still sequestered inside. Everything that he'd discovered in the study could wait, and he walked through the downstairs to the back door.

He found Nicki and her father outside by the garbage pails. Both father and daughter appeared shaken and upset.

"What's wrong?" he asked.

"Nicki was putting the garbage out and found blood," Nolan said. "Take a look for yourself."

One of the pails had its lid off, and he peered inside at a black garbage bag with a yellow drawstring. The mouth of the bag was partially open, revealing a tissue with a patch of dark-brown blood the size of a silver dollar.

"Is this exactly how you found it?" he asked the teenager.

"Uh-huh," she said.

"Did you move anything?"

"No. I saw the blood and backed away. I didn't touch anything."

"That was very smart. Do me a favor, and go into the kitchen, and see if you can find a plastic Ziploc bag."

She went inside. Lancaster took out his cell phone, and used it to photograph the bag. He took six shots, including three close-ups, as if documenting a crime scene. There could be a simple explanation for the blood, but until he discovered what that was, he was going to treat everything as possible evidence.

Nicki returned holding a Ziploc bag. Reaching into the pail, he undid the drawstring, and carefully removed a wadded Kleenex soaked with blood. Nicki opened the mouth of the Ziploc, and he placed the tissue inside and sealed it shut.

"That's a lot of blood," she said. "Did someone attack my grandfather?"

"That's hard to say. Your grandfather could have cut himself shaving," he told her. "Let's gather the evidence and not jump to conclusions, okay?"

"Sure, Jon."

"You have to admit, this looks awfully suspicious," Nolan chimed in.

"It does look suspicious," he said. "But we can't let it cloud our judgment."

"Got it."

Lancaster hoisted the garbage bag out of the pail and removed its contents, which he placed on the ground. The bag was filled with garbage and old newspapers, but no more blood. He took photographs with his cell phone, just to have a record. Then he returned the items to the bag, put it into the pail, and replaced the lid.

Holding the Ziploc, he went into the kitchen, and found a Sharpie on a desk by the refrigerator. He wrote the date and time on the Ziploc, and put it on the island so Beth would see it when she came out. At the sink he scrubbed his hands.

"Did you find anything in the study?" Nicki asked.

"Yes. I found a hidden wall safe," he replied.

"A wall safe? What's in it?"

He didn't want Nicki making any false assumptions, and decided to tell her a lie. "I didn't open it. That's for your mom and Aunt Beth to do."

"What do you think's inside?"

"I have no idea."

He dried his hands with a paper towel. As he threw the towel away, his eyes scanned the kitchen. He did not see a box of Kleenex, and he guessed the bloody Kleenex in the trash had come from one of the bathrooms. How it had ended up in the kitchen garbage was anyone's guess.

"Grab some Ziplocs," he said. "We're going to do some more snooping."

He checked the wastebaskets in the two downstairs bathrooms, and found them empty. Nicki and her father hovered behind him, saying nothing.

He went upstairs and checked the bathroom in Martin's bedroom. The trash can beneath the sink was loaded, and he dumped the contents on the floor, and had a look. A second bloodied Kleenex reared its ugly head. Nicki let out a little shriek.

"What does it mean?" she asked.

"I don't know," he said. "Let's bag it. Did you bring the Sharpie?"

Nicki said no. He placed the Kleenex in a Ziploc and sealed it. As she started to leave with her father, he said, "Be sure to notate that this came from the upstairs bathroom."

"I will," she said.

"And leave the Ziplocs in case I find something."

"You got it."

He listened to Nicki and her father go downstairs. Then, he picked up a wadded piece of toilet paper lying on the floor. It had caught his eye as he'd scoured the trash can's contents. To his relief, neither Nicki nor Nolan had noticed it.

He peeled the balled-up tissue apart. It contained a used condom and was brittle to the touch. Martin Daniels was an athletic septuagenarian, and it wasn't a shock to imagine him having sex. The surprise was the condom itself—Manforce Pink Bubblegum Flavored. He knew it was this variety because of the hot-pink color and bubblegum smell. When he was a cop, he'd busted many streetwalkers. He knew this was a favored brand, and that it also came in a variety of tropical flavors.

Had Martin been paying for sex? It was a reasonable assumption, and he wondered if it somehow played into Martin's decision to end things. He would wait until he got Beth alone before telling her, and let her decide what she wanted to do. It was going to be a painful conversation, and he wasn't looking forward to it. He sealed the condom into a Ziploc, and washed his hands before heading downstairs.

CHAPTER 5

Daniels liked to be in control. The majority of times she and Jon went somewhere, she drove. This had nothing to do with Jon's skill behind the wheel, or the fact that he sometimes drove too fast. She simply needed to be the one handling the wheel.

The highway back into town was two lanes, and lined with palatial beachfront homes. She drove with her window down, the ocean breeze tingling her face. Jon was in the passenger seat, his nose whistle faint and true.

She waited a minute before speaking. "You're holding back."

"So are you," he said.

She turned her head and stared at his profile.

"Explain yourself, " she said accusingly.

"Watch out, there's a squirrel on the side of the road," he warned.

She looked straight ahead. There was no squirrel lurking on either side of the highway, and she began to fume.

"Don't do that again," she snapped.

"Sorry. Where are we going, anyway?" he asked.

"To the sheriff's office. Should we flip a coin to decide this?"

"I'll save you the trouble. I found more than a couple of bloody tissues during my search. I didn't tell your niece or brother-in-law, but wanted you to hear it first."

"Why did you do that?"

"Because it's not pleasant."

Her eyes burned with tears. Losing her father had been awful, and she wasn't ready for more bad news. She grabbed a bottled water out of the holder and chugged it.

"Want to do this later?" he asked.

"No. Lay it on me," she said.

"Before I do that, I need to ask you a question."

They came to a traffic light. Braking, she gave him her full attention.

"Go ahead," she said.

"Do you want me working this investigation?" he asked. "It feels like your father was in a bad situation, and I could find things that will hurt you. I don't want to ruin our relationship."

"That's not going to happen."

"You sure?"

She managed a smile. Jon wasn't pretty to look at, but he was smart and honest and he could be trusted, and she hadn't found many men who had all those traits. He was a good one, and she hoped he stuck around for a while.

"Yes," she added for emphasis.

He dug a plastic bag out of his breast pocket. It landed on the dashboard, and she stared at a used condom of the hot-pink variety. Her mind raced with the possibilities of where it had come from. She swore, which was something that she rarely did.

"Fuck. Where did you find that thing?"

"In the wastebasket in your father's bathroom."

The light changed, and she goosed the accelerator. Her face was burning with embarrassment, and she stared straight ahead.

"So my dad was having sex. Big deal," she said defensively.

"I was more surprised at the condom. It's a brand I saw frequently as a cop. It's bubblegum flavored, and it's edible."

"Meaning what? That it came from a hooker?"

"That would be my assumption."

Her father was the classiest man she'd ever known, and the image of him having sex with a cheap prostitute was too much to bear. In anger, she punched the wheel.

"I'm sorry, Beth," he said.

"Don't be. I needed to know," she said. "Thank you for shielding my sister and her family from this. I appreciate that."

Jon lapsed into silence, and she sensed that the conversation was bothering him. For a long minute, neither one of them spoke.

"You found something bad in your dad's records, didn't you?" he said.

"How did you know that?" she said.

"Because you didn't argue with me about the hooker. It's a reasonable scenario, but there could be others. Your father went fishing with a group of buddies. Maybe one of them used the bedroom to have sex. It's a possibility. But you accepted that it was your dad, which tells me you and Melanie found something in your dad's records."

"Were you listening through the wall?"

"No, Beth, it's just a hunch. I suggested that your dad may have entertained a prostitute, and you didn't fight it. So what did you discover?"

"His bank accounts were cleaned out."

"How much?"

"One point two million dollars. The withdrawals were made during the past few weeks in the form of money orders. Where it went is anyone's guess."

"That's a lot of money. Do you think he was being blackmailed?"

"That's what my sister thinks. Melanie said that Dad was acting weird, and seemed to be under a lot of pressure. Extortion is certainly a possibility."

"By who?"

She'd been wrestling with that same question. Pulling into the sheriff's station, she parked in the visitor's space by the front door.

"Let's see if we can find out," she said.

- - -

Lancaster had never known a woman like Beth. She did not tolerate fools, or foolish questions, nor did she like to explain herself. He had no idea why they were visiting the sheriff, but knew that in due time he'd have his answer.

They went inside. Beth identified herself to the sergeant at the reception desk, and then she asked to speak with the detective investigating her father's death. Until a final report was filed, Martin's death would be treated as a possible crime, and was the responsibility of the sheriff's department.

They sat on a couch to wait. He wondered how much information Beth planned to share with the detective in charge. Would she tell him about the missing money, or the condom? His gut told him no. If Saint Augustine had a black mark, it was its police force, which had been featured in a pair of sobering documentaries that had run on the public broadcasting channels.

As the story went, the girlfriend of a rookie cop had been shot at point-blank range, and the evidence pointed to her boyfriend having pulled the trigger. For reasons that were unclear, the police department had concocted a story saying that the young woman was despondent, and had taken her own life. This was physically impossible based upon how the bullet had entered the dead woman's head, and the fact that the victim's jaw had been broken before she'd died. All evidence pointed to her boyfriend being involved.

But the police department had stuck to its crazy story, and no charges were filed against the boyfriend. It was the kind of coverup that gave small Florida towns a bad name, and when the Florida Department of Law Enforcement had tried to clear the air and conduct an investigation, the police had closed ranks, and made it impossible for the FDLE investigators to do their jobs. Justice had never been served.

Lancaster had seen his share of bad behavior on the force. Cops would alter evidence at crime scenes to get someone arrested, or alter testimony at trial to put a bad person behind bars. Other officers would witness these transgressions and say nothing, knowing that if they spoke up, it would ruin the cop's career, as well as their own.

This stuff happened, and it was regrettable. But he'd never heard of an entire department covering up a murder. Maybe there was an explanation for why the rookie had shot his girlfriend. Perhaps they'd been having problems, and she'd gone into a rage and grabbed his gun and tried to shoot him, and in the scuffle taken a bullet herself. A story like that was believable. The one that had been fed to the public wasn't believable, and as a result, the department wasn't trusted by other law enforcement agencies.

"Special Agent Daniels?" A man in his fifties with a detective's badge pinned to his jacket lapel stood before them. Tall and tan, he had a thick moustache and sideburns, and had his thumbs hooked into the top of his belt like a gunslinger in a TV Western. "I'm Detective Gaylord Sykes. How may I help you?"

Sykes was the epitome of a southern gentleman, with a soft drawl and easy manner. Daniels rose from the couch, as did Lancaster.

"I was hoping I might ask you a few questions concerning my father's passing," Daniels said.

"I was thinking you might come by. Please, come back to my office," Sykes said. "I'm sorry, but I didn't catch your name."

"Jon Lancaster," Lancaster said. "I'm a friend."

"Nice to meet you, Jon. Would you like a drink? We have coffee and water."

They both declined. Sykes used a plastic key to gain entry to the station, and he led them down a hallway to a corner office decorated with plaques and framed photos from various stages of his career. He'd been a cop most of his life, all of it serving Saint Augustine. He offered them chairs and leaned against the desk with his arms crossed.

"I'm sorry for your loss, Special Agent Daniels," the detective said. "I didn't know your father personally, but he had a wonderful reputation in the community. I'm sure this has been a very difficult time for you, and your family."

"I appreciate you saying that," Daniels said. "I was hoping you could let me see my father's cell phone. The police report I read said that it was found with his body."

"Actually, it was found in your father's car," Sykes said.

"May I see it?"

"I'm afraid I can't release your father's cell phone until my investigation is finished. Department rules."

Daniels gave him a look. The FBI had authority over the police, and Beth could ask for whatever she wanted. Her authority was being challenged, and Lancaster could tell that she didn't like it.

"Is the cell phone here?" she asked sternly.

"It is. Is something wrong?" Sykes asked.

"We found evidence at my father's house that there might have been a struggle."

"What kind of evidence?"

"A tissue soaked with blood. Jon put it in a plastic bag for safekeeping."

Daniels opened her purse and removed the Ziploc, which she handed to Sykes, who held it up to the light. He shifted his attention to Lancaster.

"Where exactly did you find this?" the detective asked.

"Beth's niece found it in a garbage pail by the back door," he said. "She called me outside, and I removed it from the garbage bag and put it in the Ziploc."

"That was smart. You a cop?"

"Retired."

Sykes blinked. "I thought your name was familiar. You were down in Broward, if I'm not mistaken. There's a video on YouTube of you rescuing a little girl on the side of I-95. That was one fine piece of shooting, sir."

Lancaster's career as a policeman had been defined by a commitment to protect the innocent, which he'd done every single day he'd worn a badge. Unfortunately, it was not how his career would be remembered. A two-minute video of him shooting a pair of kidnappers was his legacy, and would remain in cyberspace long after he was gone.

"Thank you," he said quietly.

"Did you find any other evidence in the house?" Sykes asked.

The Ziploc with the condom was in the breast pocket of his shirt. Before he could hand it over to the detective, Beth spoke.

"Just the bloody tissue," she said.

"I see. Well, this definitely needs to be looked into. I'll turn the tissue over to our CSI team, and see what they turn up," Sykes said. "I'll also need to get a brief statement from you, so I can add it to the report."

"Of course," Lancaster said.

"I'd like to see my father's cell phone," Daniels said. "Please get it for me."

Sykes looked uncomfortable with the request, but he did not protest. He moved around the desk, and removed a drawstring envelope from a drawer. Untying the envelope, he dumped out a cell phone, and came around the desk and handed it to her. The device looked new, with hardly a scratch or blemish on its protective case.

Beth powered up the cell phone, and the screen came to life. The screen saver was a photograph taken from the balcony of Martin's home during sunrise, the blinding sun balanced on a cloudless horizon. Lancaster imagined Martin sitting in his favorite chair reading the newspaper and deciding to take the shot. A spur-of-the-moment thing, captured for eternity.

"There are no apps on this phone. All the information's been erased." Beth looked at Sykes accusingly. "Who did this?"

"We believe your father did," the detective said.

Beth tossed the phone on the desk, clearly angry. "What led you to that conclusion, Detective?"

"Your father's body was found in a park by a hiker, who called the police. A pair of officers were sent out. They were shaken up by what they found, and called the station for help. I jumped in my car, and drove over. As you probably know, your father's corpse was badly mutilated."

"Your report said by a pack of coyotes," Daniels said.

"That's correct. It was impossible to identify his body, and he wasn't carrying a wallet or ID. But there was a set of car keys in his pocket. I walked to the parking lot with one of the officers, and tried the keys in several parked cars. I got a match, and opened the vehicle. The cell phone was on the seat, along with your father's wallet. It was on, and I saw that everything had been erased."

"Which led you to assume that my father had done it."

"I don't see how anyone else could have."

Beth's anger hadn't gone away. She rose from her chair and stared at Sykes, as if measuring him. The detective wilted under her gaze, and shrank a few inches.

"Was there anything you saw at the scene that looked strange? Anything at all?"

Sykes thought about it for a moment. He shook his head.

"It looked like a suicide," Sykes said.

"Have you investigated many suicides?"

"I'm afraid I have. There's a veterans' home in town, and some of the patients get pretty despondent, and decide to take their own lives.

They usually go off into the woods and end things on their own terms. That's what it appeared your father did."

"Do you have a copy of the pathologist's report?"

Sykes removed a copy of Martin's autopsy from a file in his desk and handed it to her.

"Thank you, Detective," she said. "Thank you very much."

– – –

Pulling out of the parking lot, Daniels erupted, and punched the wheel with a clenched fist. Her cheeks had turned crimson, and her breathing was accelerated.

"What's wrong?" Lancaster asked.

"Everything," she said in a rage. "That son of a bitch is lying!"

CHAPTER 6

"Slow down, before you hit someone," Lancaster said.

Hell hath no fury like a woman lied to. Beth slammed the brakes so hard that he might have flown through the windshield had he not been strapped in. The street was empty, and she threw the vehicle into park and turned sideways to look at him.

"Switch places with me," she said.

"You want me to drive back to your father's place?"

"Please."

Soon he was behind the wheel and using his memory to drive back to Martin's home. Beth looked ready to explode, and he found himself feeling bad for Sykes. It was a crime to lie to an FBI agent, and the detective's life was about to become a living hell.

"You want me to stop, get you something to drink?" he asked.

"No. Just be quiet, and let me calm down."

"I didn't like him either."

"Sykes is a god damn snake. He erased my father's cell phone."

"Why would he do that?"

Beth's voice cracked, and tears flowed down her cheeks. She was heading toward a meltdown, and on the next block he pulled into the parking lot of a Starbucks, and hustled inside. A minute later he emerged with a strawberry scone and a brownie the size of a small brick, which he handed to her on a napkin. In his other hand were two bottled waters, which he placed into the cupholder. She dug into the sweets.

"That was fast," she said.

"I flashed my badge and told them it was an emergency, so they let me cut in line."

"That's going to get you in trouble someday. Want some?"

"No thanks."

Soon the scone was reduced to crumbs. She bit into the brownie and emitted a happy groan. "This is so decadent. Thank you."

"How can you be sure Sykes erased your father's cell phone?"

"My father was something of a Luddite," Beth said. "He disliked computers and smartphones, and still wrote on a typewriter. He believed the digital age was making people dumber instead of building intellect. He also despised social media and refused to have his own Facebook page."

"How does this make Sykes the culprit?"

"I'm getting to that part. Last bite. Sure you don't want some?"

"I'm good. You just downed two thousand calories. How do you stay so thin?"

"I've never had a problem with my weight. A few months ago, my father called me up, and said he wanted to buy a smartphone, and would I help him. He'd gone into a Verizon store, but the salesman was useless, and just confused him. That led him to call me."

"Why would he want a smartphone if he was a Luddite?"

"My father said that Nicki had begged him to get one, so that he could have it in case of an emergency."

"Makes sense. Did you help him?"

"Yes. I came down for a weekend, and we bought a phone together, and I showed him how to operate it. Dad didn't even know how to power it up. Smartphones are designed by people who assume you've owned one before, or know that there are instruction tutorials on YouTube. My father was completely in the dark."

Beth took a drink of her water. She was back to being herself, her voice calm and measured. "The phone had several preinstalled apps, including a couple for online casinos, which really ticked him off. I tried to show him how to uninstall them, and he said, 'I don't need to learn that. You do it.'"

"He actually said that?"

"Yep. My father had to be dragged kicking and screaming into the digital age. The less he had to learn about it, the better."

"So your father didn't know how to uninstall the app on his phone."

"No, he did not. Even if he had, it wouldn't have been something that he would have done before taking his life."

He took his bottled water from the holder and screwed off the top. "Do you remember which apps were on your father's phone?"

She closed her eyes, thinking hard. "There was an app for emails, and another for text messages. He had his retirement money with Vanguard, so I installed their app so he could look at his accounts. He liked to follow hockey, and I installed a sports app. I also installed the Weather Channel app so he would know if a storm was heading his way. And he had me install an app called Gallery so he could store photos and videos."

"Of what?"

She opened her eyes. "Come again?"

"Your last sentence doesn't make sense. Your father was motivated to buy a cell phone by his granddaughter. He didn't know how to use it, and wasn't in a hurry to learn. Yet for some reason, he asked you to install an app that would let him store photographs and videos. That meant he was intending to take photos and videos with his cell phone, and store them. Of what?"

"I have no earthly idea."

"Was he into photography?"

"Not that I'm aware of."

"Bird watching?"

"No."

"Did he enjoy photographing pretty girls?"

"Are you implying that my father was a dirty old man that enjoyed taking pictures of young women? You're out of line, Jon."

"I'm just trying to help you figure out what's going on."

Beth shot him a murderous glare. He'd seen that look before, and knew the conversation was about to turn ugly. He began to back out of the space.

"Stop," she said.

He pulled back in and threw the car into park but left the engine running.

"I quit," he said.

The words stunned her, and she struggled to reply.

"You can't . . . ," she said.

"You want my help, you'll answer my questions. Otherwise, I'd suggest you call the FBI agents from the Jacksonville office, and get them to assist you."

She squeezed his forearm. "I want you, not them."

"You sure about that?"

"I'm sure."

"Warts and all?"

"Warts and all."

"Let's start this conversation over, shall we?" He turned off the ignition. "Did your father ever text you a photograph or video he'd taken? I'm betting he saw some pretty spectacular sunrises from his balcony."

"He never did that."

"Did he like to text, or send emails?"

"Hardly. When he wanted to talk, he called."

The car's interior was growing warm without the AC, and he rolled down the windows and for a long moment said absolutely nothing.

"Tell me what you're thinking," she said.

"If your father rarely used emails or sent text messages, then the Gallery app would have been the only app on his phone stored with personal information. My gut tells me that Sykes erased the phone to get rid of whatever was on that app."

"That's a stretch."

"Come up with a better scenario. I can't."

Beth chewed her lower lip. The conversation had turned uncomfortable, and was making her look at her father in a different light.

"Let's pretend you're right, and the Gallery app is the key," she said. "What do you think was stored on it?"

"Something of recent interest," he said.

"What does that mean?"

"Your father had no interest in owning a cell phone. Then he wants to buy one, and he asks you to help him. He only cared about one app, and that was the Gallery app. Something happened in his life that made him want to start taking photographs, and store them on a cell phone."

"Hold on a minute. My father didn't want a cell phone. Nicki talked him into buying one. I already told you that."

"Did Nicki tell you that, or did he?"

"He did. Do you think my father lied to me?"

"Yes, I do."

"But why would my father do that?"

"I have no idea what your father's motivation was, but I'm pretty sure he made up that story to get you to help him buy a cell phone, and install the Gallery app on it. Otherwise, he could have just bought a cheap cell phone. It would have saved him a lot of money."

"Dad wouldn't have done that. He wasn't a liar."

"Why don't we call your niece, and settle it?"

He had boxed her into a corner, and he saw a flame in her eyes. Beth yanked her cell phone out of her purse, and placed a call to her niece. She put her cell phone on speaker so they would be both able to hear the conversation.

"I'll bet you dinner I'm right," she said.

"Only if I can pick the restaurant," he replied.

"You're wrong about this, Jon."

Lancaster wanted to be wrong, but the evidence said otherwise. Nicki answered in a terrified whisper.

"Aunt Beth. You need to come back," the teenager said.

"What's wrong, Nicki?" Daniels asked.

"There are two men inside the house trying to hurt us."

"*What?* Who are they?"

"I don't know. They have ski masks on."

"Are you in a safe place?"

"Yes. I'm hiding in the panic room with my parents."

"What panic room?"

"The one Grandpa built behind the kitchen pantry."

Melanie came on the line. "Hurry, Beth! They have guns."

"Did you call 911?"

"Yes. An automated answering service put me on hold."

"Hold tight—we're coming."

Lancaster pulled out of the Starbucks with his tires screaming. Saint Augustine was a sleepy town, and he guessed the number of home invasions that took place during broad daylight was probably zero. He thought back to the pair of Russian thugs parked outside the church, and wished he'd done a better job putting the fear of God into them.

"Why would your father build a panic room?" he asked.

"I don't know," Beth said.

CHAPTER 7

Daniels wanted to kick herself. Jon had picked up on the threat that the Russians parked outside the church had posed, and she'd ignored his warning. Being an FBI agent made her deal with facts, and as a result, she'd tuned out her intuition. That was a mistake, and now she was paying the price.

Jon drove at breakneck speed down her father's street with the car's emergency lights flashing. A half block from the house, he pulled into a neighbor's driveway and parked. The neighbor was watering the yard and shot them a frightened look.

They jumped out and drew their sidearms. Daniels flashed her badge and told the neighbor there was a burglary taking place down the street, and to please call the police. The neighbor dropped the hose on the grass and ran inside.

There wasn't a sidewalk, and they trotted down the middle of the street toward her father's home. Her breathing was accelerated, and she could feel the world speeding up. Jon had been in a lot more of these situations, and she decided to follow his lead.

"Plan of attack?"

"We need to split up. I'll take the front door, you go around back, and come through the kitchen door. It should be unlocked."

"Got it."

Jon came to a sudden halt. He lifted his arms and pointed his weapon straight ahead as if aiming at an imaginary target. They were a hundred feet from the house, their view of the driveway blocked by the neighbor's wall of bushes.

Daniels stopped as well. She heard the faint rumble of a running engine.

"Is that them?" she asked.

"I think so," he said.

The Charger flew in reverse down her father's driveway, then turned in the street so it faced them. Its back end jumped, and it sprang forward like a sprinter coming out of the blocks. They were about to be run over, and she aimed at the darkened windshield.

Jon grabbed her by the shoulders, and lifted her clean off the pavement. He was deceptively strong, and he carried her off the street and straight into the bushes, his momentum allowing them to crash through.

They landed in a well-kept yard. A Jack Russell terrier charged them, voicing its disapproval. On the street, the Charger screamed past with its horn blaring, the driver taunting them. Daniels promised herself that she would pay them back for this.

She picked herself up off the ground and took a quick accounting of herself. Her clothes had been torn by the sharp branches, and she had dirt in her mouth. Jon stood beside her, his face cut in several places, the blood flowing freely.

"That was a bad idea, Beth," he said.

"Sorry. I wasn't thinking," she said. "You're hurt."

"Flesh wounds. Did you run a trace on the license earlier?" he asked.

"No, but I will. Let's go check on Melanie's family."

They crashed back through the bushes and ran down the street. The front door of the house was open, and they went inside and did a quick check downstairs. All clear.

"The rooms haven't been touched," she said. "What do you think they wanted?"

"I don't know. I'm going to have a look upstairs," Lancaster said. "Give a shout if you need me."

He vanished up the stairwell. Daniels moved to the rear of the house and entered the kitchen. Nothing had been touched there, either, and it made her wonder what the Russians' motive had been. She started to knock on the pantry wall to let Melanie know that it was safe to come out, but remembered that her sister had a concealed weapon permit, and might shoot through the wall if she thought they were in danger.

Daniels called her sister on her cell phone instead. "I'm here in the kitchen. They're gone. You can come out."

"Thank God," Melanie said.

Daniels ended the connection. The kitchen had a small butler's pantry, with opposing shelves containing canned goods and spices. The back wall swung in, and Melanie, Nicki, and Nolan emerged, looking scared out of their wits.

Daniels put her weapon down on the counter and hugged each of them. Melanie pulled a twig out of her sister's hair, and they both started to cry.

"I've never been so scared in my life," Melanie said.

Nolan took a seat at the breakfast nook. His shirt was soaked with sweat, and he was breathing through his mouth.

"Are you going to be okay, Nolan?" Daniels asked.

"I just need to catch my breath," he said. "Your father didn't get around to installing air conditioning in that room. It must have been a hundred degrees."

"Did you get a look at them, Aunt Beth?" Nicki asked.

"I saw their car. It was the guys parked outside the church," Daniels said.

"I told you so," Nicki said to her parents.

"We have the license plate, so it shouldn't be too difficult to track them down," Daniels said. To her sister, she said, "When did Dad build a panic room?"

"Three months ago. I thought he told you."

"I had no idea. Did he say why?"

"Nope. He just went and did it."

To her niece, she said, "Nicki, do you remember asking your grandfather to buy a smartphone recently?"

"It wasn't me," Nicki said.

Her father had lied to her about why he'd purchased a smartphone, and had also built a panic room without bothering to tell her. Was it a coincidence, or were the two things connected?

Daniels entered the pantry and stuck her head into the room. Small and without windows, it had walls reinforced with sheets of steel. The door was also made of steel and several inches thick, with a deadbolt and a dozen hinge screws to resist battering. Her father had never mentioned any burglaries in the neighborhood, and she wondered why he hadn't installed a security system if he was afraid of a break-in.

Nicki tugged on her sleeve. "Jon's calling you."

Daniels returned to the front of the house and stood at the bottom of the stairwell. Jon stood at the top, holding his weapon at his side. He looked worried, which was not like him. She started upstairs, and her niece followed.

"Nicki, don't come up," Lancaster said.

"Why not?" the teenager replied.

"Because it's a crime scene, and I don't want you disturbing anything."

"A crime scene? What did you find?"

"Do as Jon says, honey. It's for the best," Daniels told her.

"I won't touch anything, I promise," her niece said.

"Please, Nicki."

"Come on, I'm a part of this, too, aren't I?"

"You most certainly are. The police should be arriving any minute. Here's what I want you to do. Go to the living room window and wait for them. When they arrive, go to the front door, and bring them inside. They will need to take a statement from you, and your parents. Okay?"

Nicki mumbled disapprovingly and headed downstairs. Daniels watched her depart, then joined Lancaster at the top of the stairs.

"The study was ransacked," he said. "They left a memento."

"What kind of memento?"

"See for yourself."

She followed him into her father's study. Some men escaped the real world in their workshops or garages. Her father's lair was his study, where he spent countless hours reading books and poring over newspapers. He had spent more time here than anywhere else, and had often referred to it as his haven.

She let out a gasp. The desk had been pulled apart, its files lying in a heap on the floor. The bookshelves had been pulled off the walls and toppled over, her father's treasured books covering the floor. Many of the books had been ripped apart, and she suspected the burglars had been looking for something hidden within their pages.

As she walked around the room, she was careful not to touch anything. Her father had loved his books, and seeing them so mutilated filled her with anger. An open copy of Peter Robinson's *In a Dry Season* lay at her feet, the title page autographed. She'd gone to the author's book signing and gotten a copy for her father as a present. Dad had been thrilled, and said the book was one of his all-time favorites.

Her eyes were drawn to the wall safe. Like the panic room, she hadn't been aware of its existence. Her father had been keeping secrets from her, and she could not fathom why. She glanced at Jon, who hadn't made a sound.

"They were looking for the combination to the safe, weren't they?" she said. "That's why they tore apart his desk, and opened all his books."

He nodded.

47

"Doesn't look like they found it," she said. "I wonder if my dad wrote the combination down, or if he just kept it in his head."

"I have it in my wallet," he said. "When you and Melanie were poring over your father's financial records, I came upstairs, and had a look around the study. The combination was in a hidden compartment in his desk."

She shook her head in bewilderment. "He was acting like a spy. Did you stumble across anything that would indicate why?"

"No, but there must be a good explanation. That safe would have been expensive to have installed, same for the panic room. He must have felt threatened."

"And scared. You said they left a memento. Where is it?"

She followed him across the study. In the corner was a tarnished brass bucket that contained her father's carved walking sticks. Propped up against the bucket was a mummified hand wrapped in cloth. Its fingers were long and bony, the skin the color of ash. It looked like a Halloween prop, and she picked it up for closer inspection. The skin was cold to the touch, and she felt an icy finger run down her back. It was real.

"This is sick," she said.

"I feel the same way."

She held it up to the light and studied it. At the FBI academy she'd studied forensics and knew that a mummified body was a result of accidental exposure to chemicals, extreme cold, or lack of air, and that the body would not decay further if kept in cool and dry conditions. The hand was in good condition, leading her to believe that it probably had come from a museum. The Russians had brought the hand here intending to leave it behind. They were trying to send a message

"What does this mean?" she said aloud.

"It wasn't meant for us," he said.

Holding the hand was making her uncomfortable, and she placed it on her father's desk. "Then for who?"

"The police."

"You think they'll understand what this means?"

"I think so. Detective Sykes erased the apps on your father's cell phone. My guess is, Sykes isn't the only one on the force who knows what's going on."

"The police are involved."

"I didn't say that."

"Then what?"

"The police know what's going on, and don't want it getting out. They're conducting damage control, just like any other Florida police department."

Daniels shook her head. She didn't have a clue as to what Jon was saying.

"Florida's economy is driven by tourism," he said. "It's the state's economic engine, and drives everything from beer consumption to real estate sales. Local police departments are trained to suppress negative stories if they think it will hurt tourism. Saint Augustine is a tourist town, and will get hurt by a bad story in the newspapers."

"Are you speaking from experience?"

"Yes, I am. When I was a cop, we suppressed negative press all the time. That didn't mean that we didn't prosecute people who broke the law. We did. We just did our damnedest to keep the story out of the newspapers."

"Because bad press hurts tourism."

"That's right."

Daniels was getting a clearer picture of how things worked in Saint Augustine. She heard her niece calling and walked out of the study and went to the head of the stairwell.

She looked down to see Nicki standing below.

"What's up?"

"The police are here," her niece said.

"Keep them busy. I'll be right down."

"You got it, Aunt Beth."

She returned to the study. She was wrestling with how much information she should share with the local cops, if any at all. She decided that they were not her friends, and would only suppress any negative information she shared about her father's passing.

"The police have arrived," she said. "We need to tell them about the Russians breaking into the house, and get them to file a report, but that's all we should tell them. I don't want to answer their questions, or share any other information. Okay?"

"My lips are sealed," he said.

"Good," she said. "I agree with you—the police are hiding something. Until I find out what it is, I won't tell them any more than I have to. Please do the same."

"I'll do whatever you want, Beth."

She took a deep breath. Losing her father had been hard, but what was happening now was harder. The anxiety must have shown on her face, because Jon put his arms around her for a hug. She shut her eyes, soaking in his strength.

"You're the best," she said.

CHAPTER 8

When Lancaster had reached forty, he'd noticed how young other people were starting to look. He didn't know if it was a sign of his advancing years, or just his eyes going bad.

The cop who'd responded to Melanie's and the neighbor's 911 calls was a good example. He had a fresh, innocent face, and didn't look older than sixteen, yet he was wearing a uniform and carrying a sidearm, so he had to be at least twenty-one. He seemed intimidated by Daniels's FBI status, and kept swallowing his Adam's apple.

"So you think the men that broke into your father's house were also parked outside the church for his funeral service this morning," the officer said.

"I do, Officer Spencer. It was the same black Dodge Charger, so I'd have to assume it was the same two men," she said.

Spencer scribbled in his notepad. "Did you actually see them at the church?"

"Jon went to the car and spoke with them. He thought they looked suspicious."

Spencer shifted his gaze. "Mr. Lancaster, if you don't mind my saying, you shouldn't be playing police officer. If there's a problem, the Saint Augustine Police Department is more than capable of handling it, sir."

"I'm a retired police officer," Lancaster said.

"You from up north?"

"Broward County. I was a detective."

"Oh, well that's different. Did you get a look at them?"

"I did. They were a pair of Russian hoodlums with a lot of jailhouse tattoos. Early forties, short haircuts, heavy accents. They told me they'd done landscaping work for Beth's father and had come to pay their respects. That turned out to be a lie."

Spencer resumed writing. "Did they attend the funeral?"

"No. They took off after I confronted them."

"Sound like a pair of bad hombres. Did you get their license?"

Beth gave a shake of the head and mouthed the word, No. Spencer was looking down and didn't see it. Lancaster didn't like withholding information from the police, but this was Beth's rodeo, and he would do whatever she asked of him.

"Afraid not," he said.

"That's a shame." Spencer flipped the notepad shut. "I'm going to ask our CSI team to come out, and dust the study for fingerprints. They're busy right now, so it might not be until tomorrow. Will someone be here to let them into the house?"

"We'll be here," Beth said.

"Good enough. I'll need to take the hand to headquarters, and let the CSI team run some tests. You never know, it might be carrying some strange diseases. You can never be too careful these days."

The mummified hand sat on the edge of Martin's desk in a towel. Spencer picked it up in his arms as if it were a baby, and made for the door. If the mummified hand was carrying a disease, Spencer would have put on rubber gloves before touching it. Lancaster glanced at Daniels and saw her mouth the word, Bullshit.

They went downstairs and followed Spencer outside to his cruiser, which was parked in the driveway. Spencer placed the hand in the trunk and gently closed it. He was pale, and clearly upset.

"Officer, I want you to come clean with me," Beth said. "Why did someone put a human body part in my father's study?"

"I don't know," the officer said.

"I don't think you're being truthful with me."

Spencer chewed his lower lip and stared at the ground.

"You lied to us. The story about the hand carrying diseases isn't true, is it?"

Spencer would have made a lousy poker player. Unable to hide his embarrassment, he took off his hat and punched the inside. He impressed Lancaster as a guy who went to church every Sunday, and would only lie if there was a good reason.

"You got me," the officer said.

"You realize I could have you fired for doing that."

"Yes, ma'am."

"I don't want to do that."

"No, ma'am."

"So what's the real reason?"

"A bunch of mummified hands have shown up recently. It's upsetting the hell out of people. They appear on the front stoops of houses wrapped in towels. It's damn sick, you ask me. The mayor is worried that it will get out, and hurt our tourist business. So he asked the police chief to hide any mummified hands we find."

"How many is a bunch?"

"Counting this one, seven." He hesitated. "My bad. The number's six."

"Over what time span?"

"The last two months."

"Any suspects?"

"A couple of punks got pulled in for questioning, but they all had alibis, and swore they'd never do such a thing. We hit a wall with the investigation."

"Were the hands dropped in front of houses, or commercial businesses?"

"Houses."

"Do you know the owners?"

"I know all of them."

"Please give me their names. I may want to question them, and see if they were in any way connected with my father."

"I'll need to get permission from my supervisor."

Beth gave the officer a murderous look. She possessed a dark side that could be downright scary, and Spencer shrank a few inches beneath her gaze.

"Bad idea," she said. "By law, you're required to answer my questions right now. If you don't, I'll do more than just get you fired. Am I making myself clear, Officer?"

There was not enough ground for Spencer to stare at.

"Yes, ma'am," he whispered.

"Take out your notepad, and write down the owners' names. Include the streets they live on as well."

Spencer took out his notepad and pencil and did as told. Finished, he tore out the sheet of paper and handed it to her. Lancaster moved to his left, and read the list over Beth's shoulder. Four men, one woman, two of them doctors.

Beth read each of the names aloud, along with their addresses, then had Spencer verify that the names were correct. Then, she had him sign and date the list, so there would be no confusion later on.

"I also need your card, in case I need to ask you further questions," she said.

Spencer took out his business card, and scribbled a number on the back. "That's my personal cell. If you need to call, please use that one," he said.

"What's the number on the front of the card?" Beth asked.

"That goes to my official cell phone."

"You don't want to talk to me on that one?"

"I'm between a rock and a hard place here, ma'am. My supervisor can have me disciplined for disobeying orders, and you can get me fired for lying. I'd prefer to keep any further conversations private, if that's okay with you."

"Fair enough. I'll be in touch."

Spencer thought he was off the hook, and moved to get into his cruiser. Lancaster had not stopped thinking about the Charger parked in front of the church. Of all the puzzles associated with Martin's death, it was bothering him the most, and like the chicken in the road in Africa, it was going to nag at him until he solved its riddle.

"Officer Spencer, I have one more question," Lancaster said. "Would you mind telling me how large the police force in Saint Augustine is?"

Spencer was caught off guard by the question. "Come again?"

"How many officers are on the force?"

"About a hundred."

"Do they patrol the city and the beach?"

"Just the city. The beach has its own force."

"That's a lot of officers for one city. Why so many?"

"The city has a big homeless population. We try to get them into shelters so they're not sleeping outside. We had to add officers in order to deal with them."

"How do these officers get around town?"

"By car."

"So they're constantly cruising the city, looking for the homeless."

"That's right. It's extra work, but it keeps the crime rate down."

"I'm sure it does. Thank you."

Spencer looked rattled, and his tires squealed as he backed out of the driveway and left. Lancaster sensed another presence, and he turned around. Nicki stood in the open doorway, eavesdropping. He shot her a disapproving look, and she disappeared.

"Why did you ask him those questions?" Beth asked.

"The Charger was bothering me, but I couldn't figure out why. Now I know."

"I must have missed something. What did Spencer say?"

"That Saint Augustine has a large police force that regularly patrols the city."

"So?"

"The Charger got to the church early to get that spot, and was parked there for over an hour," he said. "Several police cruisers would surely have driven by it. The cops would have seen the same suspicious things that I did. Yet none stopped to talk with those jokers."

"The police deliberately avoided them? Why would they do that?"

"Because someone told them to."

"Sykes?"

"Could be. You told Spencer that we didn't get the Charger's license. Are you going to run the Charger down without the police's help?"

"Yes. I was going to ask the FBI's Jacksonville office to help me arrest the Russians. Care to join us?"

Lancaster enjoyed nothing more than a bust, and said yes. But first, he needed to have a talk with Nicki, and find out how much she'd heard of their conversation. This was a bad situation, and he didn't want her drawn into it any further.

Enough people had already been hurt.

CHAPTER 9

The special agent in charge of the FBI's Jacksonville office had been in Daniels's class at Quantico. His name was Erce Phillips, and they had spent many hours in each other's company, running the winding wooded trails within the base. She didn't think they'd talked more than ten minutes during the time they'd spent together, yet Daniels felt like she knew him, and hadn't been surprised to see him at the church that morning.

Daniels called the Jacksonville office, and Phillips took her call.

"I need your help," she said. "Two armed men broke into my father's house while my sister and family were there. I have the license plate of the vehicle they were driving, and need you to run a check for me."

"That's horrible," Phillips said. "Is your sister's family okay?"

"They hid in a panic room while the men ransacked my father's study."

"I'm sorry to hear that. Your family has been through enough."

"Thanks, Erce. It's been a long day."

She gave him the information and heard his fingers dance on a keyboard.

"My computer's running slow today," Phillips said. "Is this the same Charger that was parked outside the church this morning?"

"You noticed them too?"

"I thought they looked out of place. I wonder why they waited so long."

"What do you mean?"

"The funeral was at ten. It's now three thirty. Guys who burglarize houses scour the obituaries in newspapers, then park outside the church the day of the funeral. When everyone's inside, they drive to the deceased person's house, and break in. The guys that broke into your father's house waited, and risked running into a member of your family. Doesn't make sense."

"No, it doesn't. I don't think they were burglars. Nothing was stolen."

"Weird. Oh crap. My computer's frozen up. Let me call you back."

"You got it."

She ended the call. She was standing in the corner of the living room, and could hear Jon engaged in a lively discussion with Nicki in the kitchen. Nicki aspired to be a law enforcement officer one day, yet instead of emulating her aunt, had chosen Jon to be her role model. Daniels didn't have an issue with that. Jon was a strict disciplinarian, and she enjoyed standing back and watching him rein her niece in.

She entered the kitchen to find Nicki and Jon standing toe-to-toe like a pair of boxers squaring off in the ring. Nicki's face was red, and she appeared to be on the losing end. Melanie and Nolan stood a safe distance away, saying nothing.

"But I can help your investigation if you let me stay," her niece pleaded.

"That's out of the question, Nicki," Jon said.

"But I'm a good detective. You said so yourself."

"You're an *excellent* detective. That isn't the issue here."

"Then what—you just want me out of your hair?"

"We could actually use your help. The issue is, those men saw your faces when they broke into the house. They're dangerous, and you're not safe until they're arrested. I want you to drive back to Fort Lauderdale with your parents, and let us deal with this."

"I think that's an excellent idea." Melanie said. "It isn't safe here."

"I'll go pack the suitcases," Nolan said.

"But what about the dead hand you found in Grandpa's study?" Nicki said, unwilling to quit.

Her father stopped dead in his tracks and stared at his daughter.

"What in God's name are you talking about, Nicki?" Nolan asked.

"Jon found a mummy's hand in Grandpa's study," she explained. "Officer Spencer brought it downstairs wrapped in a towel, and put it in the trunk of his cruiser. He acted really upset, and when Aunt Beth questioned him, he admitted there were other cases in Saint Augustine where hands had appeared on people's property."

Nolan stared at his sister-in-law. "Is this for real?"

"I'm afraid so," Daniels said. "We don't know what it means, or how the cases are connected. The police are trying to keep the whole thing quiet. They're afraid if the story leaks out, it will have a negative impact on tourism."

"Sounds like a coverup to me," Nicki said.

Out of the mouths of teenagers came the most startling things. The kitchen fell silent, her accusation hanging like a dark cloud.

"What do you think the police are covering up?" Jon asked.

"Everything," Nicki said.

"Be more specific."

"I think the other people who got dead hands were connected to Grandpa. The Russians were trying to intimidate them. How about if I go online, and find the link? You told my CSI class that smart criminals never commit random acts, there's always a motive. Dig deep enough, and you'll find it."

Daniels had heard enough. The last thing she wanted was Nicki doing background checks on the other names that Spencer had given them, tainting the investigation by sticking her nose where it didn't belong.

"You'll do no such thing," Daniels said. "You and your parents are going to pack your things, and hit the road. Understood?"

"But—"

"No buts. This is for your own safety. Jon and I will figure out what's going on."

"But I can help."

"You're in harm's way. Jon and I can't protect your family while trying to figure this out. Please, do as I say."

Melanie put her hand on Nicki's shoulder. "It's for the best, honey."

"This is so totally unfair," the teenager said.

- - -

Daniels had a bad feeling about her niece. As she stood in the driveway watching Nolan back out, she had a clear view of Nicki in the back seat. Her niece was furiously typing away on her iPad, and she could only imagine the trouble Nicki was going to get herself into. Nolan beeped twice before driving away.

"She's just like you," Lancaster said.

"Are you saying that I caused this behavior?" Daniels said.

"You're a contributing factor."

"You're the one she looks up to."

"But you're the one she wants to be."

It was a scary thought. Her cell phone vibrated. It was Erce, calling her back.

"The Charger is owned by a local hoodlum named Arlen Ray Childress," the special agent said. "He's got a rap sheet, including arrests for trespassing and peddling weed. His current address is Saint Augustine Beach. I'll text you the info."

"Great. Are you free right now?" Daniels asked.

"I am. Would you like me to assist you with the bust?"

"I would. I want to leave the local cops out of it. I spoke with a Detective Sykes earlier, and he wasn't up front with me. I don't trust him."

"That's not good. Is the sheriff's department somehow involved?"

"I don't know what to think, I just know Sykes lied to me. The police don't respect outside authority, so I don't feel any obligation to include them."

"I hear you. Let me round up a team. We should be there in forty minutes, depending on traffic. I'll call you when we get close."

"Thanks, Erce."

She ended the call. Jon stood beside her, staring at the spot in the driveway where Nolan's vehicle had been parked. The pieces of the puzzle didn't fit, and Jon was trying to put them together. She could almost hear the gears shifting in his head.

"Making any headway?" she asked.

He shook his head. "I do know one thing," he said.

"And what pray tell is that?"

"This is all about your father's money. There's no other explanation."

"How do you know that?"

"Because a pair of Russian gangsters is involved. In my experience, the only thing Russian criminals care about is money. They're obsessed with it. If we can figure out where the money that disappeared from your father's bank accounts went, we'll have a clearer picture as to what's going on here."

Jon was being diplomatic. He'd just said that her dad had been involved with the Russians. There was no hiding from it anymore, as difficult as it was to accept. Her father had gotten himself in trouble, and it was up to them to clean up the mess.

"Let's go nail Arlen Childress," she said.

PART TWO

THE CURSE OF THE SACRED CAT

CHAPTER 10

Saint Augustine Beach was an oasis of glittering sand, with a smattering of high-rise condos upsetting the otherwise unmatched beauty. They drove for miles without seeing another vehicle. Lancaster was playing navigator, his cell phone clutched in his hand.

"Our turn is coming up," he said.

"This is pretty desolate," Beth said, manning the wheel. "Childress lives on Ridgeway, right?"

"Correct. My phone says the street is up ahead. Do you see a sign?"

"No, but I do see an unmarked road. Maybe that's it."

They came to the turn. Lancaster stared out his window at the downed street sign lying in the tall grass on the side of the road. The sign said RIDGEWAY AVENUE and appeared to have been ripped out of the ground with a piece of heavy machinery.

"This is the place," he said.

Daniels made the turn and drove at a crawl. The street was shaded by a canopy of trees, the branches dripping Spanish moss. They passed a mailbox with the address. Arlen Childress lived in a gray shingle house with a sagging front porch. A narrow dirt driveway snaked around the side of the house to the back of the property.

"I don't see the Charger," Beth said.

"It's probably parked in a garage in back," he said. "Turn around up ahead, and do another drive-by. Maybe I can spot it."

"How do you know there's a garage in back?"

"You can't live this close to the ocean and leave your car outside," he explained. "The salt water will destroy the finish."

"You learn something new every day."

She turned around and drove past the house again. Lancaster lowered his window and stuck his head out. As they passed, he spotted a converted barn behind the house, with a vehicle parked in front of it. It was the Charger.

"Bingo," he said.

Beth drove back to the highway, and parked in the shadow of a boarded-up building on the side of the road. She texted Phillips, and got an immediate reply.

"Erce and his team are a few minutes away," she said. "I've got a question for you. Why would someone go pull up a street sign? What's the purpose?"

"I've heard of people stealing street signs, and putting them in their houses," he said. "But the Ridgeway sign got thrown in the grass. Makes no sense."

"Another puzzle for the pile."

"That's one way to look at it."

They got out and stood in the shade. A minute later, an SUV pulled up, and Phillips jumped out. He was over six foot and didn't appear to carry an ounce of body fat. He'd brought four agents along for the ride. The trunks were popped, and the agents suited up. Phillips tossed each of them a bulky bulletproof vest.

"We've got helmets, if you want them," Phillips said. "Can't be too careful."

"I'll take you up on that," Beth said.

"So will I," Lancaster said.

They suited up. The helmets had thick, transparent face shields, and were similar to those Lancaster had worn in the navy. The sun was brutal, and sweat poured down his face and soaked his collar.

"We did a drive-by of the suspect's house," Beth said. "The Charger's parked in back, so we're assuming he's somewhere on the property. The street sign was ripped out of the ground, so you'll need to follow us."

"Do you think he ripped it out?" Phillips asked.

"Hard to know. Why?"

"His rap sheet made him sound like a druggie. He might be unstable."

"We'll soon find out. Ready when you are."

- - -

They drove to the suspect's house and parked on the street. Both vehicles emptied. Phillips and his team were armed with Mossberg tactical shotguns, which were absolutely lethal at close range. If Arlen Childress resisted, he'd pay for it with his life.

The agents fanned out across the front lawn. Lancaster and Beth went up the creaky front steps and saw the front door open before they had a chance to knock. An elderly man with a snow-white beard and teeth stained from chewing tobacco stared at them. Behind him, an old woman sat in a rocking chair, her face frozen in time.

"Oh my Lord, what has he done now," the old man muttered.

"FBI," Beth said. "We're looking for Arlen Childress. Is he home?"

"Arlen's out back," the old man said. "He lives in the garage."

"Are you his father?"

"Grandfather. My name's Adin."

"We need to speak with your grandson. One of these agents is going to come inside your house, to be with you and your wife. It's for your own safety."

"My wife has dementia, and doesn't take kindly to strangers. She might start yelling. Once that happens, I can't calm her down."

This wasn't good. If they didn't send an agent into the house, Adin might send his grandson a text, and alert him that a pack of FBI agents was looking for him.

"Does your wife yell often?" Lancaster asked.

"A couple of times a day," the old man said. "Why?"

"So your grandson is used to hearing it."

"You could say that."

To Beth he said, "Send the agent inside. It won't send up any red flags."

Beth motioned to one of the agents on the lawn, who hustled up the steps and moved past Adin into the house. When the old man started to object, Beth threatened to handcuff him, and toss him in the SUV. The old man shut up fast.

"Last question," Lancaster said. "Does your grandson own a gun?"

"He owns several," the old man said.

- - -

They walked single file down the driveway to the back, hugging the side of the house in case Arlen showed his face. Inside, the old woman had started shouting.

"She's got some pair of lungs," Beth said.

Behind the house was a red shingle barn that had been converted into a garage. It had a hippie feel, and was plastered with peace signs and counterculture bumper stickers. The garage door was up, and reggae music was playing at full blast. They waited to see if the shouting would draw Arlen out. Confronting him in the backyard would have been easier than entering the garage, where he would have an advantage.

They waited a minute, but he did not appear. Lancaster read each of the bumper stickers while they waited. One of them looked familiar, having once adorned his own car. It said FINS UP, and showed a shark's dorsal fin cutting through the water.

"I smell weed," Beth said. "He must be in there getting stoned."

"I think we should sneak up, take him by surprise," Erce suggested.

"There's a security camera on the side of the barn," Lancaster said. "If he's watching it, we're going to get shot."

"You have a better idea?" Erce said.

"I'd like to talk to him."

"You going to waltz in there, say hi? That's a real good way to get ambushed."

"He's a Parrot Head. So am I. I'm sure we have a lot in common."

"Like what?"

"We listen to the same music."

Lancaster removed his helmet and bulletproof vest and laid them on the ground. He carried a Glock pocket rocket in an ankle holster, which he removed and tucked in the back of his pants, cinching his belt an extra notch so it wouldn't fall out. Phillips was looking at him like he'd lost his mind, as was the rest of his team.

"Jon was a SEAL," Beth said. "He can handle himself."

Phillips's look of disbelief grew. "I hope you know what you're doing."

"I do," he said.

Lancaster started toward the garage. He moved slowly, not wanting to alarm Arlen if he was watching on a monitor. Law enforcement often acted like paramilitary organizations when dealing with suspected criminals. In his opinion, this was a bad thing, as too many innocent people were getting shot. Talking still worked, especially when dealing with people who smoked weed and listened to Jimmy Buffett.

After getting out of the navy, he'd camped out in Key West for a while, and tried to get his feet under him. A local barkeep had introduced him to the music of Jimmy Buffett, and he'd been a fan ever since, and even joined the Parrot Head Fan Club, or PHIP as its members called it. Parrot Heads drank rum and wore loud shirts and traded bootleg tapes from concerts. They were the most laid-back group of people he'd ever known, and he hoped Arlen Childress was no different.

If not, then he'd just have to shoot the bastard.

He stuck his head into the open garage. The interior was lit by a half dozen skylights. It consisted of one giant room divided by living room furniture, a dining room table, and a flat screen TV on a wall. Several towering pot plants took up a corner, and there were buds on the dining room table, being cleaned. He'd smoked dope once as a teen, and then slept for twenty hours straight. That had cured him.

"Anybody home?"

"That's far enough," a voice said.

The voice came from the right. A tall, sinewy guy with shoulder-length hair and bloodshot eyes stood against the wall, armed with a hunting rifle. He was in his underwear, and had a blanket draped over his shoulders.

"Arlen Childress? My name's Jon Lancaster. Can we talk?"

"Get the fuck out of here, and take your friends with you."

"I'm a private investigator. I just need to ask you some questions."

"Bullshit. If all you wanted to do was talk, why did you bring an army with you? I'm going to count to five, and if you're not gone, I'm going to shoot you dead."

"My friends will storm this garage if you do that, and it won't end well. Come on, there's no need for bloodshed."

"Then why did you put a gun in your pants? There's a security camera on the side of the house—I saw the whole thing. One."

"What do you think, that we're here to rob you?"

"Why else would you be here? I've got a license to grow pot, and half the scumbags in this town want to rip me off. Two."

"Is that why you tore down the street sign?"

"Boy, you're smart. Three."

"We're not here to steal your dope. You're a suspect in a home invasion. Those people outside are FBI agents, and I'm an ex-cop working this case."

"I don't believe you. Four."

"I convinced my friends not to storm the garage because I saw the Jimmy Buffett bumper sticker on the wall outside, and figured you were a Parrot Head—and a good guy. Please don't prove me wrong about this."

Arlen scrunched his face, thinking hard. He didn't want to shoot his visitor any more than Lancaster wanted to shoot him. He pointed the rifle's barrel at the floor.

"You're really a Parrot Head?" he asked.

"Until the day I die," Lancaster said.

"In the song 'My Lovely Lady,' what does she like to eat?"

"Her weight in crab meat."

"What song is this from: 'Nothing can tear you apart if you keep living straight from the heart'?"

"'Bring Back the Magic.' It's a duet Buffett sang with Rita Coolidge."

"Finish this line. 'Classy little white and red . . .'"

". . . 'turns everybody's head.'"

"You pass. How about some ID?"

Lancaster produced his wallet and showed Arlen his detective's badge. Then he pulled out a business card and, for good measure, his worn PHIP membership card.

"Put them on the dining room table, and step back," Arlen said.

He did as told. Arlen picked up his ID and had a look. He still wasn't sold, and Lancaster didn't know if it was the pot, or if he was just naturally suspicious.

"Tell one of your friends outside to hold up their badge," his host said.

"You got it."

Lancaster walked backward, not taking his eyes off Arlen, or his rifle. Turning his head, he said, "Beth, please take out your badge, and hold it so the monitor on the side of the building will see it."

"What?" Daniels said in a loud voice.

"Just do it. Please."

"Are you okay?"

"Fine and dandy."

Beth struggled to remove her badge from beneath the bulletproof vest. Finally she pulled it free and held it up to the building. Arlen moved over to a desk where a laptop computer sat and studied the screen. His expression changed, and he put the rifle into a gun cabinet and then opened a small refrigerator.

"My mistake," he said. "Tell your friends to come on in. You want something cold to drink?"

CHAPTER 11

The pot plants were a problem. There were seven of them, and that was over the legal limit for medicinal purposes in Florida. Special Agent Phillips was legally required to arrest Arlen for the plants. If Phillips did that, Arlen would ask for a lawyer and clam up, and they would be no closer to learning why two Russian gangsters had broken into Martin's house, and used Arlen's Charger as a getaway car.

They sat at the dining room table, hashing it out. Arlen had served up iced tea and bottled water and was smoking a joint to calm down. He had PTSD from a tour of Iraq he'd done while in the army, and was prone to recurring flashbacks.

"I'm assuming you have a medical card," Phillips said.

Arlen produced the card and slid it across the table. The joint dangled from his lips, its tip glowing each time he took a puff. He was a damaged soul, with one foot still firmly rooted in the past. Lancaster had known guys like Arlen in the navy. They rarely healed.

"You know the rules about the number of plants you're legally allowed to have," Phillips said. "The magic number is six, and you have seven."

"I know the law," Arlen said.

"So why deliberately break it?"

"For spillage," Arlen said. "Guys in town know I legally grow. They've robbed me a few times, stolen my plants. So I grow extra for them to take."

"It's still illegal," Phillips said.

"So is robbing me, but the cops haven't done anything about it."

"Did you file a report?"

"Bunch of times. Nothing came of it."

They were getting nowhere. Phillips didn't want to bust Arlen, but if it became known that he'd given Arlen a pass, he'd lose his job. It was a lose-lose situation for everyone involved. Beth rose from her seat at the table, and went to get another bottled water. Lancaster followed her to the fridge.

"I want you to distract your friends," he whispered.

"Why should I do that?" she whispered back.

"I'm going to fix this. Stand at the head of the table, and start talking. I need you to draw everyone's attention away from the side of the room where the plants are."

"Wait. What are you—"

"Just do it, okay?"

"Be careful here. I don't know Erce that well."

"Understood."

Beth got a fresh water and returned to the table. Instead of sitting, she stood at its head. "I'm confused about the dope. Isn't there another treatment for PTSD?" she asked. That led to Arlen repeating the treatments he'd undergone, and how his doctors at the VA hospital had decided that taking cannabis was the safest way to keep him from losing his mind.

"It's funny, but I never smoked until I got out of the army, and that's the God's honest truth," Arlen said, blowing a monster cloud.

Lancaster returned to the table. He gave Beth a wink. She'd seen his subterfuge, while the other FBI agents had not.

"I'm sorry, Arlen, but I'm afraid I'm going to have to arrest you, and confiscate your plants," Phillips said.

"Suit yourself," their host said.

Phillips read Arlen his rights and handcuffed him. Then, he told his team to take the plants outside. He planned to call for a police van to take the plants to the sheriff's department, where they'd be stored in a police property locker. Cell service was poor inside the barn, and Phillips went outside to make the call.

"I saw what you did," Arlen whispered to Lancaster.

"Keep it down," Lancaster said.

Arlen let out a stoner's laugh. Phillips returned moments later, holding his cell phone. He motioned for Arlen to come outside. Still laughing, Arlen obeyed, the lit joint dangling from his lips. Lancaster walked beside him, imploring him to keep quiet.

"You're okay for a cop," Arlen said.

"Glad you think so."

They stood by the building's scant shade and faced the pot plants, which were lined up on the back lawn. The team of FBI agents stood nearby, looking confused. From the house the old woman continued to yell.

"Hey, Erce," one of the agents said.

Phillips was still on his phone with the sheriff's department. He said, "Hold on," and clapped his palm over the mouthpiece. "What's up?"

"We got a problem," the agent said.

"What kind of problem?"

"A big problem. Take a look for yourself."

Phillips ended the call and joined his team. They talked in hushed whispers, and were clearly agitated. Arlen flashed a loopy grin.

"Thank you, brother Parrot Head," he said.

"That's not why I did it," Lancaster said.

"Then why?"

"I was a SEAL, and did several missions in Iraq. Every soldier that did a tour in that hell hole deserves a medal."

"You can say that again. Thanks, man."

Phillips stormed over to where they stood. He gave Lancaster an angry look, then stared at Daniels, trying to determine who had betrayed him.

"There's only six plants," the special agent bellowed.

"You must have miscounted," Beth said.

"You saw them yourself. There were seven plants when we entered the barn."

"I didn't count them," Beth said. "This wasn't intended to be a drug bust. When you said there were seven plants, I took your word for it. You must have miscounted. Mistakes happen, Erce."

"I don't make mistakes like that," Phillips snapped. "Your friend here disposed of one of the plants when we weren't looking."

Beth put her hands on her hips and stared him down. "He did no such thing. You made an honest mistake. No harm, no foul. Please remove the handcuffs from our suspect so we can get on with our investigation."

Phillips pulled out the handcuff keys and angrily tossed them on the ground. He rounded up his team, and they departed without so much as a goodbye.

Arlen laughed under his breath as Lancaster uncuffed him.

- - -

"How did you make the plant disappear?" Arlen asked.

They were back at the dining room table inside the barn. Using an app on his phone, Arlen made a Jimmy Buffett classic, "Son of a Son of a Sailor," play from the speakers hanging on the wall. Lancaster sat at the head of the table. He'd convinced Beth to let him take over. A bond had formed, and Arlen was in his corner.

"I dragged the smallest plant into the bathroom and flushed the leaves down the toilet," he said. "Then I broke the stem into little pieces, and hid them in the tank."

"Thanks for picking the smallest," Arlen said. "Guess I'd better clean the tank out before I flush again."

"That would be a good idea. Now let's discuss why we're here. Your Charger was spotted driving away from a home invasion a few hours ago, and nearly ran us over. The same vehicle was spotted earlier parked outside a church. A pair of nasty-looking Russians were driving it. Do you know these guys?"

"Not very well. Their names are Bogdan and Egor Sokolov."

"Are they brothers?"

"Yeah, I think so."

"Which is which?"

"Bogdan is taller, and does the talking. Egor is the short one, and does the driving. They rent my car when they come to town."

"So your relationship is a business one. How often do they come into town?"

"Three or four times a month. I met them through a car sharing marketplace called Turo. They fly into town and Uber it over here. They always bring the car back clean, and pay in cash. It's a good deal for me."

"Which airport do they fly into?"

"Northeast Regional. It's just north of Saint Augustine."

"Did they ever discuss their business with you?"

"No. Whatever they were doing, it was generating a lot of cashola. They always brought an empty duffel bag with them. When they left, it was stuffed." The joint had turned to ash, and Arlen rolled another on the table and lit up. In Lancaster's experience, cannabis was like truth serum. The more of it a person smoked, the more they were likely to reveal, the only difference being that people didn't take truth serum willingly when speaking with agents of the law.

Arlen took a hit and reflexively offered Beth the joint.

"Whoops. I didn't mean that," he said.

"I smoked once in college," she said defensively.

Arlen dropped his chin and tried not to guffaw.

"Let's get back to the Sokolovs," Lancaster said. "They've been visiting Saint Augustine and using your car to get around. Did you ever see them in town?"

"Just once. They were having drinks with a woman at a dive called the Bar None Saloon. It's on A1A, not far from here. I took an Uber over there with my buddies one night. I went up to the bar to get a brew, and caught them out of the corner of my eye, but they didn't see me."

"How long ago was this?"

"Three weeks back. The jukebox was on, but I caught a few words. They were talking in Russian. The woman kept saying, 'Nyet, nyet,' and Bogdan would shoot her down. It wasn't friendly, so I grabbed a beer and went onto the patio."

"Have you seen this woman before?"

"You bet. She was at the Tradewinds one Friday night, turning heads. I was going to buy her a drink, but my buddy told me she was bad news, so I left her alone."

"She was good-looking?"

"A real showstopper. Ever notice how Russian men look like dogs, but the women look like models? I wonder why that is."

"Why did your buddy say she was bad news?"

"She must have a bad rep. This being a small town, word gets around."

"Describe her."

"She's got jet-black hair and long eyelashes and a kick-ass body. She sits at the bar with an unlit butt in her mouth. That's her hook. She wants guys to light her cigarette, so she can strike up a conversation."

"Is she a hooker?"

"Sheriff doesn't put up with hookers. His deputies have orders to run them out of town. She likes to troll, see what she'll catch."

"What's her name?"

"Katya. My buddy Antonio took her out. Not sure why he broke it off."

"Do you have Antonio's number? We might want to talk to him."

Arlen recited his friend's number from memory, and Beth wrote it down on her notepad. Beth also asked for the spelling of Katya's name, which she also wrote down. While this was taking place, Lancaster slipped his cell phone off the table, and pressed a button on the screen. He'd been secretly recording Arlen, and planned to listen to their conversation later, to see what he might have missed.

They were done. Arlen had given them enough information to move the investigation forward. They rose from the table, and he and Arlen shook hands.

"Thanks, brother," he said.

"Anything for a Parrot Head," Arlen replied.

CHAPTER 12

"How much trouble are you in?" Jon asked.

Daniels stared at the ruler-straight highway, her hands gripping the wheel of her rental. There would be blowback from the ruse they had pulled on Phillips and his team, maybe even a formal review. The bureau did not tolerate impropriety among its agents, and her covering for Jon while he made the seventh marijuana plant disappear would be considered a major infraction.

She was in real trouble, no doubt about it.

She didn't care. Her father's death was looking more suspicious by the hour, and she was going to get to the bottom of the circumstances behind it, even if it meant pissing off every law enforcement officer on the east coast of Florida.

"Who cares?" she said.

"I do. Phillips will write up what happened, and he'll assume that I made that pot plant disappear while you were distracting him and his team. That could hurt you."

"Fifty-fifty Phillips doesn't file a report."

"You think your odds are that good?"

"I do. Busting Arlen would have silenced a valuable source. We needed him to talk, and arresting him would have accomplished the opposite. It was a judgment call."

"But you broke the law."

"I did no such thing. You broke the law. Look, I'm going to catch heat over this, no question about it. But if we break this open, all will be forgiven. My boss can be very understanding that way."

"How is J. T. doing, anyway?"

"He's back at work, cracking the whip. He's one tough SOB."

"My kind of guy."

They had come to the drawbridge that connected the beach to old downtown. It was called the Bridge of Lions, and had two marble lions guarding the entrance that were copies of the famed Medici lions from Italy. Traffic started to crawl, and she hit the brakes a little too hard, throwing them both forward.

"Sorry," she said.

"You okay?" he asked.

"No, I'm not okay," she said through clenched teeth. "I'm a nervous god damn wreck. These things we're learning about my father are tearing me apart, and I don't know what the hell to do. This isn't the man I knew."

"You're making assumptions. We don't know how this is going to turn out."

"It's going to turn out badly, Jon. I can feel it in my bones."

Red lights on the bridge began to flash. A crossing gate came down, and the drawbridge lifted to allow a large sailboat passage. Daniels threw the rental into park and fought back tears. Her father had gotten tangled up in a bad situation, one that involved gangsters and pretty young women with bad reputations. Instead of calling her for help, he'd let it spiral out of control until it was too late.

She got out and joined a group of tourists on the sidewalk, watching them take pictures of the sailboat. Lancaster edged up beside her, and handed her a tissue.

She blew her nose. "Thanks. When did you start carrying tissues?"

"I grabbed a few at the church this morning. Figured they might come in handy."

"Always thinking ahead."

"You got a call when we were talking to Arlen. Was it Nicki?"

"How did you know? My phone was muted, and in my purse."

"It vibrated against something metallic."

"I did get a call. How did you know it was Nicki?"

"She called me, too, asked me to call her back. She sounded very excited. I think she found something."

Daniels groaned. Her niece was like a bull in a china shop. She was headstrong and watched too many cop shows. These shows were good at explaining the forensics used to catch criminals, but didn't accurately portray the psychological toll of dealing with evil people. For Nicki, it was still a game.

"How do I tell her to stay out of this?" she asked.

"You already did that, and she didn't listen. Why don't you tell Melanie to take all of Nicki's devices away from her? Then Nicki won't be able to do any cybersleuthing."

"That's not going to happen, Jon. Nicki needs her devices to do her schoolwork."

"Then I guess you're stuck. Personally, I'd like to hear what she found."

"You're not helping. You know that, don't you?"

"You can't have everything, Beth. Want me to call her back?"

- - -

The red lights started to flash, and the drawbridge lowered. They crossed into town, their tires purring on the smooth cobblestone streets. Entering Saint Augustine was like taking a step back in time, the buildings rich with history and culture, and everything moving at a more civilized pace. She drove to a public lot across the street from a Spanish stone fortress called Castillo de San Marcos, and picked an empty spot. The fort was over three hundred years old, and had been built to defend Spain's interests in Florida. She called Nicki back, and put her cell phone on speaker. As the call connected, she glanced at him and said, "I don't feel good about this."

"You want me to do the talking?" he asked.

"She'll just roll right over you. She always does."

"Look who's talking."

"You think I'm a pushover? Just watch me."

Nicki answered on the first ring. She was filled with breathless enthusiasm and excitedly said hello. Before she could explain what she'd found, Daniels stopped her.

"Nicki, didn't Jon and I ask you to stay out of this? These men are dangerous."

"But I found the link!"

Daniels's eyes went wide. "You did? Tell us."

"Am I helping you with the investigation, or not?"

"Nicki, you don't get to bargain with us. It doesn't work that way. Where the heck are you, anyway? Are your parents there?"

"Dad pulled over for a pit stop. He and my mom are inside a 7-Eleven getting cold drinks and snacks. Remember what you told me, Aunt Beth? The more eyes on a case, the better chances you have of cracking it open. You told me that yourself."

"She's got you over a barrel," Jon whispered.

Daniels mouthed the words, Shut up. To her niece she said, "Here's the deal. You're on the case as of right now. But if I decide that you need to bug out, you must agree to do that. This is for your own safety, Nicki. Do we have a deal?"

"Yes, Aunt Beth."

"Splendid. Now let's hear it. I've got Jon sitting here with me."

"Okay, so here's what I found. Saint Augustine has a newspaper called the *St. Augustine Record*, which has a website with a backlog of articles. Officer Spencer said that mummified hands had been found at five different homes in the past year. It made me think that a story would have been written about it in the newspaper. Guess what? There wasn't a single mention."

"Maybe it wasn't a big enough story," Daniels said.

"They sure write about everything else. Bake sales, bicycles getting stolen, the local high school firing its basketball coach. But no mention of this. I went on Facebook, and typed the words 'Mummified hands, Saint Augustine' into the search engine. A dozen people in Saint Augustine who had posted comments popped up. They sounded scared, and were asking each other when the police were going to do something."

"Like it was being covered up," Daniels said.

"That's what it felt like," her niece said. "One of the comments was really strange. A woman asked her friend if she thought the mummified hands were linked to the museum. Her friend replied with a half dozen question marks."

"Did the woman mention the museum's name?" Daniels asked.

"No, she didn't. But I found it anyway."

"How did you do that?"

"I went to Google, and typed in the words 'Mummified hand, Saint Augustine.' A link for the Villa Zorayda Museum popped up. It's an old house that was built to look exactly like a famous palace in Spain. The house is filled with Egyptian artifacts, including the world's oldest rug. It was taken from a pyramid with a mummified hand wrapped inside, and is woven with cat hair. It's called the Sacred Cat Rug, and people think it's cursed. The museum won't let it be photographed, so there's a drawing on their site instead."

"How does this connect to the hands that showed up on people's doorsteps?" Daniels asked.

"I was just getting to that. It's believed that if a person sets foot on the rug, they'll be cursed, and die a horrible death. They claim that it hasn't happened recently, but get this. During a recent restoration of the rug, a mummified hand was found on the front steps of the museum."

"Seriously?"

"Uh-huh. Pretty weird, don't you think?"

"It could just be an urban legend."

"That's what I thought. I emailed the museum, and pretended to be a reporter writing an article about the rug. I got a reply right away. A nice woman said the story was true, and that the museum had filed a report with the police."

Daniels glanced at Jon, and saw him mouth the word, Wow! She felt the same way. This couldn't be a coincidence. Nicki had hit it right out of the park.

"This is amazing, Nicki. Thank you," Daniels said.

"Are you going to visit the museum?"

"I think that would be an excellent idea."

"Right now?"

"I don't see why not. We're parked across from the old fort. It can't be too far."

"I checked the museum out on Yelp. Several reviewers recommended a guide named Katya. They said she was really knowledgeable about the history of the rug."

Daniels shot Lancaster a look. His eyebrows went up.

"Katya with a *y*?" Daniels asked.

"That's right. How did you know?" her niece replied.

"Lucky guess. Thanks for all your help. Talk soon."

CHAPTER 13

The Villa Zorayda Museum *did* look like a palace, just as Nicki had said.

It was built in the Moorish Spanish Revival style of architecture that was prominent throughout Saint Augustine. Built on a foundation of poured concrete over a century ago, it had survived countless tropical storms and hurricanes.

The walk from the old fort had taken fifteen minutes. Along the way, they'd stopped to buy coffee, which they drank from Styrofoam cups. The city's sidewalks were teeming with out-of-towners, and they blended right in.

Beth had decided that they should enter the museum pretending to be tourists, and see what they could learn about the Sacred Cat Rug. Saint Augustine had many secrets, and announcing they were law enforcement would not work to their advantage.

An ornate sign on the front lawn said that the museum had been placed on the National Register of Historic Places in 1993. The place felt legitimate, and Lancaster guessed that there was some truth to the rug's dark history.

"Do you want to do the talking, or should I?" he asked.

"This one's yours," Beth said.

They dumped their coffee cups into a trash bin and went inside. The main lobby was two stories high and felt like a scene out of *1001*

Arabian Nights, the Moorish design on full display. The museum stayed open late during tourist season, and he purchased two tickets. A girl who looked like she was in high school stepped forward. She wore a floor-length dress and had her hair in a ponytail.

"Welcome to the Villa Zorayda," the girl said. "My name's Sierra, and I'll be your tour guide. Before we begin, please be aware that there are several exhibits where photography is prohibited. If you don't abide by the rules, your cameras will be confiscated."

"Putting mine away right now." Beth dropped her cell phone into her purse.

"Me too," Lancaster said, putting his cell phone away.

"Great! Please follow me," Sierra said.

They started on the ground floor. The building had a rich history, and Sierra shared stories from when it was a casino, speakeasy, and gourmet restaurant, while describing the original art and valuable antiques from the previous owner's collection. Sierra was older than she looked, and Lancaster guessed she was in her midtwenties. That made her closer to Katya's age, and he wondered if they knew each other.

They climbed a staircase to the second floor. The upstairs bedrooms were bigger than most people's apartments, and were filled with paintings and thick Persian rugs. There was so much stuff crammed into the rooms that it felt like an antique store.

The Sacred Cat Rug was in the last bedroom, and hung on the wall. It looked like a pregnant zebra, the body clumsily drawn, the legs poorly rendered, and might have fetched fifty bucks at a backyard sale. Its history made it important, and the curse that it carried.

"This is the museum's most famous piece," Sierra said. "It's called the Sacred Cat Rug, and is believed to be the oldest rug in the world. It's woven entirely of hair taken from cats found roaming the river Nile."

"That's a lot of cats," Lancaster said, playing the tourist.

"It most certainly is. The cats weren't harmed, and were released after their hair was taken. The Egyptians thought cats were sacred, and the penalties for harming one were severe, including being put to death. They revered cats for their ability to control vermin like rats and poisonous snakes, and considered them symbols of good luck."

Beth reached out as if to touch the rug. Sierra let out a little shriek and grabbed Beth's arm, stopping her.

"Please don't do that." Sierra spent a moment composing herself. She looked shaken and more than a little upset.

"Is this one of the exhibits that can't be photographed?" Lancaster asked.

"That's correct. No photographs."

"May I ask why not?"

"It's just the rule."

"But why? The rug isn't very attractive. The museum can't be worried about someone creating a knockoff."

"I don't make up the rules. Our tour is now completed. I hope you enjoyed yourselves, and will fill out a comment card before you leave. Have a great day."

Sierra flashed a practiced smile and moved to leave. She seemed eager to part company, and put as much distance between herself and them as possible.

Lancaster said, "Please don't leave."

Sierra halted on a dime. Her pleasant demeanor was gone.

"I read online that the rug is cursed," he said. "Is that why you don't want people touching or photographing it?"

"That's just a rumor," she said.

"There was an article in the newspaper that said a mummified hand mysteriously appeared on the museum's front steps after the rug was cleaned," he said.

Fear crept into her eyes, and her body tensed, as if preparing to take off running.

Beth stepped forward, and showed Sierra her badge. The young woman's mouth dropped open.

"Special Agent Elizabeth Daniels, FBI," Beth said. "This gentleman is Jon Lancaster, a retired police detective. We'd like a few minutes of your time."

"What's this about?" She sounded scared.

"We want to talk to you about a young woman that works here named Katya," Lancaster said. "Do you know her?"

Sierra hesitated. Then she said, "Katya's my friend."

"Have you spoken to her recently?"

She nodded.

"Your friend's in trouble, isn't she?"

"Big trouble," Sierra said under her breath.

"Do you want to help her?" Beth asked. "Because if you do, then you'll tell us everything you know."

"Okay," Sierra said.

Lancaster glanced at Beth and saw her nod. He could feel it in his bones, and so could she. They were about to break this thing wide open, and get to the bottom of what had happened to Beth's father in the months leading up to his death.

"Where can we talk in private?" Lancaster asked.

"Let's go to the Cobalt Lounge," Sierra said. "We can talk in private there."

CHAPTER 14

The Cobalt Lounge was located inside the Casa Monica hotel, the bar made of polished mahogany. Sierra picked a chair facing the entrance and kept one eye on the door. She acted nervous, and kept shifting in her chair. In Daniels's experience, that was good, since people who were on edge often had things to get off their chest. She'd changed into shorts and a T-shirt before leaving work, and brushed out her hair. She smiled timidly as a waitress approached.

"Hey, Sissy," she said.

"Well hey, Sierra, I didn't recognize you," the waitress said, happy to see her. "How you been keeping?"

"I'm doing okay. How about yourself? You still having those bad dreams?"

"Haven't had one in a while. Don't worry, they'll come back. You talk to Katya lately? I tried to call her, but her line doesn't work anymore. Did she leave town?"

"I don't know where she's run off to."

"If you happen to see her, tell her that a couple of guys were asking for her. They gave me the creeps." To Daniels and Lancaster she said, "Sorry for the chitchat. What can I get you folks to drink?"

They ordered iced tea, Sierra white wine. The waitress left, and Sierra stared at her image in the polished table. She seemed to be having second thoughts about talking to them, and Daniels decided to soothe any misgivings she might have.

"Are you feeling okay?" Daniels asked.

"Not really."

"We're here to help. Nothing is going to happen to you."

"Is that a promise?"

"Yes, it's a promise. Why does your friend have bad dreams?"

Sierra sucked on her vape like it was oxygen. "Sissy works too much, and it's invaded her head. They're called waitmares. A lot of restaurant servers have them."

"I've never heard that before. What does she dream of?"

"Crazy stuff. In one of her dreams, she has twenty tables, and her customers are yelling, wanting their meals. In the second, she's serving tables naked."

"Maybe she should find another line of work."

"Not around here. In this town, you wait tables or work in the kitchen. Before we start, can I ask you a question?"

"Go ahead."

"Is it true that lying to an FBI agent is against the law? I saw that on a TV show once, and wondered if the writers made it up."

"Knowingly lying to an FBI agent is a felony," Daniels said.

Sierra drew back in her chair. "Guess I'd better watch what I say."

"You need to be completely honest with us," Daniels said. "Don't hold back, okay?"

"If you find Katya, are you going to arrest her?"

"Why would we do that?"

"I don't know. I figured Katya was up to no good. She showed up in town a while back, started working at the museum as a tour guide. She was flat broke, barely scraping by. Next thing you know, she's got a house and she's wearing fancy clothes and pretty jewelry. I figured she was doing something illegal. Where else would the money have come from?"

"Was she prostituting herself?"

"No, ma'am. Sheriff doesn't allow hookers. Runs them out."

"Did you ask her where the money came from?"

"Sure. Said she had a sugar daddy. I said, 'What guy around here has money like that to burn?' She just laughed."

The waitress served them. The glass of wine was on the generous side, and Sierra took a big swallow. It settled her, and she said, "Thanks, Sissy."

"What are friends for?" the waitress asked.

Sissy departed, and Sierra continued to work on her wine.

"What do you know about the mummified hands that were turning up around town?" Daniels asked.

"Katya was behind that," Sierra said.

"Where did she get them from?"

"They were stored in the basement of the museum. They originally came from Egypt, and were put on exhibit, but they grossed people out, and were stored away. Katya went into the basement after work one night and stole them."

"Did she take anything else?"

"She stole a shrunken head. She stuck a cigarette between its lips, and put it out on Halloween as a prank."

Daniels's jaw tightened. Katya sounded like a twisted young woman, and she reminded herself that she and Sierra were friends. She glanced at Jon, wanting him to take over, and he jumped in without missing a beat.

"Did Katya put the hands on people's doorsteps?" Jon asked.

"Not Katya. She's not that brave. Stealing them was hard enough for her to pull off."

"Then who did?"

"Her crazy friends. That's my theory, anyway."

"What crazy friends?"

"I only met them once. Katya had a party one Saturday night, and a whole bunch of people in town got invited. It was a wild scene. People were doing Ecstasy and having sex in the bedrooms, and there was lots of weed and booze. There were three Mexican girls there I didn't know. They were rough trade."

"How so?"

"They were all tatted up, and gave off this weird vibe, like they wanted to rob us. You know the kind of girls I'm talking about?"

"I do," Jon said. "Do you think they were in a gang?"

"Maybe. Their stuff was in the bedrooms, so I got the sense they were staying. I never saw them around town, working in the restaurants or hotels, so I don't know how they made money."

"What led you to think they were responsible for putting the hands on people's doorsteps?"

"Something happened later in the party that made me realize they weren't normal. Everybody was flying high and getting down. One of the Mexican girls took her top off, and did this snake dance while holding the mummified hand from the museum. It used to be part of the Sacred Cat Rug exhibit. When the rug was found in Egypt, there was a mummified hand covered in jewels wrapped in it, which usually hangs with the rug. Katya borrowed the hand from the museum for her party. While the Mexican girl's dancing, she started slapping people in the face with the hand, like she's putting a curse on them. People didn't like it, but she wouldn't stop. It got way out of hand."

"Where is the jeweled hand now?"

"In a safe. I guess it was too valuable to keep on display."

"And when mummified hands started showing up in people's yards, you decided the three Mexican girls were responsible," Daniels said.

"Had to be. They were living in the house. And they were mean."

"Why do you think they did that?"

"To scare people. They had a scam going on, and it blew up in their faces. So they got Katya to steal the mummified hands, and dropped them on people's doorsteps. Everyone knows about the curse, so people naturally freaked out."

"Can you prove any of this?"

"I have a video of the party on my phone. Want to see it?"

"Please."

Soon a video of Katya's wild party was playing on Sierra's cell phone. Within the swirl of pot smoke and human bodies was a twirling, topless girl. She was young and curvy, and covered in blue-black tattoos. Using both hands, she clutched a shriveled human hand embedded with glittering stones like it was a magician's wand.

Her partners appeared holding a stoned-out girl. Dancing around them, the topless girl slapped the mummified hand against the stoned-out girl's face. The stoned-out girl did not approve and voiced her displeasure. Unfazed, the topless girl continued the bizarre ritual.

"Please pause this," Daniels said.

Sierra paused the video. The topless girl's back was to the camera. Between her shoulder blades was a tattoo of a five-pointed crown with an inscription that read, WE DON'T DIE, WE MULTIPLY. It was the logo of the Latin Kings, one of the most violent gangs in the country. Outsiders were the enemy, which explained the bad vibe Sierra had felt. The gang didn't accept non-Latino members, and she wondered how Katya fit in.

"I need a copy of this video," Daniels said.

Sierra sent the party video to her, via text message.

"You went to a party at Katya's house," Daniels said. "I need the address."

"Only if you promise to leave me out of this," Sierra said.

"Your name won't come up."

Sierra recited the address, and Daniels copied it in her notepad. She was finished, and glanced at Jon to see if he was done. He was breathing hard, the faint whistle impossible to miss.

"I have one more question," he said. "Who was Katya's sugar daddy?"

"I have no idea," Sierra said.

"Come on, you must have wondered. Didn't you?"

"I thought about it," Sierra admitted. "I figured it was probably some rich geezer who'd lost his wife, and was looking for a good time. Katya was the kind of girl that would grab a guy, and take him for a ride."

Daniels thought she just might get sick.

"I'm done," he said.

Sierra's cell phone vibrated. She stared at the incoming number on the screen.

"I need to take this," she said. "My mom's in the hospital. It might be her doctor."

"Go ahead," Daniels said.

Sierra slipped out of the booth and walked into the hotel lobby to take the call.

"I think she's lying," Jon said.

"She made up the story about the three Mexican girls?" Daniels asked.

"I think that part is true. She's lying about her mother being sick in the hospital. If that were true, she would have told us before she sat down."

"Is she going to bolt?"

"That would be my guess."

"Should we stop her?"

"On what grounds? She told us everything she knows."

Sierra glanced nervously at them. Her call ended, and she dropped her cell phone into her purse, then bolted for the exit. Daniels realized that she hadn't gotten Sierra's address in case she needed to follow up.

"Wait a minute," Daniels said.

She was too late. By the time she made it outside, Sierra was gone.

CHAPTER 15

Beth's rental was still parked at the fort, which was a good ten-minute hike. She asked the hotel valet how long it would take to summon a cab.

"Hard to say. They're not very reliable," the valet said.

They decided to hoof it. The cobblestone streets were choking with tourists, their milky skin and garish clothes making them easy to peg. By the time they reached the car it was nearly dark, and Beth was winded, and had to catch her breath. Lancaster could tell that she was emotionally spent, her body running on fumes. Each time they turned over a rock, another creep slithered out. Her father had been involved with some reprehensible people, yet they still didn't know why.

Lancaster typed Katya's address into a traffic app on his cell phone called Waze. Katya lived in an area called College Park. Waze said traffic was heavy, and the drive would take between ten and fifteen minutes.

"Think we should pay her a visit?" he asked.

"Only if we want to solve this," Beth said.

Soon they were stuck in traffic. Beth threw the vehicle into park, and turned in her seat to face him. "Tell me what you're thinking," she said.

"Who said I was thinking anything?" he asked.

"I did. You're onto something. Spit it out."

Beth had gotten good at reading his thoughts. Once this investigation was over, he planned to ask her how she did it. "There was a great deal of money missing from your father's bank account. My gut tells me Katya was the recipient."

"You think my father was her sugar daddy."

"I think he was in a relationship with her, and she started to blackmail him."

"Blackmail for what? Sleeping with a girl fifty years younger than him? If my father told me that, I probably would have applauded, and so would Melanie. We wanted him to date women, and enjoy himself. You can't be a hermit forever."

The revelation surprised him. Was Beth just saying that, or did she mean it?

"You wouldn't have been upset if he dated a woman younger than you?" he asked.

"I might have, but it's really none of my business," Beth said. "My father was a free spirit. If a pretty-young-thing tickled his fancy, so be it."

"I still think it was blackmail," he said. "Your father was living in a beautiful house with plenty of space. Katya could have moved in, and had a whole floor to herself. Instead, she blackmailed him into giving her loads of cash."

"I don't mean to sound like a broken record, but blackmail for *what*? What leverage would this woman have had over my father?"

"Your father told Nicki he was sorry. Your father did something regrettable, and he knew it would upset Nicki, and you and Melanie as well."

Beth rested her head on the wheel, and shut her eyes.

"Jesus Christ," she whispered.

- - -

Traffic started to move, and they crossed the bridge. Soon, her head-lights caught a sign that said COLLEGE PARK, and Beth turned down a street into a heavily forested area with houses far back off the road. After a long search, they found the address on a rusted mailbox, the house invisible from the street. Heavy metal music blared from behind the trees.

"Sounds like they're having a party," he said.

Beth blocked the driveway with her rental, and they got out. He removed a handgun from his pants pocket, slipped it behind his belt, and covered it with his shirt, which he wore untucked. They headed up the gravel driveway.

"Did you hear that?" he said under his breath.

"Hear what?" she whispered.

"Sounded like a woman crying."

"Your ears are better than mine."

There were certain sounds that if you heard once, you never forgot. He drew his handgun and held it loosely at his side, like a gunslinger. Beth removed her gun from her purse and clasped it with both hands, the way she'd been taught at the academy.

As they passed a hedge, the house came into view. It had two stories and stained shingles, and a wraparound front porch with a pair of identical rockers. It wasn't new, but it was well maintained, and it looked expensive. Katya had done well for herself.

The music was loud enough to wake the dead, and was pouring out of a curtained side window, which was cracked open. He had never understood the attraction to heavy metal, which was as soothing as listening to a jet take off.

He climbed the stairs to the front porch, making no sound. He was in warrior mode, his military training taking over. Beside the front door was another curtained window. He approached it cautiously, and brought his face up to the glass. Through a part in the curtain he peered into a living room filled with nice furniture and wall art.

"Shit," he said under his breath.

"She in there?" Beth whispered back.

"I think so. And so are the two Russkies."

The Sokolovs stood in the living room, stripped down to their waists. They were freakishly muscular and covered in hideous body art. Bogdan, the older and taller, wielded a large hammer, while Egor held a power drill. They were taking turns threatening a young woman, who sat in a stiff-backed wood chair in the room's center. A piece of duct tape hung off the side of her cheek, and he guessed one of them had ripped it away while trying to get a point across. Those were the cries that he'd heard from the driveway.

"It's Katya," he whispered.

"You sure?"

"Uh-huh. I think they're going to kill her."

He stepped aside, and let Beth have a look for herself. There was a difference between simply threatening, and threatening to kill. Katya wasn't playing along, and it didn't appear that she was going to budge. The Sokolovs' anger would turn to rage, and they would end her life.

"I'm going in. Which one do you want?" he asked.

"Bogdan, the big one," Beth said.

"He's yours. Aim at him through the window. I'll kick down the door and go in. If they don't obey my orders, start shooting."

Katya let out a scream. Lancaster took another look through the window. Egor had put the electric drill into her ear, and given it a little juice.

"Hurry," Beth said.

He went to the front door, and lifted his leg. Beth went into a crouch and aimed through the window. He kicked, and the door splintered at the frame and fell into the room. He rushed in.

"Drop your weapons and step away from the girl," he said.

Bogdan tossed his hammer to the floor and raised his arms into the air. Egor snarled and threw the power drill at Lancaster's head, forcing him to duck. It was a clever ploy. Lancaster wasn't going to shoot an unarmed man, and it gave Bogdan enough time to grab a shotgun off the fireplace mantel and get off a round. The blast did not miss by much, and Lancaster dove to the floor and returned their fire.

Beth also began shooting. The window blew apart, with shards of glass flying around him. It was distracting, but he kept shooting anyway. The Sokolovs weren't going to win any medals for bravery, and they retreated into the back of the house. Egor's torso was soaked with his own blood, and he wasn't moving very fast.

Lancaster got to his feet and dusted himself off. Chasing them was an option, except he was nearly out of bullets. From the backyard, he heard a motorbike's engine kick in.

He went to a window, and looked into the darkened backyard. The house backed up onto a wooded area, and he listened as the brothers escaped down a dirt path on a very loud motorcycle.

"All clear," he called out.

Beth came inside, and edged up beside him.

"You up for chasing them?" she asked.

"No thanks. That was an AA-12 assault shotgun. We're outgunned."

"Then why did they run?"

"I shot the little one in the stomach. If he doesn't get help, he'll bleed out."

They checked out Katya, who hadn't uttered a word. Her ear had a little blood, but otherwise she appeared unharmed. The look on her face said she was surprised to be alive, and she stood up and stretched her legs.

Beth flashed her badge. "I'm Special Agent Daniels with the FBI, and this is private investigator Jon Lancaster. What is your name?"

"Katya Pavlov," she said, her accent barely noticeable.

"Would you like us to take you to a hospital?"

She touched her ear. "I am not badly hurt. No hospital."

"We'd like to ask you some questions. Please sit down."

Katya obediently returned to her chair. Lancaster and Beth sat directly across from her on the couch.

"Who were those two men?" Beth asked.

"I've never seen them before."

"Please don't lie to us. It will only lead to trouble."

"What kind of trouble?"

"Jail."

Katya's eyes grew wide. She'd just had a power drill stuck in her ear, yet seemed more concerned about being thrown in the slammer.

"What do you want to know?" she asked.

"Same question. Who were they?"

"Their names are Bogdan and Egor Sokolov. They are my friends."

"Really. Why were they torturing you?"

She smiled thinly. "They were not happy with me."

"That much was obvious. What made them do this?"

"It's a long story."

"We've got all the time in the world."

A mournful cry interrupted their conversation. A skinny black cat crawled out from beneath the couch they were sitting on, and began to wail. Katya scooped the kitty up, and began to pet it.

"I will explain everything, but first may I have something to drink?" she asked. "My throat is very dry."

Beth glanced at him. The key to an interrogation was to keep the person being interviewed happy, within reason. Lancaster said, "What can I get you?"

"A bottled water from the refrigerator in the kitchen. And a glass."

"Coming right up."

Lancaster left the room.

- - -

Daniels felt her radar go up. Something wasn't right, but she couldn't put her finger on exactly what it was. Katya continued to console the cat. She was strikingly beautiful, and it wasn't difficult to imagine her father having a fling with her.

"Start from the beginning," Daniels said.

They could hear Jon rattling around in the kitchen, looking for a glass. Katya's expression changed, and her eyes turned cold.

"You are Martin's daughter," she said.

Daniels rocked back on the couch. Melanie looked like their mother, while she took after their father, and people were always commenting on the resemblance.

"That's right," Daniels said. "How did you know my father?"

"You could say we were lovers."

The words sounded evil coming out of her mouth. Daniels felt herself shudder.

"Martin said you might show up one day, and cause trouble," Katya said.

"Is that so?"

"Yes. He said that you were a real bitch."

Daniels's cheeks burned, and she raised her arm to slap Katya's face. It was exactly the response that Katya had been hoping for. She tossed the cat into Daniels's chest, startling her. Katya came out of her chair and leaped over the splintered front door lying on the floor, then bolted from the house.

"Jon! She's escaping!"

The frightened cat had sunk its claws into her blouse. She ran out of the house and into the street with the animal still attached to her, but it was too late. Katya had vanished in the wind.

"God damn snake!" Daniels swore.

CHAPTER 16

There was no greater frustration than having a suspect slip through your fingers. Back inside, they searched for clues that might tell them where Katya had run off to. Lancaster pretended not to hear the obscenities pouring out of Beth's mouth.

"The little shit told me that she was my father's lover," Beth said.

"She really said that?"

"Uh-huh. Then she told me that my father thought I was a bitch. I couldn't help myself, and went to slap her. That's when she threw the cat and ran."

"So it was a ploy."

"You think she made it up to rattle me? She's quite a looker. I could see my father having a relationship with her. Didn't you find her attractive?"

They were in the kitchen doing their search. He'd pulled the garbage pail out from beneath the sink and was sifting through its contents to see what might turn up. The trash was mostly empty diet soda cans and greasy fast food wrappers.

"There's a difference between attraction and romance," he said. "Based upon what you told me about your father, I'd say no, I can't see him in a relationship with her."

"Why not?"

Beth had stopped what she was doing and glared at him. There was a real edge in her voice. Katya had bested her, and now he was challenging her.

"Your father was highly educated, and he was practical," he said, treading carefully. "If he was seriously considering having a relationship with Katya, he'd think, 'She'd be fun in the sack, but what are we going to talk about afterwards? The important things in my life occurred before she was born.' It would be a travesty."

"But my father was lonely. He told me and my sister so."

"He would have found someone."

"How can you be so sure?"

"I spotted several attractive older women in the church this morning. I have to assume they were widows. Your father would have eventually met the right one, and it would have clicked. It's how things work."

"So he wasn't having a relationship."

"Not with Katya."

"Did she say those things to throw me off?"

"That's my bet." He paused. "And it worked."

Tears welled in her eyes, and spilled down her cheeks. Her emotions were being turned inside out, and she was hurting. Only one thing made a grieving person feel better, and he gave her a hug. She stiffened in his arms.

"Oh my God. We're being watched."

He spun around. It had been a day filled with unpleasant surprises. His eyes found the surveillance camera perched over the dish cabinet.

"That's strange," he said.

"What do you mean?"

"The camera isn't pointed at the back door."

- - -

Surveillance cameras were meant to record intruders. That was their purpose, unless the person who installed them had something else in mind.

The camera in the kitchen was pointed at the island in the center of the room, which was rectangular and had a marble top. It was large enough for several people to prepare a meal upon, and not get in each other's way.

"Why would you videotape someone preparing a meal?" Beth asked.

"Beats me."

Using a chair, he climbed up on the counter beneath the dish cabinet for a closer look. The camera was made by a company called Lorex, and he memorized the call letters before climbing down. Then he did a search on his cell phone, and discovered that the camera was considered high end, and ran $600. It could record in Ultra HD, the images it captured crystal clear.

"They could be watching us right now," Beth said.

"Should we wave?"

"This isn't funny, Jon. We don't know who these people are."

"Should I get 'Wild West' with them?"

"What is that supposed to mean?"

He drew his gun from behind his belt, and blew the camera off the cabinet. He did it so quickly that Beth was too stunned to react, let alone speak. He blew the smoke off the barrel and returned the weapon to its hiding place.

"You're crazy," she said.

"Admit it. You feel better."

"A little."

"Let's see how many more of these we can find," he said.

- - -

There were surveillance cameras in every room in the house.

Eleven total.

Two in the living room, two in the dining room, one in each of the three upstairs bedrooms, a camera in the study, and fish-eye cameras hidden in the ceilings of the two bathrooms. They were perched atop bookcases and dressers, and not easily seen, their lenses aimed at the center of each room. To keep Beth happy, he disabled each one by hand, as opposed to shooting them out.

"She let them watch her in the bathroom?" Beth said incredulously.

"Who?" he said, not understanding.

"Katya. This is her house, remember? She let someone install those cameras, and willingly let them watch her while she was in the bathroom. How would you feel if someone watched you take a shower, or do your business in the morning?"

"It would make my skin crawl."

"Me too. What kind of woman would allow something like that?"

He had to think about that. He'd seen some pretty grotesque behavior as a cop, the boundaries that people were willing to stretch often boggling the imagination. But he'd never seen or heard about a person doing what Beth had just described.

"Maybe she didn't have a choice," he said.

Beth wanted to go to the rental and use her laptop computer to run a check on Katya to see if she had a criminal history. Katya was no innocent, and had probably brushed up against the law before. If so, there would be a rap sheet to show for it.

Together, they repositioned the front door back in its place.

"We didn't check the basement," he said.

"You go. I'll be in the car," she said.

- - -

He'd spied the door to the basement earlier. It was located inside the kitchen pantry, and was padlocked, which he'd found strange. Was Katya keeping something hidden that she didn't want a nosy visitor to see? There was only one way to find out.

He examined the lock. It was the cheap, hardware store variety. This make of lock was easily opened. A hammer would do the trick, or the end of a screwdriver.

He rifled the kitchen drawers but came up short. But he did find a wrench, which would also work. Standing next to the door, he grasped the lock and applied pressure on one end. With the wrench, he gave a few hard taps on the other end, searching for the sweet spot where the locking mechanism was located.

He found it, and the lock popped open.

He stepped away from the door before opening it. Just in case there was a booby trap waiting for him. There wasn't, and he stuck his head into the darkened space, seeing nothing but blackness below. He flipped the light switch, and a light came on halfway down the stairwell. The stairs were made of wood, and looked sturdy.

He went down. Reaching bottom, he found himself standing in a finished basement, with a painted concrete floor and paneled walls. It was decorated like a studio apartment, with a kitchen in one corner, a small dining table, and a couch and a pair of matching chairs facing a flat screen TV on the wall. Except for the TV, there wasn't anything of value. So why the padlock?

He was missing something.

The space didn't feel right. After a few moments, he realized what it was. The basement was smaller than the first floor of the house. In most houses, the basement was the same footprint as the ground floor. Not here. The basement was smaller. Or was it? He ran his palms across the paneled wall, and applied a gentle but firm pressure.

Halfway down the wall, he felt it give. He pressed harder, and a hidden door popped open, revealing a secret room. He stepped in, and was immediately hit by the smell. It was moldy, the air foul.

Martin Daniels had built a panic room in his house. Those were common these days. This wasn't a panic room, not if the decorations were any indication. It looked like a room in a bordello, the walls painted hot pink, the lighting subdued, the pink carpet thick and furry. A heart-shaped bed sat in the room's center.

He'd once been engaged to a woman who'd wanted to honeymoon in the Catskill Mountains because it was where her parents had gone. She'd shown him a glossy full-page ad for the hotel in a bridal magazine that featured photos of a room with pink walls, a bathtub shaped like a champagne glass, and a heart-shaped honeymoon bed. It was so cheesy that he'd broken off the engagement on the spot.

This room reminded him of that ad. Since the rest of the house was wired with surveillance cameras, he assumed this room was as well. A minute later, his suspicions were confirmed when he found a surveillance camera hidden behind a painting of a naked woman hanging on the wall.

There was also dust. It covered the picture frame and the bedspread. The room hadn't been used in a while. On the night table was a small picture frame that was also covered in dust. He cleaned it off, and stared at the two smiling people in the photo. One was Katya. It took a moment for him to place her partner. An older man with a thick head of hair and a gap-toothed smile. It was Martin Daniels.

He studied the photo. He'd told Beth that her father wasn't having a relationship with Katya because it just didn't seem possible. Martin was smarter than that. But here was the evidence, staring him right in the face.

He put the photograph back on the night table. The room hadn't been used in a while. Had the relationship soured, and Katya turned on him? It was a possibility, only it didn't explain why the Sokolovs had ransacked Martin's study, or the missing money from Martin's bank accounts, or why there were mummified hands being put on people's doorsteps. The truth be known, it didn't explain a damn thing.

Taking out his cell phone, he snapped a photo of the picture of Martin and Katya, then took multiple shots of the room, including the hidden camera behind the painting. Then he left.

Leaving the house, he walked down the driveway to the road. Beth was in the passenger seat with her laptop, typing away, her eyes filled with murderous intensity. The laptop's screen was visible, and he spied Katya's rap sheet and mug shot.

He climbed behind the wheel. Beth stopped what she was doing.

"I found her rap sheet," she said.

"Great. Want me to drive?"

"Please. I need to make a few calls. Katya got busted in Fort Lauderdale on a pot charge last year. She's here on a work permit, and normally a drug arrest would have sent her home. For some reason, she got to stay. I want to find out why."

He backed out. He didn't know how to tell Beth what he'd found in the basement. She was grieving, and the news would only make things worse. He needed to figure out a way to tell her that wouldn't crush her.

"What did you find in the basement?" she asked.

"Dust," he said.

CHAPTER 17

It didn't take Daniels long to find out why Katya had been allowed to stay in the country after her arrest. She called the Broward County District Attorney's office and spoke to the prosecutor on the case, who was happy to fill her in. As she ended the call, Jon pulled into the driveway of her father's house, and killed the engine.

"Learn anything?" he asked.

"Katya's lawyer got the charge pleaded down to a simple misdemeanor," Daniels said. "She was supposed to perform a hundred hours of community service as punishment, but never showed up."

"She must have had a good attorney. Which one did she use?"

"Some hotshot named Timothy Morrell."

"You're kidding. Morrell charges five hundred bucks an hour. His clients have to put up a ten-thousand-dollar retainer before he'll talk with them."

"Where would she have come up with that kind of money?"

"Someone else must have paid him."

They fell silent. The only truism in police work was that it was impossible to learn the truth; all an investigator could do was piece together the facts, and compose a reasonable scenario. Katya's story continued to confound them, the pieces not adding up.

"What else did you learn?" Jon asked.

"Katya came here on a work permit, and was working at a bed-and-breakfast in Fort Lauderdale when she was arrested. Maybe the B&B owners paid Morrell."

"That's a stretch. Ten grand is a lot of money."

"Maybe they're nice people, and wanted to help her out."

"I have friends in the hotel business, and they don't tolerate employees that smoke pot. If the owners of the B&B paid Morrell, they probably had another motive. Did you get the B&B's name?"

"Casa Del Mar. Katya was the night manager."

"A job like that pays minimum wage. They would have let her go."

She unlocked the front door, and they went inside the empty house. Her father was fond of playing music on the loud side, and the silence that greeted them was haunting. While Jon ground coffee beans and fixed a pot, she sat at the kitchen table on her laptop, and did a search of the Casa Del Mar on the Broward Property Appraiser's website.

Jon served her a steaming mug and parked himself in a chair.

"Any luck?" he asked.

"According to the Broward Property Appraiser's website, the Casa Del Mar is owned by a couple named Boris and Svetlana Vasilek," Daniels said. "They purchased the business over a year ago, and paid a million two for it."

"Speak of the devil."

"You know these two?"

"Our paths crossed when I was a detective. Boris Vasilek has run a variety of businesses, including a car wash, a dry cleaner, and a body shop, all of which went belly-up. We assumed he was laundering money for Russian gangsters, but could never prove it. His wife, Svetlana, acts as his bodyguard. She was an Olympic weightlifter."

"If you couldn't prove it, then why assume it?"

Daniels had been trained to follow the facts, and not make assumptions. It irritated the hell out of her when Jon jumped to conclusions without having proof to back up his claims. He stirred sugar into his coffee before replying.

"I grew up with a Russian family living next door to me," he said. "They escaped the communists in the 1950s, and came here with a couple of suitcases and the clothes on their backs. They were salt of the earth, and worked their assess off. They also loved this country.

"The Russians that come to the United States today are different. The majority of them have known only one leader, and that's Putin, who's a gangster and a cold-blooded murderer. Eighty percent of them think Putin's doing a fine job, which is why he keeps getting reelected. They don't love this country, or appreciate our democracy. Their loyalties lie elsewhere."

"If they don't love our country, then why do they move here?"

"To make money."

"And you think Katya is working with the Vasileks."

"She must be. They sponsored her over here, and paid her legal fees when she got in hot water. She moved to Saint Augustine and did something they didn't like, so they sent Bogdan and Egor to clean up the mess. They're all in this together."

"It's a nice theory. Now, how do we prove it?"

"Easy. We run the Vasileks down, and make them talk."

"How? They'll just lawyer up."

"We'll do it the old-fashioned way, and show them the error of their ways."

Daniels shook her head. She loved Jon, except when he went rogue. That Jon was a different beast, and played outside the lines. He'd gotten away with it for a long time, but like any misbehavior, she knew that eventually it would catch up with him.

"I don't like your approach," she said.

"I wasn't going to include you," he said.

"Going to leave me out in the car?"

"Something like that. That way, if the Vasileks don't play ball, and someone ends up getting hurt, you won't feel any blowback."

"I appreciate you looking out for me. Do you plan to interrogate the Vasileks yourself? Or are your friends going to be involved?"

He said nothing, which was answer enough. There was a large group of ex-SEALS living in Florida who came to each other's assistance when the need arose. Jon kept in contact with many of these men, but only spoke about them in vague terms, leading her to believe that, like Jon, they made their living dealing on the fringes of the law.

"What if I forbid you from doing this? I can do that, you know," she said.

His face turned to stone. "I asked you earlier if you wanted me working this investigation. You said yes. Did you change your mind?"

"Of course not. We're a team."

"Then take my lead for once. It won't kill you."

"For God's sake—"

"We're talking about your father. So what if I step on a few toes?"

Her cell phone, which lay on the table between them, began to vibrate, and she stared at the familiar number and 904 area code. Someone at the FBI's Jacksonville office was calling her, and she suspected it was Erce, wanting to chew her out.

"That's work," she said.

"We need to come to a decision about this, Beth," he said.

"We will. Let me take this."

He rose from his chair and went outside into the darkened backyard.

"Special Agent Daniels," she answered.

"This is Erce," Special Agent Phillips said. "Can you talk?"

"I can talk. You're working late tonight. What's up?"

"We have a situation. A dead Russian gangster named Egor Sokolov was found in the bathroom of a rest stop off Interstate 95 with two bullets in his gut. The police were able to ID him through his fingerprints. I got a call from my boss because Sokolov is on the FBI's watch list. My boss wants to know if I have any idea why this guy was here, and who might have shot him. Do you know anything about this?"

"I do. We engaged Egor and his brother earlier this evening."

"Who shot him?"

"Lancaster did. We were rescuing a woman they were holding hostage."

"That explains things. Before I reply, I think it would be best if we talk. I'm free tomorrow morning, if that works for you."

Daniels ran her fingers through her hair. This was not good. If Erce leveled with his boss, and told him what she and Jon had done, she would get in hot water, and might get demoted or fired. But if Erce made up a story, and his boss found out later, it would be Erce who paid the price. It was a no-win situation for both of them.

"Tomorrow morning it is. Where would you like to meet?" she asked.

Phillips named a restaurant halfway between his office and Saint Augustine. She said goodbye and looked out the window at Jon's shadowy silhouette. He held a cell phone to his face and appeared to be on a call. She went to the window and tapped the glass. He ended the call and joined her in the kitchen.

"I need to go talk to Erce in the morning," she said. "The police found Egor Sokolov's body in a rest stop off the interstate. His brother must have dumped him there."

"My condolences."

"Egor is on the FBI's watch list. Erce's boss is sniffing around, and wants to know if he knows anything about this."

"Will Erce cover for you?"

"Maybe."

"I thought you were friends."

"We used to go running together at the academy. I'm not sure that counts as a friendship."

"Would you cover for him, if the situation was reversed?"

She thought about it. "Yes, I would."

"Hopefully he'll feel the same way, and won't throw you under the bus."

"I sure hope so. Who were you talking to?"

"Your niece. She's found another link. I told her I'd call her back."

It was the last thing Daniels wanted to hear, and she slapped her hand on the table in frustration. Jon acted amused, and he sipped his coffee and tried not to smile.

"This isn't funny," she said. "Stop encouraging her."

"I'm not encouraging her. She's just mimicking her aunt. That's what kids do—they find role models, and they imitate them." He rose from the table and washed out his mug in the sink. "It's getting late. I'd better call her back."

Daniels hated when issues were left unresolved. They hadn't decided how they were going to deal with the Vasileks; nor had she convinced Jon that breaking the law, even if it accomplished a good thing, was still a very bad idea.

Before she could speak her mind, Lancaster went back outside and shut the door behind him.

CHAPTER 18

Standing in the backyard beneath a full moon, Lancaster called Nicki back. Beth was angry at Nicki's snooping, and he suspected she was angry that her niece had contacted him, instead of calling her aunt. That had to hurt.

"Hi, Jon!" Nicki answered. "You're really going to like this."

"Are you home, or still on the road?"

"We're at home. My dad made great time driving back."

The news relieved him. Bogdan Sokolov was also on the road, and although the chances of Nicki's family and Bogdan crossing paths were infinitesimally slim, he still took comfort knowing that Nicki and her folks were back home, safe and sound.

"So what have you got for me?" he asked.

"The people in Saint Augustine that had mummified hands put on their doorsteps all knew Grandpa," she said. "It wasn't a random thing."

"You sure about this?"

"Uh-huh. I searched each of their names during the drive home, and then cross-referenced each of them against Grandpa. They all knew each other."

Lancaster thought back to his conversation with Officer Spencer in the driveway of Martin Daniels's home. "Before Officer Spencer gave us those names, your aunt told you to go inside. You didn't hide behind the front door and eavesdrop, did you?"

"Uh-huh," the teenager said.

"That's unacceptable, Nicki. You disobeyed your aunt."

"I wrote the names down too."

"You realize that was wrong, don't you?"

"Yes. But I didn't think Aunt Beth told me to go inside because she didn't want me to hear what the policeman was saying. I assumed that she wanted me out of the way because the policeman would be uncomfortable with me present."

He laughed to himself. The best investigators were always a step ahead of their suspects. Nicki had anticipated his unhappiness, and had prepared an elegant answer.

"You assumed correctly. But it still wasn't the right thing to do."

"But it got the job done," she argued. "Remember when you came to my CSI class at school, and told the story about the time you dressed up like a homeless person and hung out in a park where heroin was being sold? You said your superior was against the idea, so you went and did it on your off-hours. And it worked. You busted the biggest smack dealer in South Florida, and sent him away. How is this different?"

He could think of plenty of reasons, the main one being Nicki was a teenager, and he'd been a seasoned cop. But that argument would fall on deaf ears, so he tried another tack.

"If your aunt finds out, she'll be upset. And she'll have her feelings hurt."

"I never thought of that. Are you going to tell her?"

"Eventually. I don't keep secrets from her."

"I won't do it again." She paused. "Do you want to hear what I found?"

He smiled into the phone. "Fire away."

"Officer Spencer gave you the names of five people who had mummified hands put on their doorsteps," she said. "There were four men, and one woman. The men's names were Clarke Tuthill, Landon Padgett, John Parsons, and Peter Matoff. I did individual searches of their names, and then did group searches, and included Grandpa. I found a link where all of them were mentioned. They were fishing buddies."

"Were they good buddies, or just casual friends?"

"They were tight. They're all members of the Saint Augustine Boating Club. It's the oldest club in Saint Augustine, and has a club-house built from parts of an old hardware store. According to the web-site, annual dues used to be twenty-five cents. It's the kind of club that Grandpa would have liked. The club holds five fishing tournaments a year to raise money for charity. Grandpa and his buddies were a team. They dressed up in identical T-shirts and fishing hats, and called them-selves the Ponce de Leon Pirates. There are photos of them on the club's site. I remember seeing them at Grandpa's funeral. They sat together in the same pew."

"This is fantastic, Nicki. Will you send me the link?"

"Of course. You know what's funny? Grandpa was a real party ani-mal. In every photo he's either holding a beer or a cocktail."

Lancaster wasn't surprised. Based upon what he'd learned, there were several sides of Martin Daniels's personality that his family hadn't been aware of.

"Tell me about the woman," he said.

"Her name is Dr. Angela Sircy, and she's a heart specialist. She sits on the board of directors at Flagler Hospital, which Grandpa also sat on. I did a search of their names together, and found several photos of them. I think they were friends. I thought back, but don't remember seeing her at Grandpa's funeral."

"You could have missed her. The church was packed."

"I don't think I would have missed her. She's very tall and has flam-ing red hair. I stood with my mom and Aunt Beth by the front doors of the church, and thanked everyone for coming. Dr. Sircy wasn't there."

Nicki left the remark hanging. She wasn't giving him the full story, and he said, "Maybe she was in surgery."

"That's the exact thing I thought."

"Did you call Flagler Hospital to check?" he said.

"Yeah. I got bounced around, and eventually talked to a head nurse. I told her I was Dr. Sircy's niece, and was trying to get a hold of her. The nurse said that Dr. Sircy was on sabbatical. I thought that was weird, so I found her address and phone number in the white pages, and called her pretending I was conducting a survey."

"Did she answer?"

"She did. I addressed her by name, and she responded. When I told her I was taking a survey, she said no thanks, and hung up. I checked out her address on Google Maps. She lives right in town, and could have walked to the church. For some reason she didn't come to Grandpa's funeral. Strange, huh?"

"Very strange. We'll have to talk to her, see what's going on. This is excellent work, Nicki. Good job."

"You're not mad at me?"

It was hard to stay angry at someone who wanted to help, especially when they were as talented as Nicki was at running down clues. "I've gotten over it. Your Aunt Beth will be another story. You know how she is when it comes to following the rules."

"Rules are meant to be broken. Isn't that an old saying?"

"Goodbye, Nicki. Don't forget to send me that link."

- - -

The kitchen was empty, and he heard Beth's footsteps from the second floor as she prepared for bed. There was enough coffee left to fill his cup. He heated it up in the microwave, and returned to his chair at the kitchen table.

As if on cue, his phone beeped. He opened Nicki's text and tapped the link to the Saint Augustine Boat Club. Group photos of Martin and his fishing buddies filled the screen. The photos dated back several years, and were filled with good humor. It was obvious that these guys knew how to have a good time.

He sipped his coffee and studied the photos. There was a reason that Martin's fishing buddies had been targeted by Katya's friends to have mummified hands put on their doorsteps, and he was hoping the photos might lend a clue as to what it was.

Several things caught his attention. Martin and his buddies were in the same age bracket, early to midseventies. Dressed in shorts and T-shirts, he could see that they were all physically fit, with good muscle tone in their arms and legs. They also wore expensive watches and designer sunglasses, an indication that they had money.

Old rich guys who took care of themselves. Nothing unusual there. He sensed that there was something missing in the photos, but he couldn't put his finger on what it might be. The site contained photos of other groups who'd entered the club's fishing tournaments, and he studied those, hoping to fill in the blanks.

It didn't take long for him to find the missing element. The other group photos all included females entered in the tournaments, who appeared to be matched up with the men. Based upon the women's ages, he guessed they were either daughters or wives.

But there were no females in Martin's group. They looked like a stag party.

He went back to the photos of the Ponce de Leon Pirates, and studied them again. This time, he looked at their hands. Martin didn't wear a wedding ring, and neither did any of his friends.

He exited the site and stared into space. The Pirates were a group of single older men, dedicated to having a good time. There was no doubt in his mind that, like Martin, these guys had gotten caught up in a situation, and it had gotten out of control. That was a reasonable scenario, and he would go with it until a better one came along.

His mug empty, he rose from the table. He had enough information to move things forward. Martin's buddies needed to be talked to, and with enough persuasion, he felt certain one of them would tell him what was going on. The investigation was building momentum, except now he had an anchor attached to his leg. He knew unpleasant things about Martin's past that he needed to tell Beth without hurting her.

But what if that wasn't possible? What if the only way to tell Beth was by being brutally honest with her? That was the easiest path, but was it the best?

He was at a loss as to what to do, and he felt awful. All he could hope was that an answer would come to him soon.

CHAPTER 19

Cracker Barrel Old Country Stores were actually restaurants, and enormously popular in the Sunshine State, with over fifty locations. Most were located near a major highway, their parking lots filled with RVs and well-traveled cars with out-of-state plates.

The Saint Augustine location was packed, and Daniels and Special Agent Phillips had to wait for a table. A big-haired waitress seated them and went over the breakfast specials. Erce ordered the sausage biscuit breakfast sandwich, while Daniels got the apple and cinnamon oatmeal. The waitress left, and Erce put his elbows on the table and leaned in. It was loud enough for them to have a conversation and not be overheard.

"Someone in the bureau told me that your department conducts special training seminars for Cracker Barrel employees," he said. "Is that really true?"

She nodded. "We train the waitstaff to spot human traffickers."

"How did you get the funding for that?"

"I convinced my boss that it was a wise investment. So far, it's paid off."

"Are they the only restaurants you work with?"

"We've worked with other chains, but we've gotten the best results with Cracker Barrel's staff, so we've focused our energy with them," she said.

"What makes them better?"

"Their restaurants are located near interstates. If a trafficker is moving a victim from Miami to Atlanta, chances are, he'll stop to get a meal for himself and his victim. If he does, Cracker Barrel is often the spot. We train the employees to look for odd pairings. A girl with an older man. Or a quiet child with an overbearing adult. Is the child sad? Quiet? Staring at the table and not speaking? Those are signs that things aren't right. We also ask them to look for electronic devices."

"Why?"

"Traffickers don't let their victims have cell phones or iPads. The absence of a device can be a sign of foul play."

"Isn't all of this hard to do while waiting tables?"

"It is hard. But Cracker Barrel has a loyal staff, and they're mostly women with families of their own. These women have good instincts when it comes to spotting trouble, and they won't hesitate to report it."

Their food came. While Daniels ate her oatmeal, she gazed at the booths lining the wall of the restaurant. In one booth was a young girl accompanied by an older man. The girl wore a troubled look, and didn't have an electronic device, unlike every other kid in the restaurant. Daniels flagged their waitress and discreetly showed her badge.

"I'm with the FBI. What's the deal with the man and the girl in the booth?"

"I spoke to them earlier," the waitress said. "The girl got in trouble at school yesterday, so her daddy took her cell phone away from her as punishment. She's not happy about it."

"You believed them?"

"Yes, ma'am. They've been in before."

"Did you speak with the girl?"

"I did. She confirmed what her father said. It's all good."

"Thank you for being so diligent. You can never be too careful."

"Isn't that the truth. How's your food?"

"It's delicious," Erce said.

The waitress went to take care of another table. Erce had made short work of his meal, and wiped his mouth with a napkin.

"You've got an army of spies," he said. "No wonder J. T. likes you."

Daniels realized she was being complimented. She didn't know if Erce was being nice, or softening the blow for what he was about to tell her.

"Have you spoken to him?" she asked.

"He called last night," he said. "You would think having a heart attack would slow him down, but no such luck. He's as ornery as ever. I let his call go to voice mail, and then listened to his message."

"Am I in hot water?"

"Why else would he be calling?" Erce retrieved a voice message on his cell phone and handed it to her. "Hit the seven on the keypad to listen."

She did as instructed and placed the cell phone to her ear. J. T. Hacker was her boss and mentor, and had a voice as soothing as a just-awakened grizzly bear.

"This is Director Hacker, and I need to speak with you," the recorded voice said. "I'm told that Special Agent Daniels is in Saint Augustine, interrogating the local police over her father's death. Special Agent Daniels is perfectly within her rights if she wishes to conduct her own investigation. My concern is whether she is being accompanied by a man named Jon Lancaster. The reason I ask is, a dead Russian gangster was found in Saint Augustine with two bullets in his gut. The entry point of the bullets was within a few millimeters. That's Lancaster's trademark, and I'm guessing he was the shooter.

"Special Agent Daniels and I have had conversations about Lancaster before. I've told her in no uncertain terms that Lancaster is a liability, one that could cost Beth her job with the bureau. So far, my warnings have fallen on deaf ears. Call me to discuss."

The message ended, and Daniels shook her head. Jon had helped her bust a trafficking ring in Tampa not long ago, and he'd broken so many laws that she'd had to whitewash her final report. J. T. had privately scolded her, knowing a lie when he read one. But he'd still signed off on the report, and she'd assumed that his issues with Jon had been forgotten. She handed the cell phone back to Erce.

"What are you going to tell him?" she asked.

"That's why I wanted to meet. We need to come up with a story."

His words caught her by surprise. "You're going to lie?"

He nodded solemnly.

"Have you thought of the consequences?"

"That was the first thing I thought of," he said. "I like my job, and I don't want to jeopardize my career. But I'm still going to do it."

It was not the response she'd expected. "May I ask why?"

"Because this is your family," he said. "You have every right to get to the truth. If that means using Jon Lancaster to help you, that's okay by me."

"What about the other agents in your office? Are they going to lie as well?"

"They'll do what I tell them. Now, what are we going to say?"

It took ten minutes to construct a reasonable story. They decided that Erce would tell their boss that Daniels was conducting an investigation in Saint Augustine without Lancaster's help. Whatever Lancaster was up to, he was doing it by himself.

"Do you think J. T. will buy this?" Erce said.

"It doesn't matter if he buys it or not," she said. "The story covers our asses. I'm not responsible for Jon's behavior, and neither are you. If we disavow that he's working with me, we'll both be in the clear."

"I'll buy that. Did he shoot the Russian?"

"Yes, he did. It was self-defense. I would have shot the bastard myself if I'd had the chance. Now, let me ask you a question. If Egor Sokolov is on the bureau's watch list, then his brother Bogdan is as well. Have you run across these characters?"

"They've been on our radar for over a year," he said. "They kept slipping into town through the private airport. Had a group of young women with them. Never saw them breaking any laws, so we couldn't haul them in."

"But you wanted to."

"You bet. They've been linked to money launderers down in Fort Lauderdale named Vasilek. We figured they're running some kind of scam up here."

"How were you aware they were coming through the private airport?"

"Local drug dealers use the private airport to move product, so we monitor it with hidden surveillance cameras."

"Did you capture the Sokolovs on video when they came in?"

"Sure. My laptop's in the car. Give me a second, and I'll go get it."

- - -

Erce placed his laptop on the table so she could see the screen, and retrieved the surveillance videos of the Russians. They had been shot during the day, and showed the brothers exiting a twin-engine plane accompanied by three women wearing tight-fitting clothes. Their skin was dark, and they appeared to be either Mexican or Latin American.

Daniels still had the video of the wild party that Sierra had shared with her on her cell phone. The three women in that video had also been Latinas. She pulled the video up, and compared the three women to the trio on the surveillance videos.

It was a match.

She showed Sierra's video to Erce.

"Wow," he said. "Do you have any idea who they are?"

"They're friends of a Russian girl named Katya, who's involved with the Sokolovs," she said. "Their tattoos identify them as members of the Latin Kings."

"I've dealt with the Latin Kings. They don't mix very well."

"I know. We're not sure what the deal is. Do you have any other videos of these girls that were taken that day?"

"I think there's another. Let me look."

Erce searched the library of videos stored on his laptop. He said, "Here we go," and a new video filled the screen that showed the Latinas sharing a plastic bench. The Sokolovs stood beside them, waving their hands and talking furiously. The video had no audio, but from what Daniels could surmise, the Latinas were being lectured.

"This was taken inside the airport's terminal," Erce said.

"Same day as the other video?"

"Yes, ma'am."

She studied the three Latinas. They sat close to one another, their shoulders touching. In Sierra's video, they'd acted like wild women, while in this video, they looked cornered, and a little afraid of what the Sokolovs might do to them.

"Did you watch all the surveillance videos of the Sokolovs that were taken at the airport?" Daniels asked.

"I did," Erce said.

"How many times are these women in them?"

"Nearly all of them."

"How often did they stay?"

"Usually two or three days."

She resumed studying the video. The Sokolovs were taking turns berating the Latinas, who shrank beneath their verbal onslaught. The Russians were being abusive, and she was surprised the three women didn't stand up and leave.

The video was reaching its end, and she watched as the Sokolovs ushered the Latinas out an exit door of the terminal. They were treating them like cattle, and not fellow human beings. The door closed, and the screen went dark.

She heard the air catch in her throat. Something was wrong with this picture, and it dawned on her what it was. The Latinas had no luggage or personal belongings, not even a purse. Nor did she see the rectangular bulge of a cell phone in their pants pockets.

They had no earthly possessions.

She had seen this before, and knew exactly what it meant.

They were slaves.

CHAPTER 20

Lancaster had no trouble finding Dr. Angela Sircy. She was old school, her address and land line phone number in the white pages, and he had the Uber driver drop him off in the street in front of her two-story clapboard house. Like many dwellings in Saint Augustine, the residence reeked of southern charm, with rocking chairs on the front porch and a hand-painted sign that said BE NICE hanging on the front door.

He lifted the brass knocker and let it fall. His reflection in the front window made him frown. His shirt was rumpled, and his hair was askew. He'd cleaned himself up before leaving, but it hadn't lasted long. His mother had once likened him to Pig-Pen from the Peanuts comic strips, who had attracted a permanent cloud of dust wherever he went. Try as he might, he'd never been able to keep himself looking neat.

He heard shuffling feet inside the house. A teenage girl in braces answered the front door. With one hand, she held back a snarling Doberman, who looked ready to tear his head off. "Whatever you're selling, we don't want any. Go away," she said.

He flipped open his wallet and flashed his detective's badge. "My name is Jon Lancaster, and I'm a former detective, now a private investigator. I'm working a case in town, and was hoping to speak with Dr. Angela Sircy. Is she available?"

"Can I see that?"

He handed her his wallet. In the act of taking it, she let the pooch go, and the animal jumped on his chest with his front paws and began to lick his face.

"What's his name?"

"It's a she. Her name's Sheena, and she's a pussycat." The teen returned his wallet and reined in her dog. "Is my mom in some kind of trouble?"

"Not at all. I want to talk to her about a man she worked with at the hospital."

She made a face. "Let me guess. This is about Martin Daniels."

"It is. How did you know?"

"Because my mom said that one day, there would be an investigation into all the crazy stuff Martin was doing before he died. She said it was just a matter of time."

She had called him Martin, not Dr. Daniels, suggesting a friendship.

"How well did you know him?" he asked.

"I thought I knew Martin really well," she said. "He used to take us out on his boat, and he had us over for dinner a few times. He was an amazing cook, especially on the grill. Then it all turned to shit." She clicked her fingers. "Just like that."

"Did he and your mother date?"

"Yep. They were hot and heavy for a while. He even proposed to her."

Neither Beth nor Melanie had ever mentioned that there was a woman in their father's life, and he imagined it was yet another secret he'd been keeping from them.

"Did your mom say yes?"

Tears blurred her eyes, and she nodded. An awkward silence followed. The Dobie lay down at her owner's feet and fell fast sleep.

"Some watchdog, huh?" The teen wiped away her tears, but her sadness didn't go away. "My mom's behind the house, working on her chopper. She can fill you in."

And with that, she shut the door in his face.

- - -

There was a detached garage behind the house where a redhead wearing a long-sleeve denim shirt was working on a motorcycle with a power tool. Parts of the bike were strewn on a workbench and also on a blanket at her feet. Several of his buddies liked to work on their bikes, and they did so with a beer in one hand, and a butt in the other. Sircy took a more conservative approach, and she wore a pair of work gloves and protective goggles, her hair tied back in a ponytail. Seeing him approach, she killed the power tool and yanked off her goggles. She was in her late fifties, attractive, with a perfectly even tan that came from riding her bike on one of Florida's endless highways.

"I'm sick of you god damn Jehovah's Witnesses coming onto my property," she said. "Get out of here before I sic my dog on you."

He'd been mistaken for many things in his life, but never a religious zealot, and he promised himself that he'd ditch the clothes as soon as he could. He took out his wallet and showed his badge. "My name's Jon Lancaster, and I'm a private investigator. Your daughter was kind enough to send me back here. I'd like to talk to you about Martin Daniels."

"My daughter must have thought you were okay. She's very protective."

"She let your dog lick my face."

"It's a high honor. Who are you working for?"

"Martin's daughter."

"Which one? The nurse or the FBI agent?"

"The FBI agent. We're trying to find out why Martin took his life, and I was hoping you might be able to fill in some blanks."

She took a beer out of a cooler and swigged it. She was trying to play tough, but it was an act, and he watched a stream of beer escape down the side of her mouth. Martin's death had affected her, even if she hadn't attended his funeral.

"I'll give you the *Reader's Digest* version, Jon," she said, wiping her mouth with her sleeve. "I met Martin at the hospital where we worked. We dated, and I fell for him. He was erudite, charming, and handsome to boot. It couldn't have been more perfect. Then, out of the blue, he dumped me. I never saw it coming." Her eyes shifted to a work bench where her tools resided. On it was a framed photo of her and a smiling man sitting on a bike. It was Martin. She choked up and threw her beer at the photo, missing badly and striking the wall.

"Fuck," she swore. "Why can't I get over him?"

There was not enough ground to stare at. Hurting people was bad, but it was something else entirely to hurt those who loved you. Martin had done that, in spades.

"I'm sorry," he said.

"No, you're not," she snapped. "You don't even know me. Look, this is painful. Would you mind getting the hell out of here?"

"I have a couple of questions, then I'll go."

"I told you everything. Please leave."

"Why did someone put a mummified hand on your doorstep?"

Her legs turned to Jell-O. She stuck her other hand out, needing support, and he grabbed a stool from the workbench and had her sit on it. She was like a wounded animal, and filled with fear. He gave her a fresh beer from the cooler.

"I don't want any more beer," she said.

"Drink some anyway. It will make you feel better."

"The voice of experience." She took a swallow. "You were right. Thank you. To answer your question, they put a disgusting old hand on my doorstep to keep me from talking."

"About what?"

"Martin's problem."

Everyone had problems, but Sircy had used the singular. He helped himself to a cold one and sat down beside her. He clinked his can against hers.

"Nice to meet you," he said.

"I really shouldn't be talking about this," she said.

"But you're going to."

"Give me one good reason why I should."

"I'll give you several. Two masked men broke into Martin's house yesterday while his daughter Melanie and her family were inside. They managed to escape into a panic room. The burglars ransacked the place. They had guns."

"My Lord. Please tell me Melanie's family wasn't hurt."

"They're fine. Now, let's talk about Martin."

"Do you know who these men were?"

"A pair of Russian gangsters named Bogdan and Egor Sokolov."

She shook her head, the names unfamiliar. He pointed at the can and mimed her lifting it to her face. She gave him a wry smile.

"Are you trying to get me drunk, Jon?"

"I prefer the term buzzed," he said. "In my experience, people who are buzzed have an easier time talking about difficult subjects. Drink your beer."

She did as told. It seemed to relax her, and she winged the empty can across the room into a garbage can without touching the rim. "You remind me of Martin. You both have an unusual sense of humor. Did you know him?"

"Unfortunately not."

"A pity. Very well. Martin had an addiction for which he did not get help. I have to believe that it was a contributing factor to his suicide."

"To drugs?"

She shook her head. He was going to have to pry it out of her. He hadn't seen a lot of alcohol around Martin's house, but maybe he was hiding it.

"He was a drunk," he said.

"Hardly touched the stuff. There was no evidence in the house, I suppose."

"Of what?"

"Martin was addicted to pornography. Some people find that amusing, but trust me, it's not. Do you know what the definition of an addiction is?" He shook his head, and she said, "It's when a choice becomes a compulsion. We can enjoy these beers, and then we'll stop, while an alcoholic will drink until he passes out. That's a compulsion.

"Martin's compulsion was hardcore porn. The poor man couldn't get enough of it. He would look at images of naked women wherever he went. He did it in restaurants, at the beach, even working at the hospital. It cost him his seat on the board."

"You saw him doing this?"

"I did. At first, I just thought he had an unhealthy relationship with his cell phone, and made little of it. But then one day, I came up behind him, and . . . well, it was startling, to say the least. He couldn't have been more embarrassed, and put his phone away."

"He was looking at pictures?"

"It was a video of a naked couple in bed having wild sex. We were still dating, so I asked him what in God's name had gotten into him. That's when he confessed, and told me about his problem. I begged him to get help. He promised me that he would."

"Did he?"

"I don't think so. He dumped me a week after that."

He thought back to the hidden safe in Martin's study. There had been a laptop computer in it, and he'd been wondering what dark secrets its hard drive might contain. Now, he thought he knew. The laptop contained Martin's library of porn.

The thought depressed him. Martin Daniels was a dirty old man, and he could only imagine the hurt this was going to cause his daughters. Losing a parent was rough, but over time, the loss was healed by memories. This situation was different. Finding out your dad was a pervert was a hurt you couldn't wash away.

"What happened at the hospital?" he asked.

"Martin got caught, and tried to lie his way out of it," Sircy said. "The whole thing blew up in his face, and he lost his seat on the board. It was painful."

"How did it blow up in his face?"

"I wasn't the only person that caught Martin looking at dirty pictures. Many of his colleagues had also caught him, but were too embarrassed to confront him. We all knew, but didn't say anything."

"The proverbial elephant in the room."

"Exactly. Unfortunately for Martin, there was an intern named Demetria who was not so accommodating. Demetria was a gofer, who did odd jobs for the doctors. She was given an order of coffee for the board meeting, and she delivered it during the meeting. Martin was sitting with his back to the door with his cell phone in his lap, and didn't hear Demetria enter the room. She got a bird's-eye view of a video playing on Martin's cell phone, and she let out a shriek. She went straight to the head of human resources, and filed a complaint. That's when the shit hit the fan."

"What did Martin do?"

"He denied it. I've heard it said that if you're going to tell a lie, tell a big lie, so Martin claimed that Demetria was mistaken, and that he hadn't been looking at his cell phone when she came in."

"Turning it into a 'he said, she said.'"

"Correct."

"What tripped him up?"

"The board meetings are videotaped for there to be transparency. Martin must have forgotten the camera was rolling, because you can plainly see him take his cell phone from his lap, and flip it facedown on the table. The head of HR saw the video, and smelled a rat. She individually interviewed each board member, and the others confessed that they knew about Martin's obsession with porn."

"Did you?"

Sircy shook her head. "I couldn't stick the knife in his back. I was still carrying a torch. Still am, I suppose."

The conversation had drained both of them. He thanked Sircy for her time, and got up to leave. She pointed at his drink.

"Are you done?" she asked.

"I am," he said.

"May I have the can?"

He handed it to her, and she performed another flip over her back that landed in the trash can on the other side of the room without so much as kissing the rim.

"That's impressive," he said.

"It's an acquired skill," she said.

CHAPTER 21

Catch 27 was an elevated restaurant in the heart of Saint Augustine's historic district that served locally sourced seafood. Daniels had suggested they meet here for lunch, believing the pricy menu would keep the local cops away, and allow them to talk freely.

She sipped a glass of wine and stared into the parking lot while waiting for Jon to show up. She'd seen none of this coming. She was trained to follow her instincts, yet her instincts had failed her. Her father was a predictable man with little drama in his life, save for the holidays when he got tipsy at parties and would tell a funny story that dragged on too long, or break out in song. Those were the extent of his transgressions. Nothing in his past had prepared her for the juncture she was at now. It was almost as if she were dealing with two different people.

A car pulled into the lot. Jon got out, and the car drove away. He came inside, took a seat, and ordered a beer. After he was served, she took out a quarter, and spun it on the table.

"Call it," she said.

"Heads," he said.

It was heads.

"You go first," he said.

"I met with Erce," she said. "Our boss is hounding him, wanting to know if you're helping my investigation. J. T. isn't very fond of you."

"What's his problem? That I wear shorts most of the time?"

"Your methods bother him. The bureau constantly gets sued. If a criminal defense attorney finds out you're helping us, it could cause problems."

"It's a free country. He can't tell me what to do."

"J. T. is convinced that you shot Egor Sokolov. The bullets that entered his body were millimeters apart. J. T. referred to that as your trademark."

"And I thought it was my Jimmy Buffett T-shirts."

"This isn't funny."

"Your boss is paranoid. I'm just a retired cop."

"With a huge following on YouTube."

Back when he was a cop, Jon had engaged in a high-speed chase on I-95 in South Florida, forced a fleeing pickup off the road, then shot to death two armed kidnappers who were prepared to kill an innocent girl. Captured on video by a TV news chopper and posted on YouTube, the shootout had gone viral and garnered millions of views. There was a movie in the works with a well-known actor slated to play the lead. Whether he liked it or not, Jon was famous, and viewed by the public as a real-life Dirty Harry.

"What do you plan to do?" he asked.

"Erce is going to tell J. T. that you're running your own investigation, separate from mine," Daniels said. "I plan to tell J. T. the same thing when I speak with him. We need to keep our distance until this thing is over."

"You're making me feel like a leper."

She put her hand atop his, and left it there. "I didn't say that I wanted you to leave. Just a little separation for appearances' sake. There's too much at stake here."

"I'll do whatever you think is best."

She removed her hand. "Thank you. I also got a bead on the Sokolov brothers. They're human traffickers. The three women we saw in Sierra's video were victims."

"Are the Sokolovs pimping them?"

"Could be. Although that would fly in the face of what everyone says about the sheriff not tolerating prostitution."

"Maybe the sheriff doesn't know about it. What's Katya's role in this? Is she a victim, or also a trafficker?"

"I don't know. She's definitely under the Sokolovs' thumb, which would make her a victim. So that was my morning. How did yours go?"

Jon took a long pull of beer. He was no longer making eye contact, and she sensed that he'd found something unpleasant, and was struggling with how to tell her. She gave him some time.

"Your niece tracked down the names of the victims who'd gotten hands put on their doorsteps," he said. "Four of them were fishing buddies of your father's. The fifth was a doctor named Angela Sircy who sat on the board of directors at the local hospital with your father. I decided to talk with her first."

"That name's familiar. Did she and my father date?"

"Yes, they did. She told me things about your father that caught me by surprise."

Jon had his poker face on, and was showing no emotion. Something big and ugly was about to fall out of the sky, and Daniels suddenly wished she hadn't touched her wine.

"Go ahead," she said quietly.

"Sircy said that your father was addicted to pornography, and that she'd caught him looking at smut on his cell phone. She claimed others had as well. An intern at the hospital caught him and told HR. It led to him being thrown off the board."

"Pornography? My father?"

"I said the same thing to myself."

"Did you believe her?"

He took a swig of beer. "Not completely."

"Why not?"

"Parts of her story didn't ring true. Your father was single, and had all the time in the world to look at porn when no one was around. Her claim that he was doing it in public bothered me. He would know the consequences, and try to hide it."

"Like any other addict."

"That's right."

"What part of her story did you believe?"

"I think your father had images on his phone that he didn't want people to see. That's why his phone's memory was erased when the police found it."

"Images of what?"

"Our friend Katya."

"You think they were having a relationship?"

"I do. Dr. Sircy and your father appeared to be in love. Then your father jilted her. I'm guessing that's when Katya came into the picture. When I searched the basement of Katya's house, I found a photograph of your father and Katya together. They looked very happy."

"You told me you didn't find anything in the basement."

"I lied. I found the photograph in a hidden room. It bothered me, so I didn't tell you right away. I'm sorry."

Daniels bit her lower lip. This was hurting her, and she suppressed the urge to take her anger out on him. But that wouldn't have been fair. Jon was trying to help her and protect her at the same time, and that was never easy.

"If this is true, then Katya seduced my father, and got him into a compromising situation. Then she blackmailed him, which would explain the missing money," she said.

"Yes, it would," he said.

"So how do we prove all of this?"

"We open the wall safe in your father's study, and look at what's on the hard drive of the laptop stored inside. I'm guessing there are photos of him and Katya that your father didn't want anyone to see."

"You already opened the safe?"

He nodded and killed his beer.

"Why didn't you tell me this?" she asked angrily.

"Because as an FBI agent, you would have been obligated to share whatever you found on the laptop with Detective Sykes, since the investigation into your father's death is ongoing. I didn't want you to do that, so I kept my mouth shut."

She slapped the table. Jon had played her like a fiddle. Like his perfect aim, it was another trademark. He'd done this before, and each time she'd nearly ended the relationship. She wondered what it said about her character that they were still together.

"Please don't do that again," she said.

He threw down money and rose from the table.

"Let's go look at your father's laptop," he said.

CHAPTER 22

"Looks like we had a visitor," Lancaster said.

He removed the business card stuck in the front door of Martin's house. It was from the captain of the Saint Augustine Police Department's CSI team. He flipped the card over and read the note printed on the back.

"Crap," Beth said, reading over his shoulder. "I forgot that the police were sending a CSI team to check Dad's study for clues. Think we should call them?"

"The Sokolovs ransacked your father's study," he said, tearing the card up. "What else is there to know?"

Beth unlocked the front door, and they headed upstairs. The study looked like a tornado had gone through it, with hundreds of books strewn across the floor. There was a musty odor left by the mummified hand, and he opened the double doors leading to the balcony to air the place out.

"We still don't know the Sokolovs' motivation for doing this," Beth said.

"It's the same as ours," he said. "They wanted to look at your father's laptop. When they realized it was locked up, they got mad, and went on a rampage."

From his pocket he took the slip of paper with the combination. "15, 25, 45," he said.

Beth opened the safe and removed the laptop.

"Let's do this downstairs," she said. "The smell is bothering me."

- - -

The dining room table had been in Beth's family for three generations. They sat at the head, and Beth powered up the laptop. It was an older model Dell Latitude and made a soft purring sound as it slowly came to life.

"You didn't explain how Nicki figured out the names of the people who got a hand dropped on their doorstep," she said. "Don't tell me she was hiding behind the door when Officer Spencer shared that information, and she wrote the names down."

"Afraid so," he said. "She ran the names through a search engine and eventually figured out how they were related to your father. She's turned into a real cybersleuth."

"Did my sister or her husband know?"

"I don't think so. Nicki must have told them she was doing homework during the car ride home, when she was running down these names."

"I really want her to stop. Any suggestions?"

"I'm not a parent. How do you stop a kid from doing something?"

"I'm going to talk to my sister. Nicki needs to be reined in."

"Can it wait until we're finished? She's been a real help."

Beth gave him a hard look. "These are dangerous people, and if they find out she's onto them, who knows what might happen? This has to stop now."

"Roger that."

The laptop had booted up. On the slip of paper with the combination was a password. Maximilian$*@. Beth typed it in, and unlocked the screen.

"Max was my father's favorite dog," she explained. "Big old German shepherd he rescued out of a parking lot. Dog never left his side."

The screensaver was a sunrise taken from the balcony outside Martin's study, the glistening ocean visible just above the treetops. Beth clicked on the icon on the lower left, and a list of programs appeared. She ran the mouse over them, trying to decide which folder to open first. A single tear rolled down her cheek.

"You okay?" he asked.

"No, I'm not okay," she said.

When he was six years old, he'd walked into his parents' bedroom and found them lying naked on the bed, having sex. Thirty-six years later, the memory hadn't faded. If Beth found lurid videos of her father on the laptop, she'd never forget it either.

"Let me do this," he said.

He took the laptop and slid it toward himself, positioning it so she was no longer looking at the screen. She looked ready to fall to pieces.

"I'll let you know if I find anything of interest," he said.

"Are you suggesting that I leave the room?"

"Isn't that what you want to do? You don't want to do this."

She exhaled deeply. "Is it that obvious?"

"Yes, Beth, it's that obvious. Why don't you call Melanie, and see how she's doing? She's had a pretty rough time. I'm sure she'd like to hear from you."

"That's not a bad idea. Can I get you anything?"

"I'm good."

She rose and put her hand on his shoulder. Gave him a look that said thank you. Only after she'd left the room did he start his search.

- - -

There was nothing there.

There were no incriminating images of Martin having sex with Katya, or for that matter, any other woman. What he found instead were videos of lectures by well-known academics given at the college where Martin taught. He watched snippets of each, and found them as stimulating as staring at a fly crawling up a wall.

In the folder called "Pictures" he found photographs of Martin on his boat with his fishing buddies, photos of Martin riding his motorcycle with Dr. Sircy, and a collection of photos with Martin and his daughters and granddaughter taken during the holidays. What he didn't find was a single photo that could have been used to hurt Martin.

Not one.

He grew frustrated. If Martin was being blackmailed—and all the evidence they'd uncovered pointed to that being the case—then there were images that Martin didn't want the world to see. That was how the extortion game worked.

So where were they? Not here. Or, had he missed something?

He decided to start over. There was a reason why Martin had locked the laptop in the wall safe, and there was a reason why the Sokolovs had torn apart the study. The laptop had things on it that Martin didn't want anyone to see. If he looked hard enough, he would certainly find them.

- - -

"How's it going?" Beth said, standing in the doorway.

"Nothing yet," he said.

"No porn library, or videos of my dad having wild sex with Katya?"

Two hours had passed, and he still hadn't found the smoking gun that would explain Martin's erratic behavior. But he had found something odd, and he pointed at the screen. "Take a look at these, and tell me what you think."

145

Beth came into the room to have a look. With the mouse, he scrolled through a dozen photos of what appeared to be a fancy bed-and-breakfast. The photos were divided between the landscaped exterior, and the establishment's interior, including several of a lavish bedroom with a four-poster bed and a fireplace.

"What is this?" she asked.

"I was hoping you could tell me. On the bedroom wall there's a map of Saint Augustine. I think this place is local," he said.

"They're just photographs. Why did they pique your interest?"

"Because there aren't any other photos like this stored on his hard drive. Every single shot is either of him and his boating buddies, or family shots of you and Melanie and her family. These look out of place."

"I don't know—maybe he was thinking of buying a bed-and-breakfast. He talked about running a small business, to keep himself busy. Is that all you've found?"

"Yup. If your father was hiding a raunchy sex tape, it's not here." He shut the laptop, and Beth handed him a cold beer. She took a seat beside him at the table.

"I spoke to Melanie," she said. "She's going to have a long talk with Nicki. She thinks she knows how to get her to stop running her own investigation."

"How?"

"If Nicki doesn't quit, Melanie will pull her out of her CSI class at school as punishment. That will do the trick."

"I like it."

"Melanie found something strange. During the drive home, she went through my father's mail to see if there were any bills that needed to be paid. There was a notice from the cable company confirming that my father had canceled his service."

"Maybe he decided to cut the cord."

"That was what Melanie first thought. But then she found a notice from the local newspaper confirming he'd canceled his subscription delivery, and another from Visa saying that he'd canceled his credit card."

"People who plan suicides often tie up loose ends."

"I thought the same thing. Only the police report says my father's suicide was spur of the moment. The police came to that conclusion because Dad didn't leave a note, and two people he spoke to that day said he was in a good mood, and not despondent."

"I guess the police got it wrong."

"So what do we do now? We're back to square one."

"We still have leads to chase down. I'd like to start with something Dr. Sircy said about a video from a hospital board meeting that shows your father watching porn, and an intern catching him in the act. We need to take a look at that video, and see what's on it."

"That's a long shot. There's no guarantee that the surveillance video captured what my father was watching."

"I know it's a long shot, but we still have to check it out. Maybe we'll get lucky, and see who's in it."

"You think the video is of him and Katya?"

"Who else would it be?"

She gave him a tired look. It had been a long, frustrating day, and it was only half over. She took a deep breath, and he saw the resolve return to her face.

"I'm in," she said.

PART THREE
The Sixth Victim

CHAPTER 23

Florida was big on hospitals. With all the babies being born, as well as the growing elderly population, there were new hospitals going up in practically every corner of the state.

Flagler Hospital in Saint Augustine had recently added a new addition to meet the demand. It was built like a fortress, without a single tree to protect it from the blinding sunlight. Daniels parked on the building's shady west side and killed the engine. It had been a rough night, and she'd hardly slept. She slurped down the Starbucks coffee they'd picked up during the ride over. Jon offered her the rest of the croissant, and she shook her head.

"It's yours," she said.

He stuffed the bread into his mouth. "How long did your father work here?"

"Almost from the day he moved to Saint Augustine. The hospital's administration was happy to have him on board. He liked to say it was a marriage made in heaven."

"So he really liked it here."

"Loved it. When he retired up north, he said he felt like he didn't count anymore. That changed when he joined Flagler."

"It gave his life a purpose."

"Absolutely."

The sound of Jon's whistle caught her ear, and she realized he was onto something.

"Is that important?" she asked.

"It's another contradiction," he said. "Your father loved his job, yet he risked losing it by looking at porn during a board meeting when the other doctors might catch him. The risk outweighed the reward. Your father was smarter than that."

"Who knows what was going through his mind."

They went inside to the reception area. Daniels had decided that it would be best if she conducted the interview with the head of human resources by herself. It was important that she not be seen in Jon's company until the investigation was over, for fear her boss might find out. She asked if there was a place to get a drink, and they followed the receptionist's directions to a café that sold coffee and fresh pastries.

"I need an espresso," she said.

Jon bought espresso for her and a regular coffee for himself. Several uniformed police officers sat at a table eating breakfast, so they picked a table on the other side of the room and spoke in hushed tones.

"We still haven't figured out how the police are involved," she said.

He blew on his drink. "Maybe they're not."

"They have to be. The sheriff runs a tight ship, and runs hookers out of town. Yet somehow the Sokolov brothers were trafficking women right under his nose. To use your Spock-like logic, that's a contradiction."

"Let's hope we get a chance to ask him."

She downed the espresso like it was a shot of whiskey. It was just the extra kick she needed, and she took out her badge and pinned it to her lapel.

"Wish me luck," she said.

- - -

Leaving the cafeteria, she caught the uniforms' stares. Was it the badge, or were they just sizing up the merchandise? Any other time, she would have gone to their table, and given them a piece of her mind, but there were more important things to attend to.

Walking to the reception area, Daniels used her phone to get on the internet, and find the name of the hospital's head of human resources. It was a she, and her name was Greta Vinson.

The hospital reception area resembled a hotel check-in, with two receptionists on duty, one a young girl of no more than twenty, the other a silver-haired lady. Daniels approached holding her wallet open. Both receptionists stared at her photo ID.

"Oh my. The Federal Bureau of Investigation," the older one said.

The young one put on a brave face. "How can I help you?"

"I'm here to see Greta Vinson," Daniels said. "Would you please ring her office, and tell her that Special Agent Daniels wishes to speak with her?"

"Yes, ma'am."

The young one made the call. The older lady leaned in, breathless.

"I didn't think there really were female FBI agents," she said. "I see them on TV shows, but I figured that was just a way to get women to watch. Are there a lot of you?"

The remark made Daniels wince. The bureau's male/female ratio was a sore point to every female agent she knew. Male agents outnumbered their female counterparts five to one, with only a handful of women having leadership roles. The FBI was a good old boys' club, and showed no sign of changing anytime soon.

"No, but we're really loud," Daniels said.

The older one cackled. "I bet you are!"

The young one put down the phone. "Ms. Vinson said she will see you. Her office is on the sixth floor. Let me print you a pass."

Soon Daniels was riding upstairs in an elevator with a hospital pass attached to her other lapel. As the doors parted, she was greeted by a striking Scandinavian woman with a shock of white-blonde hair who was easily six feet tall.

"Special Agent Daniels," she said.

"Ms. Vinson. Thank you for seeing me so promptly."

"It's Greta, and I'm happy to help. Please step this way. Is this about Clive?"

Daniels shook her head, not understanding.

"The FBI planted an undercover agent here last month," Vinson explained. "One of our custodians, a fellow named Clive Croake, was a suspect in a murder that took place in Atlanta thirty years ago. DNA found on the dead woman matched Clive's DNA from a previous arrest. The undercover agent posed as a cleaning man, and tried to secretly get more DNA from Clive to confirm it was him. I think he was hoping for an empty soda can."

They entered an office with a small sitting area. They sat so they were facing each other. Vinson kicked off her shoes as if by habit.

"That isn't why I'm here," Daniels said.

"A pity," Vinson said. "Clive vanished like a puff of smoke. Which means he was probably guilty. I hope they catch him."

"Eventually, they will. It's a lot harder to hide than it used to be. Now, let me tell you why I'm here. My father was Martin Daniels."

Vinson's mouth opened, but no words came out. She took a moment to compose herself. Then she said, "I'm sorry, I didn't make the connection. You bear a resemblance to your father. You have his eyes."

"No need to apologize. It's a common last name. I'm conducting an investigation into my father's death, and was hoping you could help me."

"An investigation? Is there something wrong?"

"It appears that my father was being extorted. Were you aware of this?"

"Martin never mentioned anything like that to me."

"Did you speak with him often?"

"When he was on the board, we often lunched together."

"How often was this?"

"About once a week."

"Is it true that my father was fired because an intern caught him looking at pornographic videos on his cell phone during a board of directors meeting?"

Vinson's face reddened. "Who told you that?"

"Dr. Sircy. She told my partner that my father was a porn addict, and that he got caught many times watching it. Did you ever catch him?"

"I'm afraid so. It was in the elevator. I caught a fleeting image of a couple rolling around in the sheets. The sound was the tip-off."

"You heard something?"

"The female was having a loud orgasm. I cleared my throat, and your father put his cell phone away and said that he needed to stop opening junk email."

"Did you believe him?"

"No. I'd already heard the rumors. This just confirmed them."

"Did this occur before or after the intern complained?"

"It happened before."

"Why didn't you take action?"

Vinson shifted uncomfortably in her chair. She was a person of authority, and not used to being put in the hot seat. "Your father was such a valuable addition to our staff that I was willing to overlook his transgressions. In hindsight, that was a mistake, but I can't promise you that I wouldn't make it again."

Daniels smiled. Her father was a charmer, and had many fans. Yet for reasons she still did not completely comprehend, he'd destroyed everything by letting an obsession get the better of him. It made his demise that much more tragic.

"Dr. Sircy said that your board meetings were videotaped, and that a video exists of the incident between my father and the intern. Do you still have it?"

"I do," Vinson said. "It's on my laptop."

"I'd like to see it."

"I would have to speak with the hospital's legal counsel first."

"Why would you have to do that?"

"The video was shown during a hearing as evidence. I'm bound by privacy rules not to release it. I would need to get our attorney's permission."

"Which he probably won't give you."

"Probably not."

"Let me explain what will happen then," Daniels said. "I will go to a judge, and tell him that you didn't hand over a piece of evidence to me, which you are legally required to do, since I'm with the FBI. The judge will issue an order requiring you to turn over your laptop. I will review everything on it, and find the video myself. I'll also keep the laptop until my investigation is completed, which might be a while. I suggest you save yourself the embarrassment, and show me the video right now."

"Are you threatening me?"

"I most certainly am."

CHAPTER 24

Lancaster drank coffee in the cafeteria while cleaning out emails on his cell phone. There were hundreds, and most of them were junk or scammers posing as young women with alluring first names wishing to establish a relationship. They were obviously fake, and he wondered how anyone ever fell for them.

He got a text from Nicki. Hi, Jon! Can you talk?

He considered not responding. Nicki needed to go back to her classes, and stay out of their investigation. But there was always the chance that she'd found something valuable that would move things forward. If that was the case, then not responding would be a huge mistake.

Sure, he texted back.

Is Aunt Beth nearby?
No, I'm by myself.

His phone's screen lit up. "Hey, what's up?"

"My mom threatened to pull me out of my CSI class if I didn't stop sticking my nose into your case," the teenager said. "Was that Aunt Beth's idea?"

"No, it wasn't. But it was a good one. We're dealing with dangerous people. You could put yourself in harm's way if you're not more careful."

"But I am being careful."

"It's your mom's decision, Nicki, and you need to honor it."

"Okay. Last night, I dug up some more information about the four men in Saint Augustine who got the hands on their doorsteps. There's some interesting stuff there. Can I send it to you? I don't want it to go to waste."

A bell rang. He realized that Nicki was calling him from school. He wanted to say no, just to get her to stop, but also wanted to see what she'd unearthed.

"Interesting in what way?" he asked.

"Their backgrounds," she said. "There are a lot of parallels. They were older, like Grandpa, but they all worked, and were very successful. It made me wonder if they were being extorted, like Grandpa."

"Who told you your grandfather was being extorted?"

"I heard my mom tell my dad about all the missing money from his bank accounts. I put two and two together, and figured that was going on."

He found himself nodding. Because Sircy had said that her mummified hand was intended to keep her quiet, he'd assumed this was why the others had received hands as well. But that might not have been the case. Perhaps Martin's boating buddies were also being shaken down by the Russians.

"Send it to me," he said.

"You're not going to tell Aunt Beth, are you? CSI is my favorite class."

"I'll tell her I made the link myself, and steal your glory."

"Thanks, Jon."

He said goodbye and disconnected. He had company. The three uniformed police officers who'd been eating now stood beside his table, wearing menacing looks. The one in the middle wore a greasy butter stain on his shirt.

"Morning, Officers," he said.

"You need to come with us," the cop with the stain said.

- - -

He was taken to the parking lot and frisked. His Glock 43 drew sneers. It was the smallest handgun that Glock made, just over an inch wide and six inches long, and the cops tossed it between them like it was a beach toy.

"I wouldn't be caught dead carrying this," one of them said.

"Hell, my wife wouldn't carry something this small," the second said.

"Frisk him again, just to be safe," Butter Stain told them.

They searched him again. One of the cops stuck his hand into Lancaster's open shirt, feeling under his armpits for a hidden weapon, and busted a button.

"He's clean," one of them said.

"Good. Hands behind your back," Butter Stain said.

"Is this really necessary?" Lancaster asked.

"Shut your mouth, and do as you're told."

"Are you arresting me?"

"I said, shut up."

He put his hands behind his back and was cuffed. They walked him over to a parked cruiser and shoved him into the back seat. The interior was hot as an oven, and the cops stood outside shooting the breeze while he baked inside the vehicle. Soon his clothes were drenched in sweat and his hair was matted on his forehead.

Butter Stain got behind the wheel and fired up the engine. His partners drove an unmarked sedan with tinted windows. He followed them out of the parking lot.

"Where are you taking me?" Lancaster asked.

"You were a cop, what do you think?" Butter Stain said.

"I think you're abusing your authority."

"And you would be right."

He hadn't spent enough time in Saint Augustine to have a lay of the land, and unfamiliar street names flashed by. They came to a large park, with swings and basketball courts, and Butter Stain parked behind an aluminum storage shed. An unmarked sedan was waiting for them.

Butter Stain yanked him out of the back seat and removed the handcuffs. Lancaster watched the cops roll back their shirt sleeves in preparation for a good beating. One by one, they removed their side-arms and placed them on the hood of the sedan.

A man stepped out from behind the shed. He wore a jacket and tie and was sucking on a cigarette. He took a final hit and ground it into the dirt. It was Detective Sykes. Coming forward, he poked his finger in Lancaster's chest.

"You are the definition of a problem," Sykes said.

"What did I do?" Lancaster asked.

"What didn't you do, is more like it," the detective said. "You run around town with that pretty little FBI lady, poking your nose where it doesn't belong, stirring the pot. Martin Daniels killed himself, and nothing's going to change that. Leave it be."

"Martin was being extorted by a group of Russians," he said.

"We'll take care of the Russians in due time," Sykes said.

"The Russians have been causing trouble for a while, and it doesn't appear that you did a damn thing to stop them."

Sykes poked him again. "Leave it be."

"Fuck you."

"What are you, some kind of masochist? My boys will beat you to a pulp, make that ugly face even uglier."

"Have at it."

Sykes snarled like a junkyard dog. He moved backward while motioning with his arm. The biggest of the three uniforms stepped forward. He was corn fed, about six-four and 250 pounds, with tree-trunk arms and no neck. Lancaster, who stood five-nine and weighed 170, held his ground.

"You shouldn't have said that," No Neck said.

"Said what?" Lancaster asked.

"Fuck you. You shouldn't have said that."

"I didn't realize you boys were so fragile. Oh, by the way, fuck you."

No Neck put his hand on the lapel of Lancaster's shirt and gave it a yank, popping the buttons. "You're not funny." Suddenly his eyes went wide, and he froze.

Sykes sensed something was amiss. "What's wrong?"

No Neck pointed at the distinctive frog skeleton tattoo crawling up Lancaster's shoulder. The tattoo was blue-black in color, and had the date that it had been inked.

"He's a SEAL," No Neck said, the bravado gone from his voice. "Those guys are lethal. I don't want my eyes gouged out."

"He's no SEAL," Sykes said. "He probably got the tattoo to trick a lady into thinking he was. Only way he was ever going to get laid."

Sykes and the other two cops laughed. No Neck wasn't convinced and started backing up. Lancaster wondered if the guy had been born stupid or if he took classes. By dropping his defenses, he'd made himself vulnerable to a variety of kicks and blows, all of which would incapacitate him. He was an open target.

Lancaster rushed forward and grabbed No Neck by the arms. He kicked his legs out from under him, and gave him a shove. No Neck crashed to earth, taking Butter Stain with him on his way down. They lay on the ground, writhing in pain.

"My knee!" Butter Stain said.

Sykes cursed. Their four-to-one advantage had just been halved. He began to draw his sidearm from inside his sports jacket. Lancaster knelt down and grabbed a handful of dirt, which he tossed into Sykes's face.

"I can't see. Get him, Kenny," Sykes said.

The third cop rushed him like a mad bull. Lancaster had seen the tactic before. Kenny was going to use his superior weight to wrestle him to the ground and hold him there. It was a smart tactic when dealing with a suspect resisting arrest, but not an ex-special ops soldier. In fact, it was probably the worst choice Kenny could have made. SEALS were taught first and foremost to be practical fighters, and were trained not to engage in fancy spinning kicks or other showy maneuvers. As a result, they only focused on the effective martial arts, like Brazilian jiu-jitsu, Israeli Krav Maga, Muay Thai, and good old-fashioned boxing.

He sidestepped Kenny's charge and tripped him. Kenny broke his fall, then sprang off the ground, and threw an amateurish haymaker. He ducked the blow, then stepped in and grabbed Kenny's right ear with his right hand. He pulled Kenny's head toward him, while driving his elbow into Kenny's mouth. The sound was awful.

Holding his damaged face, Kenny sank to his knees.

Sykes was struggling to get his vision back. Lancaster reached into the detective's sports jacket, and relieved him of his weapon. Then, he scooped up the three officers' weapons that had been left on the hood of the sedan. The trio remained on the ground. Their faces were bloodied, their clothes ripped. The badges of dishonorable men.

"Give us our weapons back," Sykes said.

"So you can arrest me? Fat chance."

"You'll pay for this," Sykes said.

"You're in no position to threaten me. I'm also taking your car. I'll leave it in the hospital parking lot with the keys under the mat. I plan to tell Special Agent Daniels what happened, and I'm sure she'll relay my story to the FBI's Jacksonville office. If you pull another stunt like this, they'll come after you. Am I making myself clear?"

Sykes grunted under his breath. He was seeing clearly, and the future didn't look very promising. In a pleading voice he said, "Please don't take our guns. I'm begging you, man. From one cop to another."

Sykes and his pals would get in hot water for losing their weapons. There would be a department review that would end in them being disciplined, or even suspended. If they fabricated a story, and were later caught lying, they'd lose their jobs.

"Sure. But I want something in return," Lancaster said. "Tell me why you didn't run the Sokolov brothers out of town. From what I can see, they've been pulling bad shit for a while, yet the police haven't touched them."

"I can't tell you that," Sykes said.

"Then you're not getting your guns back."

He got behind the wheel of the sedan. The engine was running, and the interior was ice cold. He placed the cops' guns on the passenger seat, and pulled out. Driving away, he glanced into his mirror at Sykes and his goons and saw them shake their fists.

– – –

Reaching the main road, Lancaster spied a kid with a backpack on a bicycle, pedaling furiously. Had the kid seen the fracas with the cops?

Lancaster decided to follow him.

CHAPTER 25

After a mile, the kid ran out of steam, and pulled his bike into the parking lot of a convenience store named Rudy's. Lancaster sensed the kid was going to jump off his bike and make a run for it, and he pulled in and lowered his window.

"Police. Stop."

Lancaster jumped out of the sedan. The kid was straddling his bike, puffing hard. He was looking through the front window of Rudy's as if expecting someone might come outside and save him. Lancaster showed him his badge.

"Don't be afraid, I just want to talk," he said.

"You're not going to arrest me?" the kid asked breathlessly.

"I wasn't planning to. Let's start with your name."

"It's Micah," the boy said.

"Why aren't you in school, Micah?"

"Teacher's conference. We got the day off."

Micah looked about fourteen, with a curly mop of brown hair and thick glasses. He still hadn't mustered the courage to make eye contact, and looked scared out of his wits.

"What were you doing back there, Micah?" he asked.

"I like to look through the trash at the park, sometimes there's stuff that I can salvage," the boy said. "When the police cruiser drove in, I got scared, and hid."

"How much did you see?"

"All of it. You beat the boogers out of those cops. Pow, pow, pow. They didn't know what hit them. Where did you learn how to do that?"

"In the navy. They made a man out of me. Taught me how to fight."

Micah finally looked at him. He didn't act scared anymore.

"Can I see your tattoo?" he asked.

Lancaster parted his shirt so his shoulder was bared. Micah was transfixed.

"That's cool. How come it's a skeleton?" the boy asked.

"They call it the bone frog," he explained. "It signifies a comrade lost in the line of duty. I got mine after a buddy got killed during a mission in Afghanistan."

"Your friend died?"

"That's right. He was my best friend. I got the tattoo to honor him."

"What are those square things beneath the frog?"

"His dog tags." Lancaster buttoned his shirt. "You want a soda or something?"

Micah shook his head. His eyes had a faraway look as he tried to imagine what it was like to lose your best friend in a godforsaken part of the world. It was a hard concept to grasp when you were young. When it did grab you, you stopped being a kid.

"Can I ask you a question, Micah?"

The boy thought about it, then nodded.

"Did you take a video of me beating up those policemen?"

Micah grinned. Of course he'd taken a video of the fight. Any person in possession of a cell phone was an evidence gathering machine, capable of taking photos, videos, and audio of any event they witnessed.

This was especially true of teenagers, who immediately posted the images on social media for the rest of the world to see.

"I got the whole thing," he said.

Lancaster took out his wallet. From the billfold he removed two crisp fifty-dollar bills. The boy's eyes grew wide.

"How would you like to make a hundred bucks, Micah?" he asked.

"A hundred bucks? What do I have to do?" the boy said.

"Two things. First, I'll give you fifty bucks if you send me a copy of the video."

"You have yourself a deal."

Micah removed an iPhone from his backpack. Lancaster read him his cell phone number, and the boy texted him a copy of the video. Lancaster watched thirty seconds of the video and saw that the boy had captured the entire event, but had muted the audio. He handed him one of the fifties, and watched Micah stuff it into his pocket.

"I'll give you the other fifty if you'll erase the video from your phone," he said.

"You want me to get rid of it?"

"That's right. Those men might come after you, if they find out you have it. I don't want anything bad to happen to you."

Micah reluctantly agreed and erased the video. Lancaster handed him the second fifty and told him it was nice meeting him. He entered the convenience store and purchased two iced teas. Coming outside, he tossed Micah one of the drinks.

"How old do I have to be to enlist in the navy?" Micah asked.

"Eighteen, unless you have your parents' consent. Then you can be seventeen."

"How old were you?"

"Eighteen. My parents didn't want me to go." He got back into the sedan and started the engine. It was a bad way to end the conversation, and he lowered his window.

"They got over it," he added.

- - -

The Matanzas River ran the entire length of Saint Augustine, and led to the city's port. He let Google take him there, and parked in a spot on the side of the road. Taking the policemen's guns off the passenger seat, he got out, and tossed them into the water. He had taken three years of Spanish in high school, and knew that Matanzas was the Spanish word for massacre. It was a strange thing to name a river.

He drove back to Flagler Hospital. The sedan was fully equipped, and he heard a police dispatcher barking over the radio. She was looking for Sykes, and he had an urge to answer the call, and pretend he was the detective.

He decided that was a bad idea, and kept driving.

He had told Sykes that he would leave the sedan in the hospital lot, which in hindsight was a dumb thing to say. Better to call Sykes after he parked the sedan, and tell him where it was. There was the chance that Sykes and his goon squad would be waiting for him, hoping for a little payback.

But it was a slim chance.

More than likely, they'd go to a walk-in clinic to get their wounds treated, then find a diner where they could sit in a corner and fabricate a story to explain what had happened. They'd then have to memorize the story, and take turns reciting it. If one of them tripped up, they'd all go down.

As he pulled into the hospital lot, Beth called him. She sounded angry.

"Where the hell are you?"

"I had an unwanted encounter with three deputies in the hospital cafeteria," he said. "They made me leave with them."

"They kidnapped you?"

"Afraid so. It didn't end well." He paused. "For them."

"Did you beat the living daylights out of them?"

"Guilty as charged. Sykes was behind it."

"What a surprise. I'm in the hospital parking lot. Where are you?"

"I just pulled in. I borrowed Sykes's car. Are you in your rental?"

"Yes, why?"

"Don't get out. Let me scope things out, and make sure they're not hanging around. See you in a few."

He circled the parking lot and did not see any sign of the law. He parked in a visitor space and hustled over to Beth's rental and hopped in. She had the car in reverse before his door was completely closed. While she drove, he pulled up Micah's video on his cell phone and played it for her. She laughed under her breath.

"Who shot the video?" she asked.

"A fourteen-year-old kid."

"Sykes won't take this lying down."

"I'd like to think that I taught him and his boys a valuable lesson."

"Which is what?"

"Never underestimate an opponent. Sykes told me to leave town. He said we were poking our noses where they didn't belong."

"Sounds like he's running scared."

"I agree. But we still don't know of what. How did your meeting with the head of human resources go? Were you able to get your hands on the video of your father?"

"Yes. She put up a fight, but I prevailed."

Beth grew quiet, fighting back tears.

"I'm assuming you watched it," he said.

"All eleven minutes of it." Then she said, "It was awful."

CHAPTER 26

When Daniels was a teenager, she'd witnessed a tragic automobile accident. She had never forgotten it, nor the lessons she'd learned.

Melanie had been accepted at the University of Pennsylvania, and their father had decided to take the family out for a celebratory dinner. In their town was a restaurant that served authentic Northern Italian cuisine, and they'd eaten enough pasta and desserts to make themselves uncomfortable.

Her father had driven home. An Eric Clapton and B. B. King duet called "Riding with the King" played on the car stereo. Her father loved the blues, and the music was loud. He braked for the light at an intersection, which was illuminated with streetlights. With no vehicles in front of them, they had a clear view of the cross street.

A white Ford station wagon came to the intersection, slowed down, and began to turn. A Saab being driven at high speed in the opposite direction hit the Ford, destroying both vehicles. It was the loudest, most gut-wrenching noise she'd ever heard.

Her father went to help. But it was too late. The driver of the Ford was dead, as was the driver of the Saab. Daniels and her sister broke down and cried.

The police and an ambulance soon arrived, and the scene was cordoned off. Because they were witnesses, a deputy took each of them aside, and got a statement.

Back home, they sat in the living room in a state of shock. Their mother served them hot chocolate, and it soothed their nerves. They talked about the accident, and to Daniels's surprise, their recollections of what had occurred were different.

Her father believed the Ford's driver was at fault, and had turned into the path of the Saab without putting his blinker on.

Their mother said the Saab's driver was to blame. She believed the Ford had turned its blinker on, yet the Saab hadn't slowed, and caused the wreck.

Melanie believed both drivers were at fault, and that the Ford's driver hadn't used his blinker, and that the Saab was speeding.

Daniels had a completely different view. She felt that the driver of the Saab was impaired, and had crossed the middle line, and hit the Ford.

Four eyewitnesses to the same event, four different versions.

How was that possible?

To further complicate things, the local newspaper published a story claiming that a crime scene investigator had determined that the Ford's driver was at fault, and that the Saab's driver wasn't to blame. Confused, she worked up the nerve to call the paper, and spoke to the reporter who wrote the story.

The reporter was very nice to her. He explained how people's imaginations often distorted the things that they saw. This was especially true with stressful situations, when a person's eyes could play tricks on them. The only way to get to the truth was to let an impartial person look at the facts, and then determine what actually happened.

- - -

"I want you to look at the video of my father in the board meeting," she said.

They were in the local Starbucks's parking lot, drinking coffee and sharing an oversize muffin from the bakery. It had become a ritual when they were working a case, and were faced with a difficult problem. Jon stared ahead, saying nothing.

"Is that a problem?" she asked.

"Can I do it later?"

"You mean when I'm not around."

"Yes. I don't want to say something out of line, and hurt your feelings."

She popped the last piece of muffin into her mouth. Jon always left her the last piece, and he always paid. He had impeccable manners that way, and his request to view the video alone did not surprise her. "Nothing you can say at this point is going to offend me. My father had another side to him; so do a lot of men. I've accepted that. The reason I want you to watch the video is that I feel like I'm missing something important."

"How so?"

"I watched the video several times while I was waiting for you. It doesn't feel like I'm looking at my father. The behavior is wrong. Yet I can't put my finger on why. I need another set of eyes to look at it."

Jon drank his coffee in silence. She was not going to give him a chance to say no. Taking her briefcase off the back seat, she removed her laptop. Soon the video was playing, and she shifted the screen so it was pointing at him.

"My father arrived first to the board meeting. Watch what he does."

The video was in color, and showed a sunny room with a board-room table and six leather chairs. On the table were glasses and two pitchers of water. A door opened, and Martin Daniels appeared. He looked every bit the country doctor, wearing a tweed jacket with elbow patches and a striped necktie. He glanced impatiently at his watch.

"Dad couldn't stand when people were late," she said.

"So that's where you get it from," he said.

Martin cordially greeted each of his colleagues as they arrived. When all were present, he took a seat facing the camera, and poured himself a glass of water.

The meeting started.

The video had audio, and the chairperson read the minutes from the previous meeting, then read the topics that they would be discussing. It was about as exciting as watching paint dry, and Jon smothered a yawn.

"Watch my father," Daniels said.

"What am I looking for?" he replied.

"Just watch. Something weird is going on. See if you can spot it."

Jon reached across the seats and took the computer from her lap. "Do you mind?"

"Go ahead," she said.

He balanced the computer on his legs, and stared at the screen. His eyes were unblinking, his face cast in stone. A long minute passed.

"Your father looks agitated," he said. "He keeps shifting in his seat and making faces. If I didn't know better, I'd say someone was sticking him with a pin."

"What do you think is bothering him?" she asked.

"Hard to say. But he's clearly upset. He was in a good mood when he came in. Something happened after the meeting started that upset him."

"Did someone at the table make a sarcastic remark?"

"If they did, the audio didn't pick it up."

The meeting droned on. The chairperson was talking about the hospital budget for the coming year. Suddenly, her father began to tug at his collar like it was choking him. It reminded her of the comic who used to say he didn't get any respect. Only her father wasn't doing it for laughs.

"Come on, Martin," Jon said under his breath. "Tell us what's wrong."

Her father lifted the glass of water to his face. His eyes shifted around the table. Checking to be sure that the others weren't watching him. His other hand removed his cell phone from his jacket pocket.

"Your father just caved to his desires," Jon said.

"Yes, he did," she said quietly.

"Is this when he gets busted by the intern?"

"Just watch."

Her father held the cell phone below the table's edge. His eyes shifted downward as he stared at the screen. His eyes narrowed, and he looked stunned. "What a transformation," Jon said. "Did you ever see him act like that?"

"Never."

The door to the meeting room opened. It was directly behind her father, and he didn't hear it. A twentysomething woman entered the boardroom.

"That must be Demetria the intern," Jon said.

"In the flesh. This is when it gets ugly."

Demetria shut the door. In her hand was a pot of coffee. She came up behind Daniels's father, and leaned over, ready to whisper in his ear. Her eyes found the screen. Bringing her hand to her mouth, she said, "Oh. My. God."

The meeting came to an abrupt halt. Her father snapped his head up, seeing Demetria. He came out of his chair. The intern backed up, afraid.

"It's not what you think," her father said.

"You pervert!" the intern said.

Demetria grabbed the door handle. In a flash, she was gone. The other people in the room stayed in their seats, too stunned to speak.

Her father remained standing, looking ashamed. His shoulders sagged, and his body went limp. The cell phone fell from his hand to the table. For a moment the screen was visible to the camera, the images of a naked couple rolling around on a bed impossible to miss.

"She got him dead to rights," Jon said.

The meeting ended, and the others left without a word. Her father slipped the cell phone into his pocket. His world was falling apart, and he didn't know what to do.

The chairperson came around the table. They were the last two people in the room. She seemed to share her father's pain, and put her hand upon his shoulder.

"Martin, you need to get help," she said.

"It's not what you think," her father repeated.

"The cat is out of the bag. We all know about your problem with pornography. You've let it invade your professional life, and it's going to ruin you," she said.

"It's not—"

"Stop making excuses, damn it." She took a business card from her purse and stuck it into his hand. "This is a therapist that I know. Get some help, before this addiction destroys your life. It's for your own good."

"I don't have an addiction," her father protested.

"I'm not blind, Martin," she said. "Please, get some help."

Her father slipped the card into his breast pocket without looking at it. The chairperson shook her head and left. The door slammed loudly behind her.

Her father gathered his things. Then he, too, was gone.

The screen went dark.

CHAPTER 27

Lancaster stared at Beth. "Your father looked tortured in that video."

"That's exactly what I thought," she said.

"I'm no shrink, but his behavior doesn't fit the profile of a porn addict," he said.

"Are you speaking from experience?"

"Hardly. I worked the night shift as a beat cop. There was another cop who I shared a patrol car with who was addicted to porn. He used to sneak away and watch videos on his cell phone on break. He never did it in the open."

"Your partner hid his addiction."

"That's right. And he was good at it."

"My father was watching a porno in a board meeting. It was like he was oblivious to the danger he was putting himself in. It doesn't make sense."

They had hit another wall, and they both fell silent. They were missing something important. Martin's problem was right there in front of their faces, yet his motivation still remained unclear.

Beth's cell phone lit up. Special Agent Phillips calling. She let the call go into voice mail, then played his message so they could both hear it.

"Call me right away," Erce said. "Jon Lancaster has been up to his usual tricks."

Lancaster glanced at his watch. A little over an hour had passed since he'd smacked around Sykes and his posse. Bad news traveled fast in these parts.

Beth turned on the car before calling Erce back. Her phone's Bluetooth connected to the car's sound system, and they listened to the call go through over the car's speakers.

Phillips answered on the first ring.

"Hey Erce, it's Beth. I'm driving in my car. What's up?" she said.

"Have you spoken to Jon Lancaster recently?" Phillips asked.

"No," she lied. "What's going on?"

"The Saint Augustine Police Department released an official statement a few minutes ago," he said. "It seems that three uniformed officers and a detective were attempting to subdue a homeless guy when the homeless guy jumped them. One of the cops got his face rearranged, and another has a broken knee. The homeless guy also stole their weapons, and drove off in one of their vehicles. They gave a description of the assailant, and are asking other law enforcement agencies to be on the lookout."

"One homeless guy took down four cops? How does that work?"

"The statement was vague on the details."

"Who is this guy—John Rambo?"

"That's what the Saint Augustine cops made it sound like. Between you and me, I think your buddy Lancaster is responsible, and the story is a coverup."

"Really. Why do you think that?"

"Most of the homeless population in Saint Augustine have drug and alcohol addictions. There's no way a drunk, or a druggie, could pull off what these cops are claiming. And Lancaster's an ex-SEAL with a history of confrontation. The guy has no fear. I'll bet you a beer he was responsible for roughing up these cops."

"Does J. T. know about this?"

"Not yet."

"Are you going to tell him?"

"I have to. J. T. ordered me to report any suspicious activity that might be linked to Lancaster. If I don't send him the statement, he'll be all over my ass."

"Got it. Please remind J. T. that Lancaster is running solo here."

"I'll be sure to do that."

She thanked Erce for keeping her in the loop, and disconnected. Lancaster smiled to himself. Sykes and his goons had just painted themselves into a corner, and he realized that it couldn't have played out any better if he'd scripted it.

He hopped out of the car and entered the Starbucks. When he returned, he had two Double Chocolate Chunk Brownies wrapped in a napkin. Brownies were Beth's weakness, and her eyes went wide when he handed her one.

"What's this for?" she asked.

"We're celebrating," he said.

"What for?"

"We're going to break this thing wide open."

- - -

While Beth ate her treat, Lancaster replayed Micah's video on his cell phone.

Micah had been standing on elevated ground when he shot the video, his angle pointing down. For reasons only Micah knew, the audio was muted, and there was no sound.

On the video, a police cruiser and a black sedan pulled into a public park and parked behind an aluminum storage shed. Three beefy uniformed police officers climbed out of the vehicles, followed by Lancaster, who was in handcuffs, and was obviously being held captive.

Detective Sykes appeared from behind a shed after Jon's handcuffs were removed. A brief conversation between the two men followed.

"What did he say to you?" Beth asked.

"He told me we were sticking our noses where they didn't belong," he said.

"So he threatened you."

"Several times. Now comes the fun part. Watch."

The largest cop cuffed his shirt sleeves and stepped forward, ready to administer a good old-fashioned whipping. The other two cops and Sykes were sharing a laugh.

"What a bunch of mutts," she said.

The largest cop pulled the front of Jon's shirt apart. He pointed a chubby finger at Lancaster's shoulder. He said something to his partners, then started retreating.

"He saw the frog tattoo on your chest and made the connection, didn't he?"

"Good eye. It put the fear of God into him."

"It was four against one. Weren't you afraid?"

"Not of these idiots. They thought I was going to roll over for them."

On the video, Lancaster charged the largest cop, and tossed him into one of his partners. They went down, and lay on their backs, writhing in pain. He threw a handful of dirt into Sykes's eyes, then incapacitated the third cop. There were plenty of street fights on YouTube, and they always ended quickly. This one was no exception. They watched him relieve Sykes of his weapon, scoop up the cops' handguns, then hop into Sykes's sedan and drive away. It was here that Micah's video ended.

"You fight dirty," she said, licking her fingers.

"Dirty wins. Does anything you just saw match the statement the Saint Augustine Police Department released?"

"Nope. Whoever wrote that statement lied through their teeth."

"Sykes wrote the statement."

"You don't think the others had a hand in it?"

"No. Sykes is the ringleader."

"Do you want me to arrest Sykes? Based upon what I just saw, I can charge him with kidnapping, assault, and attempted battery. He'll also be suspended from the force for releasing a false statement, and eventually fired and lose his pension. He might even spend time in prison. His life will be ruined."

Lancaster ate his brownie in silence. He would have enjoyed seeing Sykes get what was coming to him. He was a dirty cop, the kind that gave police departments a bad name, and deserved whatever harsh treatment he received. But justice was never cut and dried. If Beth arrested him, Sykes would lawyer up, and they'd never find out what had happened to Martin Daniels in the months leading up to his death. That was the goal, and he needed to make sure they didn't lose sight of it.

"I don't think arresting him will get us any closer to the truth," he said. "Sykes knows what happened to your father. We need to make him open up, and talk to us."

"How? Blackmail?"

"Works for me."

Beth shook her head.

"Why not?" he asked. "We'll use Micah's video to leverage the truth out of him. Don't tell me you haven't coerced suspects before."

"I have coerced suspects, and it works wonders," she said. "But Sykes is different. He lied to us the first time we met him, and now he's lied to his superiors by issuing this false statement. Whatever Sykes is hiding, it's big enough for him to risk everything. If we corner him, he'll just come up with another story, and hope we fall for it."

He found himself nodding. Beth's instincts were right, and not being clouded by the personal nature of the investigation. He admired her for being able to do that.

"I agree. So what should we do?" he said.

"We need to figure out why Sykes is lying to us," she said. "Why is he willing to forfeit his career to cover up what happened to my father? There's something nasty going on here. It's right in front of our noses, but we're not seeing it."

"Start over."

"Yes. Start over."

"I'm game."

"But first, we need to study the video of my father during the board meeting. My father says 'It's not what you think' several times. He got caught red-handed, but he wouldn't back down. Why?"

"Because it wasn't what everyone thought," he said.

"Exactly. The video had a hidden meaning," she said. "We need to figure out what it was. Once we do that, I think we'll understand why Sykes is being a snake."

Beth's cell phone rang. She answered it and made a face. "I'm leaving right now," she said, then disconnected.

"Who was that?" Lancaster asked.

"Erce. There's trouble in River City." She started the rental and backed out. "Where do you want me to drop you off?"

CHAPTER 28

Forty minutes later, Daniels arrived at the FBI's Jacksonville office on the west side of town. The building was a four-story, yellow monstrosity inside a bland industrial park, and had no personality. Erce had been cryptic over the phone, and it had made her wonder if there was someone in the room with him as he made the call.

The reception area was cold and unfriendly. She handed her credentials to the male receptionist and announced that she was here to see Special Agent Phillips.

"I'll let him know you're here. Please make yourself comfortable."

She was too nervous to sit. She studied the smiling portrait of the director in charge hanging on the wall behind the reception area. Her name was Maria Rojas, and she had olive-colored skin and an engaging smile. Even though Daniels didn't know Rojas, she admired her. The Jacksonville office was a big operation, with seven satellite offices that reported to it, and the bureau didn't hand out those kinds of assignments to bench warmers. Rojas had earned her stripes.

To her surprise, it was Rojas who greeted her.

"Special Agent Daniels, it's a pleasure to meet you."

Rojas had a firm handshake and eyes that didn't blink. She used her security card to open a door with a security camera over it, and they walked down a carpeted hallway.

"You don't remember me, do you?" Rojas said.

They stopped at a pair of double doors leading to a conference room. Daniels studied Rojas, then shook her head.

"We spoke the morning of 9/11," Rojas said. "I was working at the FBI's office on Wall Street. When the first tower was hit, I called the Pentagon to report what happened. You were on assignment at the Pentagon that day, and picked up the phone. We spoke for several minutes. You sounded young, like me. I never forgot you."

"I remember you now," Daniels said. "A half hour after our conversation, the Pentagon got hit. What a horrible day that was."

"It made us who we are today."

"It sure did. Can you tell me what's going on?"

"J. T. is on the warpath. He wants to do a conference call with us."

"About what?"

"Your boyfriend."

Daniels swallowed the lump in her throat and followed Rojas into a conference room with blackout shades on the windows. A sixty-four-inch flat screen hung on the wall, facing a long table with chairs. Erce stood at the head of the table, looking worried. He skipped the formalities and simply nodded. Daniels nodded back.

Rojas made the TV come to life. Their boss filled the screen, sitting behind a desk littered with reports and thick memorandums. He'd recently suffered a heart attack and had ignored his doctor's advice and returned to work once he was strong enough to get around. He'd lost a lot of weight, and looked gaunt.

"Good afternoon, Special Agent Daniels. Thank you for joining us," J. T. said. "All of you, grab a chair, and have a seat. We need to have a little chat."

The words sounded ominous. They pulled chairs from the table and sat in a row, facing the screen. Daniels put her best poker face on.

"A few years ago, a college buddy of mine named Jack Potter became publisher of the *Florida Times-Union*, which as you know is the main newspaper in Jacksonville," J. T. said, staring at Daniels as he spoke. "Jack called me earlier today. It seems that the paper has a satellite office in Saint Augustine. A few hours ago, a fourteen-year-old boy came into the office, and met with a reporter. The boy had a video on his cell phone that he wanted to sell to the newspaper for a hundred dollars. After reviewing the video, the reporter decided it was a good investment, and paid the kid off."

Daniels couldn't believe it. Jon had been tricked by a kid. Micah had pretended to erase the video, then tried to sell it to someone else. The kid was a real entrepreneur.

"The reporter sent the video to his editor, who shared it with Jack. Jack was disturbed by what he saw, since the video involves several members of the Saint Augustine Police Department. He sent the video to me, and asked for my advice.

"As you know, the Saint Augustine Police issued a statement today, stating that a homeless man attacked four of their officers, and relieved them of their weapons. The video paints a different picture of things. See for yourself."

J. T. picked up a remote on his desk and punched in a command. Half of the flat screen was taken over by a second screen. The video of Jon humiliating Sykes and company began to play. It was even better the second time around.

Daniels's mind raced. J. T. was going to grill her about the video. He would want to know why the police had kidnapped Jon. And, he'd want to know if she and Jon were working the case together, and not running solo, as she'd led J. T. to believe. Every FBI agent was trained to detect when a suspect was not being forthright with them. J. T. was an expert at reading people, and had taught classes at the academy. If he caught her lying, he'd fire her on the spot.

The video ended, and the second screen went away. J. T. stared at Daniels from a thousand miles away, his eyes boring a hole into her soul.

"Special Agent Daniels, can you identify the individuals in the video?" he asked.

"Certainly. The man in the handcuffs is Jon Lancaster. The man wearing the sports jacket and necktie is Detective Sykes with the Saint Augustine Police Department," she said. "I don't know who the three uniformed officers are, but I'll guess they're also members of the Saint Augustine police."

"Were you aware of this video?" her boss asked.

She placed the tips of her fingers together, as if praying. There were more nerve connections between the hands and the brain than any other part of the body, and hand gestures were a gold mine of information during an interrogation. Steepling the hands was an indicator that the suspect was telling the truth.

"I was not," she lied.

"Did Lancaster tell you the Saint Augustine Police tried to rough him up?"

"I haven't talked to Jon in days."

"Is that a yes, or a no?"

"It's a no," she lied.

"So Lancaster didn't talk to you about it. How do you know Detective Sykes?"

"I spoke with him two days ago in his office about my father's suicide. Sykes had my father's cell phone, which he let me look at."

"And what did you find?"

"Everything on it had been erased, which I found suspicious."

"Was Lancaster present during that meeting?"

"Jon was there, yes."

"Did he say something out of line that angered Sykes?"

"I did most of the talking. I don't believe Jon said more than a few words."

"What is your take on Sykes?"

J. T. was staring at her legs. FBI agents were taught to always believe the feet, as they were the most honest part of the body. She realized she was locking her ankles, a sign that she was holding back. She uncrossed her legs, and answered truthfully.

"My take is that Detective Sykes is hiding information," she said. "I don't believe that my father erased the data on his cell phone before he took his own life. I believe that Detective Sykes erased the data later on."

"Why would Sykes destroy evidence?"

"Any answer I give you will be purely speculative," she said. "So let me tell you what I do know. There's over a million dollars missing from my father's bank account. A young Russian woman named Katya was in a relationship with my father, and appears to have been blackmailing him. I believe that Sykes is involved."

"What's the connection between Sykes and the Russian?"

"Katya was being fronted by two Russian brothers named Sokolov. The Sokolovs were trafficking young women into Saint Augustine through the private airport. I believe Sykes was being paid by the Sokolovs to look the other way."

J. T. spent a moment considering what she was saying. Daniels sat up straight in her chair, her posture confident, her face expressionless. She felt like she'd passed the test, and wasn't ready for what came next.

"Special Agent Daniels, I don't believe you're being honest with me," he said.

J. T. paused, waiting for her to reply. She wisely said nothing.

"Are you lying?" he asked.

"No, sir," she lied.

"I believe everything you've told me, except the part about Lancaster not telling you that he'd had a dustup with Sykes," J. T. said. "That just doesn't ring true."

"Why is that, sir?" she asked.

"I'm the one asking the questions, Special Agent Daniels," he said curtly.

"You've called me a liar in front of my peers," she said sharply. "I believe I'm due the courtesy of an answer."

J. T.'s face grew fire engine red. Erce and Rojas both shifted uncomfortably in their chairs. She wasn't going down without a fight.

"I've known you since you were in the academy, and I've seen the relationships you've had," J. T. said. "None have seemed to satisfy you. Your relationship with Lancaster is different. He makes you happy in a way your other suitors did not."

It was Daniels's turn to grow red.

"Really," she managed to say.

"Yes, really," J. T. said. "The most challenging aspect of our work is the shackles the system places upon us. Lancaster doesn't play by the rules, and that appeals to you. He succeeds where other law enforcement officers often fail. You like that."

"I suppose," she said.

"Lancaster is your alter ego. Which is why he told you about his encounter with Sykes. For him *not* to tell you would have been a betrayal."

J. T. had nailed it on the head. But she wasn't going to tell him that. To do so would have been professional suicide. She put her elbows on her knees, and leaned in.

"When Jon and I first started dating, we set ground rules," she said. "We agreed not to discuss current or past investigations, and so far, we haven't."

"I find that hard to believe, Beth," her boss said.

She ignored the remark. "We had to do this. Jon was a Navy SEAL, and went on a hundred and fifty missions in hostile countries. The navy expects him to adhere to his nondisclosure pledge, and will severely discipline him if he doesn't. Since a part of his past is off-limits, we decided not to discuss our cases. By doing that, neither of us will divulge sensitive information to the other."

J. T.'s face was hard as stone. It softened, and he nodded.

"I believe you, Special Agent Daniels," he said. "I apologize for questioning your integrity. I was out of line."

"Apology accepted."

"Do you know where Lancaster is now?"

"I do not."

"Can you get in contact with him?"

"I can certainly try. He's usually good about getting back to me."

"Please reach out to him. I want to see where this situation with Sykes is heading. Lancaster is linked to the bureau because of his relationship with you, and we need to keep him in check. If such a thing is possible."

"I'll do my best."

"I'm sure you will. Once you've made contact with Lancaster, please communicate through Special Agent Phillips and Director Rojas what you find out."

"Yes, sir."

"Goodbye, Beth."

The screen went dark. The air trapped in her lungs slowly escaped. Phillips and Rojas rose, and she did as well. She exchanged goodbyes with Phillips, and accepted Rojas's offer to be shown out. Rojas walked her to the parking lot. They stood in the building's long shadow, facing each other.

"That was quite a performance," Rojas said.

Rojas's eyes had a mischievous glint, her lips a faint smile. Daniels felt trapped. A woman knew when another woman was lying, and Rojas had her dead to rights.

"Oscar caliber?" she asked.

"You would have given Meryl Streep a run for her money," Rojas said.

"Do you think J. T. knew?"

"Not at all. You snowed him. Good job."

"So you're not going to tell him?"

"Absolutely not. Since the day I landed in this job, I was made aware that things weren't right with certain members of the Saint Augustine Police Department, but I couldn't pin down what they were doing. You're getting close. Keep at it."

"I will. Thanks for the support."

She had made a new friend. They shook hands, and Daniels got in her vehicle. She backed out and saw Rojas move her finger up and down. She lowered her window.

"I want you to remember one thing," the director said.

"What's that?"

"We have your back. Call me if you need help."

"I'll do that," she said.

CHAPTER 29

Lancaster had stayed in plenty of dive hotels, and the Microtel Inn & Suites by Wyndham Palm Coast ranked right up there with the best of them. Fifty bucks a night got him a noisy room with paper-thin walls and ugly striped carpet. The TV didn't work, and the internet service was spotty. The only thing to recommend the joint was that it was one county away from Saint Augustine, ensuring that he would not receive any unwanted visits from Detective Sykes or his minions.

The desk in the room faced the parking lot, which was a stone's throw from Interstate 95. In the distance, cars zipped past in a blur on the elevated highway. He had watched the video of Martin Daniels at the board of directors meeting four times, and he still didn't have a clue why Martin had behaved so strangely, or continued to maintain his innocence after being caught with his hand in the cookie jar.

It's not what you think.

He decided to deconstruct the sentence, just to see where it got him. What did Martin think the intern *thought* the video was? Two naked adults engaged in wild sex was porn. Or was it? Was the video another act, that looked like porn?

It's not what you think.

Then what was it?

He watched the video again, and focused his attention on the moment that Martin got caught by the intern. The screen of his cell phone was briefly visible, revealing two adults rolling around on a bed. The resolution was poor, and he could barely make out their bodies.

It's not what you think.

He scrolled through the contacts on his cell phone. Hector Morales had joined the Broward Sheriff's Department the same week as him. Two weeks in, Hector had gotten shot in the gut while handling a domestic dispute, and lost the partial use of his left leg. Hector had gotten a desk job, and over time, had become the department's top forensic expert. His friend picked up immediately.

"Is this Jon Lancaster, star of stage, screen, and television?"

"You got him. How you been?"

"Living the dream. I heard that Tinsel Town is making a movie about your life. Are they going to let you play yourself?"

"Fat chance. They picked some soap opera star from Australia. Guy's six-foot-two with a washboard stomach and a perfect tan. We met last month over lunch. He took one look at my stomach, and rolled his eyes."

"But your stomach is your most defining feature."

"I agree. Some men have a six-pack, I prefer a keg. But this is Hollywood, where everyone is supposed to look perfect. You know how it is."

"Sounds like a blast. So what can I do for you?"

"I have a video that I need enhanced. Think you can help me out?"

"Sure. There's a new video quality enhancer called FonePaw. I'll send you the link, and you can download it to your desktop. It's super easy to learn."

He coughed into the phone. He needed to focus his energies into reviewing the case, not learning a new software application. Hector caught his drift.

"Or, you can send me the video, and I'll enhance it myself," Hector said.

"That would be great. How long will this take?"

"I'll do it right now. Are they letting you have final say on the script?"

"You mean the producers? Not final say, but they did send me a draft."

"Was it any good?"

The script was typical Hollywood horseshit, the characters dumbed down to the point of not being lifelike, the dialogue stilted, the action scenes over the top. When he'd voiced his objections during a conference call, the producers had explained that these changes were necessary in order to appeal to foreign markets, the inference being that audiences in foreign countries were half-wits who needed to be talked to like children. He didn't believe that for a second. It was the producers who were half-wits, and needed to keep the story cartoonlike in order to understand it themselves.

But he wasn't going to tell Hector that, and burst his bubble. Hector, like many other people he knew, was entranced by the movies, and believed they were magic.

"I loved it," he said.

"Cool," Hector said. "Email me the video once we hang up. Do you want the entire thing enhanced, or just a portion?"

"Just a portion. There's a man in it, holding a cell phone. Toward the end of the video, he stands up, and holds his hand so the screen is visible to the camera for a few seconds. There are two people in a video, having sex. That's what I want enhanced."

"A sex video, huh? Sounds like the plot for another movie."

"I'm done with Hollywood, Hector. Once is enough."

"You're going to be famous, man. Just you wait."

"I sure hope not. Has your email address changed?"

"Nope, still the same."

"Then we're good. Later, my friend."

- - -

He purchased a can of Pibb Xtra from a vending machine in the hallway outside his room. Mr. Pibb had been his favorite drink as a kid, and he hadn't had one since joining the navy. It had a spicy cherry taste, and brought back a lot of memories.

He sat at his laptop and watched the video of Martin again. Martin looked like a stuffy doctor until he pulled out his cell phone and started watching porn. The expression on Martin's face changed, and his eyes took on a nervous look. Only when the intern caught him in the act did his facial expression go back to normal.

Lancaster shifted his gaze out the window. The whole scenario didn't make sense. A man as intelligent as Martin wouldn't commit an act so blatantly stupid that carried such enormous risk to his personal and professional life. Yet the act had been captured on video.

It's not what you think.

"You could have fooled me," he said aloud.

His cell phone vibrated in his pocket. Normally, he ignored his cell phone's beeps and rings, not wanting to be a slave to any device. But a vibration meant that he'd gotten a text, and since only his friends had his number, those texts were usually important.

It was from Beth. She was on her way.

He considered calling her. He was curious to hear how her meeting at the FBI's Jacksonville office had gone. But his mind was locked on Martin, and he didn't need the distraction.

He put the phone away, then watched the video of Martin again.

He noticed something that he hadn't seen before. The cell phones of the other doctors attending the board meeting lay on the table next to their notepads. Not Martin's. His cell phone resided in his jacket pocket. Like he didn't want the distraction.

Lancaster leaned back in his chair, his mind racing. Martin had deliberately put his cell phone into his jacket pocket so it wouldn't disturb him. So why had he pulled it out in the middle of the meeting, and started watching a porno? It didn't make sense.

His cell phone again vibrated in his pocket. He had a look, assuming it was Beth. And was wrong. An elderly neighbor in the condo building where he lived had texted him. Lancaster was the building's de facto cop, and was often called upon to settle disputes or deal with undesirables who managed to get past security and invade the pool area.

His neighbor had sent him a reminder that there was an HOA meeting tomorrow night in the building's recreation center. Would he be attending?

He texted her back, and said he was out of town.

He started to put his phone away. On his laptop's screen, Martin had pulled his cell phone from his pocket, and was staring at it. The look on his face was filled with uncertainty.

That's when it hit him. Martin hadn't decided to start looking at pornography in the middle of the board meeting. That was out of character, and not plausible. In fact, Martin had received a text, assumed it was important, and taken a look.

He cursed. Dr. Sircy had told him that Martin was addicted to pornography, because she'd caught her lover looking at porn on his phone. But it was a false assumption. Martin was looking at videos that were being sent to him.

He'd made a beginner's mistake. It wasn't the first time.

His first week as a cop, he'd responded to a 911 call of a woman claiming a burglar was in her home. He went through the front door to find a bloodied man holding a broken bottle. He nearly shot the guy before noticing the suspect was wearing bedroom slippers. Not a burglar, but the caller's estranged boyfriend, who hadn't done a damn thing except tell his girlfriend their relationship was over.

He'd let the 911 call cloud his judgment, and hadn't entered the house with an open mind. And now, he'd done the same thing with Martin. Dr. Sircy saying that Martin had a pornography addiction had made him believe that Martin really did have one, even though he'd seen no evidence of an addiction in Martin's house, or among the books and papers in his study, or on his laptop. No evidence at all.

He'd let a jilted lover distort his thinking. He wanted to kick himself.

He rewound the video, and watched it again, this time from a fresh perspective. As he reached the end, his cell phone rang. It was his friend Hector calling.

"Hey, Hector. Tell me you have good news," he said.

"I have good news and bad," Hector said. "What order do you want it in?"

"Give me the bad news first."

"There are two individuals in the porno on the guy's phone. A male and a female. The female's face isn't visible. Sorry."

"Any identifying marks or tattoos?"

"Yep. She has light-brown skin and a number of colorful tattoos on her back. I did a search of the tattoos, and got a hit. She's a member of the Latin Kings gang."

The girl in the video was one of Katya's friends, and he found himself nodding.

"What's the good news?" he asked.

"I was able to capture the face of the male, and blow it up," Hector said. "Guy was right in the middle of having an orgasm. Pure ecstasy."

"Was he an older guy?"

"Yes, indeed. Do you know him?"

"I think so. But I'll need confirmation. Can you send it to me?"

"Of course. It will be in your inbox in a minute."

"Thanks, Hector. I owe you big time."

"Any chance there will be a premiere of your movie in South Florida before it's released? It would be a blast to take my wife and kids to."

Lancaster liked it. The producers were regularly calling him for help with the script, and he didn't think it would be hard to finagle them into having a premiere in his hometown so he could invite his cop friends and drinking buddies.

"I'll see what I can do," he said.

Ending the call, he went into the inbox on his laptop, and waited for Hector's email to arrive. He was certain that it would be what he and Beth had suspected all along. One of Martin's trysts had been secretly videotaped and used to blackmail him. The fact that the female in the video wasn't Katya was a shock, but not entirely a surprise. Martin had been sexually active, and it wasn't hard to imagine him having sex with one of Katya's friends.

Beth's rental had pulled into the parking lot, and she got out. In her hand was a cell phone, which she called him on. He answered it.

"I just arrived," she said. "What room are you in?"

"103. I'm on the ground floor. I can see you through my window," he said. "The door's unlocked."

Hector's email appeared in his inbox with an attachment. He placed his cell phone down, and clicked his mouse on the attachment. The face of a man in full rapture filled the laptop's screen. Lancaster's mouth dropped open. The door opened, and Beth came in.

"You're not going to believe what happened," she said.

Still speechless, he continued to stare at the screen.

"What are you looking at?" she asked.

"My friend enhanced the video on your father's phone," he managed to say.

"And?"

"You're not going to believe this."

He had been wrong. The man having sex in the video wasn't her father. She came over to the desk and had a look.

"Hey," she said. "Isn't that Sykes?"

CHAPTER 30

As an investigator, Daniels had been trained to look for patterns. If a suspect committed a crime once, it could be explained as bad judgment. But if the suspect committed the same crime repeatedly, it often meant darker forces were at work.

She also looked for patterns in the men she dated. She'd once dated a guy who chose the clothes he wore to work each week by laying them out on his bed on Sunday night. When she asked if he'd ever changed an outfit on the spur of the moment, he got angry with her. Another beau had ordered the same thing on the menu whenever they went to dinner. A question about dietary restrictions produced a dirty look.

Jon was also predictable, but in a different way. He was in love with the water, and tried to be near it whenever possible. Growing up, he'd lived near a canal, where he went fishing with his friends. During summer vacations he worked as a lifeguard, and spent his days on the beach. Upon graduating high school, he joined the navy and became a SEAL. Being near the water calmed him down, and made him happy.

At his suggestion, they went to the South Beach Grill, and sat at an outside table and had drinks while listening to waves slap the sand. Daniels flipped a coin. She won, and proceeded to tell him about the video conference with her boss at the FBI's Jacksonville office, and how Micah's video had ended up in her boss's hands.

"I gave that kid a hundred bucks for that video," he said, shaking his head.

"He must have thought he could get additional money from the local newspaper," she said. "Watching it a second time was a real eye-opener."

"How so?"

"I had no idea you were still so skilled at self-defense. You could have killed Sykes and his men."

"My goal was to humiliate them, and at that I succeeded. What happens now?"

"J. T. wants you to restrain yourself. You're linked to me, and therefore linked to the FBI. He's afraid you'll really hurt someone, and it will reflect badly on the bureau."

"Is bad press all he's worried about? What about your father's death?"

"Come on, Jon. He's just doing his job."

Jon stared out at the ocean. A couple of long-haired kids were trying to break their necks on boogie boards. He said something under his breath, and a thin smile creased his lips. When he looked back at her, he'd noticeably calmed down.

"I'm not going to restrain myself," he said.

"I didn't think you would," Daniels said. "Your turn."

"We need to start our investigation over," he said. "For starters, we have to stop thinking that your father was addicted to porn, and that his addiction was driving him to watch it at inopportune times. There wasn't any porn in his study, or on his laptop, which would have been the usual hiding places."

"What about the used condom in the bathroom?"

"Your father had a healthy sex life. Nothing wrong with that."

"But he was looking at sex videos when he was out in public."

"Not by choice."

"I'm not following you. Of course it was by choice."

"Not in the way that you think." Taking out his cell phone, he held it in front of her face. "We are slaves to these devices. That's especially true when we get texts, which are almost always from people that we know. When was the last time you got a text, and didn't read it?"

"I always read my texts."

"Exactly. We all read our texts, regardless of where we are, and who we're with. We can't help it. Your father was receiving texts that contained porno videos of men that your father personally knew. That was why he was looking at them. He wanted to see who'd gotten snared in the trap."

"Back up a second. Who was sending these videos?"

"Either Katya or the Sokolov brothers. They're all in this together. They were blackmailing your father."

"So they caught my dad in a compromising situation."

"Yes. Katya turned a room in her basement into a love nest, and I believe she secretly videotaped your father having sex. Then the blackmail began. That's where all the money in your father's bank accounts went."

She considered what Jon was saying. It all added up, except the part about the videos being of her father's friends. That came out of left field.

"How are my father's friends caught up in this?" she asked.

"I think the Russians are blackmailing them as well," he said.

"Based on what?"

"Piece together what we know so far. The Sokolovs brought three young Latin women to Saint Augustine on a private plane. You told me those women didn't have any luggage, and were slaves. I think they were sex slaves."

"They were the bait."

"Correct. They were introduced to different men at wild parties at Katya's house, with the purpose of having sex with them. The men were secretly videotaped, and later blackmailed."

"Which is why there were cameras all over that house," Daniels said. "The women would get the men drunk, pull them into a room, and have sex. It didn't matter which room, because they all had hidden cameras."

"That's right. The house was rigged to trap them."

"This all makes sense, Jon. I'm on board."

"There's more."

He paused to take a long swallow of beer. When conducting an investigation, she'd learned that it was impossible to ever know the true story. All an investigator could do was take the available evidence and construct a plausible story. That story then became the truth that the case would be built upon. Jon was as good as anyone at doing this, and his theories usually held up.

"Tell me what you're thinking," she said.

"I think these men decided to fight back, and didn't pay the Sokolovs their ransom money right away," he said. "That's when the mummified hands started showing up on people's doorsteps. The Sokolovs were sending a message."

"And the men caved, and paid them off."

"I think so. Except your father. I think he must have held out. So the Sokolovs started sending him text messages that contained videos of his friends in compromising situations. It was their way of putting pressure on him to pay up."

"Do you think he gave in to their demands?"

"I do. If he hadn't, the videos of him and Katya would have been posted online by the Sokolovs, and we would have heard about them by now."

"So my father wasn't addicted to porn."

"No, he was not. He was a victim."

She wiped away her tears with a napkin. Her father was a proud man, and she could see him doing what Jon had described. In the end, he had given in to the Sokolovs' demands, and the shame of his transgressions had led him to take his own life.

"I still don't understand how Sykes plays into all of this," she said. "You don't think he was stupid enough to fall into the same trap as my father, do you?"

"I do. Sykes was also being blackmailed by the Sokolovs. The video proves it," he said.

"How can you be sure? Maybe he had a fling with one of those girls, and it got videotaped. That doesn't mean he was being blackmailed."

"No, it doesn't. But the other lies Sykes told are proof enough."

"What lies?"

"Sykes never mentioned to us that he knew your father, yet it's obvious they were acquaintances by the way your father reacted when he saw the video of Sykes having sex with the girl. Your father wouldn't have reacted like that if he hadn't known Sykes."

It was excellent deductive reasoning, and she kicked herself for not seeing it.

"Good call," she said. "What else?"

"When we talked to Officer Spencer about the mummified hands, Spencer said that there were six victims. He immediately backtracked and said there were five. That's not the kind of fact that a police officer would get confused. I think Spencer was hiding the name of the sixth victim from us."

"You think the sixth victim was Sykes."

"Correct."

It was too neat a conclusion, and Daniels shook her head. She remembered seeing a number of framed citations hanging on the walls of Sykes's office. Police officers didn't receive those unless they were good at what they did.

"I can't see Sykes being drawn to that house, and being lured into having wild sex. He's too experienced to fall for something like that," she said.

"I agree. Sykes is too experienced. I think the video was shot in another location. One where Sykes felt safe enough to let his guard down."

"Where?"

"This is just a guess."

"Go ahead."

"Remember the photographs on your father's laptop of the local B&B? It's been bugging me why he had those. Maybe one of the rooms was outfitted with hidden cameras, and Sykes was drawn there and secretly videotaped."

"You have no proof of this."

"No, but why else did he have those photos?"

"It's a stretch. You couldn't outfit a room in a B&B without the owners knowing about it. They would see the equipment being brought in."

"The owners are involved."

"That's a real stretch."

"Not really. Remember the Russian couple that sponsored Katya into this country?"

"The Vasileks."

"Right. They own a B&B in Fort Lauderdale. I'm thinking they might have done this before."

As every investigator knew, there were no coincidences in police work. But knowing something and proving it were entirely different things.

"Let's say you're right, and a local B&B was used to trap Sykes," Daniels said. "How do we find out which B&B was used?"

"Easy," he said. "We'll use the internet."

PART FOUR

Carrie, like the Horror Movie

PART FOUR

CHAPTER 31

Lancaster walked out of the restaurant and retrieved his laptop from the trunk of Beth's rental. When he returned to the patio, a fresh beer awaited him.

"You shouldn't have," he said.

"You deserve it. Now show me how we're going to do this," Beth said.

Her laptop sat on the table, the photo of the bedroom in the B&B with the four-poster bed and floral wallpaper they'd found on Martin's computer on its screen.

He placed his laptop beside Beth's, and powered it up. Taking a seat, he saluted her with his bottle and took a healthy swallow.

"I think I know what your plan is," she said.

He worked on his beer and waited for her to finish.

"You're going to visit the websites of the different B&Bs in Saint Augustine, and compare the photographs you find on the sites to those stored on my dad's computer," she said. "If you make a match, you'll know which B&B was used to trap Sykes."

"Exactly," he said.

"I think your plan is flawed."

He continued to drink and said nothing.

"Based on my own experience, most B&Bs are mom-and-pop operations, and can't afford to build or maintain websites," she said. "You could strike out."

Beth didn't know Florida the way he did. The state was the single largest tourist destination in the world, and every motel, hotel, and B&B had a presence on the internet, be it a website, Facebook page, or online booking engine.

"Bet you dinner we make the match," he said.

"You're on," she said.

Using Expedia, he pulled up the names of every bed-and-breakfast in Saint Augustine. The site showed twenty-one properties that advertised themselves as B&Bs, and offered rooms and breakfast. The first listing was called the Castle Garden Bed and Breakfast, and had a design reminiscent of the structures found on miniature golf courses. Expedia did not offer a link to the Castle's website, but Google did, and he soon was reading about its unique history. Originally a carriage house, the building dated back to the late 1800s. The last line caught his eye.

"'Every guest is sent as a gift from God.' What do you think that means?"

"The owners must be religious," she said, reading along with him.

He took the virtual tour, which allowed him to zoom in and out while the video played. As the guest rooms were shown, they studied the decor.

"I didn't see a four-poster bed or lily wallpaper," she said.

"One down, twenty to go," he said.

They worked their way through the other listings. There was the Victorian House, the Bayfront Marin House, Casa de Solana, the Cedar House Inn, the Historic Sevilla House, the Penny Farthing Inn, and fourteen more, all of which started to look very much the same, and none of which had a bedroom with a four-poster bed or lily wallpaper.

"You lose," she said. "Where are you taking me to dinner?"

"We missed one." He pointed at the screen. "The Gables Inn B&B in Palatka is not far from here. It's listed under Saint Augustine because it's so close."

"Why does that name sound familiar?"

"Palatka is home to a state prison, and a jail."

"I thought I'd heard of it. Give it a shot."

He did a search on Google and turned up nothing. The Gables Inn didn't have a website.

"You lose. I'm in the mood for a steak," she said.

"Not so fast. Let's check Yelp," he said.

She leaned back and crossed her arms. "How could a prison town support a B&B? Who would stay there?"

He typed on his keyboard. "Family members of inmates who come to visit. When I was a cop, I visited Palatka to interview inmates who had information pertinent to cases I was working on. The local motels did a good business."

Yelp was a home run. The Gables Inn had a listing, and he scrolled through the reviews. Most were lukewarm, with customers complaining about cold-water showers or finding cockroaches in their closets. Several posted photos of their stay. It was an old three-story Victorian house, the guest rooms decorated with dated furniture, most of which was chipped. The last photo was familiar, and he stopped.

"Bingo," he said.

Beth leaned in. The room on the top floor boasted a scenic view of the Saint John's River, and contained an antique four-poster bed and faded lily wallpaper. He compared the photo to the one from Martin's computer.

They matched.

"Would you look at that," she said.

"Want to pay them a visit?"

"After I buy you dinner?"

- - -

The inn's number was included in the listing. A woman named Carrie answered. She had a smoky voice and sounded a little tipsy. He spun a yarn about having stayed in the room on the top floor years ago, and was it available tonight?

Carrie checked. "This is your lucky day. The honeymoon suite is presently available. Would you like me to hold it for you?"

"Please," he said.

"How many nights?"

"Just tonight."

She quoted him a rate of $175 for the night, which was twenty dollars higher than the rate quoted on Yelp. He gave her a credit card to hold the room and hung up.

"I just got swindled," he said.

"Don't worry. I'll expense the room," Beth said.

He rose from his chair, and walked over to the railing to stare out at the beach. The pieces were starting to fall together, the puzzle nearly complete. There was no greater feeling during an investigation, and he realized they were nearing the end.

Beth joined him at the railing.

"This makes sense," he said.

"What do you mean?"

"Sykes was too smart to hook up with a woman in Saint Augustine because he knew someone might recognize him. Palatka is a different story. It's off the beaten path, and he could rendezvous with a woman there without fear of being caught."

"So you think the video of Sykes that was on my father's cell phone was secretly shot at the Gables Inn," Beth said.

"I do."

"The room would have been outfitted with surveillance cameras. That's not something that can be done without the owners knowing."

"They would have known," he agreed.

"So they're probably involved."

"That's a fair assumption."

"But why would the owners do something like that? What would their motivation be? Sykes would have arrested them if he knew he was being filmed."

Beth had found a glaring discrepancy. Why would the owners of the Gables Inn risk going to jail in order to film a police officer having sex with a woman on the sly? Even if the Sokolov brothers had paid them a few thousand dollars, the risk still far outweighed the reward. After a long moment, the answer came to him.

"Because they've done it before," he said.

"You think the owners are filming their guests?" she asked.

"What other explanation is there?"

"But why? What's the benefit?"

"Money."

"Something tells me you've encountered this before."

"I have. A sleazy motel owner in Fort Lauderdale secretly filmed his guests. It was a big money maker for him. I'll explain it to you during the drive. What's for dinner?"

"It will have to be fast food. Does something good and greasy strike your fancy?"

"Now you're talking," he said.

CHAPTER 32

Zaxby's Chicken Fingers and Buffalo Wings was a fast food chain that had only just started making it out of the southeast. That was strange, because the food was decent, and the owners had a thing for John Wayne, with one of the late actor's famous quotes hanging on the wall when you walked in. LIFE IS HARD, LIFE IS HARDER WHEN YOU'RE STUPID.

They shared a chicken finger plate and an order of boneless wings and things. Wiping her fingers with a towelette, Daniels started the engine and backed out. According to her phone's GPS, Palatka was a twenty-five-minute drive.

"Tell me about this motel owner who was secretly filming his guests," she said. "He must have been a real sleazeball."

"He was," Jon said, sucking down his iced tea. "His name was Grady Cox, and he owned a fleabag motel called the Sand Dollar. Grady was on a first-name basis with every hooker in town, and rented his rooms by the hour to them. The city finally wised up, and made it illegal to book a room for less than twenty-four hours."

"He got a law changed. What a pioneer."

"Grady fell on hard times. He needed a new source of income, or he would go out of business. One of his big money makers came from guests renting porno movies, which generated several thousand dollars a week. Problem was, he had to split the money with Hustler and Playboy, which produced the movies."

"What was the split?"

"Eighty/twenty, with Grady getting twenty."

"That hardly seems fair."

"Grady felt the same way, so he decided to film his guests on the sly, and later rent the videos to his customers."

"How did he know they'd be having sex? They might just get drunk, and fall asleep."

"He only turned the cameras on for couples on their honeymoon."

"That's brilliant."

"I agree. The videos were a huge hit. The problem with porn is that the actors are faking their emotions, and the action feels forced. Grady's videos were the real thing; his customers couldn't get enough of them. They would often rent the entire collection during their stay."

"What tripped him up?"

"A couple named Nate and Nancy Lovejoy."

"Is that their real name?"

"Would I lie to you?"

"Go on."

"The Lovejoys got married as teenagers, and took a cruise out of Fort Lauderdale for their honeymoon. The night before they departed, they stayed at the Sand Dollar. Five years later, they took another cruise, and stayed at the Sand Dollar again. They rented a video from the front desk called *Hot Teens in Love*. Guess who the stars were."

"Nate and Nancy Lovejoy."

"They went straight to the police. I was working the graveyard shift that night. They came into the station house in their pajamas."

"Were they traumatized?"

"Absolutely. They were virgins when they got married. That video was the first time they'd ever had sex, and it was pretty wild."

"You saw it?"

"Everyone in the station house saw it."

"Poor kids."

"We busted Grady the next day. He had quite an operation going. Every room in the Sand Dollar had a camera hidden in the ceiling, or behind a two-way mirror. We confiscated two hundred videos he'd made without his customers' consent."

"What a bastard."

"Now here's the interesting part, and why I brought this up in the first place," he said. "After Grady's arrest, his lawyer tried to cut a deal with the district attorney. If the state went light on Grady, the lawyer said that Grady would give us the name of the guy who outfitted his motel with the cameras."

"What value was there in that?"

"The lawyer said that the guy had approached Grady with the idea. He claimed this guy had outfitted motels and B&Bs all over the state of Florida, and that the practice of secretly filming guests having sex was widespread."

"Did you believe the lawyer?"

"We did. Grady was as dumb as a rock. He didn't have the brains to conceive a scam on his own. The guy lived in Miami. We busted him a week later at his office. Someone told him we were coming, and he set his records on fire so we couldn't get the names of the places he'd outfitted. He pleaded guilty and did eighteen months."

"And you walked away knowing that there were motels and B&Bs in Florida that were in the porn business. Do you think the Gables Inn was one of them?"

"I do."

"Based upon what? And don't tell me your gut, because I'll make you pay for dinner."

"The Gables Inn fits the profile that I drew up. The guy was outfitting a motel in Miami called the Pink Flamingo when we arrested him. The Pink Flamingo was similar to the Sand Dollar in several ways. It was privately owned and barely making ends meet. The owners had also rented to hookers before the cops made them stop."

"So your profile is a privately owned motel that's struggling to get by with owners who will break the law to stay afloat."

"That's it."

"If all of this is true, how do the Sokolovs fit into the picture?"

"This scam is well known in Florida. I'm guessing the Sokolovs heard about it, and looked around Saint Augustine for a B&B that had been outfitted. They found the Gables Inn, and struck a deal with the owners to secretly record Sykes."

Jon's logic was spotless. But that didn't mean the owners of the Gables Inn would play ball with them. A sign announced that Palatka was five miles ahead.

"We need to find the hidden camera in the honeymoon suite, and pressure the owners into talking," he said. "It shouldn't be too hard."

"But what if the honeymoon suite's been stripped clean, and the camera's gone?" she asked, hearing the doubt creep into her voice. "What then?"

"The camera's still there," he said confidently. "They're not going to stop doing something that's making money. Even if it is illegal."

CHAPTER 33

A pair of copper statues of World War I soldiers greeted them as they crossed a bridge and entered Palatka's downtown. It was growing dark, and the town had shut down for the night, the sidewalks deserted, with only a handful of cars.

The Gables Inn was on a side street that ran parallel to the river. A drive-by revealed a three-story house with faded paint and sagging gutters. It had once been pleasing to look at, but time and the elements had robbed it of its charm.

Beth parked on the next block and let the engine idle.

"So what's our story going to be?" she said.

"Want to pretend we're on our honeymoon?" he said.

She gave him a tiny smile. "Haven't you heard? Marriages between law enforcement officers never last. Let's just say we're vacationing together."

On their first date, they'd discussed why neither of them were married, even though they'd both been in long-term relationships with partners they'd liked. They'd come to the conclusion that they both put their work first, which made a permanent commitment difficult, if not impossible.

"Works for me," he said. "Since I spoke to the manager, let me do the talking."

"How do we explain our lack of luggage?"

He gave it some thought. People in the hospitality industry were wise to cops, and the absence of luggage would raise a red flag.

"I'll tell the manager that the airline lost our luggage," he said.

"That should work."

They returned to the B&B. A sign on the lawn said PARK IN BACK OR GET TOWED. A narrow driveway led to a cleared area where Daniels parked.

"Not very hospitable, are they?" she said.

They walked around to the front and climbed the steps. The house had a wraparound porch where a half dozen cats were hanging out. Lancaster tried the front door, found it locked, and pressed the buzzer. Through the glass he spied a middle-aged woman with big hair manning the front desk. Her eyes were focused on something behind the counter that he guessed was either a small TV or a surveillance monitor. When she didn't respond, he pressed the buzzer again and kept his finger down.

"That's rude," Beth said.

"Would you prefer I kick the door open?"

The big-haired woman snapped awake, as if from a deep slumber. She unlocked the front door with a practiced smile on her face. "You must be Jon. I'm Carrie, like the horror movie." She laughed at her own joke. "Welcome to the Gables Inn."

Carrie checked them in. Lancaster made sure to hide the detective's badge attached to his wallet as he pulled out his credit card. Everything was going splendidly until Carrie asked what brought them to Palatka.

"We're here on vacation, thought we'd see the sights," he said.

Carrie eyed him. Most of her guests were either visiting an inmate at the prison, or did business with the prison, and weren't tourists. He'd said the wrong thing.

"No luggage?" Carrie asked.

"The airline lost our bags," he explained.

She bit her lower lip, clearly uneasy. He needed to calm her down.

"I should have listened to the guy checking in before me," he said.

"Come again?"

"He had three pieces of luggage. He told the ticket agent that he wanted the blue suitcase to go to Houston, the black suitcase to go to Chicago, and the green suitcase to go to Los Angeles. The ticket agent said, 'We can't do that, sir.' And the guy said, 'You did it the last time I flew this crummy airline.'"

Carrie slapped the counter. "That's a good one. I'll have to remember that."

He dropped his voice to a conspiratorial whisper. "Would you by chance have a couple of toothbrushes and some toothpaste we can borrow?"

"I'm sure I can rustle them up."

"Thank you. You've very kind."

Carrie opened a drawer filled with room keys. While she searched for the key to their suite, he glanced at the reflection in the window behind her. Beneath the counter was a video monitor hidden from the customers' view. The monitor was a matrix, and had four black-and-white screens. Based upon a quick glance, the screens appeared to rotate between cameras outside the property, and some inside as well. She fished out the right key and shut the drawer. Lifting her hand to her mouth, she called out, "Hey, Dalton, I'm going upstairs to show these folks their room. I need you to cover for me."

There was no response. Carrie whipped out a cell phone and made a call. "It would take hell and high water to tear that boy away from his video games," she said. Into the phone, she said, "It's me. I need you to man the desk." She made a face. "I don't care how many points you're about to score. Get the hell out here."

She disconnected and shook her head. "I don't know what's worse. His pot smoking or those damn video games."

"Your son?" he asked.

"The one and only."

Dalton appeared. Lancaster was expecting a skinny teenager with bad skin, not a hulking thirtysomething in a sleeveless T-shirt. Dalton's eyes, which were mud brown, scanned his guests as if they were standing in a police lineup.

"Where's their luggage?" he asked suspiciously.

"The airline lost it," his mother said. "I'll be right back."

- - -

The stairs leading to the third floor were carpeted and groaned beneath their weight. On the second floor landing they stopped to let Carrie catch her breath.

"Damn job's going to kill me," she lamented.

The journey to the third floor was also a struggle, and again she had to stop.

"I should never have stopped running," she said.

"Why did you?" Beth asked.

"Because the ice cubes kept flying out of my drink."

She shrieked with laughter. It was an old joke, but Lancaster laughed along anyway. She went to the door at the hallway's end and jammed the key into the lock.

A quick tour of the honeymoon suite followed. The room looked the same as it had on Martin's laptop, right down to the bedspread. Carrie avoided mentioning the water stains in the ceiling, or the musty smell. Finished, she presented him with the key.

"I'm sure you folks would enjoy a little privacy," she said. "Come downstairs later, and I'll rustle up toothpaste and brushes for you."

"Much appreciated," he said.

She left, and he chained the door and found the remote. Powering up the TV, he found a twenty-four-hour news network, and jacked the volume up. Then he parked himself on the edge of the bed. The mattress sagged as Beth sat beside him.

"I spotted a video monitor beneath the counter when she was checking us in," he said in a low voice.

"You think they're spying on us?" Beth asked.

"I don't know, but I think we need to assume that they are. I think we should stay here for a few minutes, and act like lovebirds. Then I'll go downstairs and distract them while you search the room for hidden cameras. Sound like a plan?"

"I'm in. I don't like the looks of her son. He's a mean one."

"I'll take care of him if he acts up."

"You enjoy dealing with guys like that, don't you?"

He smiled and nodded. He'd been picked on as a kid, and had a chip on his shoulder when it came to dealing with brutes and bullies.

"Thank you for being here for me," she said. "I really appreciate it."

"Don't thank me until we're done. Then we'll party."

She placed her hand against his chin, and kissed him on the lips. It caught him by surprise, and he raised his eyebrows in question.

"Just acting like lovebirds," she said.

CHAPTER 34

They smooched like a couple of high school kids on a hot date. Jon wasn't much to look at, but he was a great kisser, and it let Daniels forget things for a little while. When they came up for air, he said, "I'd like to rip your clothes off."

"What's stopping you?" she asked.

"I'd hate to later see it on video after these people get arrested."

"Fair enough. How about a rain check?"

"Now you're talking. I'm going downstairs to engage Carrie and her son," Jon said. "Don't start looking for the hidden camera until I text you."

She heard the whistle, and knew something was worrying him.

"Dalton bothers you, doesn't he?" she said.

"He was suspicious of us from the start. I think he knows we're the law."

"But how? We're not dressed like cops."

"Do you know how many guys in Florida have done time? Over a million. Some get reformed, but most don't. One of the things they learn in the joint is how to avoid getting caught the next time they break the law. That includes how to spot a cop."

"Then maybe we should leave. I'll call the Jacksonville office for backup, and we can come back tomorrow, and bust them."

"If we leave now, Dalton will know for sure that we're the law. That will give him time to destroy any incriminating evidence on his hard drive. I vote we stay."

Jon was never one to run from a fight. He wanted to get to the bottom of what was going on as much as she did, and she gave him another soulful kiss. It caught him by surprise, and he blushed.

"Just in case they're watching," she explained.

- - -

As Lancaster came downstairs, he spied an older couple checking in. He knew they were from up north because they were dressed in jeans and long-sleeve shirts, and looked uncomfortably warm. By tomorrow they'd be wearing Bermuda shorts and T-shirts, and showing a lot of milky-white skin.

He stepped aside as they dragged their suitcases up the stairs.

"Nice place?" the husband asked.

"So far," he said.

He approached the front desk. Carrie was typing the couple's credit card information into a computer and paid him no attention; there was no sign of Dalton.

"I'll be right with you," she said.

He drummed his fingers on the desk. By staring in the reflection in the window behind her, he was able to see the video monitor hidden below. The matrix of surveillance cameras followed the couple as they entered a room on the second floor.

"All done. So you must be looking for those toothbrushes." She removed a pair of cheap toothbrushes and a tiny tube of Crest from a drawer, and handed them to him. "Let me know if there's anything else you need."

"Actually, I could use a little help," he said. "I got lost looking for the Ravine Gardens State Park earlier today. I kept following the Saint

John's River, but ended up lost. We'd like to go there tomorrow, and check it out. Can you help?"

"That's because the Saint John's flows north," she said. "It's one of a handful of rivers in the country that does that. Bet you didn't know that."

The truth be told, he did know that. He also knew that tourists regularly got lost following the river, since they assumed it flowed south like most rivers did.

"That's amazing," he said.

"Palatka used to be a major port city, and had the most beautiful hotels in the country until a fire burned them all down. Bet you didn't know that either."

"No, ma'am."

"Let me close out my computer, and I'll show you the right way."

As she shut her computer down, Lancaster removed his cell phone from his pocket. Holding it below the counter, he texted Beth the all clear.

They went outside and stood on the front porch. The night air was cool and crisp, and Carrie gave a little shudder. She lifted her hand and pointed.

"The park is a little over a mile away. There are three ways to get there. You can take River Street, or you can take Kirby Street, or you can take Crill Avenue, which is about a half mile longer, and will take you past the elementary school."

"Which route is the most scenic?"

"River Street. It takes you right past the Saint John's River. If you leave early enough, you can catch the rowing club out for their morning exercises."

"Can we walk it?"

"Sorry. There's no sidewalk."

One of Florida's great mysteries was the absence of sidewalks or walking paths on its roads. Environmentalists claimed the auto industry had engineered this in an effort to force people to drive cars, but he suspected it was due to the state's sheer enormity.

"How early does the rowing club come out?" he asked.

"They start at seven and quit right around nine, before it gets too hot."

"I think we'll take River Street."

She gave him directions. Left, right, left, right.

"Do you know what time the gardens open for visitors?" he asked.

"It's open from nine to five, three hundred and sixty-five days a year."

Enough time had passed for Beth to have cased the suite and found the hidden camera. He thanked Carrie for her help, and they went back inside to the lobby.

Dalton was kneeling behind the front desk, his eyes glued to the video monitor beneath the counter. He wore black leather and looked like a character out of *Mad Max.* The expression on his face was best described as murderous.

"I thought you were going out for a spin on your motorcycle," Carrie said.

"Change of plans." Dalton lifted his gaze and stared at Lancaster. "The room not to your liking?"

"It's fine," Lancaster said. "I was just asking Carrie for directions to the Ravine Gardens State Park. My girlfriend and I want to visit it tomorrow."

"Sure you were."

Dalton stood up and drew a handgun from his jacket pocket. His draw was lightning fast, and caught Lancaster by surprise as the weapon was aimed at him.

"You came downstairs to distract my mother so your partner could search the suite," Dalton said. "I'm watching her on the monitor right now. I knew you were cops the moment I laid eyes on you. Put your hands in the air."

Lancaster obeyed. Carrie frisked him and dropped three small handguns onto the counter. Dalton's eyes grew wide.

"Who the fuck carries three guns?" he asked.

Dalton made him sit in the swivel chair behind the counter. Carrie pulled a large handgun out of a safe, and pointed it at him.

"Shoot him if he does anything stupid," Dalton said.

"You bet I will," his mother said.

"I'm going upstairs to deal with his lady friend." Dalton headed for the stairs. As he started to go up, he stopped and glanced over his shoulder at Lancaster.

"Three guns? Why do you need three guns?"

"You can never be too careful," Lancaster said.

"I'll remember that," he said, and vanished up the stairs.

CHAPTER 35

After Jon left, Beth turned off the overhead lights, kicked off her shoes, and lay on the bed with her head propped up on the pillows. If she was being spied upon, then she needed to play the part of a tourist, and not arouse any suspicion.

She found the remote and began to surf. She spent little time watching TV, her spare hours devoted to exercise and working cold cases. The shows that flicked by were foreign to her, the fresh-faced actors all strangers.

There were several hundred channels, and as she got up into the higher numbers, she found dozens devoted to porn. They featured every conceivable sexual partnering, and had movie-inspired names like *Forrest Hump*, *The RawShank Rehumption*, and *Driving Miss Daisy (into a headboard)*. The sheer volume made her suspicious.

The last was *Shaving Private Ryan*. The promo copy boasted of a young soldier with his hot bride, the sex as wild as anything you've ever seen. Now sitting on the edge of the bed, she hit the "Pay" button.

The video began to play. A skinny kid in an army uniform, his bride in a frilly dress. Neither looked older than twenty. They ripped off their clothes and went at it.

The sex was frantic and didn't feel staged. They were really in love, and it came through with every pant and pelvic thrust.

She studied the room they were making love in. It was nicely appointed, with an ornate headboard and lots of antique furniture. Not a hotel room, more likely a private residence, or a B&B.

She sampled several other videos in the collection. She watched an interracial couple perform oral sex in a bedroom with a beautiful view of the ocean, an older couple make love missionary style in a room with a chandelier and wall sconces, and two athletic men get it on in a room with French doors that opened onto a balcony overlooking a courtyard with a bubbling fountain. As part of her job, she watched a fair amount of porn, and she knew when someone was going through the motions and faking an orgasm. These folks weren't faking.

She killed the picture. Was that the scam? Were different B&Bs secretly filming their customers, and sharing the videos? People who liked porn consumed a lot of it, often in one sitting. A library this big would generate huge revenue.

She swallowed the lump in her throat. If different B&Bs were sharing porn, there might very well be a video of her father having sex with Katya that was out there. She tried to block it out of her thoughts, and found that she couldn't.

"God damn it, Daddy," she said under her breath. She wanted this to be over, but knew that it would never truly be over. The truth—whatever it turned out to be—would be painful, and would stay with her forever. The great memories of her father from childhood would be replaced by images he'd so indiscreetly left behind.

And there wasn't a damn thing she could do about it.

Her cell phone vibrated. It was Jon.

All clear, his text read.

She hopped off the bed and started her search. There were two places to hide a camera—in a ceiling light fixture, or behind a two-way mirror. Ceiling cameras could be bought online and were easy to install, and therefore more common to find.

The honeymoon suite had a desk with a sturdy wood chair. She slid the chair beneath the light fixture in the room's center, and stood on it. The fixture screamed Pottery Barn and had a hundred glass petals. She examined each one, looking for a hidden fisheye camera. After a few minutes she decided the fixture was clean, and jumped down.

The room had two mirrors. One over the desk, the second over the vanity. She started with the mirror over the desk, and she lifted it off the wall and placed it on the bed. There was a large water stain on the wallpaper, but no camera. She replaced it.

Next was the mirror over the vanity with a carved wood frame. When she tried to take it down, she encountered resistance. The mirror was stuck to the wall with adhesive, which was odd. Why hang the mirror over the desk, and attach the mirror over the vanity?

From her purse she removed a Swiss Army knife. It had seventeen different functions, including a locking screwdriver, a wire stripper, and a two-point-five-inch double-cut wood saw. She'd gotten it after graduating from the academy. It had been a present from her dad.

She opened the wood saw and locked it into place. She dug the saw's tip into the adhesive at the mirror's corner, and began to saw away. It was slow going, and after a minute she was forced to stop to shake away the cramping in her fingers.

But she didn't quit. There was no doubt in her mind that behind the vanity was a hidden camera. Once she found it, she would bust Carrie and her brutish son, and turn their lives into a living hell.

It took another minute to cut away a small section of adhesive. She was growing impatient, and she gently pulled the mirror back a few inches. Placing her cheek against the wall, she stared behind it with one eye.

"Yes," she said.

There was a hollowed-out section with a camera pressed against the mirror, just as she'd suspected. A red light was flashing, indicating the camera was filming. She shuddered, and backed away.

She'd been caught in the act.

She grabbed her purse off the bed and removed her cell phone. She needed to send Jon a text, and alert him to the danger.

She felt a breeze, and looked up. Dalton had silently entered the honeymoon suite with a house key, and was pointing a gun at her.

A long moment passed.

"You're a cop," he said.

"I don't know what you're talking about," Daniels said.

"Liar."

"I'm not lying."

"Ordinary people scream when you point guns at them. Cops don't. They play it cool, and try to talk their way out of it. You're a stinking cop."

"Why are you doing this?"

"Because you came here to arrest us, and I'm not going to let you do that. Open your purse and empty it on the bed. Nice and slow."

She did as told.

"Now kneel, and put your hands behind your head."

Again she obeyed.

Dalton jammed his gun behind his belt, and sifted through her things. He ignored the pepper spray in the small, stainless steel container, possibly thinking it was perfume. He pulled her ID from her wallet, and whistled through his teeth.

"FBI. Wow."

"You want to talk this over?" she asked.

"Talk what over? You don't have any chips in the game."

"You planning to kill me?"

"It crossed my mind."

"The bureau doesn't take it well when one of their agents is murdered. They'll come after you, and they'll do it hard. I'll cut you a deal."

"What kind of deal?"

"A detective from Saint Augustine named Sykes was secretly filmed in this suite having sex. If you tell me who was behind that, we'll go light on you."

"What does that mean?"

"I'll talk to the prosecutor, and ask that you get probation for helping me. You won't spend a day in prison. Come on, Dalton, work with me."

"You can't guarantee that, and you know it."

"I'll fight for you."

He laughed silently at her, his eyes dark and soulless.

"I'm going to make you suffer, just like your partner," he said.

Something inside her snapped.

"What did you do to Jon?" she said.

- - -

Carrie leaned against the counter to wait. She used both hands to hold her weapon.

"You shouldn't have come here," she said.

"Does that thing have a safety?" he asked.

"Hell, no. A safety on a gun will only slow you down. I learned that in my first concealed weapons permit class. Safeties are for wimps."

"I guess that makes me a wimp, then."

"Do your guns have safeties?"

"You bet. I don't want one accidentally going off, and shooting someone when I'm out in public. Whoever told you that about safeties was an idiot."

"You're just afraid I'm going to shoot you."

"You have no reason to shoot me. I haven't done anything wrong."

"You're looking to cause trouble. That's enough reason for me." She reached beneath the counter and touched a control on the monitor. The picture changed, and they both watched Dalton enter the honeymoon suite and draw his weapon. Beth emptied her purse on the bed, then sank to the floor with her hands on her head.

"Looks like he's going to shoot her," Carrie said.

Lancaster swallowed hard. "Why?"

"He did time in prison, swore to me he'd never go back."

"He'd kill a person for that?"

"Damn straight."

He jumped up, turning sideways as he did. She pumped a bullet into the chair's upholstery, missing him by inches. He grabbed her wrists and twisted them so the gun's barrel was pointed at the floor. She got off another round, which sounded like a cannon going off. They wrestled, and he pulled her down and brought his knee up into her face. It produced the desired effect, and the gun fell from her hands and her eyes rolled back into her head. He couldn't tell if she was out cold, or faking it, and he put her down on the floor and placed his foot on the back of her head and kept it there.

He looked at the monitor, fearing the worst. Beth was standing, and holding what looked like a lipstick in her hand. She used it to spray Dalton in the face with a foreign substance that he guessed was pepper spray, causing Dalton to hold his face in agony.

Make the bastard pay, he thought.

Carrie let out a pitiful groan. "I can't breathe."

He pulled her off the floor. Blood soiled her face and ran down her chin. He pulled a tissue from a box and gave it to her. She tore it in half and plugged her nostrils. It made her look grotesque.

"You broke my nose," she said.

"Be thankful I didn't break your neck," he said.

A loud noise interrupted their conversation. The couple who'd just checked in came barreling down the stairs with their luggage, and hustled past them.

"You folks have a nice night," he said.

The front door slammed shut. Carrie had started to sob. He handed her another tissue and saw that her face was starting to swell. Carrie pointed at the monitor.

"What is she doing?" she asked.

"What are you talking about?"

"Look."

He shot a glance at the monitor. Dalton was on his knees, his head rocking from Beth's ferocious blows. He wondered what Dalton had said to provoke her.

"Make her stop," she pleaded.

"How do you expect me to do that?"

"Call her! She's going to hurt him."

He called Beth on his cell phone. On the monitor she paused, and started to answer the call. Seeing his chance, Dalton struggled to his feet. Beth grabbed a brass lamp off the nightstand, and smashed it into his skull, then used the lamp to beat him some more. Dalton went into a fetal curl and didn't move. The punishment was over the top, and bordered on sadistic. It wasn't the Beth he knew at all.

"She's killing him," Carrie wailed.

"Sure looks that way," he said.

CHAPTER 36

It wasn't long before the inn's remaining guests departed, the sound of Dalton getting the daylights beat out of him too much to bear. One couple stopped at the front desk to make an inquiry. They were Asian and appeared to have just rolled out of bed.

"Can you recommend a place not so noisy?" the husband asked.

"Try the Microtel off I-95 south of here," Lancaster suggested.

The couple left. On the monitor, Dalton lay unconscious on the floor. Beth stood over him holding a glass of water, which she poured onto his face. Dalton blinked awake. Seeing Beth hovering over him, he lifted his arms in surrender.

"See, he's not dead," Lancaster said encouragingly.

"But he's hurt. Look at him," Carrie moaned.

"He's a big boy. He'll get over it."

Dalton struggled to get up, and appeared to be in distress. Unfazed, Beth pointed at the door, then kicked him in the ass for good measure. They walked out of the picture. Moments later, Lancaster heard them coming down the stairs. He was going to have to get Beth alone, and confront her. She had stepped way over the line.

They came into the lobby, single file. Seeing him, Beth halted, and brought her hand to her mouth. Her eyes filled with tears.

"What's wrong?" he asked.

"He told me he'd shot you," she said.

Then, she kicked Dalton in the ass again.

- - -

Carrie rose from her chair, and attempted to comfort her son. Dalton's mouth was a bloody mess, and one of his front teeth was chipped. She shot Beth the evil eye.

"Look at me like that again, and I'll cuff you," Beth said.

Carrie led her son to the swivel chair, and helped him sit down. She balled up several tissues, and pressed them gently against his busted lip. Dalton stared sullenly at the floor, and seemed to be weighing his options. If he cooperated with them, he might avoid serious prison time. If not, he'd spend a long stretch behind bars.

"Are you going to play ball with us?" Lancaster asked.

"Yeah, I'll play ball," Dalton said.

"How long have you been filming your guests without their knowledge?"

"About ten years. Another B&B owner approached us with the idea. Said it was a real money-maker."

"What's his name?"

"Lynch. That's what everybody calls him. I don't know his first name."

"Was Lynch secretly filming his guests?"

"Yeah. Lynch was part of a network. He couldn't rent the films taken in his place to his guests because they might recognize the furniture, so he shared them with the network. In return, he borrowed films from the network, and rented them to his guests."

"Are you part of the network?"

"Uh-huh."

"How much money does this generate for you?"

Dalton looked to his mother for help.

"It's a third of our revenue," Carrie said.

"There are close to forty pornographic videos for rent on the cable TV in our room," Beth said. "Did they all come from the network?"

"Yes, ma'am," Dalton said.

He was being respectful, which was usually a good sign. Lancaster pulled a can of soda from the minifridge behind the desk, and gave it to him.

"Put that on your lip. It will bring down the swelling."

"Right."

"How many B&Bs are part of the network?" Beth asked.

"I don't know," Dalton said.

"How can you not know? You're in business with them."

"I'm in business with Lynch. I don't know the others."

"Explain how the deal works."

"Lynch has a password-protected site with a video library. For every video a member contributes, they can borrow one for free. I never checked how many other B&Bs were involved."

Dalton's answer didn't ring true. He was a criminal, and had to know that it wasn't smart to enter into a criminal enterprise without knowing your partners.

"I think you're lying to us," Beth said.

"May God strike me dead if I am," he said piously.

The conversation had stopped being productive. Lancaster decided to try a different tack, and said, "Explain the deal with Sykes to us."

"Sure," Dalton said. "About a year ago, two Russian brothers rented a room. The next morning over breakfast, they pulled me aside, and said they knew that we were secretly videotaping guests. They told me that they wanted to videotape a guy with a girl, and blackmail him. They made me an offer I couldn't refuse, so I agreed."

"Was their name Sokolov?" Lancaster asked.

Dalton thought about it. "I think so."

"How did they know your inn had hidden cameras? Who told them that?"

Dalton's mouth opened, but nothing came out. He had tripped himself up, and was scrambling to come up with an answer that wouldn't get him in any more trouble.

"They must have discovered the cameras on their own," he said weakly.

"Wait a second. The vanity mirror in my room was glued to the wall," Beth said. "I had to use a saw knife to pry it loose. Are you telling us that the Sokolovs cut a mirror in their room away from the wall, and found the camera?"

"I don't know."

"Of course you know! You would have found the mirror when you had the room cleaned later that day. You're lying to us."

"I'm not sure how they knew."

"Did Lynch tell them?"

"He could have. Come to think of it, that's probably how they knew."

Dalton gave them a sheepish look, as if that would put an end to the questions. Beth slapped her hand on the counter, and he jumped out of his chair.

"Is Lynch working with the Sokolovs?" she asked. "Are they using the B&Bs in the network, and blackmailing people?"

"Beats me."

"What are you afraid of, Dalton? That Lynch will find out that you gave him up? Let me tell you something, my friend. That is the least of your worries right now."

Beth wasn't seeing the big picture. Dalton's problem wasn't with Lynch; it was with the other B&B owners who were part of the network. If they found out that Dalton had squealed, they might seek revenge. Dalton was going to spend the rest of his life looking over his shoulder, and it scared him.

"I want a lawyer," he mumbled.

"That's not going to help you," Beth said.

The can of soda slipped out of Dalton's fingers, and fell between his feet.

"Shit," he swore.

He bent over to retrieve it. As his left hand picked up the can, his right went under the chair. His mother stood with her back pressed to the window, giving her son a clear shot at their visitors in the event he decided to make a last stand.

Guys like Dalton watched too many cop shows, and too many action movies. Through endless exposure, they'd been brainwashed into believing that when things got rough, they could blast their way out. It was bad advice, but they believed it anyway.

Dalton tore away the gun attached to the bottom of his chair. Then he sat up straight. His eyes stared at the barrel of the gun in his face.

Before Dalton could get off a round, Lancaster shot him dead.

CHAPTER 37

Daniels went to the second floor and knocked on doors.

"Anyone home?" she called out.

No answer. She visited the third floor and repeated the ritual. The inn's guests had cleared out. Which was exactly what she had hoped for.

She spent a moment composing herself before heading downstairs. She had thought Dalton had shot Jon, and that her boyfriend was dead. Finding Jon alive had been like being hit by a cattle prod. It had jolted her in a way she'd never been jolted before.

She went to the first floor. Jon and Carrie were behind the counter, standing next to Dalton, who was sprawled dead in the swivel chair. His mouth was catching flies, his eyes open in disbelief. Jon was forcing Carrie to look at him, and accept the reality of the situation. It was an old cop trick, designed to bring a suspect to their knees.

Beth locked the front door, and lowered the shade. If they were going to get Carrie to talk, they needed privacy, without intrusions. She went into the living room.

"Ready when you are," she said.

Jon led Carrie into the living room, and had her sit in a wingback chair. Carrie was sobbing, and holding her head with her hands.

"Do you have any idea how much trouble you're in?" Jon asked.

"I didn't know there was a gun under the chair," she blubbered.

"Of course you did."

"I swear I didn't."

"You're lying." Jon knelt down, and spoke in her ear. "Do you think I wanted to shoot your son? Do you?"

"I don't know."

"I didn't, and that's the God's honest truth."

The first time they'd dated, Jon had confided to her the number of people he'd shot to death in his life. As a Navy SEAL, as a police officer, and now as a private citizen, he'd been forced to use deadly force many times, and the body count was high. Each time had been justified, but that hadn't made the task any easier.

"Look at me," he said.

Carrie gazed at him. The tissue was gone from her nose, her nostrils caked red.

"The gun was taped beneath your chair, " he said.

"I didn't know it was there," she said emphatically.

"Are you saying that Dalton put it there without you knowing?"

"He must have."

"You led your son to that chair, and had him sit down. Then, you stood with your back against the window so he'd have a clean shot. You knew the gun was there, and you knew what your son was going to do. That makes you an accomplice to attempted murder. You're going down hard, Carrie."

"No!"

"Do you like air conditioning? Well, you can kiss it goodbye, because the state prisons in Florida don't have any. You're going to spend the rest of your life roasting to death. Sorry, my friend. But that's the way it is."

There was an art to putting the screws to a suspect, and Jon had the routine down pat. Carrie shrank in her chair and balled her hands into fists. She was about to cave, and help them.

"My son was running the show," Carrie said.

"How so?" Jon said.

"My son was evil. He slapped me around when he got liquored up, so I did whatever he wanted."

"He was abusing you."

"Yes. He was a monster."

Dalton hadn't been dead ten minutes, yet Carrie was already throwing her beloved boy under the bus. Jon had done his job; now Daniels needed to close the deal. She pulled up a chair and sat beside their suspect.

"Let me help you, Carrie, " she said.

Carrie looked into Daniels's face and waited.

"You shouldn't be punished for your son's transgressions," Daniels said. "But right now, things don't look good. You need to play ball with us. Will you do that?"

"What do you mean, play ball?"

Daniels leaned in. Their legs were nearly touching, and she could smell Carrie's fear pouring off her skin. It had a stinky odor, like rotting garbage.

"Your son filmed a police detective having sex with a woman," Daniels said. "His name was Sykes, and this film was used to blackmail him. Were you aware of this?"

Carrie said that she was.

"Two Russian brothers named Sokolov talked your son into doing this," she said. "We want you to tell us what the arrangement was."

"You mean the payment?" Carrie asked.

"That would be a good place to start."

"They gave my son five thousand dollars up front, and five thousand dollars when he emailed the film to them," Carrie said. "That was the deal."

"Do you have their email address?"

Carrie's mouth clamped shut. She shook her head.

"What about their phone number?" Daniels asked.

Carrie again shook her head.

"Would it be on your son's cell phone? Or his laptop?"

"I don't know where my son kept things."

"Are you sure about that?"

Carrie folded her hands in her lap. She was holding back, which Daniels found strange. If Carrie wound up going to prison, she would most likely end up dying there. A jail cell was no place for an older person to live out their final days.

A crash behind the desk made them jump. Daniels went to have a look. Dalton had slipped out of the swivel chair, and hit the floor. A pool of blood had started to form and would soon engulf the entire area behind the desk. They needed to get a CSI team here to deal with the mess. But first, they needed to get Carrie to open up.

Daniels returned to her chair in the living room.

"He's still alive, isn't he?" Carrie sobbed.

"I'm sorry, but your son is dead."

"What did I just hear?"

"His body is growing stiff, and he fell out of his chair."

Carrie looked at the ceiling, and said a silent prayer.

"Are you going to help us, or not?" Daniels asked.

"I'm not going to say anything else," Carrie said.

"Why not?"

"Because I don't want to die."

"You're not going to die."

"I will if I listen to you. They'll kill me."

"The Russians?"

"Damn straight."

"You have nothing to be afraid of," Daniels said. "One of the Russians is already dead, and we're going to arrest his brother soon. They won't cause you any harm."

Carrie hissed at her. "You don't know nothing."

Jon stepped in. "Why don't you educate us? What don't we know?"

"You think there are just two Russians behind all of this? You don't know nothing, and I'm sure as hell not going to educate you."

"How many more are there?"

"Plenty."

"Give me a number."

"At least a dozen. That's what Dalton told me. And one of them will slit my throat if I start talking to the likes of you. So screw your god damn deal. I'll take my chances in court."

CHAPTER 38

There was a loud banging on the inn's front door. Lancaster said, "Let me get it," and passed Beth his gun. He found four uniformed cops standing outside with their sidearms drawn. He opened the door and said, "Good evening, Officers."

"We got a report of gunshots," the officer in charge said. "We need to come inside."

The officer in charge looked older than his years. The job was eating him up, the way it did most guys. Lancaster had been down that road, and felt bad for him.

"My name is Jon Lancaster, and I'm a private investigator. My partner is Special Agent Beth Daniels with the FBI. We had an altercation with one of the owners of the inn, a man named Dalton, which resulted in him being shot to death."

"Who did the shooting?" the officer in charge asked.

"I did. It was self-defense."

Another cop muttered, "Good riddance," under his breath.

"Enough of that," said the officer in charge. "Where's your gun?"

"Special Agent Daniels has it. She's in the living room with Dalton's mother."

"Was anyone else injured in this altercation?"

"No, sir."

"Before we have a chat with Carrie and get her side of things, I want you to explain what Dalton was doing that led you to put that sorry son of a bitch out of his misery."

Lancaster hid a smile. Everything was going to be all right.

"We had reason to believe that Dalton was secretly filming guests engaged in sexual activity, so we registered as guests, and my partner searched our room," he said. "As expected, there was a camera hidden behind a mirror. We tried to interview Dalton, but he refused to talk. When Special Agent Daniels went to arrest him, Dalton drew a gun that was hidden under the chair he was sitting in. That's when I shot him."

"That sounds like something that dumbass would pull," the officer in charge said.

"I take it Dalton was a problem."

"Some guys are born failures; Dalton aspired to it. He's been arrested for every stupid thing you can imagine. Never met a bad idea that he didn't like."

"What about the mother?"

"Carrie's also got a record, mostly petty stuff."

"She told us that Dalton was the mastermind."

"That sounds about right. I need to speak with your partner."

Lancaster led the officers into the living room. Carrie hadn't moved from her chair, and was now wearing plastic handcuffs. The miserable expression on her face suggested that she was having second thoughts about not playing ball with them. Beth was typing a message on her cell phone. She hit "Send" and put the phone away. She'd pinned her badge to her shirt to let everyone know who was in charge.

"I'm Special Agent Daniels," she said. "Your timing is impeccable."

"Why is that, ma'am?" the officer in charge asked.

"Because my partner and I are about to rip this place apart, and we can't do that while Carrie is present," she said. "Please take her to a cruiser, and hold her until we're done."

The officer in charge spent a moment processing this.

"You're throwing us out?" he asked.

"In a manner of speaking, yes. This is an FBI investigation until I turn the reins over to you. Am I making myself clear?"

"Loud and clear. Would it be okay if we had a look at Dalton?"

"I don't see why not."

Lancaster led the officers behind the desk. Dalton's blood now covered a large swath of the floor, and one of the cops accidentally stepped in it. His partners laughed under their breath while he cleaned his shoe with a tissue. Cops in rural areas didn't see much in the way of real crime, and as a result, had little experience in dealing with the serious stuff. Beth was wise to send them outside.

The officers took Carrie off their hands. Lancaster stood at the front door, prepared to lock it once they were outside. The officer in charge lingered behind.

"You did this town a favor shooting that dumb bastard," he said.

"Glad to be of service," Lancaster said.

"Why was Dalton filming guests? Was he in the porn business?"

Lancaster hesitated. For all he knew, the Sokolovs were paying the local cops to look the other way, and the question was designed to see how much he knew.

"I have no idea," he said.

– – –

Back in the living room, he found Beth studying her phone.

"The director of the FBI's Jacksonville office is sending a forensics team to help us out," Beth said. "Let's see if we can find Dalton's computer or his cell phone. The Sokolovs' contact info should be stored on one of his devices."

"He's probably carrying his cell phone," he said.

"Then we'll start there," Beth said.

They got behind the counter. Lancaster hopped over the pool of blood, and stood behind the dead man. Sticking his hands beneath Dalton's armpits, he lifted him off the floor while Beth searched his pockets. A cracked leather wallet landed on the counter.

"That's all he's carrying," she said.

She dumped out the wallet's contents. It contained several thousand dollars in crisp hundreds and a driver's license, but no credit cards.

"Dalton did all his business in cash," she said.

"He's probably also using burner phones," Lancaster said.

"We still need to find his cell phone. We'll start on the ground floor, and work our way through the rooms. It has to be here somewhere."

"I've got a better idea. I'll be right back."

Lancaster went outside to find the four officers on the lawn, shooting the breeze. Carrie sat in the back of the cruiser with the windows shut and the engine running, enjoying the nice cool air conditioning courtesy of taxpayer dollars. Yanking open the back door, he told her to get out. When she refused, he dragged her out.

"You're hurting me," she said.

"No, I'm not. Stand still."

Her eyes were filled with venom. "I'm going to make you pay for killing my boy. Just you wait."

"Is that a threat?"

"You can take it to the bank, mister. I'm going to rip your heart out."

Her dress pockets produced nothing of value. He made her climb back into the cruiser. She was not done with him.

"You think I'm kidding? I can hurt you and that FBI lady in ways you never dreamed of," she said.

He slammed the door in her face. The officers were watching with curious looks.

"Where's her purse?" he asked.

"It's on the front seat," one of them said.

He retrieved Carrie's purse off the front passenger seat. Her cell phone lay inside, the battery dying. It wasn't password protected, and as he walked up the path, he scrolled through her contacts, and pulled up her son's cell phone number.

Beth awaited him in the living room. He showed her Carrie's phone and placed a call to Dalton's cell phone.

"You're brilliant," she said.

"I'm just smarter than I look. The call is going through. Listen."

The sound of a man belting out a country and western song came from the rear of the inn. They followed the music to a small, windowless office with a schoolhouse desk, and a cheap folding chair. Dalton's cell phone sat on the desk, the ringtone Garth Brooks's "Friends in Low Places."

"Nice work," she said.

- - -

Dalton's laptop also sat on the desk, and Beth attempted to access the hard drive. In the right-hand corner of the screen appeared a blue padlock icon.

"It's encrypted," she said dejectedly.

She went into Dalton's emails and discovered that his history had been scrubbed, and that his contacts file was empty.

"There's nothing here. Any luck with the phone?"

The cell phone had little in the way of stored information. It was a bare-bones device used for calls and texts only.

"It's a burner. There's nothing of value on it," he said.

They searched the office. Underneath the table was a shoebox filled with cheap phones. They powered them up, hoping that Dalton had gotten careless, and left a scrap of information that might prove helpful in their investigation.

No luck. Each device had been scrubbed clean.

"Another dead end," Beth said.

She tossed the burner in her hand back into the box. Criminal investigations were solved by tireless resolve, but along the way you needed to catch a break. The gods of fortune were not smiling down on them.

"Someone told me that the FBI employs hackers who can break into encrypted devices," he said. "Is that true?"

"Yes, we do. But it's off the record."

"Why?"

"Many criminals use an algorithm called AES to hide information on their devices. Our government also uses AES to protect sensitive information. If an FBI hacker broke into a criminal's device that had AES, and the information was used in court, we'd have to explain how the hacking was done, and that would jeopardize national security. To avoid that, our guys work in secret, and the bad guys never know they've been hacked."

"Let me guess. You sneak the laptop out of the evidence room, and your guys hack its hard drive. Then you put it back, and hope no one notices."

"That's exactly what we do."

"No one's ever caught you?"

"Nope. We do it over the weekend. Works like a charm."

"Can you hack Dalton's computer this way?"

"I can try. I'd have to put in an official request, and explain why it's necessary. I'd have to prove that I've exhausted all other options."

"How long would that take?"

"About a week."

"That long?"

"That's fast for the bureau, Jon."

He didn't like it. Too many things could happen in a week. A smart defense attorney could get the case thrown out by a judge over a technicality, or the laptop could get damaged while being handled by the cops.

But he didn't say anything. Using FBI hackers was their last resort, and they needed to run with it. Beth got a text, telling her the Jacksonville team had arrived.

"I better go meet them," she said. "Would you mind cleaning up?"

"Not at all."

- - -

As he put the burners back into the cardboard box, he wondered if they'd missed anything. Perhaps a scrap of paper in Dalton's wallet held a clue, or there was a notebook in his bedroom. It was a big house, and they needed to turn it upside down.

The burner Beth had tossed in frustration lay in pieces inside the box. The back of the burner had popped off, and exposed the electronics. A tiny object behind the wires caught his eye. It was coin-shaped, and painted black to avoid detection.

"Whoa," he said to himself.

He removed the broken burner for a closer look. The coin-shaped object looked like a transmitting device, which made no sense. Dalton was using burners so his activities couldn't be traced, and would have never willingly had a transmitting device installed into one of them.

Maybe Dalton hadn't known about it. Maybe the Sokolovs had given him the burner with the transmitting device so they could keep tabs on him.

The object was soldered to the burner, and he used his fingernail to pry it free. It was the size of a quarter, and twice as thick. He scratched away the paint. The manufacturer's insignia—a calligraphic capital C— stared back at him.

Now he was really confused. The company was called Callyo; it made some of the most advanced mobile tracking technology in the world, and worked exclusively with law enforcement agencies. The Sokolovs weren't the ones monitoring Dalton. They couldn't have gotten their hands on these devices, or gained access to the technology needed to make them work.

It was the cops who were monitoring Dalton.

CHAPTER 39

Daniels found Jon hunched over the desk upon returning. Instead of cleaning up, he had taken apart the burners, and neatly laid the pieces across the desk.

"You're not going to believe this," he said without looking up.

"Try me," she said.

"Each one of these burners is equipped with a Callyo transmitting device," he said. "How well do you know Director Rojas?"

"I just met her today."

"Do you trust her?"

"I do. Why do you ask?"

"Someone was monitoring Dalton, and my bet says it was the Jacksonville office of the FBI. They somehow got these burners into Dalton's hands and were tracking him."

She examined one of the burners and found the transmitter hidden behind the wiring. There were a variety of mobile tracking devices used by law enforcement to monitor criminal behavior. Callyo was unique in that it had been created to monitor human traffickers, the information it gathered invaluable in sending traffickers to prison.

"Let me ask her," she said.

Daniels returned to the living room. Rojas was overseeing an agent taking photographs of Dalton's corpse, and did not see her approach.

Daniels pulled her to the side, and handed her one of Dalton's burners. Rojas immediately spotted the transmitter.

"Are you running an operation here?" Daniels asked.

Rojas shook her head. "Not mine."

"Then whose operation is it? The transmitter is made by a company called Callyo, and is only sold to law enforcement agencies. You familiar with these guys?"

"I've heard of them. Their technology helps catch traffickers."

"That's right. This looks like a cheap burner, but it's actually a sophisticated digital phone. Every call or electronic communication that's made off this phone is sent to the cloud, and is logged into a database with a date and time attached to it. It also records the caller's latitude and longitude and attaches it to the log. You can't do any of these things with a burner, which is why traffickers use them."

"That must be great in court."

"The data is overwhelming. Whenever I've used it, I've gotten a conviction."

"If it's only available to law enforcement agencies, then the Florida Department of Law Enforcement must be running the operation."

"Wouldn't they have let you know?"

"That's the rule. I guess it got broken here."

"This operation has been going on for a while."

"Really? What led you to that conclusion?"

"My partner found ten burners in a cardboard box beneath Dalton's desk. Most traffickers use a burner for a month, then buy a new one."

Rojas made a face. Human trafficking cases fell under the FBI's jurisdiction, and the FDLE could not legally conduct an investigation without informing the bureau, and keeping them regularly apprised of their progress.

"Would you call your contact at the FDLE? I need to see the data they have on Dalton," Daniels said.

Rojas pulled out her cell phone, and made the call. She was steaming, and looked angry enough to bite the head off a live chicken.

"My pleasure," she said.

- - -

The call was a short one.

"The director of the FDLE's Jacksonville office swears to me on a stack of Bibles that they aren't running surveillance on Dalton," Rojas said, putting her phone away. "He was surprised when I told him how long the operation has been going on."

"Could another FDLE office be running the sting?"

"Those guys are very careful about not treading on each other's turf," Rojas said. "I would say that the answer is no. He did mention the National Center for Missing and Exploited Children, and wondered if it might be their operation through Team Adam."

"I didn't know that Team Adam ran covert operations," Daniels said. "I've worked with them in the past, and they've always been transparent."

"That's been my experience as well," Rojas said. "My guy at FDLE said there's an ex-cop out of Fort Lauderdale who's a member of Team Adam who has a reputation for not playing by the rules some of the time. He thinks this guy might be responsible."

Daniels realized that Rojas was referring to Jon. She had hit another dead end.

"Thanks for the assist," she said.

"Happy to help," Rojas said. "I'll need to get a statement from you and your partner before the night is over."

"Will do."

- - -

Angel's Dining Car in Palatka bore a strong resemblance to a grounded submarine. A hot-dog shaped building with a foundation of concrete blocks, it sat in the middle of a parking lot, and claimed to be the oldest diner in the Sunshine State.

Daniels studied the extensive menu. The big sellers appeared to be the fried okra, fried green beans, and frog legs. They also served breakfast all day long.

"You go first," she said.

Jon ordered the Black Bottom, which was a mixture of scrambled eggs, bacon, and ground beef, all served on a toasted potato bun.

"What strikes your fancy?" the waitress asked.

"I'll have the same, and a cup of coffee," Daniels said.

They fell quiet after the waitress departed and enjoyed the down-home smells coming out of the kitchen. It was a friendly place and felt genuine.

"You hungry?" Daniels asked.

"Starving," Jon said. "I know I'm not supposed to feel that way, but I do."

"What do you mean?"

"Shooting people is supposed to make you feel awful, and rob you of your appetite. I heard a psychologist say that at a murder trial."

"How did shooting Dalton make you feel?"

"Bad at first, but I got over it. Sort of like accidentally running over a squirrel. It goes back to something that happened to me in the navy."

Part of Jon's training as a SEAL was an oath he'd taken that prohibited him from talking about his missions. When he did, it was usually in vague terms.

"You want to talk about it?" she asked.

He absently played with his napkin. "We were on a rescue mission in Central America, and a guy with a machete jumped out of the bush, and tried to cut my head off. I had no choice, and put him down. I got so upset that I didn't eat for days.

"My commanding officer took me aside. He told me that if the guy had killed me, he didn't think he'd be having any issues putting down food. My CO said, 'Don't waste your emotions on the enemy. Save them for the victims.' That stayed with me."

Their food came. Her mother had told her never to eat anything bigger than her head. Daniels decided to ignore her mom's advice, and dug in.

"We need to find out which law enforcement agency was running the surveillance operation on Dalton, and get our hands on those records," she said between bites. "I'm going to put in a request to subpoena Callyo's records first thing tomorrow."

"I'm sure Callyo will fight you in court," Jon said.

"On what grounds?"

"They sign confidentiality agreements with all their customers. Callyo's lawyers will argue that if they release Dalton's records, it will be opening Pandora's box, and they'll have to turn over records to every sleazy criminal defense attorney that requests them. It's a strong argument."

"You think I could lose?"

"Yes. Even if you win, Callyo's lawyers will file an appeal. The case could drag on for months."

The food no longer tasted very good. Daniels wiped her mouth, and tossed her balled-up napkin on her plate. Jon wasn't having any issues, and kept eating.

"I have another idea," he said.

"Does it involve breaking the law? If so, then just do it, and don't tell me."

"It doesn't involve breaking the law. Thanks for asking."

"I'm all ears. What is it?"

"When the Callyo technology was first being rolled out, the company's owner gave a presentation to Team Adam in Washington. I introduced myself afterward, and he gave me his contact info. Why don't I call him?"

"He's not going to turn that data over, based upon a phone call."

"No, but he might tell me who his client is. Then you can contact them, and request Dalton's information. Since you're with the FBI, they'll have to comply."

Jon wasn't telling her the whole story, and she wondered if he'd taken Callyo's owner for a few beers. That was his style, and it had made him a lot of friends.

"It's worth a shot. Call him," she said.

- - -

Callyo's owner was a laid-back guy named Chris Bennett. Back in the rental, Jon gave him a call, and left a message on voice mail. New companies with crime-fighting technology were popping up every day, and competition was fierce. It was all about customer service, and Beth wasn't surprised when Bennett called back a minute later.

Jon put his cell phone on speaker and placed it into the cupholder. "Hello, Chris. This is Jon Lancaster. We met last year after your presentation to Team Adam."

"Good evening, Jon. You're based out of Fort Lauderdale, correct?"

"Good memory. I'm sitting in a car with Special Agent Daniels of the FBI, and I have you on speaker phone."

"Good evening, Special Agent Daniels," Bennett said.

"Hello, Chris. Nice to meet you," Daniels said.

"Same here. What can I do for you folks tonight?"

"We're conducting an investigation in Palatka, and happened across a box of burner phones with your tracking technology," Jon said. "The suspect who had these phones is named Dalton, and is connected to a human trafficking ring. We assumed the Jacksonville office of the FBI was running the operation, but that isn't the case."

"Is it an FDLE operation?" Bennett asked.

"The FDLE has no knowledge of the operation. We've hit a dead end, and were hoping you could tell us whose show this is."

"I sign confidentiality agreements with all my clients," Bennett said. "If it is one of our jobs, I can't share the data with you."

"We don't expect you to break an agreement with a client," Daniels said. "We just need to know who the client is. We'll take it from there."

"Got it. Okay, let me see if this is one of our jobs."

"How could it not be?" Jon asked. "Your tracking equipment is in the burners."

"It could be a Chinese rip-off," Bennett explained. "China doesn't recognize our trademarks or patents, and we get ripped off by companies we compete with. It's the price of success these days. Give me a couple of minutes. Back at you."

The phone went silent. They leaned back in their seats to wait. She heard the faint whistle, and knew that Jon was upset.

"What's wrong?" she asked.

"Who said something was wrong?" he replied.

"You're clearly upset about something."

"I didn't know I was so obvious to read."

"Or maybe I'm just really good at it. Tell me."

"Carrie threatened me. She said I could take it to the bank."

"Don't tell me you haven't been threatened before." She reached across the seat and slapped his leg. "Dalton is dead, and his dear mama is going to jail. You're safe."

"This was real. She's going to enact some kind of revenge for my shooting her son. She said she was going to rip our hearts out."

"Was I included in her threat?"

"Yes. It was directed at both of us."

"Do you think she might have family in Palatka?"

"Her family doesn't worry me. But the Russians do."

Bennett's voice came out of the cell phone. "Sorry this is taking so long. We have six active jobs in Florida. Each has a different account manager, and I need to speak to each of them to find out who's running this operation. I shouldn't be much longer."

"Take all the time you need," Daniels said.

The phone went silent.

"Tell me why the Russians worry you," she said.

"Carrie refused to cut a deal because she's afraid the Russians will kill her while she's in jail," Jon said. "That means she knows things about the Russians' operation that are worth having her killed over. Make sense?"

"I'm with you so far."

"Carrie has leverage over the Russians. When she's in jail, she'll have her lawyer send them a message. In return for her silence, she'll ask them to carry out her threat."

"Do you really think she's capable of that?"

"I killed her son. She's capable of anything."

"How is she going to rip our hearts out?"

"I haven't figured that part out yet."

Daniels considered what Jon was saying. Carrie looked like a doting old woman, but she was just as guilty as Dalton, and probably just as ruthless. To underestimate her would have been a mistake.

Bennett came back on the line.

"Hey, there," the founder of Callyo said. "I just got off the line with one of my account managers. The Palatka operation is his. Sorry I didn't recognize it, but we've got over a hundred jobs around the country we're running right now."

They had hit so many dead ends. Now, finally, they were going to break the investigation open, and get to the truth. If there was a greater feeling, she didn't know what it was. She glanced at Jon. He was thinking the same thing, his eyes dancing.

"Did your account manager tell you who the client is?" Daniels asked.

"Yes, he did," Bennett said. "Our client is the Saint Augustine Police Department."

Daniels sat up straight in her chair.

"Bastards," Jon swore under his breath.

"Are you sure?" she said into the cell phone.

"Positive," Bennett said. "My account manager emailed me the contract, which I'm looking at right now. Twelve months ago, the Saint Augustine Police Department hired us to supply tracking devices hidden in burner phones for an investigation that is still ongoing. Is that a problem?"

"We met with the Saint Augustine police a few days ago, and the operation was never mentioned," she said. "Who in the department are you working with?"

"Let me look. The name should be on the contract."

The line went mute. Daniels shook her head angrily. She would have bet her paycheck on who it was, but still needed Bennett to confirm.

"It has to be him," she whispered.

"Must be," Jon whispered back.

"Found it," Bennett said. "The point person for this job is Detective Gaylord Sykes. Do you know him?"

It was all Daniels could do not to scream.

"We sure do," she said.

PART FIVE

CRIME AND PUNISHMENT

CHAPTER 40

Sykes watched the spinning carousel while sipping from his flask.

The carousel had appeared right around the time he'd joined the police department. It had been owned by a member of the Ringling Brothers Circus, who'd paid a small fortune for it in the early part of the last century. It had been moved around the country, and had eventually found a home here in Saint Augustine.

His daughter, Regina, had loved the carousel. On weekends, he'd brought her to the park to play. For a handful of change, she'd ride on a painted horse while the calliope piped out music that could be heard for miles. Sometimes, she chose instead to ride the camel that was part of the carousel's menagerie. The camel wasn't pretty to look at, and hardly any of the kids ever rode it, except Regina. He often wondered why the owners hadn't replaced it with a horse. But they hadn't, and it was still there.

He took another sip of whiskey, and felt it burn going down. It was a bad way to start the morning. But it took the edge off, and like the pills his coworkers took for high blood pressure and hypertension, he liked to think it was doing him some good.

The radio on the dashboard barked.

"Sykes? Are you at Davenport Park? Please pick up."

One of the minuses of working for a small-town police department was that everyone knew where you were, all the time. He pulled the radio off the clip on the dashboard and pushed the button.

"Good morning, Tiffany. Yes, I'm at the park. What's up?" he said.

"We just got a 911 call. A body was found at the Old Jail. Can you handle?"

Sykes could see the Old Jail from where he was parked. It was one of the stops on the trolley tour of the city and was now a museum. A long time ago, a rich man named Henry Flagler paid for the jail to be built north of downtown. So as not to strike fear in the hearts of the public, Flagler had decided to disguise it, and built it to resemble a posh hotel. Few tourists ventured out of the historic downtown these days. If not for the trolley tours, he had to believe the Old Jail would have been shuttered a long time ago.

"I can handle it," he said. "Does it look like foul play?"

"Gunshot," the operator said.

"Self-inflicted?"

"They didn't say."

Sykes hadn't dealt with a homicide in a while. Most of the deaths were suicides of patients from the local VA hospital who seemed to lose hope the older they got.

"Tell them I'll be right there."

He took another pull of whiskey before backing out. In the theater of his mind, he saw Regina flash by, waving to him as she galloped past on her wooden horse.

It was all he could do not to wave back.

- - -

Mannequins dressed like a chain gang lined the road in front of the Old Jail. It hearkened back to a time that most people in the city would have liked to forget. Sykes wished they'd take it down, but no one had ever listened to what he had to say.

The museum didn't open for another hour, and he had his pick of parking spaces. He swished mouthwash and spit it on the ground as he got out.

A fake sheriff greeted him at the door, packing a six-shooter. Local actors served as tour guides, and often got carried away, locking mouthy kids in cells or sticking them in the "Bird Cage" jail cell behind the building. Sykes had lectured the guides several times, and knew most of them by name. The fellow at the door was new.

"Who are you?" Sykes asked.

"My name's Gamble. I started last week," the fake sheriff said.

"I've never seen you before. Where are you from?"

"Gainesville."

"College boy, huh. What did you study?"

"Acting and drama."

"What brings you here?"

"I answered a job posting online. I needed the work."

The story rang true. But Sykes wanted more. "Is that pea shooter loaded?"

"No, sir. It's just for show."

Sykes drew back his sports jacket to reveal the gun strapped to his side. "Mine isn't. Am I making myself clear? Leave that thing in its holster at all times."

"Yes, sir," the fake sheriff said.

"Glad we're on the same page. Now where's this body?"

"In the back by the gallows. Follow me."

Gamble led him down a hallway to the back of the building. The jail had been built by the Pauly Jail Building Company, the same people responsible for constructing Alcatraz in San Francisco, and it was designed like a small fortress, with concrete walls and steel ceilings.

During the jail's more than sixty years in operation, no prisoner had ever managed to escape.

The gallows was another sore point. It evoked the days of public executions, and lynchings. Men needed to die with dignity, even bad men, and he wanted to see it removed. He stepped into the backyard and was blinded by the sunlight. As his eyes adjusted, he discovered that a small gathering awaited him. Special Agent Daniels, that sneaky bastard Lancaster, and four FBI agents with badges pinned to their lapels. He didn't see anyone from the police department, and wondered why that was.

"Put your hands in the air," the fake sheriff said.

"Don't tell me—you're one of them," Sykes said.

"I sure am. But I did take acting classes in college. They come in handy."

The fake sheriff frisked him, and took away his sidearm and the backup gun he wore on his ankle. He decided to play stupid, and see where it got him.

"Would you folks mind telling me what this is all about?" Sykes said.

Daniels stepped forward. "Don't you know? You're under arrest."

"For what? Not paying my property taxes on time?"

"For starters, lying to an FBI agent multiple times."

"I was completely honest with you," he lied.

Her forefinger jabbed him in the chest. The look in her eyes made him swallow hard. "You have no friends here," she said.

- - -

The cellblock resembled a steel cage, with cells lining the two walls, a small common area with a badly pocked table, and a pair of benches. The table and benches were screwed to the floor so the inmates couldn't break them apart, and turn them into weapons. There was no air conditioning, the air still and warm.

Sykes was made to sit on a bench. The FBI agents and Lancaster stood on the other side of the picnic table, while the fake sheriff guarded the door. Sykes was still annoyed that he hadn't seen through the guy's disguise. He would turn fifty-five soon, and wondered if he was starting to lose his edge.

One of the FBI agents picked up a cardboard box from the floor, and placed it on the picnic table. Daniels reached into the box and removed a handful of cell phones, which she placed in a row on the table. She did this until the box was empty.

Sykes felt sweat trickle down his back. These were the burners that he'd used to track Dalton over the past twelve months. He guessed the FBI had arrested Dalton, and during a search found the burners. It probably hadn't been very hard for the FBI to contact the people at Callyo, and trace the burners back to him.

"Recognize these?" Daniels asked.

"Never seen them before," he lied.

A second cardboard box was taken off the floor, and put on the table. Daniels removed reams of printed paper as thick as a phone book, and slapped them down in front of him.

"How about this?" she asked.

Sykes leafed through the papers. It was a transcript of the data that Callyo had collected on Dalton, and included every phone call, text, and email, along with the date, time, and his geographical location when he made the communication. Sykes's name was on the cover page as the point person of the operation. He was cooked.

"Yeah, I recognize these papers," the detective said.

"This is your operation, yes?" Daniels said.

"Yes, ma'am."

"You've been monitoring Dalton's activities for the past year, correct?"

"Yes, I have."

"Good. Now we're getting somewhere."

Sykes took a deep breath, waiting. He expected Daniels to pull out his bank records, and slap them on the table. Those records would be the knockout punch, and prove how deep he'd gotten himself into this mess. He'd let greed get the best of him, and now he was going to pay for it.

But Daniels didn't do that. Instead, she took out a small notepad, and a pen, in preparation for questioning him. The FBI didn't use tape recorders during formal interrogations for reasons he'd never completely understood. It was old school, and not with the times.

"I'm going to ask you some questions," Daniels said. "How you answer them will determine what we do with you. Am I making myself clear?"

His mind raced. The FBI hadn't bothered to search his house. If they had, they would have discovered his bank records, and realized what was going on. In their haste to arrest him, they'd failed to cover all their bases, and as a result, they were still partially in the dark. They would eventually find out what he'd done, but it might take a while.

Daniels looked tired and run-down. The woman had been through a lot. If he helped her, she might cut him some slack. He needed to fall on his sword, and confess. He'd throw the others under the bus, and try not to implicate himself.

It was the only shot he had, and he was going to take it.

"Loud and clear," Sykes said.

"Good. But know this. If I catch you telling a lie, I'll throw your ass in jail so fast it will make your nose bleed," Daniels said.

"I won't lie," he lied.

CHAPTER 41

Daniels placed a bottled water on the table. She wondered if Sykes had figured out why they'd brought him to the cellblock to conduct their questioning, as opposed to the FBI's Jacksonville office, or the police station.

"That's for you," she said.

Sykes took a long swallow. The cellblock was heating up, and he looked like he was melting. The jail wasn't air conditioned, and there was little in the way of cross-ventilation. It was hard to imagine living under these conditions.

"Are you ready to start?" she asked.

Sykes nodded.

"Tell us the circumstances leading up to your decision to monitor Dalton. Start from the beginning, and don't leave anything out."

"Can I take my jacket off? I'm burning up."

"Go ahead."

The detective rose from the bench, and removed his sports jacket. Jon stood in the corner, watching the detective's every move. Sykes avoided his gaze, and sat back down.

"Okay, so here's what happened," Sykes said. "Because Saint Augustine is a tourist town, we're vulnerable to a certain breed of criminals, like con men and prostitutes. We employ two undercover cops whose sole job is to be on the lookout for these people. They hit the bars at night, and know people in the hospitality business, who tend to be a pretty good source of information."

"Their names," Daniels said.

Sykes gave her the names, then resumed. "About a year ago, my guys started to see these hot young Latin women in the bars, hitting on older guys. They saw these women take older guys home for the night, which of course got them suspicious."

"Did you arrest them for prostitution?" Daniels asked.

"We did not. No money was changing hands, at least not in public. We assumed the transaction was taking place in a hotel room. Turns out, that wasn't the case either. My guys had beers with one of these Romeos, and learned that he hadn't paid for the sex, which he claimed was pretty wild."

"Sounds like a set-up."

"It *was* a set-up. These ladies had a friend, a young Russian woman who worked as a tour guide, who was making the introductions. "

"Her name."

"Katya."

"So Katya was pimping these Latin women."

"That's correct. Folks in town liked Katya, so no one was suspicious."

Daniels knew bullshit when she heard it, and she slapped the table. "Young women don't have sex with strange men unless they're getting something in return. Don't play us for fools, Detective."

"I'm not playing anyone," Sykes said defensively. "People liked Katya because she was dating your father. It had a halo effect, if you know what I mean."

Daniels's cheeks burned. Her father had let himself be used in more ways than one. "You're saying their relationship paved the way for Katya to work her scam."

"That's right. Your father was used. A month later, my under-cover guys heard a rumor. Our Romeos were being blackmailed by two Russian brothers named Sokolov. They had videos that had been secretly taken at Katya's house with the Latin girls. The Russians were threatening to destroy these men's reputations if they didn't pay."

"How big were the ransoms?"

"Hundreds of thousands of dollars."

"What did you do?"

"I found out who the victims were, and talked to them. None of them were willing to press charges. I guess they were afraid of the consequences. That's when we started running surveillance on the Sokolovs."

"How did that go down?"

"The Sokolovs brought their ladies into Saint Augustine every week on a private plane, and rented cars privately through a company called Turo. They used one guy pretty regularly, so we went to his place, and planted a tracking device on his car, which let us watch where the Sokolovs went."

"What was the guy's name they rented the car from?"

Sykes searched his memory. "Arlen Childress."

"What kind of car?"

"A Charger."

So far, Sykes was getting a passing grade. "Keep talking," she said.

"The Sokolovs did their business in Saint Augustine, but at night they stayed in Palatka. I guess it was safer for them that way," the detective said.

"Where in Palatka?"

"The Gables Inn."

"Dalton's place."

"Correct."

"How did you get Dalton to use the Callyo burner phones?"

Sykes smiled thinly, pleased with himself. "The Sokolovs gave them to Dalton."

"Come again?"

"The Sokolovs used burners to avoid being traced. They were buying them from a shop in Palatka, so we talked the store's owner into stocking the Callyo phones, which had special bar codes on the packaging. When one of the Sokolovs purchased a burner, it was scanned at checkout, which let us know which phone they had. We contacted Callyo, and they activated the transmitter in that particular phone."

"What was Dalton's role?"

"He was the Sokolovs' point person. He made sure they were taken care of when they came to town, the girls as well."

"Taken care of how?"

"He kept rooms open, and brought takeout food to them. He also bought drugs for them. The girls were pretty doped up."

Daniels ran her thumb up the side of the transcripts. She'd stayed up late poring through Dalton's communications between the Russians and various drug dealers in the area, and knew that Sykes was telling the truth. But that didn't explain why he hadn't mentioned the operation when they'd talked in his office.

"Why didn't you share this?" she asked. "Were they blackmailing you?"

"I don't know what you're talking about," he said.

The detective had told his first lie. If he wasn't careful, she'd slap handcuffs on him, and let him bake in a cell for a while. "There's a videotape of my father in a board meeting at the hospital, looking on his cell phone at a video of you having sex with one of the Latinas. Why don't you tell us about it?"

Sykes seemed to shrink before their eyes. He was sweating like he was about to be hanged from the gallows in the courtyard, and he spent a moment composing himself.

"I got trapped," he said quietly. "My wife died a few years ago from cancer. It's not easy being alone."

She let an appropriate amount of time pass. "Go on," she said.

"One of the Latinas was named Lissette Diaz. She came into head-quarters one day, asking for help. She offered to turn on the Sokolovs if we'd put her into witness protection. It sounded intriguing, so I talked to her. Lissette lived in south Florida, and was a member of the Latin Kings. She and two other Latin Kings girls got arrested for shoplifting. While they were in the county lockup, they met Katya, and became friends."

"What was Katya doing in jail?"

"Recruiting. Katya would get arrested on a minor charge, and spend a few days in the lockup, getting to know the other women. She offered to help them get work as strippers at a men's club in Fort Lauderdale when they got out."

"Which club?"

"I don't remember. It was owned by a Russian gangster named Sergey."

"Go on."

"Lissette and her friends went to work for Sergey when they got out. They started as strippers, but soon were turning tricks. Lissette said it was crummy work, but the money was good. One day Katya introduced them to the Sokolovs, who told the girls they had a scam that would make them rich. Katya was moving to Saint Augustine to work in a museum and live in a house the Sokolovs had outfitted with hidden cameras. Once Katya got settled in, the girls would come up, and stay with her.

"Katya would take the girls to bars, and introduce them to rich men. The girls would seduce the old boys, take them to the house, and have sex. Every room had hidden cameras, so it really didn't matter where they chose to do it. The videos would later be used for blackmail.

"Lissette was getting nervous. She didn't think the Sokolovs were going to pay her, and might even kill her. So she came to the police. I decided she was being truthful, and we struck a deal. She would wear a wire, and collect evidence. The night before she was to start, we went to dinner. I got drunk, and she started rubbing my leg beneath the table. One thing led to another, and we snuck off to Palatka and had sex."

Daniels shook her head in disbelief. It felt like the truth, but it wasn't the whole truth. Sykes looked away, ashamed.

"Let me make sure I have this straight," she said. "You had sex with an informant at the Gables Inn, which was owned by Dalton, who was under your surveillance."

"Yes, ma'am."

"Do you actually expect us to believe this?"

"It's true. Look, I'm not proud of it. Lissette did the driving that night. She parked behind the inn, and we went in through the back door, and snuck upstairs and got naked. I didn't realize where I was until the next morning."

Sykes stared at the table. Avoiding eye contact was often a sign of deceitfulness. But there was also the chance he'd made an error in judgment that he now regretted. It wouldn't be the first time a man had compromised himself for sex.

"When did they start blackmailing you?" she asked.

"The next day. Lissette was supposed to come to my office, and get wired up. She pulled a no-show, so I called her. She said, 'Look in your inbox,' and hung up. She'd emailed the video to me." Sykes spent a moment looking at each of them. His gaze came to rest on Daniels. "I knew I was screwed. But I didn't shut down the operation. I was going to build my case, and nail those assholes. Once they were in jail, I'd tell my boss about the video, and retire. It was the only honorable way out of the mess I'd created, and that's the God's honest truth."

Sykes had fallen on his sword, and admitted his guilt. Most cops that got caught breaking laws didn't take that route. Her opinion of him changed.

"Last question," she said. "Why was your sex video sent to my father? What purpose did that serve?"

"I don't know. But I can guess."

"Go ahead."

"The victims refused to pay. We heard the Sokolovs talking about it on the surveillance. Then the hands started appearing on their doorsteps. The victims caved, except your father. He threatened to go to the police. That was also on the surveillance. The Sokolovs must have sent him my video to silence him."

"My father never came to you?"

"No, ma'am."

"So the threat worked."

"It would seem that way, yes."

The sound was as distinct as a distant train whistle, filled with fury and unbridled rage. Jon came out of his corner, straight toward Sykes. Deceptively fast, he went around the bench, cuffed Sykes in the head, and sent him sprawling to the floor.

"You're a god damn liar," Jon roared.

CHAPTER 42

It took three agents to pull Jon away. Sykes remained on the floor, shielding his head with his arms. The detective had not uttered a word in protest. Had he lied to them? Daniels certainly hadn't seen it.

But Jon had smelled the deception, and it had brought out the worst in him. He aimed a well-deserved kick at the detective's head.

"You're a piece of shit," Jon said.

"Cut it out." To Sykes she said, "Get up."

Sykes dragged himself off the floor, and returned to his spot on the bench. His hair stuck up on his head, his lip bloodied from his fall.

"Did you just lie to us, Detective?" Daniels asked.

"Everything I said was true," Sykes said.

Jon lunged at him, the agents holding him back. "Two days ago, you told us that you didn't know Martin. Now you're telling us that Martin never came to you."

"That's right," Sykes said. "I didn't know him, and he never filed a formal complaint with the police. So what?"

"When Martin watched the video of you and Lissette having sex, he freaked out. He *knew you*. You're not telling us the truth."

Sykes's eyes went wide. Trapped by his own words, he had nowhere to go. "I want an attorney," he declared.

Daniels cursed under her breath. It was impossible to know how much of what Sykes had told them was true, or cleverly fabricated lies designed to protect his skin. Under any other circumstances, she would have ended things, and let him call a lawyer; but this was her father they were talking about, and she was not prepared to go silently into the night.

"Let him go," she said.

The agents released their grip on Jon, who jumped forward.

Sykes let out a muted cry. "Get away from me!"

Grabbing the detective by the shoulders, Jon dragged him toward the cell door. "I'm going to hang your sorry ass from the gallows by my shirt."

"Help me!"

Daniels and the agents didn't move. No one liked this tactic, but sometimes it was the only path forward. The gallows were directly outside the cellblock, and Jon yanked the cellblock door open and dragged Sykes kicking and screaming toward it.

"I'll talk!" Sykes said.

Jon kept dragging him toward the gallows. "You said that before."

"On my wife's grave."

Jon put on the brakes. "So help me God, if you're lying . . ."

"I'll tell you everything."

Jon retraced his steps, and tossed Sykes onto the bench. The detective's chest heaved up and down as he gasped for breath. Jon cuffed him in the back of the head.

"Start talking."

"Martin was on our radar from the beginning," Sykes said. "We weren't sure if he was a part of the scam, or just an innocent dupe."

"Which was he?"

"He was a pawn. That Russian bitch had him wrapped around her little finger. He was pussy-whipped." He glanced at Daniels. "Sorry, ma'am, but it's the truth."

Daniels fumed. "Why didn't you tell us this when we came to see you?"

"I was afraid you'd be angry with me," the detective said.

"Why would I be angry?"

"Your father came to me, and said he wanted to press charges. He'd secretly tape-recorded several of his telephone conversations with the Sokolovs. It was enough evidence to put them away for a long time."

"What did you do with this evidence?"

"I burned it."

"You did what?"

"I put it in the fireplace in my house and burned it. Martin was willing to accept responsibility and admit his mistakes. I wasn't. It was as simple as that."

"You betrayed him."

Sykes nodded ruefully. "Not the proudest day of my life, but that's what I did. Your father told the Russians that he'd gone to the police, and was going to fight back. The Russians responded by sending him the video of me with Lissette."

"To silence him," Daniels said, seething.

"Uh-huh."

The detective fell silent. Jon cuffed him again. The blow was hard enough to snap Sykes's head forward.

"Stop hitting me," he protested.

"You're holding back, which is as good as lying in my book," Jon said.

"Who said I was holding back?"

"I did. The fact that you betrayed Martin wasn't the end of the world. Martin could have picked up the phone, and called his daughter. If he was willing to admit the affair to you, then he would have done the same with her. So why didn't he?"

"You're asking me?"

"Yes. And I think you know the answer. It was Nicki, wasn't it?"

"Who's Nicki?"

"His granddaughter. Martin spoke to her a day before he took his life, and told her he was sorry. I didn't know what that meant, but I do now. The Russians were going to send the blackmail videos to Martin's granddaughter, whom he adored. Martin couldn't bear the thought of that, so he drained his bank account, and paid them off. Does that sound about right?"

"Yes," the detective said.

"Who gave the Russians Nicki's email?"

"Katya did. She stole Nicki's personal information off Martin's computer."

"Who told you that?"

"Lissette sent me an email. She said that the Sokolovs had shut Martin down."

"How did you feel about that?"

"Relieved. I wanted the whole thing to go away."

"I'm sure you did. Last question. Why did Martin take his life after paying the Sokolovs off?"

"I have no idea."

Jon put his hand on the back of Sykes's neck, and drove the detective's face into the table. Sykes was wise enough to turn his face sideways at the moment of impact, which spared him a broken nose and losing a number of his front teeth. Jon pulled him back up.

"The Sokolovs weren't done with him, were they? They had found his Achilles' heel with Nicki, and were going to continue to blackmail him. Isn't that right?"

Sykes was breathing hard and said nothing.

"Lissette told you that. Or maybe it was Martin. It doesn't really matter, because you didn't do a damn thing about it. You just wanted the whole thing to go away."

Sykes continued to be mute.

"And when the call came that an apparent suicide had been found by a hiker, you were hoping that it was Martin, weren't you?"

Still nothing. Jon grabbed the detective by the back of the neck. It was enough to get Sykes to break his silence.

"I liked Martin. He was my friend," Sykes said.

"You didn't like him enough to help him," Jon said. "You stood by, and let these animals torture him. You're a god damn disgrace."

"What about our deal?" Sykes asked.

"No deal," Daniels said. "Get him out of here."

- - -

Sykes was dragged out of the cellblock by the FBI agents. Daniels remained behind with Jon, telling the agents she needed a moment to herself. When they were gone, she buried her head in Jon's chest, and wept.

"Sykes could have done something. He could have helped my dad," she cried.

"I'm sorry, Beth. At least now we know the truth," he said.

"When you were hitting him, I was thinking, Please kill him. Please."

"But then you would have arrested me."

Jon held her with one arm. In his other hand was his cell phone, which he punched a number into. In a rage, she tore the device from his hand, and tossed it onto the floor.

"How can you be so heartless?" she said.

"There's no time to waste. We have to move quickly."

"What are you talking about?"

He retrieved the cell phone and finished dialing the number.

"Put that damn thing away!" she said.

He had to leave a message. "Carlo, this is your old buddy Jon. I need help. Call me ASAP." He pocketed the phone and gave her his full attention. "Pull yourself together."

"Don't talk to me like that."

"You're letting your emotions mess with your head. Why did we pull this routine on Sykes? Why didn't your team just arrest him, and interrogate him normally? Because we were threatened last night, and we determined the threat was real."

Daniels blinked. "We didn't ask Sykes about that."

"We didn't have to. He already gave us the target."

She brought her hand to her mouth. "Nicki?"

"Correct. Katya stole your niece's information off your father's computer, which I'm sure included Nicki's physical address. That's how Carrie plans to rip our hearts out. She's going to tell the Russians to go after your niece."

"But they're blackmailers. Killing kids isn't what they do."

"Normally I'd agree with you, but this situation is different. I shot Bogdan's little brother, and he's not going to let that score go unsettled."

Daniels wiped away her tears. "I'll call my sister now. I'm sorry I yelled at you."

He got a call and answered it. "Hey, Carlo. Some friends of mine need protection. Are you available?" He placed the phone against his chest. "Give me Melanie's address."

CHAPTER 43

"Do I look okay?" Beth asked.

They were outside the Booty Call, a sleazy strip club in Fort Lauderdale, basking in the lurid pink neon sign that flashed GIRLS! GIRLS! GIRLS! to passing motorists. It was past midnight, the middle of the week, and business was slow, the lot only a third full. A few miles away, Carlo and his men were guarding Melanie and her family.

Beth had dressed down for the occasion, and wore tight-fitting jeans and plenty of makeup. It made her look sexy in a trashy way, not that Lancaster was going to tell her that.

"Perfect for the occasion," he said. "Is your team in place?"

"They were the last time I checked."

"Please check again. I don't want this blowing up in our faces."

Beth texted her team, and got an immediate response. "All set."

He offered her a stick of chewing gum, which she declined. "Think of it as part of your disguise," he said. She smiled, and moments later blew a large bubble.

They entered the club. A woman with enormous cleavage tried to collect the entrance fee. The music was deafening, and he had to shout in her ear.

"I'm here to see Sergey," he said.

"Nobody here by that name. Ten dollars a head," the woman said.

"Tell him Jon Lancaster wants to see him." He faced the security camera in the ceiling, and waved. "Hey, Sergey! I need to talk to you!" To the woman he said, "We go back a long way. Please tell him."

The woman slid off her stool and moved to the other side of the lobby. She made a call on her cell phone while her back was turned.

Beth leaned into him. "How do you know this guy?"

"He was a snitch that I used a few times."

"He won't be suspicious?"

"On the contrary, he should be happy to see me."

The last time he'd gotten together with Sergey, the diminutive Russian gangster was being squeezed by a pair of drug-dealing Broward County detectives who were forcing his dancers to move cocaine being stolen out of the sheriff's stockade. Sergey was a seasoned criminal, and knew the score. While these types of arrangements were lucrative on the front end, they often proved deadly, as bad cops were known to put bullets into their partners if things broke bad. Lancaster had worked his magic, and gotten the smuggling operation shut down, forever earning Sergey's love.

"We're buds," he added.

The woman returned. "Sergey says ten minutes. Go have a drink. You still got to pay me."

"In your dreams," he said.

- - -

Entering the club was like a descent into hell. The pulsating music made his head throb, and the strobe light hurt his eyes. The girls dancing naked on the elevated stage looked strung out, their faces emotionless.

He did a head count while paying for their drinks. Fourteen guys drank at the bar, six more around the club. There was a bouncer built like a linebacker, and two male bartenders. If his memory served him correctly, two of Sergey's thugs hung out in back, and would enter the club in case of trouble. The magic number of bad guys was five.

He watched the girls doing pole dances while counting his change. Had their parents envisioned this when they'd signed their little darlings up for gymnastics or dance school? Probably not. He found Beth waiting in a booth.

"Cheers," he said, clinking glasses.

"What kind of wine is this?" she asked.

"It's a patriotic place. Red, white, and blue wine. I got you red."

"Thanks. None of the dancers look like the girls that the Sokolov brothers brought to Saint Augustine to work their scam."

"How can you be so sure?"

"They aren't showing any Latin Kings tattoos."

He sipped his beer. When working a case, they complemented each other; the things he missed, Beth picked up on. If the relationship didn't work out, he supposed they could open a private investigation firm once she grew tired of the FBI's bullshit. The Donna Summer song ended, and the stage lights began to flash.

"Fire drill?" she asked.

"They're about to switch dancers. It keeps the customers interested."

"Do you have a membership?"

If you wanted to solve cases in south Florida, you had to frequent the bars and clubs. The patrons and employees were great sources of information, and could be persuaded to talk for a few drinks, or a generous tip.

"I get around," he replied.

The new lineup pranced onto the stage, and started bumping and grinding. His eyes locked on the last girl in the line.

"Lissette Diaz just came in. Last girl on the left," he said.

"I'm not seeing the right tattoo," Beth said.

"Hold on."

He went to the bar and ordered a gin and tonic. While the bartender did the mixing, he edged up to the stage, holding a twenty in his hand. He motioned to the dancer he believed was Lissette. She came over in a flash.

"This is for you," he said.

"Want to stick it in my G-string?" she asked.

"From behind. I'm an ass man," he said.

She giggled and spun around. As he slipped the currency into the purple floss separating her cheeks, he got a good close-up of her back. On her right shoulder was the distinct Latin Kings tattoo, covered by a heavy application of makeup. It made sense. A lot of guys hit on dancers in clubs, but no guy would hit on a girl who was part of a gang.

Lissette spun around, blew him a kiss, and pranced away. He paid for the drink and returned to the booth. Beth wore a wry smile.

"Looks like you made a new friend," she said.

"It's her," he said.

- - -

The club bouncer approached their booth. No neck, refrigerator body. It was the same thug whose thumb Lancaster had torn up several months ago during an unpleasant encounter. The cast was gone, which was usually a good sign.

"How's your hand?" he asked.

The bouncer frowned. "I remember you."

"I'm Jon. This is Beth. Sorry, but I forgot your name."

"You're not funny."

"Don't be a hater."

The bouncer motioned for them to follow him. Lancaster found it amusing that Sergey had sent the same thug that he'd roughed up. He guessed that Sergey was trying to teach the guy a lesson, which seemed to be the Russian way of doing things.

Sergey's office befitted a corporate CEO. Mammoth desk, a large wall covered in HD video monitors, and the newest addition—a portable bar. The little gangster sat in a swivel chair, staring intensely at the monitors.

"Make yourselves comfortable," he said without turning around. "Andres, make our visitors a drink. What is your pleasure?"

There was a sitting area next to the desk. Beth plopped down on the leather couch and got comfortable. "I could use a scotch, straight up."

Lancaster sat next to her. "Beer works for me. A cold glass, if you have it."

Andres's eyes flared, and he started to say something. His judgment got the better of him, and his angry response stayed buried. Sergey told him to shut the door after the drinks were served. Andres gave them a parting scowl.

Lancaster raised his glass to his lips. A tiny particle dislodged off the bottom and rose to the top, where it fizzled and popped. It could have been nothing, or it could have been a knockout drug. Revenge being a dish best served cold, he placed the glass on the coffee table. Beth did the same with her drink.

"How's business?" he asked.

"My employees are robbing me blind," their host replied. "The bartenders steal from the till, the girls take whatever isn't nailed down. I'd like to shoot all of them, but then I'd have to shut down. Who is your lady friend? What does she do?"

"My name's Elizabeth, and I'm a dancer," Beth said.

"Wonderful. Two dancers quit at my other club. When can you start?"

"How about tomorrow night?"

"You have yourself a deal."

Lancaster had thought the Booty Call was Sergey's only operation. Perhaps the other members of the Latin Kings were dancing at the second club, instead of here with Lissette. He grabbed his beer and edged up to Sergey's chair.

"I thought this was your only club," he said casually. "Did you expand?"

"Yes, and I'm getting ripped off there as well."

Sergey pointed a remote at the monitors. One by one, the screens changed, showing the interior of the second club. It was smaller, with a horseshoe-shaped stage, and a bar running against the wall. Two Hispanic dancers were bumping and grinding for the sparse crowd. It was all about tips, and their G-strings were hurting for cash. In desperation, one girl got on her knees, and ran her tongue against her partner's buttocks. Her shoulder turned to the camera, exposing the Latin Kings branding.

"What's your new club called?" Lancaster asked.

Sergey did not respond. Lancaster waited a beat before looking at his host. The Russian gangster was staring at Beth with a murderous intensity.

"She's a cop, isn't she?" he said, seething.

"How could you tell?"

"She doesn't look like a slut."

Beth rose, and flashed her credentials. "FBI. Jon tells me you're a reasonable guy. Play ball with us, and we'll go light on you. Our interest is with your partners."

"You come into my club, and threaten me? Big mistake." Sergey's hand fell onto the laptop on his desk. His fingers were a blur. "I'm alerting my men."

"So am I." Beth sent a text on her cell phone. "You lose. See for yourself."

Sergey switched monitors back to the Booty Call. The patrons had subdued the bouncers and bartenders, and were handcuffing them. They'd slapped badges onto their shirts, and several were wielding firearms. Sergey's men were outnumbered three to one.

"Those are your men," Sergey said.

"Good deduction," Beth said.

"Why didn't you tell me?"

"And lose the element of surprise? I wasn't born last night, asshole. You're under arrest. Put your hands where I can see them."

Andres entered the office without knocking. "We are under siege."

"Go in there and fight them!" Sergey roared.

"I quit," the bouncer said, and walked out.

CHAPTER 44

The willingness of a suspect to talk was directly related to the number of charges against them. In Lissette Diaz's case, this included blackmail, extortion, and prostitution, which combined could land her ten to fifteen years in the big house.

Lissette was led out of the Booty Call with the other dancers, and made to get into a van. She wore a baggy sweatshirt and shorts, her wrists shackled. She looked scared.

"What do you think? Will she talk?" Daniels asked.

They were standing in the parking lot beneath the cloudless night sky. Jon had grabbed a fresh beer from the bar in Sergey's office, and it was nearly gone. He waited until Lissette was in a van before replying. "It all depends on how we squeeze her."

"You have something in mind?"

Jon explained his plan. It was sneaky, and just might do the trick.

"I'm in," she said.

"Let her sit for a few minutes. Then pull her out."

"Why? To torture her?"

"She's done time. Let her remember what it's like not to have your freedom."

- - -

They took her to a swanky gastropub that stayed open late and served pricy pub grub and endless refills of a local brew called Funky Buddha. They let her order off the menu, and she picked the calamari tower and beef sliders appetizers. It was an hour before closing, and the place was quiet. The waiters and waitresses stood at the bar, chatting away.

Their drinks came. Lissette had ordered an IPA with a high alcohol content. Daniels hated the bitter taste of IPAs, and she'd decided that they were popular because they got you drunk quicker. Her phone vibrated. It was Melanie. She excused herself and walked away to take the call.

"Hey! Are you okay?" she asked.

"We're fine. Carlo handed us off to your team, and they put us in a suite at the Bahia Mar," Melanie said. "Nicki keeps sneaking outside to the hallway to talk to the agents standing guard."

"About what?"

"She wants to become an FBI agent. Please tell me you'll talk her out of it."

"Do you really think she'll listen to me?"

"Well, she certainly won't listen to me."

"I'll try. Is that why you called?"

"Always cutting to the chase. No, I called because I wanted to see how your investigation was going. Are we going to be able to go home anytime soon?"

"I sure hope so. I'm interrogating a suspect right now. I'll call you in the morning, and give you an update."

"Our father really screwed up, didn't he?"

Daniels wiped away a tear. "Dad got caught up in a bad situation. I'm not going to blame him for what happened, and neither should you. He was human."

"Thanks, Beth. Good luck with your interrogation."

Daniels returned to the table. The food had arrived, the calamari a tower of fried seafood doused in a magic sauce, the sliders sizzling hot.

Lissette ate her fill and wiped her mouth with a napkin. "I'm twenty-five years old, and I've been in jail four times," she confessed. "You tell me what you want to know, and I'll give it to you."

It was a wonderful opening line, but Lissette's sincerity was in doubt. Taking out her cell phone, Daniels pulled up a video of Sykes giving a taped confession at the FBI's Jacksonville office. Sykes's clothes were rumpled, and he sported gray stubble on his chin that clashed with his jet-black hair. She stuck the phone in Lissette's face.

"Let's start from the beginning," Daniels said.

Lissette's playful demeanor evaporated. "You arrested Sykes?"

"I'll ask the questions. But yes, we did arrest Sykes. And he was smart enough to give us a full confession. You're in a world of trouble, Lissette."

Lissette placed her hand against her chest in surprise. "What did I do?"

"You brought those girls from the Latin Kings gang to Saint Augustine for the purpose of blackmailing a bunch of rich old men," Daniels said. "That's human trafficking. Each girl you brought will bring you ten years in prison. Add five more years for extortion and prostitution, and you're looking at over thirty years."

Daniels had overstated the crimes against Lissette, which was part of the ruse. Lissette brought her napkin to her mouth. She looked ready to puke. "Did Sykes tell you that?" she asked accusingly.

"Yes. He said you were running the operation, " Daniels said.

"He's lying."

"Why would Sykes lie to us? What did he have to gain?"

"Sykes hates me. He fell in love with me, and wants to pay me back."

"If you weren't running the operation, then who was?"

"Katya."

"Who?"

"He didn't tell you about Katya?"

Daniels shook her head. She looked at Jon, and he also shook his head. This was Jon's gambit—to pretend they didn't know about Katya, and make Lissette believe that Sykes had implicated her in crimes she hadn't committed. Lissette threw her napkin onto her plate and looked ready to explode.

"That fucking prick! He's trying to destroy me!"

The waitstaff grew quiet, and stared at them. Daniels lowered her voice. "Why don't you give us your side of things, then?"

"My pleasure," Lissette said.

\- - -

Daniels's cell phone had a special app that let her record conversations. She hit the button and positioned the cell phone so the speaker was pointing at their suspect.

"Start from the beginning," she said.

"I met Katya while I was in jail," Lissette said. "The gang I ran with threw me away, and she recruited me."

"What do you mean, they threw you away?"

"I joined the Latin Kings when I was fifteen. I became one of their girls, and worked as a prostitute. When I turned twenty-four, they cut me loose, along with two other girls. We went out on our own, and got busted. That's when I met Katya."

"What was she in jail for?"

"Weed."

Lissette explained how she and her friends became strippers at the Booty Call, and how after a few months, Katya introduced them to the Sokolov brothers, who talked them into blackmailing a bunch of rich old geezers in Saint Augustine. Her story was identical to the one Sykes had told, leading Daniels to believe it was true.

"Katya ran the show," Lissette said. "Me and my friends were just . . ."

"Pawns," Jon said.

"Yeah—we were pawns. She used us. Story of my life."

"Okay. So Katya recruited the older men that you and your friends had sex with," Daniels said. "How did that work?"

"Katya introduced us to these old rich guys at different bars, and we'd take them back to the house, and screw their brains out. Katya was wired, which made it easy."

"What do you mean, she was wired?"

"Katya had a lover named Martin. I think he was a doctor or something. Martin was a cool guy, and had a bunch of rich friends. Katya used him to get to the friends."

"Tell us about Martin," Jon said.

"He was a widower, had a lot of money. Katya said he was lonely."

"Was Katya in love with him?"

"No. Katya used him. That was how she was. Hardest bitch I've ever known."

The words gave Daniels pause. Her father had been played. It wasn't a complete surprise; growing up, he'd empty his wallet to beggars with hard-luck stories, then hit up an ATM so he could pay for dinner. He was vulnerable to a fault, which she'd always found endearing, until now.

"Was Martin blackmailed as well?" Jon asked.

"Yes," Lissette said. "He didn't want to pay at first, and even went to the police. But eventually he caved and paid up. Katya boasted to us when she got her cut. Said she was going to buy a new car when she got home."

"How much was her cut?" Jon asked.

"Fifty grand. That was the Sokolovs' deal. We'd get twenty percent of the money when the geezers paid up."

Daniels glanced at Jon. He was frowning. They were thinking the same thing. If $50,000 was 20 percent, then the total was $250,000. Yet $1.2 million was missing from her father's bank account. Where had the rest of it gone?

"Did you know that Martin committed suicide last week as a result of being blackmailed by Katya and the Sokolovs?" Jon asked.

Lissette's face crashed. It was the kind of emotion you couldn't fake.

"I didn't know," she said.

"These are horrible crimes," Jon said, boring down on her. "People's lives are being ruined because you and your friends took advantage of them."

"I was just a pawn."

"Prove it."

Lissette lifted her hands in a helpless gesture. "How am I going to do that?"

"We want Katya. Tell us how to find her, and we'll cut you the sweetest deal you've ever seen. If not, you'll go down for her crimes."

"That's not fair."

Jon rubbed his two fingers together. "That's the world's smallest violin. Take it, or leave it."

Lissette fell silent. As a member of the Latin Kings, she'd been indoctrinated in a code that prohibited her from snitching on another criminal, even if that criminal was her worst enemy. The police were the real enemy, and she wasn't supposed to help them.

Except the Latin Kings had cut her loose. Had she aged out from being a prostitute? If that was the case, then she owed her former gang nothing. Daniels tried to read her face, but couldn't tell what she was thinking. A gentle nudge was in order.

"The restaurant's going to close soon," Daniels said. "What do you want to do?"

CHAPTER 45

Lissette sang like a canary. Katya and Bogdan were hiding out in a boat at the Bahia Mar Yachting Center, and they were planning to motor over to the Bahamas in a few days and stay there until the dust settled.

The irony was not lost on Lancaster. Beth had moved Melanie and her family to a suite at the Bahia Mar, thinking they would be safe. Instead, she'd brought Melanie that much closer to the person who wished to harm her daughter.

They took Lissette to the police station on Broward Boulevard and booked her, then drove to the Bahia Mar. During the drive, Beth called the chief of the FBI's North Miami office, and requested a team. Hanging up, she called her sister.

"We need to move you again," she said. "I'll explain when we get there."

The Bahia Mar was a landmark, known for housing spring breakers and being the fictional home of Fort Lauderdale's most intrepid sleuth, Travis McGee. Lancaster waited in the car while Beth went inside and brought Melanie and her family downstairs.

From where he sat, he could see the yachting center. It was the size of a small city, and the chances of Bogdan venturing into the hotel and running across Melanie or her family were slim. But it still could happen, and they needed to take every precaution.

"The bad guy is staying in the yachting center?" Nicki said breath-lessly. "Can we stay, and watch you arrest him? It would be way cool."

Nicki was sandwiched between her parents in the back seat. Beth spun around, and gave her a freezing look. "You can't be serious."

"I've never seen a bust before. I could do a presentation at school, and explain how it went down," Nicki said.

"Were you planning to take a video on your phone?"

"That's a great idea. I could shoot it from the hotel balcony, and give a running commentary."

"This man is armed and dangerous," Beth said. "You will be nowhere near the yachting center when he's arrested."

"Do you think there will be a shootout?"

"That's enough, young lady," her mother scolded her.

- - -

Lancaster stayed in the car while Beth moved her sister's family into the Courtyard by Marriott on A1A. He was a fan of Travis McGee, and had read all of the McGee novels with their color-laden titles. While he'd enjoyed them, the stories rarely resembled the real world, where lingering questions remained after a case was solved. Lisette had said that Martin had paid $250,000 to the Sokolov brothers, yet $1.2 million was missing from Martin's bank accounts. Somehow, nearly $1 million had disappeared, and he had a feeling that they might never learn where it had gone.

Beth got in the car and slammed the door.

"My niece is driving me crazy," she said. "Let's go."

He headed south on A1A. "May I make a suggestion?"

"Go ahead."

"Take Nicki to a firing range, and spend an afternoon target shooting."

"And what will that accomplish?"

"It will humble her. Hitting a target is hard, and most people can't do it. She'll fail, and it will bring her down to earth. Then you'll be able to reason with her."

She leaned over and kissed his cheek. "That's not a bad idea. Thank you."

– – –

The team from the FBI's North Miami office was jammed into the harbormaster's office in the Bahia Mar Yachting Center when they arrived. There were six agents, four males and two females, with sidearms strapped to their sides. The harbormaster, a bronze-skinned, chainsmoking lady named Camille, had an open log on her desk.

"This is high season. I've got two hundred and fifty boats docked here," Camille said, her face enveloped in a bluish cloud. "You need to do better than the owner's name if I'm going to find the one you're looking for."

"He's Russian," Beth said. "Does that help?"

"Do you know how many Russians have boats docked here? Fort Lauderdale is every oligarch's playground during the winter. Over fifty have Russian ties, and they all use company names to rent slips. I need more information to find this guy."

Lancaster thought back to their conversation with Lissette. She'd told them that Bogdan's boat was named after his mistress, and he wondered if they'd misunderstood her. Taking out his cell phone, he typed the words "Russian" and "mistress" into Google. A long list of porn sites came up featuring Russian ladies engaged in female domination, and he scrolled down before finding a site with a literal translation. The word *kira* meant ruler and mistress in Russian.

"Is there a boat docked here named *Kira*?" he asked.

Camille ran her finger down a column in the log. "Yes, sir. It's in slip 142. It's registered to a company called Kompromat."

Another search revealed that the word *kompromat* was defined as damaging information used for blackmail and extortion. Bogdan had a warped sense of humor.

"That's our guy," he said.

- - -

The yachting center was so large that they needed a map to find Bogdan's yacht, which Camille drew up for them. Lancaster inquired about the yachts moored to either side of the *Kira*, and learned that both were owned by Europeans staying in the hotel.

It was four a.m. when they left the harbormaster's office, and the yachting center was dark. Night arrests were never easy, and Beth marched her team back to the parking lot and had them suit up in body armor, in case Bogdan decided to go out in a blaze of glory.

She offered Lancaster a vest, and he declined.

"It will only slow me down," he said.

"Put it on, anyway. I don't want you getting shot on my watch," she said.

Her voice was stern, and he reminded himself that Beth was in charge. As he suited up, she addressed the team. "Jon's been here before, so I thought it would be best if he explained what to expect," she said.

The six agents turned to face him.

"The yacht center is forty acres, and it's easy to get lost," he said. "There's a three-thousand-foot parallel dock, and another five thousand feet of floating docks. Based upon the harbormaster's map, Bogdan Sokolov's boat is moored on the parallel dock, which isn't well lit. I'll lead the way, if you want."

The team seemed good with his offer.

Beth said, "You're on."

Everyone drew their firearms, and headed down the dock. Over the years he'd experimented with different makes of concealed weapons, and kept coming back to the Glock 26. It could be hidden anywhere on his body, and packed a mean punch.

The dock's boards groaned beneath their feet. Where was a loud, annoying sea gull when you needed one? Many of the vessels were of the mega variety, with interiors larger than most homes and full-time crews. Living in Fort Lauderdale his entire life, he'd been exposed to the rich and famous, who vacationed here during the winter to escape the cold. He'd never experienced wealth-envy, except when he was around yachts like these. They cost more than a private island, yet from what he'd seen, they were hardly used. He wondered who the owners were trying to impress, or if they just liked squandering their money.

They passed a yacht where an all-night party was underway, complete with waiters in tuxedos serving drinks, and a woman in a white evening gown plucking a harp. The music was soothing, the notes dancing lightly across the water. There was enough light coming from the vessel for him to read the slip's number.

"We're getting close," he said under his breath.

Beth and her team were right behind him.

"Have you ever boarded a boat during a bust?" she asked.

"I once boarded a boat owned by a drug dealer, and nearly got shot," he said. "My footsteps gave me away. The harbormaster said that the yachts adjacent to the *Kira* are empty. I suggest we board them, and see if we can spot Bogdan inside his vessel. That way, he won't be able to blindside us."

"Sounds like a plan."

They soon reached the *Kira*. He'd been expecting a yacht with all the amenities, and was disappointed to find an old houseboat. They were a familiar sight on the Intercoastal waterways, and usually filled with partiers. This model was sixteen feet wide and sixty feet long, with a rooftop bar with a canvas top, a flybridge, and twin 90-horsepower Yamaha outboard engines. The windows were dark, with no signs of life.

Beth split her team in two. The agents boarded the adjacent vessels, and used small flashlights to peer into the *Kira*'s interior. The intrusion of light was greeted by a soft crying sound, which everyone heard.

"Sounds like a dog," Beth said under her breath.

"Can't be," he whispered back.

"People that own boats don't have guard dogs?"

"Some do, but they take them with them when they go on shore. If they don't, the dog might jump in the water, and drown."

The crying grew louder. A word became discernable. *Help.*

"Where is that coming from?" she asked her team.

One of the agents pointed at an open window in the center of the boat.

"It's coming from here," the agent said.

"Can you see what's inside?"

"No. There's a sheet over the window."

"We're boarding. Cover us," Beth said.

They hopped over the guardrail onto the flybridge, and cautiously approached a sliding glass door covered by a curtain. The door was locked, and Beth used the butt of her gun to break the glass. She fitted her hand through, and unlocked the door.

"Going in," she announced.

- - -

Jon followed her, and hit the light switch. They were in the galley. The sink was stuffed with dirty dishes, the garbage pail overflowing. The crying had stopped.

Beth walked out of the galley down a hallway. It had doors to either side, and she opened the first one, and flipped on the light. It was a small room with a queen-size bed and a night table. Like the rest of the boat, it had zero personality, the walls without photographs or artwork.

She opened the other doors off the hallway, revealing more bedrooms. The last door was locked, and she put her ear to the wood.

"I hear something. Sounds like a moan," she said.

"Want me to take the door down?" he asked.

"Be my guest."

He threw his weight against the door and popped a hinge. The rest was easy, and he removed the door and placed it in the hallway. Beth entered cautiously and turned on the light. The room was empty save for a woman bound to a metal chair. Chains circled her ankles, and were attached to thick concrete blocks. A plastic bag covered her, held down by a bungee cord. Self-preservation is our greatest instinct, and the woman had sucked the bag into her mouth, and gnawed holes into the plastic with her teeth. The holes were tiny, and she was barely breathing.

Lancaster undid the bungee cord and removed the bag. The woman's hair was matted against her forehead, hiding her face, and he wiped it away. It was Katya. He gave her a gentle slap, and her eyes popped open.

"Remember us?" Beth asked.

Her chest heaved up and down. "You're Martin's daughter."

"That's right. Did Bogdan do this to you?"

"Yes. He killed the others as well."

"What others?"

"He shot the Vasileks and the other Russians who were working with them. He apologized before he shot them, said he needed to tie up loose ends."

"That was nice of him. Where is he?"

Katya clamped her mouth shut. Russian criminals were a strange breed. Their allegiance to their partners was sacrosanct, even when their partners turned on them.

"Why are you holding back? He tried to murder you. He's not your friend."

"And neither are you! I want a lawyer."

A thundercloud passed over Beth's face. She looked ready to scream, and she looked to Lancaster for help. Beth was bound to a set of rules that he'd abandoned a long time ago.

"Leave us alone," he said.

Beth's eyes narrowed. "Why? What are you going to do?"

"I'm going to charm her into telling me."

"What the hell does that mean?"

"It means, go into the hall, and make sure none of your team comes in here."

"You can't lay a hand on her, Jon."

"No scars?"

"This isn't a game."

"Please go into the hall. This won't take long."

The battle was always the same. Beth's conscience wrestling with her heart. This time, her heart won out, and she marched out of the room.

- - -

"Last chance. Are you going to tell me where Bogdan is?" he asked.

Katya hissed at him like a snake. "Screw you."

"Wrong answer."

He placed the plastic bag over Katya's head so the punctured side was in back, and secured it around her neck with the bungee cord. When she tried to scream, he put his hand around her throat and squeezed. Her eyes bulged. He bid her goodbye in Russian.

"Dasvidaniya."

She torqued violently in her chair. Her breathing, at first frantic, began to diminish. He leaned in, and stared at her through the plastic. Their eyes locked.

"Be smart. Save yourself."

He released his grip on her throat. When no response was forth-coming, he said, "Lissette told us where to find you. She sold you out. She was the smart one."

Katya looked at him differently through the plastic. Had she and Lissette not gotten along? They were both young and beautiful, and there was every reason to think that jealousy had played a role in their relationship. It was worth a shot. Taking out his cell phone, he pulled up the photograph he'd surreptitiously snapped of Lissette eating dinner a few short hours ago, her chin greasy with food, and showed it to her.

"Lissette cut a deal, and now she's free. Tell me where Bogdan is, and you'll walk out of here. Hell, I'll even buy you dinner. What do you say?"

Katya was hardly breathing. A sound escaped her lips that sounded like yes. He undid the bungee cord and pulled away the bag. She spent a few moments sucking down air.

"Out with it," he said.

"Bogdan is in the hotel, top floor, room 1801," she said.

He started to leave. She shrieked indignantly. "Let me go. That was our deal."

"I lied," he said.

CHAPTER 46

The Bahia Mar was an iconic South Florida landmark, which was a nice way of saying that it sorely needed a facelift. Daniels stood at the front desk with the sleepy-eyed night manager, a middle-aged Cuban who'd been napping when she walked in.

"What room is he in?" the night manager asked.

"1801. Last name Sokolov."

The night manager two-finger typed an ancient computer. "Here we go. Bogdan Sokolov. He's a regular guest, and has a boat docked in our marina."

"That's our man."

"May I ask why you're looking for him?"

"No, you may not. Is there any way to know if he's in his room?"

"There most certainly is." He typed another command. "Whenever a guest enters their room, it registers on our system. They're called door counters. We installed them to stop kids here on spring break from holding parties in their rooms. Okay. According to the system, the door to 1801 was opened at 2:37 a.m."

She checked the time. It was 4:39 a.m. Two hours ago.

"Can you tell me if he was coming, or going?"

"Sure. We can review the surveillance video from the hallway." He exited the screen and opened up another application. "I'll bet you a dollar he's dealing drugs."

"Why do you say that?"

"I work nights, and see him come in with young girls. They're always messed up. I assumed he was picking them up in a bar, getting them high, and bringing them here."

"Did you ever think of reporting him?"

"To who?"

"The police?"

"The police are bad for business. I could get fired if I did that."

A surveillance video taken in the hallway outside room 1801 appeared on the computer's screen. It was of poor quality, and she squinted to read the time stamp in the bottom right-hand corner. It was the same time the night manager had said.

The video ran for thirty seconds before Bogdan and a young girl wearing skintight jeans and a halter top appeared. The girl had whiskey legs and was holding on to Bogdan for dear life. He kissed her on the mouth before keying the door. They both went in.

"Let me see that again," she said.

The night manager replayed the video. As Daniels watched, she created an order of events. Bogdan had tied up Katya and put a plastic bag over her head. Rather than watch her die, he'd left the marina and gone to a bar, where he'd picked up a floozy, fed her drugs, and brought her to his room. Most people who committed murder felt some kind of remorse. Not this animal.

"Thank you," she said.

- - -

Her team stood by the bank of elevators. The elevators were small, and she decided they would take two to the eighteenth floor.

Jon stood off to the side. He understood that he wouldn't be joining them. He deserved to go—without his help, they wouldn't have found Bogdan—but having a nonagent on the bust was against bureau rules.

"I'm sorry, but you need to stay here," she said.

"Maybe I can get a beer at the bar," he said.

"You're not mad, are you?"

"At you? Never. I'd just like to see his face when you break down the door."

"I'll describe it to you later over a drink."

She squeezed his arm and went to join her team. There were three agents in each of the two elevators. She got on with the team that had the battering ram. The door slid shut and the car ascended, the cables creaking as they rose.

"This elevator is older than me," an agent with gray hair quipped.

The cars arrived simultaneously on the eighteenth floor. The first team checked out the hallway, and confirmed that it was empty. Daniels motioned for the agent with the battering ram to take down the door. Suddenly, a man in pajamas holding an ice bucket emerged from a room. His eyes went wide.

"FBI," Daniels said. "Make yourself scarce."

The man returned to his room and silently shut the door.

"Do it," she said.

The door to Bogdan's room was of the same vintage as the elevator, and imploded from a single hit. They entered with their weapons drawn. The room was a studio with a balcony that faced the ocean. Bogdan and his lady lay naked on the bed, smoking a joint.

"You're under arrest," Daniels said.

Bogdan crushed the joint into an ashtray before getting out of the bed. His body was a carnival of tattoos, and it was hard to tell where they ended, and his actual flesh began. He lifted his arms into the air to show that he didn't have a gun. There was one hidden somewhere in the room; Daniels could feel it in her gut.

"Freeze!" she said.

Bogdan shuffled backward. He said something in Russian, pretending that he didn't understand English. His lady friend pulled the sheet up over her head.

"Stop moving."

Bogdan ignored her, and kept retreating. There was a hideous scorpion tattoo over where his heart was. Daniels aimed at it.

"Is this how you want to go out?"

More Russian came out of his mouth.

"I know you speak English," she said. "Clasp your hands behind your head, and get on your knees. So help me God, do it!"

Bogdan stopped moving. He smiled, unafraid.

"Would you really shoot an unarmed man?" he asked in perfect English.

"I have before," she replied.

His smile vanished. "Then why don't you do it?"

"Because that's not what I'm planning to do. We have enough evidence to put you away for a long time. I've already got your prison picked out."

The cocky expression left his face. "Where is that?"

"It's a supermax prison in the Rocky Mountains called ADX Florence. Twenty-three hours a day in a sound-proof cell. No phone, no TV. You'll go crazy in no time."

"You would like that, wouldn't you?" he snarled.

"Nothing would make me happier."

"Well, I am sorry to disappoint you."

Before she could reply, Bogdan turned around, and walked onto the balcony. It was a still night, and no one had realized that the slider was open. Reaching the guardrail, he put his hands over his head as if preparing to dive, and pitched himself over. Daniels got there just in time to see the impact.

Rot in hell, she thought.

CHAPTER 47

They stayed up all night searching the *Kira* for evidence. The Sokolovs had blackmailed scores of elderly men, and Lancaster knew that a notebook or digital device with records of the money they'd extorted from their victims had to exist. But as hard as they looked, Beth and her team couldn't find it.

"God damn it," she swore. "Their records must be somewhere."

Lancaster stood on the dock. He'd abstained from the search for the same reason he hadn't helped with the bust. Bureau rules.

"You need to take a break," he said.

"Don't tell me what to do," she snapped.

"But I have coffee."

"Why didn't you say so?"

She joined him on the dock, and he handed her a steaming cup of coffee he'd bought from a vending machine next to the harbormaster's office. She sipped it, said, "That tastes awful," and downed the rest. Her shoulders were sagging from an invisible weight, and he wondered if she'd hurt herself, then realized it was exhaustion.

"I'm going to find those records if it kills me," she said.

The investigation was over, only it wasn't over. Nearly $1 million from Martin's bank account was still unaccounted for. Like a jigsaw puzzle with a hole, the final piece needed to be found before the puzzle could be put in its box and stored away.

"You need some sleep. Come on, Beth. Take a break."

"Not on your life," she said.

- - -

There was no better sunrise than the one Lancaster saw that morning. It broke the ocean's surface with the fury of a newborn planet, the night sky and all its stars vanishing in the blink of an eye. Beth and her team were still hunting for the Sokolovs' bank records, their voices carrying from different parts of the houseboat. He had stayed up because that was what men in love did, no matter how futile the search may be.

He would have bet good money the records weren't on the boat. He didn't know why he knew this, but he did. The money was safely tucked away in an offshore bank account, or a safe deposit box, and would probably get moldy before it was discovered.

Beth appeared on the flybridge, looking as good as a person could look when they hadn't slept. She jumped onto the dock, holding her cell phone.

"You can't be serious." Beth had different tones of voice. This was her Melanie tone, used exclusively when talking to her sister. "Did you tell her no?"

He smelled roasting coffee. A roach coach had appeared next to the harbormaster's office. He was their very first customer of the day.

When he returned, Beth was still on with Melanie. He shredded the paper bag and handed her a coffee and a fresh Danish. She covered the mouthpiece.

"I need real food. Where are you taking me for breakfast?"

"Now you're talking," he said.

- - -

James Swain

They walked up the street to the Casablanca Café. Over the years, different immigrants had run the place, first Cubans, then Venezuelans, and now Brazilians, who were some of the friendliest people he'd ever encountered, their smiles wide and genuine. They sat at a sidewalk table with an umbrella, and ate omelets while watching the dog walkers stroll by. The food had the desired effect, and calmed Beth down.

"Let me guess. Nicki is up to her old tricks," he said.

"I've created a monster," she said.

"What did she do this time?"

"I called Melanie and told her that Bogdan was no longer a threat, so she and Nolan checked out of their hotel and went home. During the drive, Nicki asked my sister if we'd figured out where her grandfather's missing money had gone."

"Why did you tell her about that?"

"I didn't, and neither did my sister. We're guessing she must have overheard one of our conversations, and surmised the rest. The kid is sharp."

"It's genetic. So what did Melanie tell her?"

"Melanie told her the truth, which is how she and Nolan are. So Nicki says, 'I bet I can figure out where the money went.' So of course my sister exploded."

"Why did she explode? We could use some help."

Beth's fork hit the plate. "What are you saying? That we should enlist Nicki's aid again? If you don't mind, I'd rather that Nicki forget about this."

An aging Labrador sauntered past, sniffing the ground for food. He'd had a Lab as a kid, and had a soft spot for the breed, so he slipped the pooch a hash brown.

"That's not going to happen, and you know it," he said. "Your niece likes to solve problems; that's why she's drawn to CSI work. Telling her no will only make her want to do it more. Why don't you let her loose, and see what she finds?"

If looks could kill, he would have been pushing up daisies.

"I don't think so," Beth said through clenched teeth.

"Did I say something wrong?"

"That would be an understatement."

"Will you tell me what?"

"Figure it out."

He picked at his food. Was Beth afraid that Nicki would find the money trail, and make her look bad in the process? Beth wasn't petty, and would have welcomed bringing the case to a close. No, there was something lurking beneath the surface that he wasn't seeing, and after a long, reflective moment, he realized what it was.

Beth was afraid of the unknown. If Nicki found the lost money, it might very well lead to another awful truth about Martin. Perhaps Martin had a harem of women he was supporting, or he'd gotten involved in another illegal activity. As adults, that kind of information was hard to take; for a teenager, it could be devastating. Better if Beth were to find where the money went, and come up with a story that she could tell her niece.

"I get it," he said. "I'm sorry."

"So what do I do?" she said.

"Tell Nicki that tracing bank records is off limits, and could land her in serious hot water, like getting expelled from school. She doesn't want that on her record, does she?"

"I like it. Can tracing bank records really land her in trouble?"

"I have no idea. But if you say it firmly enough, she'll believe you."

Beth got a call from her sister, and decided to take it on the sidewalk across the street, where there would be less chance of being overheard. Lancaster cleaned his plate, and accepted the waitress's offer of a refill on his coffee. His own cell phone started to make noise, and he glanced at its screen.

His newsfeed had sent him a breaking story. Reading it, his heart sank. A cop in north Florida had taken his own life. It was a sickening trend. More cops died by their own hand than in the line of duty. Exposure to trauma, accidents, and shootings led to mental health issues, which went unnoticed until it was too late. He'd lost several buddies this way, and always kicked himself for not being more aware of their anguish.

The story didn't offer many details, and left out the officer's name until next of kin were notified. He did a search, and found a more thorough report on a site called Patch. The officer was a thirty-year veteran who'd recently been suspended. Yesterday, the officer had posted a note on Facebook, and apologized to all his friends for the pain he'd caused them. Sometime after that, he doused the walls of his living room with gasoline, and set the place on fire. He parked himself in a recliner, and put a gun to his temple. With his home engulfed in flames, he ended his life.

It was how most cops checked out. With a gun.

The reporter had posted a video showing the smoldering remains of the house. It had been burned to the ground, with only the stone fireplace remaining.

The officer's car sat in the driveway. It had managed to escape the inferno, and was all that was left. It looked eerily familiar, and he called his friend at the Department of Motor Vehicles and did a quick check on the license plate.

Beth crossed the street and returned to the table. She took a hard look at him.

"You don't look well. What's wrong?" she asked.

"Sykes committed suicide last night," he said.

CHAPTER 48

"If Detective Sykes was such a terrible person, why wasn't he kept locked up?" Nicki asked that evening at the dining room table in her parents' home. "A guy like that shouldn't be walking around, should he?"

"He *was* in jail, but he made bail," Jon explained.

"Shouldn't the police have kept him in jail? He broke a lot of laws, didn't he?"

"Unfortunately, that's not how the system works," Jon said. "In the eyes of the law, a person is innocent until proven guilty. Unless the crimes the person committed are heinous, most judges will allow a suspect to stay out of jail until trial."

"Even really bad people?"

"Yes, even bad people."

"I think the judge made a mistake," Nicki said.

Daniels wiped her mouth with a napkin. The dinner had been delicious, her sister's culinary skills on full display. She didn't often feel jealous of Melanie, but this was one of those special times. Facing her niece, she said, "The judge set a very high bail. Sykes was able to pay it, so he was released."

Melanie served them dessert. Homemade crème brûlée.

"Do many people kill themselves after they pay bail?" Nicki asked.

They hadn't discussed the case over dinner, but instead had talked about Nolan's medical practice, and Melanie's volunteer work at the Shriners Hospital. The past two weeks had been rough, and it was time for the family to put things behind them.

"Some people do," Daniels said. "The director of the FBI's Jacksonville office told me that Sykes lost his daughter, and that he suffered from depression."

"Is that why he did it?" Nicki asked.

"That's what everyone I've spoken to thinks."

"But you can't be sure."

"You can never be one hundred percent sure. But it's a good assumption."

Daniels ate her dessert, hoping it would end the conversation.

"How much was the bail he had to pay?" Nicki asked.

Melanie and Nolan gave their daughter reprimanding looks. Nicki ignored them, and focused her attention on her aunt. She was like a dog with a bone, and wouldn't let go of something until her curiosity was satisfied. Jon stepped in.

"Why is that important?" he asked.

"You said his bail was high," Nicki said. "From what I've read about police work, it doesn't pay very well, and many policemen struggle financially. I was just wondering where he would have gotten the money to pay it."

Jon glanced across the table at her. The expression on his face said that Nicki had a valid point. Where had Sykes gotten the money to pay bail, and walk out of jail?

"His bail was three hundred and fifty thousand dollars," Daniels said.

"Wow. That's a lot of money. I wonder where it came from."

The dining room fell silent. Jon shrugged as if to say, Who the hell knows? It was yet another question that would probably go unanswered. Nicki spooned dessert into her mouth and emitted a happy noise.

"This is really good, Mom," she said.

- - -

Jon's ocean-facing apartment in downtown Fort Lauderdale was above most retired cops' pay grades. The building was new, and had plenty of modern conveniences, including a state-of-the-art security system and an emergency generator capable of keeping the place running for several days in case of a hurricane.

Jon's unit had two spacious bedrooms, a gourmet kitchen, and a balcony with an unobstructed view of the Atlantic. Hollywood had paid Jon big bucks for his life story, and he'd bought into the building while it was still under construction.

Everyone who lived in the building knew Jon, and they often leaned on him when there was a problem. As they waited for an elevator to arrive, an elderly man wearing tennis shorts and a floppy hat hurried over to them.

"Jon—just the man I was looking for. Got a minute?"

Marty was a transplanted New Yorker who ran off a different clock. For him, a minute was more like twenty, with Marty doing most of the talking.

"Sure, Marty. What's up?" Jon said.

"That whack-a-noodle on the moped was riding around on the property last night. He came right up behind my wife, and scared the daylights out of her."

"Did you call security?"

"By the time I did, he was gone. The guy's a menace."

The elevator had arrived. "I'll be up in a few," Jon said.

Daniels went up, and let herself in with the spare key. She poured herself a glass of white wine, and went onto the balcony with her laptop. Nicki's comments about Sykes's high bail had gotten the wheels turning. Was Sykes's $350,000 bail part of her father's missing money? If so, then Sykes wasn't a victim like he'd so adamantly claimed.

The FBI's Jacksonville office had sent her the crime scene report, and she decided to start there. Sykes's neighbor had smelled smoke and come outside to see the flames, so he'd called 911. By the time the fire trucks arrived, Sykes's house and its contents were destroyed. The firemen had later discovered Sykes's body beneath the rubble. The local pathologist had done an autopsy, and said that Sykes had died from a self-inflicted gunshot wound. The pathologist had ID'd the body using dental records.

The local cops had questioned the neighbor, who was the only witness. His name was Kyle Benn, and he was a retired postal worker, and a widower. Benn was part of the neighborhood watch group, and had told the police that he liked to sleep with his windows open, just in case there was a burglar canvassing his property.

Daniels immediately saw a discrepancy. Benn was a busybody, who knew his neighbors' business. So why hadn't he heard Sykes's gun discharge? Had his TV drowned out the sound? Or were their houses far apart, and the sound hadn't carried?

Those were two logical explanations. But was either correct?

She continued reading. Benn had given the police a chronology of his evening. Dinner at seven, walk the dog at eight, then read a book. That ruled out the blaring TV.

Benn's address was in the report. She googled it, and a photo taken from the street outside the house appeared. Benn lived in a modest ranch with a carport. His neighbors to either side were very close by.

She reread the pathologist's report. There was no doubt that the body was Sykes, and that he'd shot himself in the head. So why hadn't Benn heard the gunshot?

She got a call from Jon and answered it.

"I was just starting to worry about you," she said.

"The guy with the moped showed up," he explained. "Marty and I went outside to talk with him, and he bolted. We ran him down, and now we're waiting for the cops."

"Is he a threat?"

"I found a stun gun in his backpack. He might be a neighborhood vigilante, or he could be a stalker. I'm going to let the police deal with him."

"You didn't answer my question."

"Yes, I think he's a threat. He jumped at Marty like he wanted to kill him. As we used to say in the navy, he needs to be neutralized."

Jon never ran away from a fight. It was one of his more endearing qualities.

"I've been on my laptop, reading the police report of Sykes's suicide," she said. "Something isn't adding up. I want you to take a look at it later."

"Will do. A cruiser just pulled in. I'll be upstairs as soon as I can."

She disconnected. Sykes's address was also in the police report. On a hunch, she googled it, and a photo appeared on her screen. A typical ranch house on a small plot of land. The landscaping was immaculate, the shrubs neatly trimmed, and several mature oak trees in the yard afforded the dwelling plenty of shade. She went on Zillow and got an estimate of the house's worth in today's market, which was $200,000.

She poured another glass of wine and parked herself on the living room couch. Sykes appeared to live within his means, so how had he made bail? There was a chance he'd inherited money, but in her experience, financial windfalls usually led to upgrades, like new houses or major renovations. That wasn't the case here.

She sipped her wine. It wasn't adding up. She needed a fresh set of eyes to look at these reports.

Come on, Jon. Get your ass upstairs.

CHAPTER 49

Moped Man did not go quietly.

He had an outstanding warrant in Miami for indecent exposure and attempted rape, and the cops had to subdue him while reading him his rights. As their cruiser disappeared into the night, Marty examined the bike, which was in bad shape.

"Think I should throw it away?" his neighbor asked.

"I think you should pull the VIN number, and see if it's stolen," Lancaster said.

"But it's a piece of junk. The owner can't be missing it."

"The owner might be poor, and depend on this bike to get to work. If I'm right, you'll make the guy's day by returning it."

Marty patted him good-naturedly on the shoulder. "That's what I like about you, Jon. You're always looking out for the little guy."

His neighbor said goodnight and walked the bike into the building. Lancaster was about to follow when he got a text from Nicki, asking if he could talk. He suspected she meant without Beth being present, and he answered her with a simple yes. A moment later his phone rang, and he went into the lobby to answer it.

"Hey, there," he said. "Isn't this a school night?"

"I know, I should be doing my homework, but I needed to tell you something," the teenager said. "Please don't tell my aunt that I called you."

"You're putting me in a bad spot, Nicki. I don't keep secrets from Beth. I'm going to give you a pass this time, but in the future, this has to stop. Understood?"

"Yes, sir."

"Is that a promise?"

"Yes, it's a promise."

"Okay, now tell me what's on your mind."

"No one knows where my grandfather's money disappeared to. Well, I think that there are people who know, and that you and Aunt Beth never talked to them."

Her words stung. He tried to leave no stone unturned when working a case. Beth was equally thorough, and ignored little. Now Nicki was suggesting that they'd missed something important. It happened to the best investigators, and he swallowed his pride and said, "Who's that?"

"The other men that got dead hands put on their doorsteps," Nicki declared. "They were also being extorted, and were friends of my grandfather. They know."

"How can you be so sure?"

"Because my grandfather would have told one of them."

"You think so?"

"Yes. For my twelfth birthday, my grandfather gave me a copy of *The Three Musketeers*. On the title page he wrote an inscription that said, 'One for all, and all for one. Never forget that, Nicki!' He told me that a person could live by those words, and lead a meaningful life. My grandfather was loyal to his friends. They know."

Nicki was right; Martin's buddies probably knew where the missing money had disappeared to. But that didn't necessarily mean they wanted to talk about it. Martin was dead, and so were the Sokolov brothers, and so was Sykes. The whole stinking mess was over, and he felt certain that Martin's friends wanted to put it behind them.

"It's worth a shot," he said, not wanting to tell Nicki his true feelings.

"I emailed you their names a few days ago," she said.

"I'm sure I still have it," he said.

"I'll resend the email. You need to talk to them."

- - -

His cell phone vibrated as he entered his apartment. Nicki's email had arrived. He opened it, and had a quick look at the names, then put his cell phone away.

He smothered a yawn. He hadn't slept in days, and his body felt ready to quit. He'd promised Beth that he'd take a look at Sykes's police report, and hoped he could keep his eyes open long enough to give it a careful read.

"Beth? Where are you hiding?"

"In the living room, having a glass of wine," she replied.

He poured himself a cold beer. He once read an interview with a famous mystery writer who said that if he ever ended a novel with his protagonist entering his house and saying, 'Honey, I'm home,' the character would be retired. That was a shame, because coming home to Beth was a more pleasant experience than entering an empty apartment. He found her resting on the couch, her laptop lying on her stomach.

As he sat, her eyelids fluttered.

"Everything okay?" she asked.

"The guy on the moped was wanted. He's spending the night in jail. How about you?"

"The police report of Sykes's death doesn't pass the smell test. Look at it."

He took her laptop and tapped a key. The screen saver vanished, and a police report took over. "What am I looking for?"

She answered him with a snore. He put his beer and the laptop aside, and lifted her legs so she was horizontal. She mumbled thanks without opening her eyes.

He moved to the balcony. If you lived in Florida long enough, anything below seventy degrees felt chilly, and he shivered as he drank his beer and stared at the ocean. Before he bought this place, the real estate agent had shown him the floor plan, and he'd realized that this unit would never have a building erected in front of it. The view was his, and his alone.

He slogged through the police report. Not many cops had taken creative writing classes, and the writing was as dull as dirt. Something about the report had bothered Beth, and he wondered what it was. Perhaps it was the nosy neighbor not hearing the gunshot. That was a red flag, but the neighbor was elderly, and might very well have been hard of hearing. He decided to wait until morning to ask her.

At the report's end was Sykes's autopsy. Sykes had ended his life with a gun, which wasn't surprising. In his experience, most cops chose this route, probably because they'd been around firearms, and knew that it was quick and painless.

At the bottom of the page, the pathologist had signed off. The handwriting was doctor typical, and impossible to decipher. Beneath the signature line, the pathologist's name was printed in block letters, and he stared at it.

Dr. Peter Matoff.

The name rang a bell. Pulling out his cell phone, he opened up Nicki's email, and looked at the names in the list of men in Saint Augustine who'd been blackmailed by the Sokolov brothers. The last name caught his eye.

Peter Matoff.

It was an unusual last name, and he didn't think there was more than one Peter Matoff living in Saint Augustine. Just to be certain, he did a search on Google, and was proven correct by a site called WhitePages. There were nineteen Peter Matoffs living in the United States. Only one lived in Saint Augustine. The man who'd done the autopsy on Sykes was also one of the blackmail victims.

That was a problem. There were sixty-seven different counties in Florida, and each county had its own autopsy protocol. While he didn't know the exact procedures in Saint Augustine, he felt certain that Matoff wouldn't conduct an autopsy on a policeman involved in a case where he was a victim.

He stared into the darkness, thinking hard. Sykes had killed himself at home, so the sheriff would have told Matoff that it was Sykes, and not a John Doe. To avoid a conflict, Matoff should have asked for another pathologist to conduct the autopsy.

But Matoff hadn't done that, and had performed the autopsy himself.

Why?

He went into the kitchen to get another beer. Beth was on the couch, having a bad dream and talking to herself. Upon returning to the living room, he knelt down beside her and whispered in her ear. She stopped twisting and turning, and fell into a deep sleep.

Her handbag lay on the floor. Tucked in a side pocket was Martin's autopsy report, which Sykes had given to Beth during their visit to his office. Normally, these reports were emailed, which allowed them to be distributed to other people to read. But Sykes had chosen to give Beth a hard copy. It hadn't felt strange at the time, but it did now.

He returned to the balcony and read Martin Daniels's autopsy report. Beth had used a yellow magic marker to highlight the gun that

Martin had used to kill himself. It was a vintage WWII handgun, which had never made any sense.

He came to the bottom of the report. The pathologist's name was scribbled and impossible to read. But it was instantly familiar, as was the name printed beneath it.

Dr. Peter Matoff.

PART SIX

Wasting Away Again in Margaritaville

CHAPTER 50

Lancaster waited three days before returning to Saint Augustine. He made the trip alone, Beth having returned to her job in DC. He hadn't shared his suspicions with her, fearful that he might set off all sorts of false alarms.

He took a prop job into the Jacksonville Airport, rented a car, and drove to Saint Augustine, which took forty-five minutes. He spent the rest of the day driving around the city. The town was swarming with news crews filming stories, and he did his best to avoid them. Bad things happened every day, but when a cop was involved, the media would dig as hard as they could, hoping the story would sprout legs and become a cottage industry, producing true crime books and podcasts. Journalism was a noble profession, but at the end of the day, it was still about the money.

Late in the afternoon, he drove to the sheriff's office and parked in a visitor's space. He wasn't going to win any popularity contests here, but it was a risk that he had to take. He needed to get to the truth, and the Saint Augustine police were the best people to help him accomplish that.

The lobby was quiet, and he smiled at the uniformed reception-ist behind the bulletproof glass. She raised a finger for him to wait. A surveillance camera was watching him, and he gazed into its lens, still smiling.

She ended her call. "Can I help you?"

"My name is Jon Lancaster. I'd like to speak with Sheriff Soares," he said.

"Is he expecting you?"

"I'm afraid not."

"No appointment?"

He shook his head.

"Sheriff Soares is a very busy man. Please contact his secretary, and schedule one. Have a blessed day."

She steepled her hands, as if praying for him. He passed a Team Adam business card through the slot, which had the National Center for Missing and Exploited Children's logo prominently displayed. A moment passed as she studied it.

"I know who you are," she said quietly.

Bad news traveled fast. He lowered his voice. "Sheriff Soares needs to hear what I have to say. Would you be so kind as to tell him I'm here?"

"I'll do that. Have a seat."

The waiting area had a small couch and three rows of stiff plastic chairs that were screwed to the floor. The clientele had to be pretty rough to nail down the chairs, and he parked himself in one. He watched the receptionist make the call, while silently counting to himself.

After thirty seconds had passed, a door sprang open, and a big hunk wearing a uniform emerged, walking with a limp. It was one of the deputies that he'd roughed up, No Neck, and he rose from his chair. His head barely reached the deputy's chin.

"You've got a lot of flipping nerve, coming here," the deputy snorted.

"I need to speak with your boss."

"When hell freezes over."

"You'd be surprised. How's the leg?"

"Why do you care?"

"Because I'm not the asshole you think I am."

The deputy chewed on that one. "It's healing."

"How are your friends holding up?"

"Not so good. Kenny's nose is busted in two places, and Bobby Joe's got three busted ribs. They both got suspended."

"How did you get so lucky?"

"Sheriff Soares is my uncle."

"It's nice to have friends in high places."

"My uncle's busy. Come back tomorrow."

"Will he be here? Or out fishing?"

The deputy hid a grin. "Come back tomorrow, and find out."

"Tell your uncle that I need to speak with him about Sykes."

"My uncle doesn't want to talk with you. Can I make myself any clearer?"

"I found something."

The deputy's face turned to stone. "Come again?"

"I think I know what Sykes was up to."

"Really. Why don't you tell your buddies at the FBI? The pretty one's your girlfriend, isn't she? Why come here?"

It was an excellent question that could only be answered with the truth. "I used to be a cop, and part of me will always be a cop," he said. "I want your uncle to hear this first, before the FBI or anyone else. It might help him."

"Help him how?"

"Sykes was dirty. Dirty cops have a way of taking down innocent cops when they fall. Sometimes, they even take down the people in charge, if you know what I mean."

The deputy stared at the wall. "You must have heard the news."

"What news?"

"The governor has asked the Florida Department of Law Enforcement to conduct an investigation. A bunch of pencil dicks are going to turn this place upside down, and figure out how Sykes was able to get away with things for so long. They'll be looking for a scapegoat. My uncle is a goner."

"Maybe not."

"Don't bullshit me. You were a cop, you know how the FDLE works."

"I do. The FDLE is at the beck and call of the governor, who can call them off whenever he damn pleases."

The deputy mulled it over. Then he looked at Lancaster. "What are you saying? That the information you have is strong enough to make the governor call them off?"

"That's right."

"And you're giving us first dibs on this information."

"Correct. But, if your uncle won't talk to me, I'll have to go to the FBI. Now, what do you say? Will you ask your uncle to give me ten minutes of his time?"

"No, I won't."

He had run out of road, and moved toward the door to leave. He felt the deputy's hand on his arm, gentle but firm.

"No need to ask my uncle anything," the deputy said. "I'm going to tell him to talk to you. If I put it that way, he won't have a choice, now will he?"

CHAPTER 51

The FBI put in long hours. Special agents worked a fifty hour minimum week, and often seventy to ninety hours a week when on assignment. An agent was considered on duty twenty-four hours a day, seven days a week, and often worked holidays.

None of that had ever bothered Daniels, who sat in her make-shift office in the basement of the bureau's DC headquarters, reading through reports of active investigations that her department was conducting. Despite their best efforts, human trafficking was on the rise, the traffickers as clever at moving human beings across the border as the drug cartels were at moving contraband.

She let out a violent sneeze. The dust was wreaking havoc on her sinuses. Her office on the fifth floor was getting a much-needed face-lift, but in the meantime, she would have to suffer in this windowless hole.

Her cell phone vibrated on the metal desk. The caller had a 904 area code, which was Jacksonville and Saint Augustine. She got robocalls from all over the country, and had been fooled before into answering them. She decided to take a chance and answered it.

"Can I help you?"

"Special Agent Daniels? This is Director Rojas in Jacksonville. Do you have a minute to talk?"

"Of course. Nice to know I'm not the only one working late tonight."

"I work late most nights, and I'm sure you do as well. Did you have the chance to read the report I emailed you this morning? I'd like your opinion before I submit it."

Rojas was referring to the report on Sykes that her office had prepared and was about to submit to their bosses. It was not uncommon for the FBI to weigh in when an officer of the law crossed the line. While these reports offered little in the way of new information, they often highlighted things about the suspect's behavior that may have led them to break the law. For the folks in the bureau's behavioral science division, these insights were invaluable.

"I haven't read it. I was going to do so tonight."

"Of course. I'm sure you're buried in work."

Daniels had been raised to believe that it was better not to say anything than to tell an outright lie, which she'd just done. "Let me rephrase that. I started to read your report, but had to stop. The section about my father was painful, which I'm sure you can imagine."

"I'm sorry if it upset you," Rojas said. "Since you interviewed Sykes, I thought it would be best if you had a look."

"No need to apologize. I'll read the report when I get home, which should be in a few hours. I'll let you know what I think."

"Thank you. The second thing I need to talk to you about is Jon Lancaster. Were you aware that he's in Saint Augustine, talking to the police?"

Daniels sat up straight in her chair. Jon had called her last night, and they'd spoken for nearly an hour. Not once had he mentioned a trip to Saint Augustine.

"Are you sure?" she asked.

"Positive. He flew in this morning, and was spotted driving around Saint Augustine in a rented car. I looked at the surveillance videos, and confirmed that it was him."

Because Jacksonville was a port city, the FBI's antiterrorism unit video monitored every ship that came in, as well as every passenger who arrived at the airports. It was impossible for anyone to slip in, and not be spotted.

"How did you find out he was talking to the police?" she asked.

"His behavior seemed odd, so I had an agent tail him. Lancaster pulled into the sheriff's office at four o'clock."

Daniels checked the time. It was past six.

"Is Jon still there?"

"Yes, he is."

"Is your agent watching him?"

"My agent's sitting in his car across the street, watching with a video dash cam. The images are being sent to my laptop, which I'm looking at right now."

It didn't make any sense. Why had Jon traveled to Saint Augustine without telling her? And why was he talking to the sheriff? She heard her name, and looked up to see another agent who'd been sent to the basement standing in her doorway.

"Let me call you back," she said, and disconnected. "What's up?"

"We're going running in the morning," the special agent said. "Care to join us?"

She hadn't run in weeks, and her body needed the workout, only something told her that she might be getting on a plane in the morning, and heading back to Florida.

"I'm swamped. Thanks for thinking of me, " she said.

"Maybe next time," the agent said.

She watched him walk away. Rising, she went to the door and shut it, then returned to her chair. Rojas picked up on the first ring.

"Things have changed since we last spoke," Rojas said. "Lancaster just walked out of the sheriff's office accompanied by six deputies. Sheriff Soares is with the group."

She stiffened. "Is Jon under arrest?"

"I don't think so. They're standing in the parking lot, having a discussion. Everyone appears to be getting along."

"What do you think is going on?"

"Your guess is as good as mine. Lancaster just shook the sheriff's hand."

"They shook hands?"

"Correct. It appears the chat is over. Lancaster got in his rental, and is driving away. The deputies are in their cruisers, following him. Sheriff Soares is getting into an unmarked vehicle and joining the procession."

"Do they have their flashers on?"

"No, they do not."

Daniels was stumped. This made no sense at all. Without thinking, she said, "Would you ask your agent to follow them, and see where this little parade ends?"

Rojas coughed into the phone. "I work with Soares on a regular basis. If he finds out that I had an agent tail him, there will be hell to pay."

"Sorry."

"May I make a suggestion?"

"Go ahead."

"Why don't you call your boyfriend, and ask him what the hell's going on? And after he tells you, please call me back, and fill me in. Because I'm dying to know."

Rojas sounded angry, which she had every right to be. Jon hadn't gone to Saint Augustine to take in the sights. He'd found something important, and instead of taking it to the FBI, he'd gone to the sheriff instead. It was a slap in the face, both to Rojas and to her, and Daniels could feel her cheeks burn.

"I'll do that," she said.

CHAPTER 52

Florida had one of the largest veteran populations in the country. Over a million of its citizens had served in a war, and now bore the scars, both visible and psychological, that armed conflict left upon the courageous few who fought.

The VA Hospital in Saint Augustine looked to be brand new, the trees that lined the parking lot propped up by sticks until their roots grew strong enough to hold up their weight. As Lancaster exited his rental, he spotted a pair of deer grazing in the adjacent preserve. It was a pastoral setting, and he was certain that the veterans who lived there appreciated the tranquility, but a part of him wished the building was out in the public, by the side of a highway, with walls made of glass, so that ordinary citizens who passed it would be reminded that for many of the brave men and women who fought them, wars never ended.

Sheriff Soares and his deputies pulled in moments later. Lancaster had been thinking how he wanted to handle this, and he pulled the sheriff aside.

"If it's okay with you, I'd like to talk with him first," he said.

Soares twirled the toothpick in his mouth. He was the epitome of a cracker, the back of his neck burned to a crisp by the unrelenting sun.

"What good is that going to do you?" Soares asked.

"We don't know the whole truth. If I reason with him, maybe he'll confess."

"In my experience, guilty men don't confess."

"He may have been coerced into this. Let's give him a chance to do the right thing. We have nothing to lose."

"Except our precious time. What the hell. Okay, give it a shot."

Soares told his deputies to wait by their cruisers. Then the sheriff and Lancaster entered the hospital and approached the main reception area. Soares was a man of manners, and he removed his black campaign hat before addressing the receptionist.

"Good afternoon. We're here to see Dr. Peter Matoff. Is he in?"

"Why hello, Sheriff Soares. How have you been?" the receptionist asked.

"Fair to middling," the sheriff replied.

"I can't believe the things I read in the newspaper about Detective Sykes. Who would have known he was such a bad person?" the receptionist said.

Soares coughed into his hand. The receptionist caught his drift, and opened a three-ring binder on her desk. She ran her finger down the page. "Dr. Matoff alternates his days between his duties here, and his private practice. According to my log, he's here today. Would you like me to call him, and let him know he has visitors?"

"Please don't," Soares said. "Where's his office?"

A cloud passed over the receptionist's face. Her eyes drifted to the wall of glass by the entrance, and to the deputies standing at stiff attention in the parking lot. It was then that she knew that something was terribly wrong.

- - -

The door to Matoff's office was shut. Soares rapped loudly, then hitched his thumbs in his belt to wait. To Lancaster he said, "I still think you're wasting our time."

"Let's hope you're wrong," Lancaster said.

"But my gut tells me you'll try and reason with him, while all I'm going to do is threaten the son of a bitch. So have at it."

"Thank you."

"How long were you a cop?"

"Fifteen years."

"Do you miss it?"

The door swung in before he could reply. Matoff stood in the doorway, wearing a rumpled navy suit and a necktie with its knot undone. He was a thin man with a mop of unruly white hair and droopy eyes. Seeing the sheriff, he feigned surprise.

"Why hello, Sheriff Soares. What can I do for you today?" Matoff asked.

"We need to have a chat," Soares said.

"I was just leaving. Can this wait until tomorrow? I've had a long day."

"We need to talk now."

Matoff swallowed a lump in his throat. "Should I assume this isn't a social call?"

"You assume right."

"May I ask who your friend is?"

"This is Jon Lancaster, and he's assisting me with an investigation," Soares said. "He's got a couple of questions he'd like to ask you. It won't take long."

Matoff hesitated. He acted like he wanted to call a lawyer, only that would have been an admission of guilt, so instead he'd try to talk his way out of it. It was a classic mistake made by people who didn't fully understand how the law worked.

"Well, all right. Come in, and make yourself comfortable," Matoff said.

- - -

The blinds on the office windows were drawn, the air stuffy. Matoff sat at his cluttered desk, while Soares and Lancaster remained standing.

"Fire away," Matoff said, forcing a smile.

Lancaster opened the blinds, flooding the room with light. The office faced a water fountain behind the building, where over a hundred patients had congregated. Many were in wheelchairs, while others used walkers to get around. The majority were old and frail, and appeared to be near their final hour.

Lancaster sat on the edge of the desk, his posture friendly.

"You're the pathologist here at the VA, correct?" he asked.

"That's right. I've held the position for twenty years," Matoff said.

"And you also maintain a private practice in town."

"Correct."

"And, you also work for the sheriff's department."

"On occasion, I perform autopsies, as I'm sure Sheriff Soares has told you. I also assist in investigations when medical advice is necessary."

"Are you the only pathologist who works with the police?"

"No, I'm not," Matoff said. "I share that duty with another pathologist, Dr. Mark Torgove, as I'm sure Sheriff Soares also told you."

"I believe that's common practice, isn't it? Most police departments work with two pathologists in case a problem arises."

Matoff's face turned to stone. He pretended not to understand.

"I don't know what you mean," he said.

"Let me explain. When I was a detective, we had two pathologists on call. If a person died and an autopsy was needed, the pathologist would first find out who the deceased was. If the pathologist happened to know the person, he'd excuse himself, and the other pathologist would take over. You don't want to be slicing open a person you know, even if they are dead. Does that sound about right?"

The blood had drained from Matoff's face, his skin ghostly pale. When an answer was not forthcoming, Lancaster glanced at Soares.

"Is that how it works in Saint Augustine?"

"That's standard operating procedure in the whole county," the sheriff said. "We don't expect pathologists to perform autopsies on friends. It's too damn painful."

Lancaster resumed looking at Matoff. "So that's the deal. You don't slice open people you know. But for some reason you did. Not once, but twice."

"I don't know what you're talking about," Matoff said.

"Then let me refresh your memory. You performed an autopsy on Martin Daniels after he committed suicide, even though you and Martin were close friends, and belonged to a group that went fishing together. Correct?"

"But I didn't know it was Martin!" Matoff protested. "When his body was brought into the hospital, his face had been eaten away by a coyote, and he was unrecognizable. It was only after I compared dental records that I knew it was him."

"That wasn't what Detective Sykes told me," Lancaster said.

Matoff sank into his chair as the words took hold.

"I was present when Sykes was interviewed by the FBI. Sykes said that a car was discovered in the park where Martin's body was found, and that Sykes ran a check on the plate, and he identified the vehicle as Martin's. This happened well before the body was brought to the hospital. You're telling us you didn't know this?"

Matoff shut his eyes, then reopened them.

"No," he said.

"You also did the autopsy on Sykes after the detective burned to death in his house," Lancaster said. "Why didn't you pass that off to the other pathologist?"

"Because I didn't know Sykes," Matoff said.

"Oh yes you did," Lancaster said. "You were being blackmailed by the Sokolov brothers, who put a mummified hand on your doorstep. The Sokolovs were blackmailing several other prominent men, including Sykes. You were talking with each other, and trying to stop the Sokolovs from ruining your reputations. Isn't that right?"

"No—I didn't know Sykes," Matoff said lamely.

"You're lying. If the police look through your emails and cell phone records, they'll find communications between you and Sykes. You knew him, just like you knew Martin Daniels. So why did you perform their autopsies?"

Matoff buried his face in his hands. He'd painted himself into a corner, and there was nowhere left to hide. Lancaster got a bottled water from the minifridge and told him to drink it. It seemed to calm him down, and Soares took over.

"We've got you dead to rights, Doc," the sheriff said. "Jon here thinks you're an innocent victim; I'm not so sure. Why don't you tell us your side of things, and let us help you? It will work out better in the long run."

Matoff lowered his hands. He was weeping.

"All right," he whispered.

- - -

Once Matoff started talking, it was impossible to get him to stop, the words flowing out in a river of guilt, his fear of being caught no match for his conscience.

When he was finished, he gazed sheepishly at Soares and Lancaster.

"I'm sorry for what I've done." Matoff extended his wrists, as if expecting to be handcuffed. Soares shook his head, then motioned for him to rise.

"You're not going to arrest me?" Matoff asked.

"I agree with my colleague. You were a victim," Soares said. "You're going to have to face your family and friends, not to mention the state medical board. That should be punishment enough. I want you to come over to my office, so we can get a confession on video. We can pick up dinner on the way. That work for you?"

Matoff said of course. Soares put his hat on, and left the office. As Matoff started to follow, Lancaster stopped him. Listening to the doctor confess, he'd decided that Matoff had probably never done a bad thing in his life before this, and had simply gotten caught up in a situation that was out of his control. That was the thing about evil that few people understood. Its allure was hypnotic, and its power was all-consuming.

"I know this was hard," Lancaster said. "Thank you."

"If I'd only spoken up sooner," Matoff said regrettably.

"You know what they say. Better late than never."

"I suppose."

"One more question. Where in the Keys?"

"I honestly don't know."

They went outside. The sun had gone down and the parking lot was pitch dark, the only light coming from the cruisers' headlights. Matoff got in Soares's vehicle and they departed, followed by the deputies in their cruisers. Lancaster was pulling out when he got a call from Beth. He wasn't ready to talk with her, and let it go to voice mail.

She called right back. If he didn't answer, she'd keep calling and calling. She could be relentless that way.

"Hey," he answered.

"Where have you been? I've texted you a dozen times," she said angrily.

"Sorry. It's been a long day."

"Were you planning on telling me you were in Saint Augustine, or that you'd met with the sheriff this afternoon? What the hell is going on, Jon?"

"Who told you I was in Saint Augustine?"

"A little bird. Now tell me what's going on. And don't you dare bullshit me."

Relationships, if they were meant to last, were based upon trust. Without that bond, they disintegrated. He wanted to tell Beth the truth for no other reason than he wanted their relationship to last. He loved her, and believed that she loved him. But he still hadn't put all the pieces of the puzzle together. There was one more person he needed to speak with. Until he had that conversation, he was just guessing.

"I'm chasing down a lead," he said.

"What lead? God damn it, what did you find?"

"I can't tell you."

"It's about my father, isn't it?"

He gripped the wheel and struggled with a reply.

"Let me call you tomorrow," he said.

"Answer me! You learned something about my father."

"Please, Beth."

"If you don't tell me what it is, I'll never speak to you again."

Yes you will, he thought.

"I'll call you tomorrow," he said.

Beth started cursing like a sailor, and he wondered how much harm he'd done to the relationship. Maybe it was over, or maybe she'd love him that much more when it was all said and done. He disconnected and hit the gas.

CHAPTER 53

Three days later

Every five or six years, the Florida Keys went through a transformation. This change had nothing to do with the economy, or an influx of new arrivals eager to put their stamp on the Conch Republic. Rather, it was a result of a major hurricane ravaging the Keys like a runaway train, and tearing down every weary structure in its path.

The latest home-wrecker was Irma, a Category 4 monster that ripped apart four thousand homes, many beyond repair. Manufactured homes and RVs took the worst hit, with residents forced to rent tiny spaces in order to survive. Several thousand people had lost their homes and were now living this way. If you wanted to track one of them down, you needed to know who to ask, and where to look.

Bobby's Monkey Bar in Key West was the epitome of a dive. The exterior looked like an adult video store, with walls painted a horrendous shade of pink. Inside, smiling stuffed monkeys hung from the ceiling while a drunk lady in a bathing suit sang karaoke on the makeshift stage.

Lancaster had driven down that morning, and needed a drink. Kirk the bartender was just the man he needed to speak to. Kirk's ratty T-shirt said, ASK MY ADVICE AND YOU'LL END UP DRUNK.

"Hey, Jon, good to see you. What's your pleasure?" Kirk asked.

"A cold, refreshing beer," he said.

"If my memory serves me correctly, you have a fondness for IPAs."

"I'm impressed. You pick the brew."

Kirk filled a chilled glass and slid it toward him. The bar was busy, as were all the bars in Key West, the town a drunk tank sitting atop a giant sponge. Lancaster took a long swallow and exhaled pleasurably.

"The older I get, the better that tastes," he said. "Did you get my message?"

Kirk had been living in Key West for decades, and was wired into the town gossip. He was *the* source for information, provided he knew you, and trusted you.

"Now that you mention it, I did," he said. "When did you get into skip tracing?"

"I'm not skip tracing. This is a one-time thing."

"You're not working for a bail bondsman?"

"No, sir."

"Good. I hate those assholes."

Kirk went to serve a pair of leather-clad bikers who'd come in. The drunk lady was mutilating Springsteen's "Born to Run," which was not an appropriate song for the area. Key West was on the country's southernmost tip, and if you left it, there was no place left to run to. Kirk came back and refilled his glass.

"Thanks. So, what have you got for me?"

"Calm down. You just got here," Kirk said. "Why don't you take a load off your feet, and soak up the atmosphere? It'll do you good."

Normally, he would have agreed. No one in the Keys was in a hurry, and any job was expected to be put off until tomorrow. But this was different; he was about to fit the last piece into the puzzle, and the urgency was killing him.

"I'm not here on vacation," he said. "I want to get this done before dark."

"Have it your way. Should I cash you out?"

"Please. How much do I owe you?"

"Eight bucks."

He fished two hundreds out of his wallet and placed them on the bar.

"Keep the change," he said.

Kirk found a pen and scribbled an address on the back of a coaster, which he gave to him. "This won't be easy to find. A lot of buildings got blown away by the storm, and the new ones aren't on Google Maps. You're going to need to poke around."

"That's my specialty. Poking around."

"Good luck. Don't be a stranger."

- - -

Key West was second to none when it came to community, and sparkling blue water. He found the address by asking a man walking his dog, and parked a block away. He spent a few minutes getting a feel for the area before knocking on the front door. A woman wearing a fluffy pink bathrobe answered, a tall boy in hand.

"Sorry to bother you. I'm looking for Danny O'Brien. Is he here?"

"That all depends on who's asking," she said.

"My name's Jon Lancaster. Danny and I are old buddies. He told me to look him up if I ever made it to Key West."

"Danny's giving a paddleboard lesson right now. What's in the bag?"

He showed her the six-pack he'd bought from the local minimart. He offered her one, and she killed the tall boy and popped the fresh can.

"Much obliged. Danny lives in the back," she said. "You can wait until he comes home. Don't make any noise. I'm about to take a nap."

"Yes, ma'am. Thank you."

The clapboard garage had been recently converted into an apartment, the paint still fresh. The door was ajar, and he said, "Anyone home?" before entering. The interior was around four hundred square feet, with a George Foreman grill for cooking, a daybed, and a black cat sleeping on the AC unit. He popped a beer and stuffed the rest into the fridge. A stack of flyers sat on a table. He grabbed one and headed outside.

He sat on a rusted chair beneath the shade of a banyan tree and read the flyer while sipping his beer. *Lazy Dog Paddleboard Tours. Two-hour eco tours, paddle yoga, and paddle fit classes. Paddleboarding is easier than it looks—come take a class!* At the bottom of the page was an email contact, but no phone number.

He heard footsteps and rose from his chair. A man with a neatly trimmed white beard and tanned legs came around the side of the house. He wore clamdigger swim trunks and a long-sleeve shirt to protect him from the sun, and held a glistening paddleboard and an oar by his side. Seeing his visitor, he froze.

"May I help you?" the man asked.

Lancaster held up the flyer. "Your landlady said I could wait until you came back. I'm interested in learning how to paddleboard, and heard you were the local expert."

The man rested the paddleboard and oar on the side of the garage, and offered his hand. "I'm Danny O'Brien. Nice to meet you."

"Same here."

"Have you ever paddleboarded before?"

"This would be my first time."

"It's easier than riding a bike, and lots of fun. You'll get the hang of it in no time. I charge fifty dollars an hour, and provide all the equipment. Cash only."

"Sounds like a deal. Can we start this afternoon?"

"Of course. Sorry, but I didn't catch your name."

"It's Jon. Jon Lancaster."

O'Brien blinked, and then he blinked again. The blood drained from his face, and he looked like he might pass out. Lancaster helped him into the chair.

"You're Beth's boyfriend," he whispered.

"That's right."

"How . . . did you find me?"

"It wasn't very hard. Let me get you a cold beer. I brought some with me."

He went into the apartment and rummaged through the cabinets. His host impressed him as the type of guy who drank his beer out of a glass. He went outside holding a mug with a foaming head, and gave it to him.

"Here you go."

Lancaster found another rusted chair and positioned it across from his host, and watched him drink. The beverage was consumed in a series of long, desperate gulps.

"It's nice to finally meet you, Dr. Daniels. Beth's told me a lot about you."

"Call me Martin. Does Beth know that I'm alive?"

"No. I wanted to find you first, before I told her."

Martin stared into the depths of his glass. The ruse was over, and he seemed uncertain how to proceed, so he asked the obvious. "Who told you I was here?"

"Dr. Matoff said you were hiding out in the Keys. He confessed to filing false autopsy reports, and claiming that the bodies of two veterans living at the VA who'd committed suicide were actually you and Sykes."

"The Keys are a big place. How did you know where to look?"

"Because I've looked before. When a fugitive hides in the Keys, he avoids the smaller islands, and goes to Key West, which has a larger population. I have a friend here who was able to track you down."

"So my behavior was predictable." Martin's eyes were moist, and when he spoke again, his lips were trembling. "What tripped us up? We thought it was a perfect plan."

"I was suspicious from the start," he said. "The autopsy report said that you shot yourself with an antique World War II revolver, yet there were no firearms in your home. Where did the gun come from? And why did you choose one from World War II? When Dr. Matoff explained that the body was actually a World War II veteran who'd used his favorite gun to kill himself, it all made sense."

Martin shook his head sadly. "I actually thought the same thing, at the time. But we were in a rush. Sykes wanted me to disappear. He said it would solve a lot of problems. So I agreed. Was that the only clue?"

"Sykes's apparent suicide was also suspicious," he said. "The autopsy report claimed he'd set his house on fire, then shot himself. That seemed like overkill. It made me wonder if the body was Sykes, or if it had been burned to hide its true identity."

"Another screwup. You must think we're real amateurs."

"Not really. You fooled a lot of people."

Martin looked despondent. The gravity of what he'd done—and what was about to happen to him—had settled in. "I considered suicide. It would have been easier."

"Maybe not. Everything happens for a reason, Martin. Want another beer?"

Martin stared at the ground and mumbled, "No thanks."

"Dr. Matoff told us that Sykes was running the show. He said Sykes was getting a cut from every hooker in town, until Sheriff Soares ran the hookers out. Sykes needed a new scam, so he connected with the Sokolov brothers, and they started extorting you and your friends. Is that how it was?"

"Yes. Sykes was the mastermind. Although none of us knew it at first," Martin said. "We thought he was just another victim, like us. It was the perfect cover."

"When did you find out otherwise?"

"Sykes came to my house a few weeks ago, and told me to pay the Sokolovs off. That's when it dawned on me what was going on."

"He went to the homes of the other victims as well. Didn't he?"

"Yes. He told them to pay, or else."

"Dr. Matoff showed us a text where Sykes threatened him. Were you threatened?"

Martin was drawing into himself, and no longer making eye contact. He shifted uncomfortably in his chair and did not reply.

"Please answer the question. Did he threaten you? We found bloody tissues in the house."

"Yes. He became violent, and hit me in the face and bloodied my nose, so I threw him out," Martin said. "That night, he texted me, and said that if I didn't play ball, he'd drive down to Fort Lauderdale and kidnap my granddaughter. I believed him. I told him I'd pay, but I wanted something in return."

"Which was to disappear."

"That's right. I couldn't live with myself anymore."

"So you took off, and Sykes staged your suicide. Do you know where Sykes went?"

"He has a place outside of Cabo San Lucas. Probably there."

The sun came out from behind the clouds, and the air turned hot. Martin closed his eyes and shuddered as if he'd caught a chill. Tears were running down his cheeks, his conscience tearing him apart. "Do you know what the worst kind of lie is, Jon? It's the one that we tell ourselves. That was what my relationship with Katya was. A bright, shining lie. She was young enough to be my granddaughter, yet I allowed myself to fall in love with her, and let my feelings poison my thinking. I didn't care if my behavior hurt my family, or my friends. Or if it would destroy my reputation. All that I cared about was being with her. I even kept seeing her when the extortion started. That's how far gone I was."

"We all make mistakes, Martin."

He slowly opened his eyes. "Thank you for saying that. The problem is, I kept making the same mistakes, and dug myself a hole I couldn't get out of. The inability to learn from one's mistakes is a neurological problem that is treatable, yet I refused to correct my own problem. I failed myself. And I have no one but myself to blame for what happened. It's all on me." He kicked the empty can sitting next to his chair, and sent it clattering across the backyard. "May I ask you a question?"

"Go ahead."

"Are you going to arrest me?"

"I'm no longer a policeman. I can't arrest you."

"Did you bring a cop with you to do the job? Maybe out on the street in a car?"

"I came alone. I just wanted to talk to you."

"And talk we did. You're a good man. I can see why Beth's attracted to you."

"I appreciate that, Martin."

Martin came out of his chair and got his paddleboard and oar. Without a word, he walked down the driveway to the cracked sidewalk in front of the house, took a left turn, and headed down the street, with Lancaster trailing a few steps behind. They walked to a vacant lot, which had a cutoff that took them down to a deserted beach.

The beaches of Key West were small and filled with sharp rocks that would cut your feet, and Martin carefully maneuvered his way to the shore. Once there, he kicked off his sandals and peeled off his shirt. His body was bronzed and trim, and as he waded out into the surf, Lancaster realized what was happening. Martin was going to paddle out a ways, pick a tranquil spot, and dive in. He would go down to the bottom and stay there for a while, beholding the colored fish and coral reefs, and when his lungs felt ready to burst, he'd open up his mouth and be done with it. The final journey.

Lancaster tossed his watch and cell phone on the sand, then waded out as well. By now, Martin was waist deep in the water, and preparing to climb upon his board. He shot Lancaster a disapproving look that said, That's far enough.

"Please don't do this."

"Give me one good reason why I shouldn't."

Lancaster could think of many reasons. Beth and Melanie were at the top of the list. And of course Nicki. And all the friends in Saint Augustine who cared deeply about him. Those were good reasons, yet they weren't good enough. Martin was so ashamed that he'd convinced himself that only by ending his life could he erase that shame.

But what exactly had Martin done? Although stupid and vain, it wasn't a crime to have a relationship with a younger woman, or to continue to love her, even when she didn't love you. Nor was it a crime to fall prey to a ruthless extortionist, or to protect a loved one from the same extortionist's threats. Martin's only crime was that he'd betrayed himself, and couldn't live with his conscience.

Lancaster took a chance, and waded closer. When they were nearly touching, he put his hand on Martin's shoulder. Martin looked at his hand, and then at him.

"Say it," the older man said.

"You did nothing wrong," Lancaster said.

Martin started to protest. Lancaster cut him off.

"I looked at the evidence. You were the victim, which makes the things you did excusable. The sheriff in Saint Augustine isn't going to arrest Dr. Matoff, and he won't arrest you. It's Sykes he wants."

"But I did so many bad things . . ."

"For a reason."

"But I hate myself. That's why I came here, and created a new identity. I can't stand to look at myself in the mirror in the morning. Do you know how that feels?"

"Your heart betrayed you. It happens to the best of us."

A school of fish swam between their legs. Then, in a flash, they were gone.

"What are you saying? That I can just start over?"

"Yes. It's like running a race. You take one step at a time."

Martin shook his head. "It's not that easy."

"I didn't say that it was."

Lancaster reached for the board. He took it as a good sign when Martin didn't resist. They waded back to shore, and he retrieved his cell phone and pulled up Beth's number. He handed the cell phone to Martin, who stared painfully at the screen.

"You want me to call my daughter."

"That's right. She's suffered terribly, so you should start there."

"What should I say? That I'm sorry for being such a horrible father?"

"Tell her you love her. That's your first step."

"Do you think she can ever forgive me?"

"Yes, Martin, I do."

They stood there for a while. So long that the sky changed color, and the temperature dropped. Martin took several deep breaths and shuddered, like an animal shedding its skin. Then, with his eyes fixed on the horizon, he pressed the "Call" button, and lifted the cell phone to his face.

ABOUT THE AUTHOR

James Swain is the Amazon Charts best-selling author of more than twenty mystery novels and has worked as a magazine editor, a screenwriter, and a novelist. His books have been translated into a dozen languages and have been selected as Mysteries of the Year by *Publishers Weekly* and *Kirkus Reviews*. The author of two previous novels in the Lancaster & Daniels series, *The King Tides* and *No Good Deed*, Swain has been nominated for five Barry Awards, has received a Florida Book Award for fiction, and was awarded France's prestigious Prix Calibre .38 for Best American Crime Writing. When he isn't writing, he enjoys performing close-up magic. Visit him at http://jamesswain.com.